13.5.2024.

Th~~...~~ and the Rose

Jean Plaidy, one of the pre-eminent authors of historical fiction for most of the twentieth century, is the pen name of the prolific English author Eleanor Hibbert, also known as Victoria Holt. Jean Plaidy's novels had sold more than 14 million copies worldwide by the time of her death in 1993.

For further information about our Jean Plaidy reissues and mailing list, please visit
www.randomhouse.co.uk/minisites/jeanplaidy

Praise for Jean Plaidy

'A vivid impression of life at the Tudor Court' *Daily Telegraph*

'It is hard to better Jean Plaidy . . . both elegant and exciting'
Daily Mirror

'Outstanding' *Vanity Fair*

'Plaidy has brought the past to life' *Times Literary Supplement*

'One of our best historical novelists' *News Chronicle*

'An excellent story' *Irish Press*

'Spirited . . . Plaidy paints the truth as she sees it'
Birmingham Post

The Thistle and the Rose

JEAN PLAIDY

arrow books

Published by Arrow Books in 2006

3 5 7 9 10 8 6 4

Copyright © Jean Plaidy, 1963

Initial lettering copyright © Stephen Raw, 2006

The Estate of Eleanor Hibbert has asserted its right
to have Jean Plaidy identified as the author of this work.

First published in the United Kingdom in 1963 by Robert Hale Ltd

Arrow Books
The Random House Group Limited
20 Vauxhall Bridge Road, London SW1V 2SA

Random House Australia (Pty) Limited
20 Alfred Street, Milsons Point, Sydney,
New South Wales 2061, Australia

Random House New Zealand Limited
18 Poland Road, Glenfield,
Auckland 10, New Zealand

Random House (Pty) Limited
Isle of Houghton, Corner of Boundary Road & Carse O'Gowrie,
Houghton 2198, South Africa

Random House Group Limited Reg. No. 954009
www.randomhouse.co.uk

A CIP catalogue record for this book is available from the British Library

The Random House Group Limited supports The Forest Stewardship
Council® (FSC®), the leading international forest-certification organisation.
Our books carrying the FSC label are printed on FSC®-certified paper.
FSC is the only forest-certification scheme supported by the leading
environmental organisations, including Greenpeace. Our
paper procurement policy can be found at
www.randomhouse.co.uk/environment

MIX
Paper from
responsible sources
FSC® C016897

ISBN 9780099493259 (from Jan 2007)
ISBN 0 09 949325 X

Typeset by SX Composing DTP, Rayleigh, Essex

Printed and bound in Great Britain by Clays Ltd, St Ives PLC

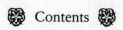

Contents

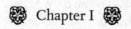

Chapter I

THE BETROTHAL

In an apartment of that royal palace which recently, by the command of the King, had had its name changed from Shene to Richmond, three children were ranged about a blazing fire. Outside the January wind buffeted the octagonal and circular towers, threatening to sweep away the little chimneys which looked like inverted pears.

The eldest of the three – a girl just past her twelfth birthday – had taken off the net which held her beautiful reddish golden hair, so that she could have the joy of letting it fall over her shoulders and down to her waist. The boy, who had the same rosy complexion and bright gold hair, watched her sullenly. She was delighted with herself; he was displeased. As for the other child, a little girl not quite six, she was intent on watching the pair of them, very conscious of the fact that on account of her age she was of small account in the eyes of her twelve-year-old sister, Margaret, and ten-year-old brother, Henry.

'The fact is,' Margaret was saying, 'that you are angry because I am to have a marriage and because I shall be a queen before you are a king.'

'Queen of Scotland!' sneered Henry. 'That barbarous land!

Nay, my sister, I tell you this: I am displeased because it seems to me unfitting that *my* sister should so demean herself by such a marriage.'

Margaret burst out laughing. 'What airs you give yourself, Henry. I declare that since you became Prince of Wales you believe you are a king already. And think of this, brother: Had our dear Arthur lived you would never have been a king at all.'

Henry scowled. It was like Margaret to take an unfair advantage. She was telling him that he showed too much pleasure in his new state and not enough sorrow for the death of their brother.

'It matters not how or why a man wears a crown,' he muttered. 'It only matters that he does.'

'So you are glad Arthur is dead!'

'I did not say that.'

'You imply it.'

'You lie.'

'I do not lie.'

Mary began to whimper. She hated quarrels between her brother and sister; they were always threatening to arise, partly because Margaret and Henry were so much alike. If Margaret's hair were cut off – which she would never allow because it was her greatest beauty and she was very proud of it – and she were dressed like a boy, there would be Henry all over again. And it was not only in appearance that they resembled each other. They were both headstrong, wilful, loving to indulge themselves, furious with any who opposed them. Mary secretly took Henry's side because he made much of her. He often told her how pretty she was and that she was his favourite sister.

'Now you see what you have done,' complained Henry. 'You have frightened Mary. Come here, Mary. I will sing to you if you like. I will play my lute.'

'Oh yes, please.'

Margaret regarded them scornfully.

'And you must say none sings like he does, none plays the lute to compare with him, and you are the luckiest girl in the world to have such a brother. That is the payment which will be asked of you for his attentions, little sister.'

'Heed her not,' Henry reassured the little girl. 'She is angry with us because she has to leave our beautiful Court for that of a barbarian.'

Margaret lost a little of her bravado. She had her qualms. It could be an ordeal at twelve, when you had not a great experience of the world, to be called upon to leave your home for that of a husband you had never seen.

Henry saw the change in her demeanour and made the most of his advantage.

'I never cared for Scottish alliances.' He imitated the tone of one of his father's ministers and stood ponderously, long legs apart, hands clasped behind his back, an expression of wisdom on his round, rosy face.

'I wonder you do not discuss this matter with the King,' Margaret put in sarcastically.

'I might do so.' Henry was playing for Mary; it was possible that she would not find it difficult to imagine her wonderful brother already advising the King.

'Go and seek an audience at once,' Margaret suggested. 'I am sure our father will be eager to listen to your counsel.'

Henry ignored his sister; he began to pace up and down before the fire. 'In the first place,' he said, 'I like not these

Stuarts. I like not their lax morals. You will be going to a man who has had a host of mistresses and, some say, married one of them. A pleasant state of affairs, madam, for a Tudor!'

Margaret folded her arms across her breasts and laughed gaily. She was aware of mingling apprehension and excitement; she had become conscious of her body at an early age; her governess and nurse said of her: 'She should marry young.' It was different for Henry, who was as eager for manhood as she was for womanhood; they were lusty people, these young Tudors. They must have inherited that quality from their maternal grandfather; they had often discussed gossip they had heard about him. Great Edward IV – handsome, tall, golden and very like them in appearance – whose greatest pleasure had been the pursuit of women. His daughter, their mother, was mild and docile; their father lusted after gold and possessions so exclusively that he had no lust left for anything else. So, thought Margaret, Henry has undoubtedly inherited his tastes from his grandfather. Have I? She believed so; and that was fortunate, for it meant that in spite of certain natural fears she could look forward with excitement to marriage with a man noted for his sensuality.

It was amusing to see Henry in this mood. His little mouth was prim; because he liked to be the centre of attention, and since, as this was her marriage which was about to take place, *she* must necessarily be, he was going to show his displeasure by disapproving of the morals of her bridegroom.

'He will have to give up his mistresses when *I* arrive,' said Margaret.

'If he would not do so while negotiating with our father for the marriage, depend upon it he will not when he has achieved his purpose: alliance with the Tudors.'

Henry said the last sentence as though he were making an announcement like a herald at a tournament. He had become very insistent on the homage due to the Tudors since he had become the heir to the throne.

Of course, Margaret thought, that had changed everything. He was surrounded by sycophants, all eager to be friends with the boy who would one day be King; and Henry did not appear to see what their flattery meant – but perhaps he did though, and loved it so much that he would accept it eagerly no matter what lay behind it.

Little Mary was watching him with adoring eyes. It was easy enough to be a hero in the eyes of a five-year-old little girl.

'Our grandfather had many mistresses, and he was a great King,' Margaret reminded Henry.

'But these Stuarts! Even their castles are draughty.'

Margaret shivered. 'So are ours.'

'And the winters are hard, north of the Border.'

'I shall know how to keep myself warm.'

'And' – Henry narrowed his eyes and his mouth grew tight – 'I remember – though others do not – that your bridegroom has been overfriendly with a certain traitor.'

'A traitor!' squealed Mary. 'Oh, Henry, what traitor?'

'You are too young to remember, but two years ago Perkin Warbeck was a prisoner in our Tower of London, and there he was tried and found guilty; after which he was taken to Tyburn and hanged by the neck until he died. Do you know what this traitor planned to do? To pass himself off as the Duke of York, our mother's brother, thereby claiming that he had more right to the throne than our father. Vile traitor that he was. And this James, whom your sister is so proud to marry, received him in Scotland, gave him honours and allowed him to marry his own cousin. There! Do you understand now why I see no matter for rejoicing in this marriage of our sister?'

Mary turned solemn eyes to Margaret. 'Oh, Margaret, is it indeed so?'

'Do you doubt me then?' roared Henry.

'Oh no, Henry. *You* are always right!'

'He is not,' snapped Margaret. 'And that is all ancient history. Perkin Warbeck deceived James Stuart as he did others. It is over and nothing to do with my marriage.'

'I beg leave to say that it has a great deal to do with your marriage.'

'Then I am surprised you do not forbid our father to consent to it,' Margaret mocked.

Henry's face flushed scarlet. 'When I am King . . .' he muttered.

It was unfortunate for Henry that at this moment the door was flung open and his words were overheard by the last person he wanted to hear them.

The King had entered the room with his wife and a few attendants. King Henry VII was no lover of ceremony; his clothes were a good deal plainer than those of many of his courtiers; his face was pale and shrewd, and no one would have suspected he was the father of those pink and gold children who were clearly disconcerted to be so interrupted.

Henry thought scornfully that a king should make his entrance to a fanfare of trumpets; his garments should dazzle with their magnificence; he should tower above his followers. When I am King . . . his thoughts went on, for that was their persistent theme since the news of Arthur's death had been brought to him.

He bowed to his parents, and the girls curtsied.

6

'That time is not yet, my son,' said the King coldly, 'though it would seem you are unbecomingly eager for it.'

'Sire,' began Henry, embarrassed, 'I was but explaining to my sisters . . .'

The King lifted a hand. 'I rejoice in your healthy looks,' he said, 'and would that your mind kept pace with your body. You should pray that the time will not be yet for, my son, you are an infant in princedom and have much to learn of kingship.'

'I know this, Sire,' murmured Henry, 'and I will endeavour to learn quickly – so to please you.'

'My daughter,' said the King; and Margaret came forward.

Her father did not smile – he had rarely been seen to do so – but his glance was approving.

The vitality of these children of his never failed to delight while it surprised him. He had lost Arthur and Edmund, it was true, but the ruddy looks of these three reassured him. If the child the Queen now carried had this same blooming health, and it were a boy, he would cease to mourn for the death of Arthur. There was, of course, no reason why there should not be more and more. Both he and the Queen were young enough to add to their brood.

He went on: 'The Scottish nobles are now arriving at the Palace. You should be ready to receive them. This is no time for nursery games.'

'No, Sire,' murmured Margaret.

The Queen stepped forward and took her daughter's hand. Elizabeth of York tried to hide the apprehension she was feeling. It was only a little more than twelve years ago that this bright girl had been born to her in the Palace of Westminster; she remembered the November mists which hung over the river and seeped into the room; she remembered holding the tiny child in her arms and rejoicing in her, forgetting the disappointment in her sex which it seemed must overshadow all female royal births. A sister for Arthur – a healthier baby than her little brother.

And now soon there would be another. The present pregnancy worried the Queen. She was filled with foreboding perhaps because she, more than any, knew the weakness of her own body. Childbearing had taken its toll and, although she could remain fruitful for several years to come, she thought with dread of future pregnancies.

There was none to whom she could confide this fear. Her daughter was too young to understand; moreover could she complain to her of a fate to which, by very nature of her own position, Margaret could herself be condemned? It was a great responsibility to be a royal princess, one whose duty it was to provide sons – a task which seemed extremely difficult for royal princesses and amazingly simple for humble subjects. Could she explain to her husband? Henry would never understand that anything could be of importance except the piling up of wealth, the strengthening of the country, so that the Tudor, who sat somewhat uneasily on his throne, should maintain his place. There was reason for disquiet. The recent affairs of Lambert Simnel and Perkin Warbeck had shown that; but with his usual sound good sense Henry had dealt with those impostors in a manner befitting his kingship. But such matters were disturbing to him.

And now ... a match with Scotland. An excellent proposition. Perhaps that would mean an end to the senseless border warfare which harried their peoples. Perhaps the Alliance would so strengthen the friendship of the two countries that they would live amicably together during the years ahead.

And my daughter Margaret would be responsible, pondered the Queen. Pray God that she may be a wise counsellor to her husband.

She would speak with Margaret, try to impress upon her the importance of her duty.

'Come and prepare yourself to meet the envoys from the Scottish Court,' she said.

'The Prince of Wales should also grace the assembly with his presence,' said the King with a slight lifting of one corner of his mouth to imply mockery.

Margaret glanced at her brother. Now was the time for him to declare his dislike of the match, to state boldly before his father what he had told his sisters.

Henry's lower lip jutted out slightly. He opened his mouth as though to speak; but when he looked up into his father's stern face, he changed his mind. He was not yet King of England.

❀ ❀ ❀

In the Queen's great chamber in Richmond Palace a dazzling company of men and women had assembled.

With the Queen were her daughters, the Princess Margaret and the little Princess Mary. Margaret, in her state robes, looked slightly older than her twelve years; her naturally rosy complexion seemed even more dazzling than usual and her eyes shone with excitement. Everyone in this assembly was aware of her, for in the ceremony which was about to take place she would be the central figure.

A fanfare of trumpets sounded as the King, accompanied by the Prince of Wales, entered the chamber. Such a fanfare must have satisfied even young Henry. He looked smug, Margaret thought, and well pleased with himself. Had he already forgotten how much he disapproved of the Scottish match, or was he going to make a formal protest? No, he never would. There was one person at Court of whom Henry went in great fear, and that was his father. He might strut like a young bantam before his sisters and his friends – but in the presence of Henry VII he never forgot for one moment that he was but a ten-year-old boy who must mind his manners.

With Henry and his father were the Archbishops of Canterbury and York; and they were immediately followed by the Scottish lords who also had their parts to play on this occasion.

Margaret's gaze rested on Patrick Hepburn, the Earl of Bothwell, who was to stand beside her and take the vows; for he had been chosen to act as proxy for his master. There he stood, accompanied by the Archbishop of Glasgow and the Bishop Elect of Murray, a poor substitute, she was sure, for the King of Scotland, whom she had heard was possessed of great charm and handsome looks.

Now that they were all gathered together, the purpose of their meeting was ceremonially announced and the Archbishop of Glasgow opened the proceedings by turning to Henry VII and asking: 'Does Your Grace know any impediment on your part to this wedlock, other than is here dispensed withal?'

The King replied that he did not.

Then the same question was asked of the Queen who gave similar answer.

It was then demanded of Margaret whether she knew of any reason why she should not make an alliance with the King of Scotland.

'I know of none,' she answered; and as she spoke she could not resist flashing a look of mockery at her brother. He knew of reasons, if he had been speaking the truth to his sisters when they were alone. But Henry was solemnly staring ahead and pretended not to notice her glance.

Now it was the turn of her father to ask the same questions of the Scotsmen. Margaret caught her breath. Was it really true that her prospective bridegroom had contracted a marriage with his mistress? What if one of the Scottish lords spoke up and said so? Would that be an end to this marriage?

But the Scots were assuring the King of England that there was no impediment to the marriage, and the Archbishop of Glasgow turned once more to Margaret.

'Are you content, of your own free will and without compulsion, to marry my master?'

Margaret spoke the words which she had rehearsed with her mother. 'If it please my lord and father the King and my lady and mother the Queen, I am content.'

'It is our will and pleasure,' pronounced the King.

Now her hand was laid in that of Patrick Hepburn who was declaring with the utmost earnestness: 'I, Patrick Earl of Bothwell, procurator of the right high and mighty Prince James, by the Grace of God King of Scotland, my sovereign lord, having sufficient power to contract marriage *per verba presenti* with thee, Margaret, daughter to Henry by the Grace of God King of England and Elizabeth Queen of the same, do hereby contract matrimony with thee, Margaret . . .'

Margaret's gaze had strayed once more to her brother; she was flashing a message to him: Why did you not speak when there was time? It is too late now.

But the young Prince of Wales refused to interpret her glances. He was showing a great interest in everything that was going on and endeavouring to look as pleased with the proceedings as his father did.

The Archbishop of Glasgow was attracting her attention and whispering: 'Repeat after me.'

She nodded slightly and, following him, began: 'I, Margaret, first daughter of the right excellent, right high and mighty Prince and Princess Henry, by the Grace of God King of England, and Elizabeth, Queen of the same, wittingly and of deliberate mind, having twelve years complete in age in the month of November which be past, contract marriage with the right excellent, right high and mighty Prince James, King of Scotland, for the person of whom Patrick, Earl of Bothwell, is procurator; and I take the said James, King of Scotland, unto and for my husband and spouse, and all others for him forsake during his and my lives natural; and therefore I plight and give to him in your person, as procurator aforesaid, my faith and troth.'

As she completed those words there was a sudden burst of music from the royal trumpeters and in an adjoining chamber minstrels began to play.

Princess Margaret of England had now become the Queen of Scotland.

❀ ❀ ❀

Life was exciting for Margaret — full of colour, full of splendour. It was rarely that King Henry encouraged extravagance at his Court but this was, after all, the occasion of his daughter's marriage and he must impress the Scottish visitors with the wealth and power of England.

'A waste of good money,' he told his Queen. 'Banquets . . . jousts! I did not know until this time what a feckless band of courtiers were mine. They welcome the opportunity to flaunt their wealth in senseless pageants.' His eyes narrowed and Elizabeth guessed that he was noting the spendthrifts and devising ways in which the wealth they were so eager to throw away could be diverted into the royal coffers.

Poor fools, to spend more than was necessary. Did they not yet understand the manner in which their royal master's miserly mind worked? Constantly he was thinking of gold for his exchequer. Taxes, fines, they were good methods of swelling it. He wanted more and more gold; he would never be satisfied; just as he wanted more and more children, that he might bargain for concessions from the royal houses of Europe. The Scottish marriage . . . then marriages for Henry and Mary and all the others who would follow.

Oh no, no, she thought. There could be no more. But how could she explain to him? Her duty was to provide him with children – counters for bargaining in state politics, in the same way that it was for his ministers to devise laws for diverting his subjects' wealth into the royal exchequer.

She knew that she was looking ill; her sister Katharine had told her so. But Henry would not notice. She must go on unfalteringly doing her duty as he did his.

'A few more days of this jousting,' she said to soothe him, 'and the celebrations will be over.'

He shook his head sadly. 'We must not give the impression that we are a poor nation. There will be reports circulated as to how we celebrated our daughter's marriage. But, since her husband will be eager for her to join him in Scotland, we might cut short the merrymaking.'

Elizabeth shivered. 'She seems so young. Not much past her twelfth birthday. We shall miss her.'

'Yet I fancy she is old for her years.' The King dismissed the matter comfortably. 'And you'll soon have another to take her place. Pray God this time it is a boy.'

'I trust it will be so.'

The King gave her one of his rare smiles. 'And if it is another girl, we'll not despair. There's time ahead of us.'

She turned to glance out of the window. She could not trust herself to look at him lest he see the fear in her face.

It had been a great day of jousting. Margaret had sat in a place of honour, the Earl of Bothwell beside her; she had applauded the skill of Charles Brandon and the Duke of Buckingham, while young Henry watched broodingly. In his imagination he was jousting with the knights, surprising them all with his skill. It was a great trial to be but ten years old and a looker-on.

Margaret had become grown up since that ceremony in their mother's chamber. He noticed that she was treated with a new deference; he was envious; and when his father was not present he acted as though he were already the King. All his friends indulged his whims; after all, was he not Prince of Wales, destined one day to be King? If he wished to anticipate that day it would be a foolish man who gainsaid him.

Little Mary was delighted with the jousting. She sat with her brother and asked eager questions while he looked after her tenderly; but all the time he was watchful of Margaret who had temporarily usurped the place of honour which he felt should rightfully be his.

After the jousting there was a banquet, and it was Margaret who again sat in the seat of honour, who was Queen of the pageant.

Henry could not understand his father who, in his drab garments, did not look like a king, and sat a little apart from the company with a tired expression in his eyes as though he found all the splendour and fun rather silly.

The Queen sat beside the King and she looked as though her thoughts were far away, and although she was smiling, the smile was forced.

Oh, how different it will be when I am King, thought young Henry.

Margaret, with a dignity new to her, distributed the prizes to the champions of the joust. There were silver bowls and golden cups; and the victors bowed low and kissed her hand when she presented them. She looked very lovely with her young face glowing, and clearly enjoyed being a Queen.

As soon as the prize-giving was over, the pageant began; and because such scenes were rare at the Court of Henry VII they seemed especially delightful. Never it seemed had morris dancers danced with such zest; the ballet was an enchantment, particularly as the six ladies and six gentlemen who took part were all masked and there was the fun of guessing their identities.

And when it was over, the time had come for the King to present gifts to the Scotsmen, and there was an awed silence as the magnificence of these was revealed. For the Archbishop of Glasgow there was a cup of gold and six silver pots, twenty-four silver bowls and a basin and ewer of the same precious metal together with a receptacle for holding hot ashes for the purpose of keeping the feet warm.

It was clear how it hurt the King to part with such treasures, but he did so with an air of resignation as though to say: This much would I do for the good of England. More cups of gold were presented together with crimson velvet bags full of golden coins; and many of the King's courtiers marvelled that the King could part with what he loved best in the world.

The Queen looked on through a haze of pain. It can't be long now, she was thinking. I never suffered like this before. What is going to become of me?

For a few seconds the great hall faded from her sight; she moved forward in her chair; but everyone present was too intent on the magnificent gifts which the King was bestowing to notice the Queen. And when these were all presented she was sitting upright once more, very pale and exhausted – but she had looked ill for some time and her looks surprised none who happened to glance her way.

It was late January when the Queen's barge was rowed along the river to the Tower of London. She was determined to have her lying-in at the palace there, and eagerly she awaited the birth of her child.

Her sister Katharine was with her; this was the one person who could give her most comfort.

'Stay with me, Kate,' she said. 'You remember the days when we were young. They are not really so very long ago, are they, and yet how distant they seem! I shall shortly be thirty-seven – not a great age, and yet when I think of the days when our father fought for his throne, and of how our little brothers disappeared in the Tower and Uncle Richard took the throne, it seems as though I have lived a hundred years.'

'You should not brood on the past, dear sister,' Katharine told her. 'Think of the future. When your little son is born he will bring you great delight. You are fortunate in your children.'

'I often wonder what their lives will be like. My little Margaret . . . how will she fare in Scotland, with a husband who is twice her age and already an experienced lover by all accounts?'

'His age, although twice that of Margaret, is not great . . . she being so young.'

'That's why I tremble for her. She is so young and headstrong.'

'I do not think you need fear for your children, Elizabeth. They are all strong-willed and well able to care for themselves. Margaret . . . Henry . . . and even little Mary. They remind me so much of our father.'

'I am glad of that.'

'And the new child . . . I wonder if he will resemble them.'

Elizabeth caught her breath in sudden pain. 'I think we shall soon be able to judge,' she said. 'Kate, my time has come.'

❦ ❦ ❦

It was Candlemas and the Queen lay in her state apartments in the Palace of the Tower of London. The King was at her bedside; he was disappointed. He had been certain that this time they would get a boy. But at least the child was alive, and that was a good augury for the future.

'A girl,' he mused, 'and we have two girls already. Pray God the next will be a boy.'

And I still abed with this one! thought the Queen. But she did not protest; she had never protested against the King's desires. He had been a faithful husband and, if he had rarely shown her the warmth of affection, he had never shown her the coldness of cruelty.

'I should like to call her Katharine after my sister,' she said.

17

'Katharine let it be,' murmured the King. 'It is as good a name as any.'

She looked up into his shrewd face. What did a name matter? Elizabeth, Jane, or Katharine – whatever she was called the little girl would have to play her part in the destiny of England when she was called.

Margaret had ceased to be the centre of attraction. The jousts were over; there were no more banquets. A gloom hung over the royal palace.

From a window of her apartments at Richmond she had watched the barges sailing along the river; many sailed down to the Palace of the Tower.

Henry came and stood at her side; even he was subdued.

'Is she very ill, do you think?' he asked his sister.

Margaret nodded.

'Skelton told me that Dr Hallyswurth is now at her bedside.'

Margaret was suddenly afraid. Her mother was grievously ill and her illness was due to the birth of their little sister; and the bearing of children was the direct result of marriage.

First came the jousting, the banquets, the feasts and the dancing; and then the nuptial rites; and if one were fruitful – and one must pray that one might be – this terrible ordeal, which often resulted in death, was the next step. Not once only must it be faced . . . but again and again.

Her mother was very ill – many believed she was dying – and it was because she too had had a wedding, as Margaret had, and because it was her duty to give her husband children.

It was a sad thought when one was twelve years old and just married.

She felt envious of her brash young brother, who would one day be King in his own right – not because of a marriage he had happened to contract – and who would not have to suffer as their mother had.

'I wish I were a man,' she said vehemently; and she watched the slow satisfied smile spread across her brother's face.

A barge stopping by the stairs caught her attention and she said: 'Look! Someone is alighting. He may bring news from the Tower.'

They ran from the room and down to meet the messenger, but when Margaret saw the expression on his face she felt sick and wished that she had stayed in her apartments, because before he spoke she knew.

'My mother is dead,' she said in a whisper.

The messenger did not answer, but bowing, stood humbly before her; and in that moment Margaret was too filled with sorrow for the loss of her kindly mother to harbour fears for her own future.

So the Queen was dead and it seemed that the little Katharine would not long survive her. The King had shut himself away to be alone with his sorrow, but those who knew him believed he would already be making plans for a new marriage. It was not that he did not appreciate his Queen who had been a good and docile wife to him; he would never forget that through their marriage the White Rose of York and the Red Rose of Lancaster had mingled harmoniously. It had been a good marriage, but it was over, while the need to provide England with sons was still present. Young Henry was a fine healthy boy – but now that Arthur was gone he was

...my boy; and death could strike quickly and suddenly as he knew well.

There was mourning throughout the Court where there had been gay wedding celebrations; and on the day when Elizabeth of York was laid in her grave the scene was in sad and bitter contrast to that of a few weeks before.

Through the city, from the Tower to Westminster, rode the melancholy cortege, and the newly wed Queen of Scotland knew that many of her father's courtiers watched her furtively and asked themselves whether this was not an ill augury for her wedding. On the other hand, was that a certain relish – equally furtive – which she detected in the eyes of the Scottish lords? Were they telling each other that only young Henry stood between Margaret and the crown of England now? And since Elizabeth of York could no longer give the King of England sons, that was a matter of some moment for those who had the good of Scotland at heart.

Was there a little extra deference in their demeanour toward's her?

If so, Margaret did not notice. During those sad days she forgot that she was a newly created Queen; she was merely a twelve-year-old girl sorrowing for a mother who had never shown her anything but kindness.

One could not mourn for ever. That long winter was passing and with the coming of May the King sent for his eldest daughter.

'Your husband grows impatient for his bride,' he told her. 'It is time you joined him.'

'Yes, Sire,' answered Margaret.

'Preparations shall begin,' the King told her. 'Make yourself ready. In June we will leave Richmond together, for I plan to accompany you on the first stages of your journey.'

Fear showed itself briefly in Margaret's eyes. Now that the time of departure was coming near she did not want to go. It was pleasant being a queen in her father's Court where she had spent her childhood, teasing Henry, flaunting her new importance before little Mary; but to go away to a foreign land was a different matter.

The King did not notice her fear. His mind was on other matters. He wanted a new wife, more children for whom advantageous marriages should be arranged. When he looked at his daughter he did not see a tender young girl so much as a means of keeping the peace with the tiresome warlike people who had made trouble at the Border for as long as any could remember.

The marriage pleased him; therefore Margaret pleased him.

'You may go now,' he told her gently. 'Remember what I have told you.'

She curtsied and left him; then she hurried to her bed-chamber.

She told her attendants that she had a headache and wished to rest, and when she was alone she began to weep silently.

'I want my mother,' she murmured into her pillows, for now, when she would never see the Queen again, she realised that from her alone could she have received the comfort and understanding of which she was in such need.

So Margaret, remembering that she was a bereaved little girl, forgot that she was also Queen of Scotland; and for a long time she lay sobbing because she had lost her mother.

To the Court, however, she showed a brave face, and on the sixteenth day of June, riding beside her father, acknowledging the cheers of the people who had come to watch her pass, she left Richmond Palace on the first stage of her journey to Scotland.

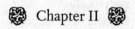

Chapter II

THE BRIDEGROOM

James IV of Scotland was not awaiting his bride with any great excitement. His counsellors had advised him that the marriage was for the good of Scotland and he must needs agree to it.

And so, he thought, I must take this child to wife.

Not so long ago he would have refused to do so, no matter that she was the daughter of the King of England and peace between the two countries was desirable. He had been in love and had made up his mind whom he would marry; and so deep had been his feelings that he would have insisted on having his will.

But passions ran high in Scotland and lives were cheap.

I should have taken greater care of her, he told himself again as he had a hundred times before. Then he would have been the husband of another Margaret.

But the deed had been done and there was no going back. He had now to think of greeting this child whom they were sending him from over the Border, for it was no fault of hers.

They were saying that England and Scotland were united at last; and the Rose and the Thistle could now grow happily side by side. But could that ever be achieved? Was even the union of Tudor and Stuart capable of working such a miracle?

James stroked his auburn curling beard, and his hazel eyes were momentarily melancholy.

He had lost the Margaret he loved, and now must endeavour to make a success of union with her namesake.

And even as he prepared himself for the journey which would end in his meeting with his bride, he was thinking of his first meeting with that other Margaret at Stobhall, her father's mansion on the banks of the Tay.

The banks of the Tay! The wild water cascading over the rocks; the sound of birdsong, and the trees in bud! And beside him, Margaret. Never had he believed such happiness existed in the world.

To be fifteen again . . . and in love for the first time. For the first and last time, he had told her; for she was the only one he would ever love.

She had listened earnestly, believing him. Then he had been a handsome youth. Not dark like his father; not yellow-haired like his Danish mother. It was said that he had inherited the good points of each, and the result was auburn hair which shone as gold in the sunshine; and hazel eyes that could be serious but more often merry; the sensitive mouth of a poet, sensual as a lover's; and a hint of recklessness in the expression which hinted he would be brave in battle.

Margaret was tall and golden-haired and all the world seemed as beautiful as the banks of the Tay to the lovers.

In the beginning they strolled among the trees while he talked to her of his childhood which had been a strange one. He tried to explain to her how he and his brothers had lived almost like prisoners in the Castle of Stirling.

'Whenever I see Stirling I shall remember. What a prison! There it stands on that precipitous hill, and my brothers and I used to look down from our windows on to the Forth. We were always expecting our father to come. We talked continually of him. I remember so well that whenever a stranger came to the castle and he was tall and handsome we would run to him and ask him if he were our father. "Please, please, sir," I used to say, "tell me you are my father." And always I was assured that he was not.'

'Poor James. How strange it must have been.'

'My mother tried to console us. We were fortunate in her.'

'The King has behaved badly not only to you, James, but to the whole of Scotland.'

Had anyone else made such a statement he would have been shocked, for he and his brothers had always been taught that kings should not be judged by their subjects; but since she was Margaret who could do no wrong, he listened.

'I have heard it said that it is no easy matter to be a king,' he replied with a hint of melancholy.

'You will be the best King Scotland has ever known.'

She gave him such adoring looks that he believed her.

'Queen Margaret,' he said, and kissed her hand.

He saw her eyes shine with the excitement he shared; at fifteen it had been pleasant to play their game of make-believe.

'It may be soon that you are crowned King of Scotland, James.'

'Nay, my father has many years before him.'

'But the nobles have risen against him.' She was well aware of that because her father was one of the rebel leaders, and it was for this reason that they had brought the heir to the throne from Stirling to Stobhall.

'It is not good that there should be civil war in Scotland.'

'It will not be for long.' She was repeating what she had so often heard. 'And the King spends too much of the nation's wealth on his favourites, and has mixed brass and lead in silver money and passed it off as pure silver. That is a bad thing to do.'

James shrugged his shoulders and, putting an arm about Margaret, kissed her; there were more pleasant things to do on a sunny afternoon than talk of the misdeeds of his father.

'You must not forget that you will soon wear the crown.'

They sat down on the bank and James thought fleetingly of his father.

'Perhaps he was led away by the company he kept. My mother told me that his greatest friends were a musician, a tailor and a smith at one time, and that he set great store by his astrologers.'

'He believed all they told him,' Margaret affirmed. 'That was why he was afraid of you and your brothers as well as his own brothers.'

'I remember my mother telling me that when I was born the position of the stars and planets showed him that harm would come to him through me. As if I would ever harm him!'

'You would never harm anyone. You are too kind and gentle. You will be the greatest King Scotland has ever known.'

They kissed once more and as he laid his hands on her shoulders, he was trembling with excitement, but he did not know what he wanted to do, so he dropped his hands and stared at the river.

'He had a dream,' he said, 'and when he asked his astrologers to interpret it, they replied that the royal lion of Scotland, in course of time, would be torn by its whelps. That was why he lived in fear of me.'

'A father – and a king – in fear of his son!' scorned Margaret. Then she touched his cheek with her finger. 'And such a son.'

He caught the hand and kissed it. He was overcome by a gust of passion but, acutely conscious of his inexperience, he hesitated. There was a bitter sweetness in fifteen-year-old love that would never be equalled at another time of his life, he knew. She drew away from him. 'They will find a bride for you from some foreign country,' she said sadly. 'They will need to make some useful alliance.'

'They have found brides for me before.' He snapped his fingers. 'That for their foreign marriages! When I was very young it was decided I should marry the Lady Cecilia, second daughter of King Edward the Fourth of England, but when Edward died his daughter was no longer considered a worthy consort. There was a new king on the throne – Richard the Third. I know because my mother insisted that I learn what was happening in other countries and particularly in England.'

'It is a necessary part of the education of one who is to be King,' Margaret reminded him.

'And Richard had a niece, the Lady Anne Suffolk, and he was eager for her to marry me. But it was not long before the Tudor Henry the Seventh had ousted Richard from the throne and then Lady Anne, like Lady Cecilia, was no longer a worthy match for me. Foreign marriages! They often come to naught.' He boasted: 'When I am King I shall choose my own bride and I know who she will be.'

Margaret sighed and leaned against him. Why not? She was after all a Drummond and an ancestor of hers, Annabella Drummond, had married Robert III of Scotland.

'Oh, James, would you indeed?'

'You may trust me,' he assured her. 'I would I were King now . . . But no . . . I don't.'

His brows were drawn together. He wanted to see his father, to tell him what nonsense it was to think that *he*, his eldest son, James, who wished to live in peace with everyone, would ever dream of harming him. James was imagining a pleasant scene when he would be brought face-to-face with his father and would heal the rift between him and his nobles; then he would take Margaret by the hand and say: 'Father, this is the lady I have chosen to be my bride.' There would be great rejoicing throughout Scotland, for the discord would be healed by this marriage; Stirling would be the scene of joyous festivities and he would ride through the streets to Edinburgh, and there would be tournaments in the fields about the Castle and Holyrood House.

It was such a pleasant dream that it was a pity to wake from it. But he did not wish to be King since that must mean his father would be dead. He hated the thought of death; it would always remind him of the death of his mother.

Margaret understood; she pressed her lips tightly together because she knew it would hurt him if she said what was in her mind; she must not repeat what she had heard her father and his friends say, which was that it would be a good day for Scotland if James III were dethroned and his son set up in his place.

Everyone at Stobhall talked of it. She had discussed it with her sisters, particularly the younger ones – Anabella, Eupheme and Sibylla. It was for this reason that her father had brought the young heir to the throne to Stobhall, that he might be here in the hands of his father's enemies when the need arose.

'I hate death,' whispered James. 'And my father would have to die before I could be King.'

It was only about a year ago that his mother had died, and he was still aware of the void that had made in his life. It had changed the tenor of his days and he could still wake in the night and shed tears for the loss of his kind and tolerant mother.

And when she was no longer there his father's enemies had decided to make him their figurehead. He should have protested, he knew; but Lord Drummond had brought him to Stobhall and here he had found Margaret.

She was impatient of the course the talk was taking, for she did not wish to make him melancholy.

'Let us take off our shoes,' she said, 'and dabble our feet in the water.'

She cried out in mock dismay as the cold water splashed about her ankles; she held her skirts above her knees, as James splashed into the river after her and she pretended to run from him.

He caught her, as she intended he should.

'Why, James the Fourth,' she cried, 'how bold you are!'

'Is that your opinion then, Queen Margaret?'

They embraced there, while the water played about their ankles, and were astonished by their sensations. They were fifteen and people of their age who lived in the early sixteenth century in Scotland were invariably sexually awakened. They had both led more sheltered lives than most young people, and they felt in that moment impatient with their innocence. They seemed bound more closely together because they must lead each other, because they must explore together.

He drew her from the water and they lay on the bank together.

'This is the happiest day of my life,' said the future James IV of Scotland.

But even as they lay there on the bank they heard the sound of urgent voices calling the Prince.

'Heed them not,' whispered James. 'They will go away.'

But the voices came nearer and Margaret struggled free of his arms and leaping to her feet smoothed her hair, straightened her rumpled gown.

He rose and stood beside her, and thus the messenger from Stobhall found them.

'I implore Your Highness to return to the house without delay,' James was told, and he caught the excitement in the voice of the man who addressed him.

Important events were close; he could not guess how important; but as he walked back with Margaret he sensed that the idyll on the bank of the Tay had been more than temporarily interrupted – perhaps it would be lost for ever.

❀ ❀ ❀

He felt the remorse even now, looking back over the years. What should I have done? he asked himself, as he had so often. Should I have refused?

But Margaret's father was among those who pointed out his duty, and Margaret herself stood by with shining eyes watching him, telling him by her glances that he was no longer a boy.

They were persuading him where his duty lay and among them were some of the most powerful lords of Scotland: Angus, Argyle, the Humes and the Hepburns. And he gave way. Many a time he had said to himself: 'I was but a boy of fifteen.' Yet he could never forget that he had allowed himself to ride out with them, while the red and gold banner of his ancestors had been held over his head.

There was one point on which he never ceased to thank God that he had insisted. 'None is to harm my father,' he had declared. 'If the battle goes in our favour he is to be brought to me.'

They had soothed him with gentle words, telling him that he was their leader and his word was law.

And thus he had ridden to Sauchieburn which was but a few miles from Bannockburn, the very spot where, nearly two hundred years before, the Bruce himself had defeated Edward II of England and restored independence to Scotland.

The horror of the battle of Sauchieburn stayed with him. Somewhere among the opposing army had been his father, the man who had shut himself away from his son because he believed that he would one day do him harm. Had this old prophecy been fulfilled? James wanted to cry out: But if you had been a natural father to me, if you had let love, not fear, govern the relationship between us, we would not be here this day at Sauchieburn fighting against each other.

He heard that his father had sent to Edinburgh Castle and ordered that the sword which Robert the Bruce had carried at Bannockburn should be brought to him, that he had said: 'As it served the Bruce then, so shall it serve me now.'

And he had ridden into battle on the fleetest horse in Scotland, the Bruce's sword in his hand.

James believed then that Sauchieburn would haunt him all his life; and it was true that his dreams were even now disturbed by the sound of the trumpets and the clash of spears. They had not allowed him to enter the thick of the fight – nor had he any heart for it – but he sat his horse fearfully watching, as he had in those days in Stirling Castle, for a man of noble bearing who might be his father.

And when they had come to him and told him that the enemy was routed and the victory was his he had felt the childish tears well into his eyes and he wanted to cry out: How can I rejoice when my victory is my father's defeat?

'Where is my father?' he demanded.

But no one knew.

'It would seem, my lord, that he left the battlefield before the end. He may well have escaped to the Forth and left Scotland in one of Sir Andrew Wood's ships which were waiting there to help him in such an emergency.'

'I must know what has happened to my father,' James insisted.

He asked that he might be alone. Then he knelt in the privacy of his tent and prayed that his father might be safe, that they might meet and all differences between them be dissolved.

He was in Stirling Castle when Lord Drummond and others of the rebel lords brought a stranger to him. This was one of the most handsome men James had ever seen – tall, with an air of fearlessness.

James went forward eagerly holding out his hands.

'Sir,' he cried, 'are you my father?'

When the man put his hands over his eyes to hide his

emotion, Drummond said sourly: 'Nay, my lord, this is Sir Andrew Wood. He has come ashore because his friends have hostages of ours for his safekeeping. He has been sheltering our enemies on his ships in the Forth.'

Sir Andrew removed his hand and said firmly: 'I am not Your Highness's father, but I am his true servant, and I shall continue to be the enemy, until I die, of those who are disloyal to him.'

Drummond said: 'If you know where the King is, it would be well for you to say.'

'I know not,' was the answer.

'But some of my father's men have found refuge in your ships?' James put in eagerly.

'That is so, my lord.'

'Are you sure my father is not among them?' asked the boy pleadingly.

'Yes, my lord. Would to God I could tell you that he is safe with us, but he is not and I know not where he is. If I knew I would tell you; but I fear the worst, and I trust that one day will see the hanging of the traitors who have cruelly murdered him.'

'Murdered!' cried James, his face turning pale with horror.

But the lords had seized Andrew Wood and hustled him from the apartment.

❧ ❧ ❧

Murder! pondered James, and then the remorse began.

Some days passed before he learned what had really happened to his father at Sauchieburn, and he felt sick with horror when the tale was recounted. His father had left the battlefield before the end, being advised by his generals that he should escape to the Forth where, while there was yet time, he could find shelter with Wood's fleet. To stay would be to die in the field; to escape would be to live to fight another day.

A few miles from the battlefield, near a millstream, he met a woman with a pitcher which she had come to fill. Seeing the horse and rider making straight for her, and fearing they would trample her underfoot she dropped the pitcher and ran. The pitcher rolling under the horse's hoofs so startled the terrified animal that it shied and stumbled, its weary rider was thrown and lay unconscious in the dust while the horse went galloping on.

The story had been slowly pieced together by the people who had witnessed it. James heard how workers had come from the mill and carried the King inside, how he recovered consciousness and when the miller's wife – a forceful woman – had asked his name, answered: 'James Stuart is my name, and this morning I was your King.'

'Saints above us!' the miller's wife had cried. 'We have the King under our roof. And dying maybe. A priest! Fetch a priest for the King.'

She dashed out of the mill and began to run to the priest's house, but before she reached it she saw a rider coming from the direction of Sauchieburn. 'Stop!' she cried. 'The King is in our mill. He is sorely hurt and needing a priest.'

The man drew up and said: 'I am a priest. Lead me to him.'

The miller's wife led him back to the mill, shouted for a boy to take his horse and then took him into the mill where the King was lying on the floor.

'I am a priest,' said the man, kneeling beside the King.

'Welcome,' murmured the King.

'Are you mortally wounded?'

'I think not, but I wish to confess my sins and to ask pardon for the faults of a lifetime.'

Then, so quickly that none of those about him realised what was happening until it was done, the man drew his sword and, saying, 'This will give you pardon,' plunged it into the King's body.

Withdrawing it, he walked out of the mill, took his horse from the boy who held it, mounted and rode away. And none ever knew his name.

Young James was in his apartment at Stirling Castle when the nobles came to him. He was astonished by their solemn looks.

'What news?' he asked.

Lord Drummond was kneeling before him as he heard the shout which resounded through the room: 'Long live the King!'

James recoiled. 'My father . . . ?' he began.

'Sire, you no longer have a father. Long live James the Fourth of Scotland and the Isles.'

It was then he heard the story of his father's end; but he could not share their joy. He could only tell himself that never again would he look into the faces of handsome strangers and wonder whether at last he was face-to-face with his father.

Already he seemed to feel the crown weighing heavily on his head. His father defeated by his enemies and murdered by them! Not until that moment had he understood how they had involved him in their treacherous conflict, and there was deep sorrow in understanding. His father had died and it might seem that he himself bore some responsibility for that death.

I believe I shall never know complete peace again, he told himself.

In the weeks that followed his accession, so great had been his remorse that he had even forgotten Margaret. Night and morning he had prayed for the soul of his father in the Chapel-Royal at Stirling Castle.

'How can I atone for my father's death?' he demanded of his confessor.

'Pray . . . pray for forgiveness,' was the answer.

But he found only brief comfort in prayer, and soon afterward he took to wearing an iron belt about his doublet, which was heavy and caused him great discomfort.

But he felt happier wearing it. It was a way of doing penance for the murder of his father.

That had happened long ago and one could not grieve for ever. He had quickly discovered that it was pleasant to be a king. His friends, important men such as Argyle, Hailes, Lyle and Hume, were eager for him to enjoy life and to leave tiresome state matters to them.

'Why,' they said, 'you are the King; and living as you did in Stirling Castle, what chance did you have of enjoying your life?'

He changed; he was no longer retiring, but discovered himself to be a high-spirited boy, and there was hunting and hawking over the glorious countryside; there were balls and banquets to be arranged; dancing to be watched and indulged in. His father was buried in state at Cambuskenneth Abbey and lay there with his wife, so there was nothing more his son could do for him, except to wear the iron belt now and then to remind himself and the world that he still regretted the manner in which his father had died.

There had been days when pleasure had been constantly with him; he remembered the occasion when Margaret Drummond had joined him at Linlithgow Castle and he had ordered gold, azure and silver cloth to make her a gown which would dazzle all who saw it; and when she sat with him in the place of honour at the table, the masked singers, luters, and harpists performed for them alone.

Had he followed his own inclination he would have married Margaret then as he had promised to; but there were jealous men about him who were determined that the Drummonds should not become too powerful and, although Margaret and he were allowed to enjoy each other's company in the weeks immediately following his succession, excuses were made to part them.

And he had allowed it to happen – just as he had allowed his father's enemies to place him at their head. He could always make the excuse: 'I was but a boy.' To become a king would naturally overwhelm one so young; it was understandable that he should find life more absorbing than it had been in Stirling Castle or at Stobhall. He became interested in the governing of his country; and the lords of Scotland were too quarrelsome ever to live in peace with one another, so there was continual strife. Was it for that reason that he allowed himself to drift away from Margaret? Or was it because he had discovered that the longings she had aroused within him could be stimulated – though not with the same tenderness or delight – by any pretty woman? Now that he was King there were so many to smile on him.

Women – more knowledgeable than Margaret – beckoned him continually. He hesitated for a while, remembering his first love; then he hesitated no longer and he knew that, of all the sports and pastimes which delighted him, nothing would appeal to him quite so strongly as making love to women.

His advisers laughed at him. They would not have it otherwise. Let him chase women who would keep him occupied, preventing him from dabbling in state affairs. What could better suit their purpose?

''Tis kingly in a man to love women,' they told him. 'A habit of all good kings – and a custom the Stuarts ever observed.'

So there need be no remorse. He forgot to sigh for Margaret; he even forgot his remorse for his father's death. Those were the carefree years.

Women! A succession of women – highborn ladies and tavern wenches. He had changed from that inexperienced boy who had dallied with Margaret Drummond on the banks of the Tay.

Yet being sentimental, he looked for one particular woman. Women there would always be, but among them he sought always the perfect mistress. He thought he had found her in Marian Boyd, the daughter of the Lord of Bonshaw – comely, witty, a charming mistress. He had been faithful to Marian for months, and she had borne him two children of whom he was very proud. He gave Alexander and Catherine the name of Stuart, for he was not ashamed to recognise them as his own. He took time from his state duties to visit them often, for he loved playing with children and he was determined that his children should never be treated by their father as he had been by his.

Marian might have remained his chief mistress had it not been for Janet Kennedy.

Janet was different from any other woman he had ever known. Redheaded and tempestuous, already she had been the mistress of Archibald Douglas, Earl of Angus, known as the Great Earl and Bell-the-Cat, one of the most notorious of all Scottish lords. It had been an achievement therefore for James to take her from Angus, even though he was a king and Angus a mere earl.

Angus had always been a leader in the country's affairs, and had earned the nickname Bell-the-Cat, by which he was always known, some years before when the English had threatened to attack Scotland and certain of the nobles refused to stand with James III to repel this enemy. When James had been preparing to march to the Border, certain of his own countrymen such as Huntley, Angus, Lennox, Gray and Lyle were gathering together an army to pursue the King's and present certain demands to him before they joined forces with him against the English. When they were deciding who should present the demands, Lord Gray told the fable of the mice who planned to put a bell about the cat's neck to warn them of its approach. All very well, was the answer, but who should bell the cat? It was Angus who spoke up: 'I will bell the cat,' and forever after he was known by that name. Shrewd, brilliant, Angus never failed to seize an opportunity which would advance the Douglases.

After the death of his wife he became enamoured of redheaded Janet, daughter of Lord Kennedy, and she remained his mistress until she became the King's.

They were thrilling days and nights James spent in Janet's company. She combined ambition with passion, and her possessiveness was a little alarming, for James was a man who liked to live on good terms with all about him. He wanted his own way and where women were concerned there was a compulsion within him to take it, but he continually endeavoured to extricate himself from a difficult situation by diplomacy rather than by quarrels.

He was deep in his love affair with Janet Kennedy when Margaret Drummond came back into his life.

It was some twelve years since they had dallied on the banks of the Tay, and Margaret had grown into a serene and beautiful woman. She had never married, she told him, but there were no reproaches; *she* understood perfectly that a king could not marry where he wished, but the boy who had made his promises at Stobhall had not. She had never ceased to love him. 'Why,' she said, 'I shall always remember that I once had your love . . . your first love, and that is enough to make me happy for the rest of my life.'

Now James saw what he had lost, and that Margaret could make him happy as neither Marian nor Janet ever could. Serene, disinterested, she could be passionate, giving wholeheartedly of her love and never demanding any favours in return; which was, he saw now, the only way to love. It had taken him years of experience to discover this. They were no longer very young, since they were both approaching their twenty-seventh birthdays.

'Nothing shall ever separate us again,' declared James vehemently. 'I am King now and shall not be diverted from my purpose.'

It was Janet who temporarily diverted him. When he tried to explain to her, she faced him with a blazing desire which he was unable to resist and that which was meant to be a brief farewell was a night of such wild passion that he began to wonder whether even Margaret could free him from the spell Janet Kennedy had cast over him.

'Can she love like this?' demanded Janet.

Janet was wily. That night their son was conceived. A lover of children could not be indifferent to his own child.

He continued to see Janet, and Margaret did not complain. She was the perfect mistress; always kind, always understanding.

I will keep that promise I made all those years ago, James told himself. I will marry Margaret.

And so they had moved slowly towards that tragic climax. He was going to marry Margaret Drummond. She had already borne him a daughter who was named after her and who James insisted should be known as the Lady Margaret Stuart. Janet's son was born two years after Margaret's, and James loved these two children so dearly that it was difficult for him to say which he loved the more. And if he could not discard a mistress, how could he discard a child?

Memories of his own childhood were often with him. He was not going to let his little James suffer as *he* had. Therefore he must pay visits to his son, and it was natural that the boy would be with his mother; so during those years of indecision, both Janet and Margaret continued to hold sway over him – Janet by the violence of her emotion, Margaret by the serenity of hers.

But it was Margaret whom he loved; and he decided that before his marriage with her he would make a clean break with Janet.

When he visited her and told her of his proposed marriage she veiled her heavy-lidded eyes and threw back her flaming hair, but she did not look at him.

'I am determined,' he told her. 'And this must be the end between us.'

'And our son?'

'Do not think I shall ever forget him. He shall be created Earl of Moray; and you shall not be forgotten either. I shall bestow on you the Castle of Darnaway and the forests surrounding it. It shall be yours unless you marry or live with any other man. In which case it would revert to me.'

Janet closed her eyes and nodded. The Earldom of Moray. The Castle of Darnaway. It was a good reward.

She said quietly: 'I believe there is good hunting in the forests of Darnaway.'

He smiled. Let her believe that he intended to hunt there and visit her when he did so. Better not to say he intended never to see her again when he was married to Margaret Drummond.

'It is indeed good.'

Then she threw her arms about him and laughed in her wild way. Well, there had to be a last time and he had been prepared for this. What was one more night among all the rest that were left to him?

Farewell Janet, he had said to himself when he had ridden away next morning.

❋ ❋ ❋

He often wondered afterwards what part Janet and her family played in the tragedy that followed. But he could not be sure and Janet might have been guiltless, for there were others to oppose the marriage.

When the news was brought to him he remembered the long-ago occasion when he had heard of his father's death.

Margaret was at Drummond Castle, making preparations for her wedding. Her four-year-old little daughter, Lady Margaret Stuart, was with her there; so were two of her sisters

– the two youngest: Eupheme who was married, not very happily, to Lord Fleming, and Sibylla who was unmarried.

The three sisters sat down to breakfast one morning; a few hours later all three were dead. One of the dishes which had been served to them contained a deadly poison.

So grief struck him for the second time. I shall never forget Margaret, he mourned; as once before he had told himself he would never forget his father's death. He was distracted by his grief, but his first thought was for his child, and impetuously he set off for Drummond Castle and took the little girl to Edinburgh Castle. He himself would watch over her.

He often wondered who had done this foul murder, but there was no means of knowing. There were some who declared that Lord Fleming, heartily sick of his wife Eupheme, had intended to dispose of her and had carried off her two sisters at the same time.

No one really believed that. There were so many who were opposed to the King's union with the Drummonds. Already there was a faction who believed that Scotland could best be served by a marriage with Margaret Tudor, the daughter of the King of England. Such ruthless nobles would not care that in killing Margaret they had to kill her two sisters also.

Lurking in James's mind was the thought of the Kennedys. Was it possible that wild Janet and her family had found some means of destroying the woman who had displaced her? Did they plan to put Janet in her place?

He did not care; he was not a vindictive man. Nothing he did now could bring back Margaret.

He listened with indifference to the arguments which were

put before him. A political marriage was the duty of a king. He must contemplate the good which could come to Scotland if there were means of making peace with the old enemy across the Border.

Nothing brought peace between countries as easily as marriage in the royal houses.

He knew they were right. Let the negotiations with Henry VII go forward.

This had been done and now, mourning Margaret Drummond as he believed he would do all his life, he prepared himself to meet that other Margaret who was journeying north to share his throne.

🌸 Chapter III 🌸

THE THISTLE AND THE ROSE

On a sunny June day, four months after the death of her mother, Margaret, Queen of Scots, set out from Richmond Palace accompanied by her father. Crowds had gathered in the countryside through which the cavalcade was expected to pass, and Margaret could not hide her delight to find herself the centre of such pageantry.

She was young and beautiful. She still mourned her gentle mother, but she had seen little of her during her lifetime and it seemed to her quite a long time ago that Elizabeth of York had died. So much had happened in between; there had been all the excitement of preparing her wardrobe – and how she loved those silks and damasks, those purple and crimson velvets! How she enjoyed the homage which was paid to her! Life was too good for mourning.

Let young Henry purse his little mouth and tell her she was frivolous; she could not care. He would have been equally excited if all the pother was for him.

She had heard stories of her husband and she liked what she had heard. She was longing to be with him. He was handsome and fearless; he loved hunting and the tournament; he was devoted to music.

'He has everything that I would ask of a husband,' she told her friends.

Riding out of Richmond, she did not look back once, nor did she ask herself when she would see those towers and turrets again. She was certain that life in Scotland was going to please her, and that she was going to feel no regrets for the past.

She was a charming figure in her riding dress of green velvet edged with purple tinsel; and when the people saw her on her white palfrey they cheered heartily for their lovely young Princess who was already a queen and whose marriage was going to bring peace to the country. Margaret smiled, acknowledging the cheers. Like Henry she was never bashful but delighted to hear the applause of the people.

There was a litter for her when she should tire of riding; it was magnificent, being covered with cloth of gold and trimmed with gold fringe; on it were embroidered the royal arms of England. She also had a chariot which brought gasps of admiration from all who saw it. It was lined with bearskins and painted with the arms of England, and the trappings of the horses and the hammer-cloths were of black and crimson velvet. Her litter-men wore the Tudor colours, green and white, and painted on them were the combined arms of England and Scotland.

They came by easy stages to Colleweston in Northamptonshire where the King planned to take leave of his daughter. This was the seat of Margaret's grandmother, the Countess of Richmond, after whom she had been named.

The Countess had prepared a great banquet to celebrate the arrival of her beloved son and granddaughter; and here there was revelry for over a week.

But it was soon time to continue the journey and there, in the hall of Colleweston, Margaret bade farewell to her father and grandmother. All the nobility who had accompanied them, and those who had assembled for the occasion, watched the ceremony of farewell.

The King embraced his daughter and gave her words of advice; he also gave her an illuminated book of prayers in which he wrote: 'Remember your kind and loving father in your good prayers. Henry R.'

Margaret was moved by this gesture, and in that moment she remembered that she was leaving her home and, in spite of all the pomp and pageantry which surrounded her and the fineness of her wardrobe, she felt apprehensive.

How could she know what this new land to which she was going would be like? Her father and family would be far away and she would be at the mercy of her Scottish husband.

But when they had left Colleweston and the journey began again she found that, now that her father was not present, she was treated with even more respect, and, her fears being dispersed, her spirits quickly rose.

All through England she was given homage. In every town and village the bells rang out as she approached. The lords of the districts greeted her and bade her welcome, and everywhere she went she was treated as a queen.

All marvelled at her beauty and her charm, her brilliant Tudor colouring, her vitality, good health and high spirits. On through Lincolnshire to Yorkshire, here to be greeted by the High Sheriff, Sir William Conyers, by Sir Edward Savage, Sir Ralph Rider, Sir John Milton, Sir John Savile and Lord Scrope –

all the worthies of the district who must come and pay homage to the daughter of their King. When she reached the City of York the gates were thrown open and the Lord Mayor marched at the head of the citizens to greet her, while the Earl of Northumberland magnificently attired in crimson velvet, with jewels glistening at his collar and on his sleeves, led the nobility. The trumpets sounded and minstrels sang to welcome her.

She revelled in the ceremonies which awaited her in that ancient city. In cloth of gold, wearing a girdle encrusted with precious stones, not only encircling her waist but falling to the hem of her gown, she visited the Archbishop of York in his palace where she heard mass; and afterward the nobility was presented to her. She would have liked to linger in the beautiful city, but she had to remember that her bridegroom was waiting for her.

It was a wonderful journey with homage all the way; a perfect horsewoman, she could ride for hours without feeling the least tired; and if she wished for a change there was her splendid litter or her even more sumptuous carriage ready for her.

And at last they reached the Border.

This was an important moment. The people here cheered more wildly than anywhere else, for it was comforting to see sparkling processions instead of ravaging hordes of savage men determined on destruction.

'Peace for evermore!' That was the cry. And this beautiful girl – no more than a child – with her round, rosy face and her glittering, golden hair, was the reason for it.

'Long live the Princess Margaret,' they cried. 'Long live Margaret, Queen of Scots!'

She had learned how to receive the acclamation of the

crowd, for she was a gracious lady now, not a shy young princess.

Lady Darcy, whose husband was the Captain of Berwick, received her at the gates; she was feted and flattered and a banquet was prepared for her. There was music and dancing for her entertainment; there was sport, and wild dogs were brought out to fight great bears. Later Margaret prepared herself for her entry into her husband's country.

Sparkling with jewels, her eyes as brilliant as any gems, her cheeks scarlet with excitement, she was a lovely sight on her white palfrey; and the ceremonial moment had come; the gates were flung wide and Margaret passed out of England into Scotland.

❦ ❦ ❦

She looked about her eagerly. The country of which I am Queen! she told herself. It was exciting to see it for the first time. This was the scene of many a bitter fight. How wonderful to contemplate that now it was a scene of rejoicing.

The first halt was at Lammermuir, and the curious people came out to look at their Queen and gasp with admiration at her youth, beauty and finery.

She was greeted at Lammermuir by the nobles of the district and although they could not have been more loyal she noticed that their clothes lacked that magnificence which had been a feature of those of the English lords. There was no gold or tinsel on their doublets, although the material of which they were made was of a good quality velvet or camlet.

Here she received a present from her husband – fruits which he believed she would find refreshing during her journey. Margaret, who was young enough to be hungry in any circumstances, devoured them with pleasure; and although it was now necessary to say goodbye to the English nobles who had escorted her from their Northern domains across the Border, she did so without regret; and her journey continued to Fastcastle. This meant passing through wild scenery such as Margaret had never before seen; and from her apartments at Fastcastle she could look down on the bay below to St Abb's Head, from the jagged rocks, black and unscalable, to the Wolf-Craig rising high and forbidding above the castle. It had been a slow journey, for the crossing of Lammermuir had been dangerous; Margaret had been warned of the bogs which lurked on the rough heath, and special guides had been hired to get them safely across.

Margaret felt that night that she was indeed in a strange new land in spite of the warm welcome she had received from Lord and Lady Home who lived at Fastcastle.

She spent only one night under that roof and the next morning took the road to Haddington; and before nightfall she and her cavalcade had reached the convent of Haddington where the Abbess was waiting to welcome her. Here she stayed for the night with her women, chief among whom were Lady Lyle, Lady Stanley, Lady Guildford and the Countess of Surrey; the men of the party could not, of course, stay at the convent so they were conducted to the Grey Friars.

The people of Haddington came out to watch the procession leave, and now there was an added excitement in the Queen's suite; the meeting with the King must be close at hand and, although Margaret did not believe for one moment that he would be displeased with her, she was eager to look her best for the meeting.

They were to reach the Castle of Dalkeith by midday and as

this was only seven miles from Edinburgh it seemed certain that on this day the meeting of the royal bride and groom would take place.

They were within half a mile of Dalkeith Palace when Margaret suddenly felt displeased with her appearance. She brought her palfrey close to that of Lady Guildford, who was known as her lady-mistress, and said: 'How do I look?'

Lady Guildford answered that she must have been aware of the admiration which she had aroused; it was well deserved.

'But I think I should look my very best, and I am not pleased with this gown. Who knows what will be waiting for us at Dalkeith?'

Lady Guildford saw the point of this. The first meeting was a great occasion, and it was just possible that the King would have ridden the seven miles from Edinburgh to meet his bride informally before he must do so in public.

'What does Your Grace propose to do?' Lady Guildford asked.

'Change here into my best gown and ride the rest of the way in the litter.'

'Change here on the road!'

'Why not?'

'Whoever heard of a queen changing her gown in her litter by the roadside!'

'They will after today,' said Margaret, 'for that is what I propose to do, and I'll have no interference.'

Lady Guildford pressed her lips firmly together. She had seen signs of obstinacy in her young mistress since they had begun this journey. Margaret resembled her brother Henry more than ever. Like him, she had a will of her own and had been waiting only until authority was hers to use it.

There was no gainsaying her; the procession was halted; the gown was brought from her baggage and her ladies surrounded her litter while she changed her travelling gown for one of dazzling magnificence.

Thus she rode into Dalkeith in velvet and tinsel, her eyes sparkling with anticipation, the flush of health and excitement on her rounded cheeks.

The Earl and Countess of Morton, castellan and castellaine of Dalkeith, were waiting for her and, as she passed through the gateway the Earl bowed low and presented her with the keys of the castle.

Lady Morton led her to her apartments and, when Margaret had expressed her pleasure in them and the loyalty of the Countess and her husband, she was left with her ladies to prepare herself for the banquet which was to follow.

While Lady Morton was receiving Margaret's thanks there was a commotion in the courtyard below. Lady Morton turned pale and, forgetting she was in the presence of the Queen, ran to the window. Then she turned to Margaret and said: 'The King is here.'

'The King . . . my husband!'

Margaret's eyes were wide and she trembled a little. Then she thought of the magnificent sight she must present in her dazzling gown, and she could not resist throwing a look of triumph at Lady Guildford. There! Was I not right! she seemed to be saying.

She ran to the window, but he had already entered the castle.

'He will come straight to Your Grace,' murmured Lady Morton.

Margaret smoothed the folds of her gown; she put up a hand to touch her shining hair. There was no time to ask for reassurance that she looked her best, but she did not need it because she knew she did.

The door of the apartment was opened and there he stood. Her heart began to beat fast and a sudden joy came to her, for he was so handsome in his velvet hunting clothes, although there was nothing ornate about them, for he had come straight from the hunt, without ceremony, perhaps to let her know that this was an informal visit.

He is beautiful, she thought; and she believed that she loved him, so happy was she to be in Scotland and already his wife.

He was flushed from the chase and perhaps he shared in her excitement, for after all, was he not meeting his wife for the first time even as she was meeting her husband? His eyes were hazel, his hair dark auburn, and she now believed all those who had told her that he was the handsomest King in the world.

He was smiling – and it was the kindest and most tender of smiles – as he came towards her. She made a low curtsy and he raised her with both his hands, and drawing her to him, kissed her.

She could not take her eyes from him. He appealed to her senses in a way which was entirely new to her; it did not occur to her that there was scarcely a woman who came into contact with him who did not share her feeling in greater or less degree. She was inexperienced and had received so much adulation that she believed he shared every emotion she herself felt. She did not stop to ask herself whether a man past thirty – and such a man – might have had many adventures in love.

James, whose years of kingship had taught him that it was always wise outwardly to observe convention, turned from his bride to greet her attendants. He took all the ladies by the hand

and kissed them and then accepted the greetings of the men with the utmost courtesy.

And all the time he was thinking: She is but a child. Poor little girl! So eager. So determined to do her duty. Little Margaret Tudor! Oh, why could it not have been that other Margaret? *My* Margaret!

Having greeted the company, it was now fitting for him to give his attention to his bride, and he returned to her, took her hand and drew her apart. Seeing his desire to talk with her, the rest of the company kept their distance, and James, smiling down at her, said: 'But you are beautiful . . . more beautiful than I dared hope.'

'And all they said of you is true.'

'What did they say of me?'

'That you were the handsomest King in the world.'

He laughed. 'I should have been afraid, had I known, that after such a glowing description I might disappoint you.'

'You do not disappoint me.'

Her eyes were glowing, her lips slightly parted. James – connoisseur of women – knew the signs. She would be no prude. It would be no hardship to do his duty. He was glad to discover in her a sensuality which might match his own.

'I trust,' he said, 'that you will be happy in Scotland.'

'I know I shall . . . now that I have met my lord.'

'Do you always make up your mind on such a short acquaintance?'

'Always.'

'Is that wise?'

'I can only trust my inclinations, which rarely betray me,' she answered.

He took her hand and kissed it.

By sweet Saint Ninian! he thought. We must join the others, lest we come to the lovemaking before we have time to get abed.

He compared her with that other Margaret. This one would never be serene. He was uneasily reminded of Janet Kennedy, for he sensed a certain wild passion in this young girl – although it was not yet full awakened – which might equal Janet's. That made him think of his Margaret, sitting down to her last breakfast with her sisters. Was it possible that Janet had had a hand in that? If he really believed that, he would never see her again. But this was not the time to think of that – nor was any time, for it was past and done with. But he did feel a little uneasy to be reminded of Janet by this little Tudor girl whom he had been obliged to marry for the sake of his country's peace.

'Come,' he said, 'we must not neglect our friends. And I'll swear there is food and wine waiting for us.'

She sat beside him at the table, which was laden with good food and wine, and all the time she was conscious of him beside her.

'I must return to Edinburgh for the night,' he said, 'and you must retire early to prepare yourself for the ceremonial entry into our capital.'

'I am sorry you must return to Edinburgh without me.'

He laughed and touched her hand lightly. This was in the nature of a caress. His hazel eyes were bright with tenderness; she did not know that this expression was invariably in his eyes when he looked at a woman – even though she were a fishwife in the market or a tavern girl.

'It was a little unseemly of me to come in this way,' he told her, 'but I was so eager to see my bride. I wanted to assure her that she had nothing to fear.'

'I should never be afraid of you,' she told him. 'You are kind and good, and the happiest woman in Scotland is the Queen.'

He smiled again and said: 'You make prettier speeches in England than we do in Scotland. I trust our rough manners will not offend you.'

'You . . . rough?'

'You will see,' he warned her, but there was mockery in his gaze, and she was more deeply in love than ever.

She danced for him, taking Lady Surrey as her partner; she was eager to show him how accomplished she was. She remembered the occasion when she and Henry had danced together at the marriage of their brother Arthur and Katharine of Aragon, and how all present had said none danced in such a sprightly manner as they did. She remembered how her father and mother had watched them, with smiles of contentment on their faces, so grateful were they for their good health and spirits.

But then she had danced as a child, trying to outleap Henry; now she danced as a woman, gracefully, seductively.

The King applauded her and, when she returned to his side, told her he was charmed with his bride.

'But the hour grows late,' he said, 'and I must return to Edinburgh; for remember we have not yet sworn our marriage vows to each other except by proxy. Until we have done so, alas, we must part.'

'Soon,' she answered, 'we shall make those vows.'

'I am glad that you look forward to that occasion even as I do,' he replied.

When he said farewell, Lady Guildford wanted to warn her charge that she should not show her feelings so frankly, but that lady realised that it was not so easy to advise the Queen of Scotland as the Princess of England.

Margaret lay dreaming of the future. She was dancing before him with Lady Surrey, and suddenly he rose and partnered her himself, holding her tightly. His handsome eyes were ardent; he was telling her that he had never dreamed she could be so beautiful. Willingly she submitted herself to his embrace; she was growing very warm; she felt that she was suffocating.

Then she was awakened by a flickering light in her apartment and she was coughing because of the smoke.

She hurried out of bed as Lady Guildford ran into the room.

'Your Grace! Rise quickly. There is not a moment to lose.'

'Is the castle on fire?'

'I fear so.'

She was hurried into a gown and out of the apartment; there she was joined by her ladies, and she saw the Countess of Morton was with them.

'Come quickly down to the hall, Your Grace,' said the Countess. 'Something terrible has happened. The castle is in danger.'

As they hurried down to the hall they heard shouts from without. Now the angry glow seemed all about them and they could hear the crackle of flames.

They were joined by the Earl and some of his men.

'It started in the stables,' he said. 'I'm afraid they're completely burned. But I believe we have saved the castle. There is no need to fear. We can remain here. The fire is under control.'

It was a wretched night, for although she returned to her apartment she did not sleep; she stood for a long time with her ladies at the window watching the smouldering remains of the stables, and when news was brought to her that her two white palfreys had been burned to death, Margaret threw herself on to her bed and wept like a child.

Her dear palfreys whom she had loved so much, who had carried her so far!

'I shall never have palfreys that I love so much,' she mourned.

❀ ❀ ❀

But in the morning there came a tender message from the King. He had heard of the disaster which had befallen his bride and was much concerned. He was coming to see her that very day but first he suggested that, as Dalkeith had been unlucky for her and she could not be as comfortable there as it was his desire she should be, he wanted her to leave at once for Newbattle Castle which was not far off; and there she would stay until her entry into Edinburgh and their true marriage. 'Only a few days it will be, long enough for me to court you in a fitting manner.'

She brightened up when she heard that message and immediately she and her train set out for Newbattle.

She was so far composed as to have settled into the new residence and was playing cards – which she loved to do – in her apartments when a visitor was announced.

She started up and cried out in delight to see him. Now he looked more like a king, in black velvet jacket with a crimson velvet border and an edge of white fur.

Margaret returned his kiss, and he sat down with her and commiserated with her over last night's unfortunate occurrence.

She told him about her white palfreys and wept. 'For they were dear beasts,' she said, 'and I loved them.'

'My Margaret has a tender heart,' said the King. 'But do not weep, for it grieves me to see you do so. There will be other palfreys and we should rejoice that you are safe.'

She blinked away her tears and said that he made her happy.

'Why,' he answered, 'you know nothing of happiness yet. Only wait until we are married in the sight of my people.' He clapped his hands. 'Could we not have a little music? I fancy, my love, that you like it, even as I do.'

The minstrels began to play and the King asked Margaret to dance for him with Lady Surrey as she had at Dalkeith, which Margaret was happy to do; and watching her radiant face, which such a short while before had been so sad, the King told himself that she was only a child after all.

Being a lover of music, he himself must perform, and this he did with great skill on the clavichord. Margaret clapped her hands and declared that she had never heard such playing. Then he took a lute and played to her so sweetly that she was completely charmed.

'I am sure,' said James, 'that there are others in the company who can amuse us.' And Margaret signed to Sir Edward Stanley to play the clavichord and sing.

'A wonderful English ballad,' commented the King, and called one of the gentlemen who had accompanied him from Edinburgh to Newbattle. 'The two of you sing together,' he commanded.

And they did so, harmonising so perfectly that everyone present applauded with enthusiasm – not only for the singing but because that was a symbol of the new friendship between the two countries.

But once again James must take his leave. As he left he whispered to Margaret: 'Would I could stay this night with you.'

He almost meant it. She was so young and fresh, and he was tiring of the mistress he had taken since the death of Margaret Drummond. 'Alas, kings and queens must conform to the rules laid down for them . . . much as they would wish otherwise.'

Margaret's flushed cheeks and shining eyes told him that she shared his wish.

'A few more days . . .' he murmured.

And she repeated: 'A few more days.'

She insisted on accompanying him out to his horse, and he with his followers and she with hers left the apartment together.

He embraced her once more and then leaped on to his horse without putting his foot into the stirrup – a feat which everyone applauded. He turned, pulling off his hat, and bowed his head to Margaret before he galloped away.

These pleasant days of courtship were the happiest Margaret had ever known. The King would ride out to Newbattle; she would play for him on the lute and clavichord as he had for her; and everyone noticed how attentive he was, and how he always remained with his head uncovered in her presence.

Always there was conversation and music, and at last came that August day when she was to make her ceremonial entry into Edinburgh.

Her women were dressing Margaret in a gown of cloth of gold edged with black velvet; they were placing about her neck pearls and precious stones, when the Countess of Surrey came in to tell her that a gift from the King had arrived. This was two palfreys to replace those which she had lost in the Dalkeith fire.

Margaret clasped her hands in pleasure.

'Do you know,' she said, 'I believe I have the best husband in the world.'

The ladies exchanged glances. It was true James was handsome, charming, courteous and kind; but they had heard certain scandalous gossip and they were inclined to believe it was true; and they did wonder how their high-spirited and headstrong little princess would act if and when she discovered there was truth in this gossip.

In the meantime it was well that she should enjoy her ignorance.

Riding in her litter, Margaret was met by James on the road to the capital. She was filled with delight when she saw him approaching, because he looked magnificent. His jacket was made of cloth of gold, and it opened to show that it was lined with purple velvet; about it was a border of black otter fur; his waistcoat was of purple satin and there were pearls and precious stones about his person, while his scarlet hose added an extra touch of colour; and he looked very fine on a horse whose saddle and harness were of gold, and bridle and headgear of shining silver.

As he approached he sprang from his horse, and coming up to the litter, kissed Margaret. Then leaping on to his horse, he turned and rode beside the litter, while his gentleman-usher took out the sword of state from its scabbard of purple velvet and carried it before the King.

James was smiling at Margaret. 'Are you prepared to enter your capital city?' he asked.

'I am longing to do so.'

'I am going to take you in on my horse,' he told her. 'It is meet and fitting that I should do so!'

'You mean I shall ride pillion?'

'Why not? It is what I wish, and it is what the people will wish. Will you be afraid on such a fiery horse as mine?'

'I would never be afraid if you were there.'

'Ah, Margaret,' he told her, 'you are too trusting.'

He was frowning. 'I would never forgive myself if you were thrown,' he went on. Then he shouted to one of his men to mount behind him pillion fashion to see how the horse reacted to the extra weight.

When it was clear that the horse was not pleased with the arrangement, the King said: 'Nay, I'll not risk this. Bring one of the Queen's palfreys.'

The palfrey was brought and when the King had mounted and Margaret had been placed on the pillion, they prepared to journey into Edinburgh.

But there was much to be seen before they reached the city, for the King had determined that his people should show his bride a royal welcome. In a meadow about half a mile from the city they must pause and watch a joust between two knights, which had been staged for their benefit; when this was over a tame deer was released and a greyhound set to chase it.

It seemed that all the citizens of Edinburgh had come out to see the fun, for the roads were lined with people who cheered the King and Queen.

They were met by the Grey Friars who carried with them the cross and some holy but grisly relics which the King and the Queen kissed. Then as they approached the entrance to the city the trumpeters, whom Margaret had brought with her, blew a fanfare and the Scottish minstrels and trumpeters joined in with the triumphal music.

An 'angel' appeared and presented the keys of the city to the new Queen; Margaret took these with a smile and turned to see that the precious relic, the arm of St Giles, was being presented to her to kiss.

When this was done they entered the city where more pageantry awaited them; Margaret felt dazzled and found the quiet of the church of Holyrood, to which James had led her, rather pleasant. Here she knelt with James at the altar and afterwards was presented to the great nobles of Scotland, among whom were such famous people as Huntley, Argyle and Lennox.

The ceremony was almost over and the King had brought his bride to his Palace of Holyrood.

They did not dine together, but later the King came to her apartments to see if she were comfortable, and there was music and dancing.

Margaret heard the city bells ringing; she knew that the streets were hung with tapestry and that all the nobility of Scotland were in Edinburgh because the following day she, Margaret Tudor, would be married to the King in the church of Holyrood.

This was her wedding day.

Margaret stood by the font, in the church of Holyrood, a dazzling figure in a gown of gold and white damask, the border of which was crimson velvet; on her head was a glittering crown, and her rippling golden hair on which she could sit with ease hung loose. About her neck was a collar of pearls. Her ladies who accompanied her were almost as richly dressed; on her right stood the Archbishop of York and on her left the Earl of Surrey.

The King was approaching, slowly, ceremoniously, accompanied by nobles in brilliant costume. He looked so handsome that Margaret could not resist the temptation to gaze at him. The white damask and gold suited his tawny colouring; and the black velvet border of his jacket and the crimson satin slashes on his sleeves, matching his scarlet hose, gave a touch of startling colour. When he saw Margaret he removed his black velvet bonnet, in which glowed a great ruby, that his head might not be covered in her presence and all could therefore see the respect in which he held her.

His eyes, as they rested on her, were above all reassuring. And she thought: This is the happiest moment of my life. I am to be married to him in very truth at last, and I know this to be but the beginning of all my joy.

They stood together before the Archbishops of York and Glasgow, and the ceremony of marriage was performed. Then the bulls from the Pope, consenting to the union, were read aloud; and when this was done the trumpets blared forth in triumph.

Margaret and James were married.

They sat side by side at the banquet and the King commanded that the Queen should be served before he was.

In spite of her ecstasy Margaret could still feel hungry, and she tackled the boar's head, brawn and ham and all the other delicacies with a zest which seemed to amuse her husband.

When the banquet was over the company left the dining hall for another room that was hung with tapestries and cloth of gold, and here the King and Queen led the company in the dance.

And so the evening passed until it was time for the King and Queen to retire together.

Margaret was happy; the King was well content.

She was young and beautiful and, as he had guessed, had been an apt pupil in those arts in which he had long excelled. It was pleasant to find a sensuality which matched his own, and if he had not continued secretly to mourn for Margaret Drummond he could have been a happy man.

Margaret with all her Tudor egoism, never doubted for one moment that the King was as delighted with her as she was with him. He had given her on the morning after the wedding night the domains of Kilmarnock as a morrowing gift.

During the weeks which followed she devoted herself to pleasure with an energy which those who had followed her from England had only seen surpassed by her royal brother. Each day she held a council of her ladies to discuss what she should wear; she danced and sang, she hunted, practised archery; and always she was eager for those hours when she could be alone with her bridegroom.

After some weeks of this merrymaking James intimated that the celebrations should come to an end and it was time he showed the people of Scotland their Queen. Then began the royal tour. From Edinburgh to Linlithgow and from Linlithgow to Stirling, to Falkland, Perth, Aberdeen and Elgin. Each night they would come to rest in some mansion, convent or abbey where there would be dancing, music, card-playing or religious ceremonies.

One of the greatest difficulties was the transport of Margaret's wardrobe, for the purpose of which special carters had to be employed.

'Do you need so much?' asked James gently.

'Indeed I do,' Margaret firmly told him.

Many would have been exasperated; not so James. He merely shrugged tolerant shoulders and the carters were engaged.

By Christmas they were back in Holyrood Palace where Margaret threw herself into arrangements for Christmas festivities with all her youthful enthusiasm. Holyrood should see festivities such as it had never seen before. There should be pageantry and dancing such as she and Henry had often longed for during the Christmas celebrations which had taken place in their father's Court. It was wonderful to escape from that miserly caution which had been a part of her early life. Margaret was determined to have gaiety, no matter what the cost. Harpers and luters, fiddlers and pipers, trumpeters and dancers filled the state apartments with their music.

And when the Christmas feasting was over, there was the New Year.

James's present to his wife on the first day of the New Year was a heavy ducat of gold weighing an ounce, with two sapphire rings; and the second day of the New Year he gave her two crosses studded with pearls.

To Margaret's chagrin the New Year festivities were brought to an abrupt end by the death of James's brother, the Duke of Ross; and when the burial ceremonies were over, James told his bride that he must leave her for a while. She must understand that as King he had certain duties to his country. He would write to her and she must write to him, but for a few weeks they must be parted.

Margaret embraced him tearfully and implored him not to stay long from her side. He assured her that he would return as soon as it was possible for him to do so. The first of the King's absences had begun.

During the periods when he was absent from his Queen, James sent her letters and gifts. He deplored the fact that they could not be together, and Margaret occupied herself in hunting and archery and sometimes in the woods she would run races with her attendants. The days passed pleasantly enough but she yearned for James.

When he returned he was as affectionate and charming as ever, but during a visit to Stirling Castle, Margaret made a discovery.

James was always eager to go to Stirling, and she had said to him: 'I believe this to be the favourite of all your palaces, and this surprises me since you spent so much of your childhood there. So your memories cannot be unhappy ones.'

'Do I love Stirling best?' he mused. 'I wonder. At this time I do. Next week I may love Linlithgow or Holyrood House or the castle of Edinburgh. I fear I am a fickle man.'

'As long as your fickleness is only for your castles I care not,' laughed Margaret.

She did not notice that he looked momentarily melancholy.

The next day she saw a little girl in the hall of the castle. The child was beautiful and in the charge of a highborn lady. Margaret called the little girl to her and asked who she was.

Her lady guardian seemed confused and said that she was lodged in the castle temporarily.

'My name is Margaret,' the child told the Queen.

'Margaret! How strange. So is mine.'

'You are Margaret too! What else? I am the Lady Margaret Stuart.'

'That is a name which arouses my interest,' answered the Queen.

'She is such a prattler, I fear, Your Grace,' said her guardian. 'And, I fear, a little spoiled.'

'I am not,' answered the child. 'My father says I am not.'

'And who is your father, my child?'

'My father is the King,' was the disconcerting answer.

Margaret knitted her brows and looked at the woman, who lifted her shoulders and murmured: 'She is but a child, Your Grace. You know how children prattle on . . . without sense.'

'Then if your father is the King, who is your mother?' asked Margaret suddenly, ignoring the woman and addressing the child.

'She was Margaret too,' the child told her. 'I am named for her.'

'Is the child's mother here?' asked Margaret.

'No, Your Grace. Her mother is dead.'

'She is not,' declared the child. 'My father says she is not dead, and will never die.'

'Oh come . . . come . . . you weary Her Grace.'

Margaret did not seek to detain them; she watched the woman take the child's hand and lead her away.

She went immediately to the King, who was in his own apartments playing his lute. Imperiously she said: 'James, I wish to speak to you . . . privately.'

James regarded her somewhat lazily and, seeing that she was truly agitated, signed to his friends to leave him.

'Well?' he said when they were alone.

'There is a child here – Margaret – who says she is your daughter. I know that this is not so, but I like not that she should proclaim herself to be. I want you to stop this.'

James was silent for a while; then he strummed a few notes on his lute. The time had come. He would have to explain.

'The child speaks the truth,' he said. 'She is my daughter.'

'Your daughter! But . . .'

'I was to have married her mother, but she . . . died. She was poisoned with her two sisters when at breakfast.'

Margaret's blue eyes opened wide and the colour flamed into her cheeks. He noted that the fact that his mistress had been poisoned did not shock her so much as that she had existed.

'So . . . you had a mistress!'

'My dear Margaret! What do you expect? Not one . . . but many.'

'And . . . a child!'

'Children,' he corrected her.

She was angry. She had been hoping for signs of her own pregnancy and there had been none. And now he . . . her own husband . . . admitted not only to having had mistresses . . . but children.

'I am glad you know,' he said. 'I visit them often. They are after all my own flesh and blood and I have always promised myself that my children should never be treated by their father as I was by mine – perhaps in the hope that they will never have to suffer the remorse I did for the part I played in my father's end.'

Margaret stood up and went to the door. She was so angry that she knew she must escape because she had a great desire to fly at him and fight him with all her strength. She had been cheated. She saw that she had been young and foolish and that her naivety must have been apparent to him. She felt insulted and her Tudor pride was in revolt. She had loved him too deeply, too trustingly.

He did not attempt to detain her. He shrugged his shoulders and turned idly to his lute. He strummed without hearing; the recent scene had made him think of that other Margaret and the longing for her was almost too great to be borne.

❁ ❁ ❁

Margaret could not rest until she discovered more about her husband's premarital love affairs. She insisted on her Scottish ladies telling her all they knew. So the King had been so enamoured of Margaret Drummond that he had wanted to marry her against the advice of his ministers; and she had borne him a daughter, that child, Lady Margaret Stuart, who was so petted and pampered at the King's command. And there were two children by a certain Marian Boyd: Catherine and Alexander; and the young Earl of Moray – who had been given this title when he was scarcely two – was the King's son by Janet Kennedy.

What a family! And he so proud of them – sneaking off to visit them on the pretence that he was engaged on state affairs! And what was worse, leaving his wife in order to do so!

All her *amour propre* – which was very strong in the young Tudors – was in revolt.

She now saw her husband in a new light. He was not the person who in her girlish imagination she had believed him to be. This marriage of theirs could well be one of convenience to him. She had been cheated.

Yet when he came to her again – tender and kind, yet not repentant – her wounded pride was submerged by her need of him. He had aroused in her that latent sensuality which must be appeased no matter how hurt her pride.

She was passionate in her demands; and there was a new

determination within her; she must have a child; and *her* child must be more important to him than any of his others, for the son she bore would be the future King of Scotland.

James was sorry that his wife was hurt by her discovery of his illegitimate family, and he blamed himself for not having broken the news more gently to her. He could not be sorry that he had these children, for he doted on them and it was a matter of great disappointment to him that, so far, Margaret had shown no signs of pregnancy. When she did, he assured himself, she would be more serene.

One of his greatest pleasures was to visit his children, and he planned to have them all together in one nursery, acknowledged as his, so that he could supervise their education and give them honours which as royal Stuarts he believed should be theirs.

Meanwhile he decided to compensate Margaret for the shock she had suffered and, since she was such a child and there was nothing that pleased her more than balls, plays and ballets, there should be more of these entertainments.

He brought a gift of jewels – that could always delight her – and told her that he was arranging a ball in her honour and asked how she would like that.

She clasped her hands in ecstasy and her young face lighted with pleasure.

'And you will be there, James?' she asked eagerly.

'Indeed I shall be there.'

'For it would be no pleasure to me if you were not.'

He embraced her and thought happily: She has recovered from the shock. She accepts the children as natural.

At the same time he wondered what she would say if she knew of those lapses from fidelity which had occurred since his marriage. She was so naive in many ways. Probably it was due to the fact that her father had been a faithful husband; it was said that Henry VII was a cold man – well, James IV was not. Women were as necessary to his comfort as money was to Henry VII's.

Margaret would have to learn this, but he trusted she would not have to make the discovery until she was ready to. In a few years' time she would become accustomed to the fact that he must have his mistresses. He would try to explain that they in no way affected his feelings for her. She was his wife and it was their duty to get children. But ever since he had been a very young man he had made no effort to curb his sexual desires; and he could not begin now. He was gentle and tolerant with her and would remain so as long as she did not attempt to restrain him.

Then they began to plan the entertainment. There should be masked dancers because it was always such fun to watch disguised performers. And there should be a play. There was one of the Queen's attendants who was a past master at coaching players. This boy, who had come with Margaret from England, was called English Cuddy by the Scots.

'I shall command English Cuddy to begin making arrangements at once,' declared Margaret.

'So much energy you have, my little one,' said James.

'But it is such fun to play for a masque.'

'When you have children you will think of other things.'

He looked at her searchingly. Was there no sign? Her face darkened because she was thinking of those other children and how she would like to banish the Lady Margaret Stuart from the Court.

'I intend to have many children,' she said. 'And when my son is born I am going to ask a favour of you. Will you grant it?'

'I think I should be ready to grant you any favour when you give me the heir to the throne.'

'I shall want him to have all that is best in Scotland.'

'That is easy. So he shall.'

'And I do not think he should have to meet the children of ... harlots.'

James looked puzzled. 'What mean you?'

'Margaret Stuart for one ... and I know there are others who might try to force themselves into his company.'

James's face was a dull red; for the first time in her life Margaret saw that he was angry.

'Do not dare to say that again,' he said. 'The Lady Margaret Stuart's mother was a great lady. She was possessed of many qualities which are lacking in the daughters of kings.'

Then he left her.

Margaret went into her bedchamber and threw herself on to her bed where she wept violently, for her emotions were invariably violent.

Her fit of sobbing did not last long; she roused herself and tried to remove the stains of weeping. Tears were futile; one day she would have her own way, but first she must learn how.

❦ ❦ ❦

When next she was in the company of her husband, Margaret behaved as though the scene had not taken place. James was relieved and ready to meet her more than halfway. He reminded himself again and again that she was but a child and he expected too much of her.

He gave her more presents; rich damasks and velvets to make the clothes with which she enjoyed adorning her person – and the result was enchanting, he had to admit. He should congratulate himself on his good luck, for he had a beautiful young wife who was overflowing with love for him while so many kings had to marry plain and even deformed women for the sake of their kingdoms. He merely had to remind himself that she was a self-willed child and that he was some seventeen years older than she was, which should make him tolerant.

So those celebrations were particularly gay, James playing the clavichord with his wife and singing with her as they played their lutes. They led the dancing together; they laughed uproariously over English Cuddy's play; and when at last they retired they made passionate love; and Margaret was so happy that she forgot to be jealous of those children.

Wait, she told herself. Surely soon I shall be pregnant. Then I shall not care how many illegitimate children he may have had in the past.

❁ ❁ ❁

There was no reason why the fun should not continue. English Cuddy and Scotch Dog (a certain James Dog whose talents were similar to Cuddy's) put their heads together and devised more original and brilliant entertainments.

It was during one of these days when entertainment followed entertainment that a messenger arrived at the Palace and asked to be taken to the King.

The man was brought to James when he was playing the lute to the Queen, and seeing how travel-stained and agitated the messenger was, James immediately laid aside his lute. One of his most endearing characteristics was his immediate sympathy with any in distress, however humble they were, and his concern to do all in his power to help them. It was this quality which had made him the most popular of the Stuart Kings.

He therefore made the man sit in his presence, and sent for wine to refresh him.

'And while it is being brought, tell me what brings you here.'

'I come from Darnaway, Sire,' said the messenger. 'My mistress, the Lady Bothwell, commanded me to come and tell you that she is sick unto death and begs that you visit her on her deathbed.'

James gasped with dismay. The Lady Bothwell was his fiery Janet Kennedy on whom the Bothwell estate had been bestowed in exchange for all the lands her lover Angus had given her. Janet . . . who had been so vital . . . sick unto death! It was unthinkable, and what of little James, their son?

'I shall go to her without delay,' said the King.

Margaret had risen and stood beside him. She laid her hand on his arm.

'Who is this Lady Bothwell?' she asked. 'And why should she send for you in this way . . . as though she were a queen and you her subject?'

James looked at her coldly and said: 'She may be dying.'

Then he turned and strode from the apartment.

Margaret had to shake the woman to get the truth from her. The foolish creature was trying to pretend she had no notion who this Lady Bothwell was.

All the Tudor fury was in flame.

75

'Who is she? Tell me that!'

'I . . . I . . .'

'It will be the worse for you if you do not say.'

'Your Grace . . . Your Highness . . . she was Janet Kennedy.'

'Janet Kennedy? And what is she?'

'The daughter of Lord Kennedy, Your Grace.'

'What is she to the King? That is what I mean?'

Silence. But silence could tell so much.

'You know!' shrieked Margaret. 'And how many sons did she bear him? Tell me that.'

'It was only the one, Your Grace . . . only the little Earl of Moray.'

Margaret slapped the woman's face in fury.

'And he goes to see her now. He leaves me, to go to see her. The wanton creature. I hate her. I hate them both, I tell you!'

She turned and ran to her apartments.

And there once more she flung herself on to her bed and wept. Lady Guildford came to her. 'Your Grace . . . Your Grace, this is not the way to behave.'

She did not answer. Instead she raised herself and clenched her fists, pummelled her pillows, with an expression which showed that was how she would have liked to beat Janet Kennedy.

'You must remember that you are a queen, Your Grace.'

'A queen . . . ah! And a woman. A woman deserted by her husband! Do you not think I understand the meaning of those absences? And all except me knowing . . . I alone in ignorance. I was not enough for him. He must have these sluts. I would kill them. I will not have him in my bed again.'

'Hush! Hush! There will be those to listen. There will be those to carry tales.'

'I care not.'

'But you must care. Remember, my dearest, you are the Queen of Scotland.'

Margaret's face crumpled suddenly and she began to cry softly. Lady Guildford put her arms about her shaking shoulders and sought to soothe her.

'I loved him so much,' sobbed Margaret. 'You could not understand how much.'

🏵 Chapter IV 🏵

THE CURSE OF SAUCHIEBURN

During the months which followed, Margaret appeared to be resigned. She had lost her innocence and those about her said: 'She is growing out of childhood.' A certain hardness had crept into her expression. She was no longer in love with the King; the romantic ideal had gone but the need for sexual satisfaction was as strong as ever and that side of their relationship appeared to have undergone no change. But both James and Margaret were deeply affected by the knowledge which had come to her. Margaret was on the defensive, but James was more light-hearted because he had never enjoyed deceiving his wife and could not help being glad that the need for deceit was over. He was a man whom no one woman could hope to satisfy, and the sooner his wife realised this, the better for them both.

The absences from home were more frequent, but during them he never failed to write tender letters inquiring after his wife's health, and these were often accompanied by some charming and costly gift.

Margaret would say to herself with that grim cynicism which had developed since her discovery: 'He must indeed be enjoying the woman to suffer such qualms of conscience.'

It was not a situation which could be endured for ever by a proud Tudor, but as yet Margaret – still so young – saw no way for her except endurance. But, that some way would be shown to her, she had no doubt.

It was not that she wanted revenge; she wanted only to restore her pride in herself. She discovered that she did not care enough for James to desire that revenge. To her he was merely the means of satisfying a need which was becoming more and more important to her as she grew more mature. Let him then supply this need. She would use him for this purpose and wait until she knew what she must do to establish herself in her own right – as a woman, as a Tudor Queen.

This was the time of growing into maturity. She was wise enough to understand that. Foolishly she had been prepared to adore her handsome husband; from now on she would never forget that nothing in her life could matter so much as Margaret Tudor.

Outwardly she appeared to be a high-spirited girl, not cowed but wisely accepting what could not be prevented. James was delighted with her, and when he came home from his travels the reunions were gay and pleasant occasions. The apartments of Holyrood House rang with laughter and music – which they both enjoyed; there were occasions when James entertained in his own apartments and Margaret in hers, but if James found an entertainer of talent he would send him or her immediately along to entertain the Queen. A female minstrel who was known by the name of Wantonness was an example of this. Wantonness had amused James; therefore Margaret must enjoy her singing. It was the same with O'Donnel, an Irish harper, and a luter known as Grey Steil.

James took advantage of his wife's complacency to have Margaret Drummond's daughter, Lady Margaret Stuart, brought to Edinburgh Castle, but when Margaret heard that the child was there her restraint broke down temporarily, and before her English attendants she demanded to know how she was expected to deal with such an affront.

Lady Guildford suggested that she might remonstrate with the King, provided she remained calm enough to do so.

'He dotes on that child,' retorted Margaret. 'And I know why. He still remembers her mother. He believes that had she lived he would have been faithful to her! As if he would! As if he could ever be faithful to any woman!'

'Your Grace should remember that it is better not to show your anger.'

'That's one lesson I've learned,' retorted Margaret grimly.

Still, she could not resist talking to the King.

They were planning a masque and were discussing the merits of English Cuddy and Scotch Dog and whether Wantonness should be summoned to sing with the other minstrels, when Margaret said suddenly: 'James, do you think it wise to have Margaret Stuart at the castle?'

'But why not?' he asked, surprised.

'I know how devoted you are to her, but she is still a bastard.'

James said coolly: 'I have decided that she shall be acknowledged as my daughter, and I swear by St Ninian that nothing shall deter me.'

'But . . .'

He had become a king suddenly and Margaret was aware that however courteous he was he would rule Scotland alone. Then she knew that there was one thing she wanted to do; that was rule Scotland herself. She understood in that moment of revelation that if James had taken her advice she could have readily forgiven him his philanderings. But he would not be advised; his gentle demeanour was a shield which hid a man determined to have his way. He was no husband for a strong-minded woman. She thought enviously of her brother Henry who on their father's death – which could not be long delayed – would be absolute ruler of England.

'I think little Margaret finds it lonely at the castle,' went on James, 'and I have for some time believed that it would be an excellent idea to gather my family together under one roof. I am therefore having young Alexander Stuart brought to the castle . . . temporarily of course. In time I intend to send him and his brother, Moray, abroad to be educated. I have a great respect for Erasmus and I want him to take charge of their education.'

Margaret could not remain calm. She laughed aloud suddenly. 'Alexander Stuart, bastard son of Marian Boyd and the King of Scotland – a mere boy, and Primate of Scotland! Don't you think that's a little ridiculous, James?'

James gave his lazy smile. 'One favours one's own flesh and blood, my dear. Parents are notoriously fond and foolish.'

'Such fondness and foolishness can have dangerous results when employed by kings.'

'I see no harm done. Wait until you give me a son. For him there will be the crown of Scotland.'

'I might have more opportunity of doing so if you did not fritter your manhood away on other women.'

James laughed aloud and, reaching for her, held her in an embrace, which was mocking yet tender.

'Why, my dear, I had thought we gave ourselves the

opportunity many a time; but if you feel we should be more assiduous . . .'

She wished that she could be aloof, make conditions; but how could she when her sensuality demanded to be assuaged?

She felt herself laughing, growing slack in his arms; and when he made love to her she was willing herself to be fruitful.

At last it had happened.

The whole Court was delighted, but no one more than the King. Margaret was seventeen and healthy, and James had proved that he could sire strong children. Now he would have a legitimate child and, if it were a boy, a new prince for Scotland; and if it were a girl . . . well, there would be boys to follow.

He was now spending more time with his wife; during his occasional journeys, letters came even more frequently than they had before; gifts were showered upon her, and Margaret was happier than she had been since the first weeks of her marriage.

James had insisted that she pass the months of her pregnancy in Dunottar Castle, in the county of Kincardine, which was more like a fortress than a residence, set on a rocky plateau which jutted over the sea. He often visited her there and made sure that she was surrounded by entertainers who could keep her amused; her minstrels, luters and harpers were commanded to make her days lively; and English Cuddy and Scotch Dog were in residence to make plays for her diversion.

There was a certain amount of unrest in Scotland at this time and some of the dissatisfied lords were contemplating rising against the King; therefore, said James, it pleased him to know that his Queen was in a safe place.

Margaret wondered how much time he devoted to state affairs and how much to his mistresses. There was a new name which was being whispered throughout the Court: the Lady of A. Previously Margaret would have exerted her ingenuity to discover the identity behind that sobriquet. Now she did not bother. What did it matter with whom the King dallied? The Lady of A could cause her no more qualms than Janet Kennedy or the dead Margaret Drummond.

She was longing for the birth of her child because she felt that when she was the mother of the heir of Scotland her position would be strengthened. She looked into the years ahead and saw herself making that son entirely hers. And who knew, when the time came for him to rule, he might be more ready to listen to Margaret Tudor than his father was.

She lay on her bed in agony.

So this was giving birth. How long had she lain in this state chamber at Holyrood House while the pains beset her body and the heir to Scotland refused to be born?

She was thinking of her mother who had lain in the Palace of the Tower of London, who had suffered so much pain, which had been the prelude to death.

But her mother had been twenty years older than she was; and she, Margaret, had many years before her . . . if she survived this ordeal.

She heard whispering; her women were talking of her in hushed, reverent tones. Were they the voices of people who knew themselves to be in the presence of death?

The pain was coming again, so fierce that she lost

consciousness, and when she regained her senses it was to hear the cry of a child.

'A boy!' She heard the joyous cry throughout the apartment; and, ill as she was, a great exultation came to her.

James was delighted. He showered presents on all her women; he stared down with reverence at the boy in the cradle.

Then he came to kneel at his wife's bedside.

Margaret looked at him dazedly. She was not sure where she was and imagined she was with her brother and sister in Richmond Palace.

'Henry . . .' she whispered, 'you are not yet . . .'

James was alarmed.

'The Queen is ill,' he said. 'She should be rejoicing now, her ordeal over, her son in his cradle. What ails her?'

He sent for the physicians and implored them to use all their skill. He was filled with remorse for the manner in which he had neglected her. He demanded to know what ailed her and why she, who had been in such rude health before and during her pregnancy, should be so ill now that her ordeal was over.

'It is a malady which occurs often after childbirth, Sire,' said the doctors.

'And she will recover?'

They tried to reassure the King, but he saw through their pretence.

If she died he would be stricken with remorse. He remembered how he had suffered at the death of his father; he did not want to suffer so again.

He would travel to the shrine of his favourite saint at

Whitehorn in Galloway, and there plead for his Queen's restoration to health.

Footsore and weary, James arrived at the shrine of St Ninian. The journey, made on foot, had been rough, and he was glad of this. If Margaret died he would feel some remorse for his infidelity. Poor child, she had been wounded by it in the beginning. He would begin to wonder whether her loss would be the punishment for his sins.

He remembered afresh the regret he had suffered after his father's death. He did not want to endure the like again. If Margaret recovered, and this would be due to St Ninian, he would go into retreat for a while with the Grey Friars at Stirling. There he would fast, pray and meditate for a few weeks, and come out feeling purged of his sins.

He never regretted building that monastery, for it had often provided his tortured conscience with the balm it needed.

Margaret and his courtiers were never very pleased when he went into retirement. He feared his Margaret was a little pagan at heart; he had seen how her attention strayed during religious services, and he noticed that if she could gracefully avoid attending them she did so. As for his friends at Court, they were too fond of gaiety to enjoy those seasons when, out of respect for the King's temporary monastic existence, they too must live soberly.

He had taken with him on this pilgrimage only four of his favourite minstrels; he enjoyed travelling about his country informally, because he believed it gave him an opportunity of discovering the true state of affairs. He had always wished to see things as they really were, so that he could improve the lives of his subjects.

He often thought ironically that he would not be a bad king but for certain failings which he found it impossible to conquer. He was never the worse for drink; he never indulged in gluttony; he would devote much of his time to the study of laws which could benefit his country; then he would meet a woman and forget duty to state, wife and all, in his pursuit of her.

Often he said to himself: 'If I could have married Margaret Drummond I would have been a satisfied husband who never strayed,' as he used to say: 'If I could have known my father, talked with him, understood him, I would never have had this terrible blot on my conscience.'

He was a man of contrasts – deeply sensual yet spiritual; logical in certain matters, extremely superstitious in others; going alternately to the monastery and the bed of one of his favourites; capable of wisdom and folly.

Having reached the shrine, he made his offerings and asked that Margaret might be restored to health; then because he and his little band were so weary he commanded that horses be hired to carry them back to Holyrood House.

He was noted for his friendliness to those who surrounded him, and he was always pleased to throw aside dignity whenever possible; so the minstrels rode beside him and they all chatted in an easy fashion.

One of them said: 'I hear, Sire, that Bell-the-Cat is paying court to Lady Bothwell again. They say that he is prepared to offer her marriage.'

'Is that so?' said James.

'Why, yes, Sire. The Earl has suffered pangs of jealousy on the lady's account, so I've heard tell.'

James was silent, thinking of Janet Kennedy – red-haired

and fiery. They had had good times together and he would never forget Janet as long as he lived; his memories of her were as evergreen as those of Margaret Drummond, though for a different reason.

He wondered if she remembered that he had given her Darnaway on condition that she did not take another lover. He had been harsh. As well imagine himself without a mistress as Janet without a lover.

And yet . . . he still hankered after her; and he still visited her – to see the boy, he would say, when he set out; and he did go to see the boy; he doted on his son; but it was meet and fitting that the boy's mother should live with him, so when he saw the boy he saw her too.

James smiled, thinking of arriving at the door of her house, of her sweeping down the staircase to greet him – mocking, her eyes blazing with the passion they both could not help arousing in each other; the vitality sparkling in her.

They would talk for a while of the boy's future; the boy himself would be sent for; and after a while he would be sent away because the need to be alone together would be too much to be gainsaid.

And now Bell-the-Cat was paying court again!

He imagined the old fellow, who must be some twenty-five years older than himself, calling on her, bribing her with offers of land . . . and honourable marriage. James had to admit that there was a virility about the Earl which, in spite of his age, remained with him.

Janet . . . with a lover!

Memories surged in and out of his mind. Janet's red hair and white naked body; Janet's eyes that looked green in passion. No, he would not lightly let her go to Bell-the-Cat.

He decided to make a divergence; they would not yet return to Holyrood. He had made his pilgrimage for the sake of his wife; now he must indulge himself by a visit to a mistress whom he could never entirely forget.

Margaret's health began to improve – so it was said – from the moment James had reached the shrine of St Ninian, so she owed her recovery to that saint, and when she was well enough must pay him the homage he would look for.

As the baby had been baptised with great pomp and christened James, Margaret left him to the care of his nurses while she travelled along the coast of Galloway to the shrine of St Ninian. Her husband accompanied her, riding on horseback beside her litter; she must travel thus for, although she was no longer in danger, she had not yet regained her good health.

She found the journey trying, and when she returned to Stirling, continued to feel weak; this was particularly alarming because James hated to see her sick and went even more often on his travels. He was seeing Janet Kennedy very frequently now as well as the Lady of A; and Margaret had learned that another woman, Isabel Stuart, daughter of Lord Buchan, had borne him a daughter whose name was Jean.

It was true that she had her own little James now, and it was a matter of great contentment to her to remind herself that of all the King's children, her little James in whom his father delighted was the one who was of real importance.

But the rude health which Margaret had hitherto enjoyed seemed to have deserted her. There were days when she was obliged to keep to her bed; she felt resentful of this, but Lady Guildford assured her that the ordeal of childbirth had been so great that she must expect to take a few months to recover.

She could not of course prevent James from taking mistresses; but Margaret was becoming wily; she was not sorry that there were several mistresses; if there were one only she would need to feel anxiety.

Christmas came and was celebrated with music and dancing at Holyrood House; and if the Queen was less energetic than before, the King was more assiduous in his desire for her comfort. Wantonness, Grey Steil, English Cuddy and Scotch Dog were at their best, and the King's fool, Currie, with his wife Daft Ann, set the King and Queen laughing uproariously.

Thus time passed until that February when the little Prince James was one year old.

The Court was at Linlithgow Palace. James had returned from hawking and was ready for the feast which lay waiting for him in the great hall.

Margaret, with her women, greeting him and his companions on their return, was a little sad because she no longer felt well enough to accompany him on such expeditions.

The great hall looked magnificent, prepared as it was for the evening's entertainment. Tapestries from Holyrood had been hung on the walls, and the logs blazing in the huge fireplace crackled and spat comfortably. The silver platters, the goblets and bowls on the table shone in the firelight, and in the minstrels' gallery sweet music – which was never lacking in the King's presence – was being softly played by his favourite minstrels.

The table was placed on a dais at one end of the hall exactly opposite the minstrels' gallery, and under the place where the

King and Queen would sit was a carpet, although the rest of the hall was strewn with rushes. Servants were scurrying in and out of that door which led to the kitchens and butteries, and the smell of appetising foods was everywhere.

James looked with appreciation at the Queen, who greeted him so warmly and asked him how he had fared at the hunt. He took her hand and led her to the table where one of his servants was waiting with a bowl that he might wash his hands.

Margaret and he seated themselves and the feast began.

One of the noblest of James's courtiers carved for the royal pair. Margaret ate heartily but James, sitting there taking the pieces of meat in his fingers as his carver handed them to him seemed more interested in the minstrels' music than in food.

It was always thus at table; James was no great trencherman; nor did he show much interest in the wine which was placed before him.

Wantonness began to sing, and it was clear that her song charmed him; he turned to Margaret and asked her opinion.

Margaret replied that Wantonness never failed to please; she was wondering whether during the hunt he had paid a visit to one of his women.

They were washing their hands after the meal when a messenger from Stirling Castle, where the little Prince was staying, came into the hall and made his way immediately to the King and Queen.

Margaret and James grew immediately grave when they heard what he had to say. The little boy had become fretful and his nurses could not comfort him. Now it seemed that he had a fever.

James said: 'We will leave at once for Stirling.'

Within an hour they were on the road.

Margaret was brokenhearted.

'Why,' she demanded angrily, 'should this happen to me! His bastards flourish and my son must die. Why should *I* be unfortunate?'

Lady Guildford tried to soothe her. 'Your Grace, many children die in Scotland and England. The little Prince had every care. And you are young. You will have other children.'

During the weeks that followed the death of the little heir of Scotland, Margaret refused to be comforted. It was so unfair, she kept proclaiming. The children of his mistresses were full of health and vigour, and the thought of them was a continual torment to her; and when her own son had been born she had found some comfort . . . but that was no more.

James mourned the loss of his son with her, but reminded her that no railing against fate could bring him back to them. They would have more children and in time they would forget this unhappiness.

He sought to comfort her in every way he could; he spent time in her company; he suggested that she should arrange entertainments to divert her. Let her call together Cuddy and Dog; let Grey Steil write a new song for Wantonness to sing.

Margaret could only shake her head and mourn; but she clung to him and within her was a faint exultation. At least she was keeping him away from his women.

Political affairs were taking up a great deal of the King's attention. The King of France was anxious for his friendship and, since the marriage between Scotland and England, had tried to woo James with prophecies of the advantages a friendship between their two countries could mean. James knew that Louis was eager to break the Scottish alliance with England; and, because France and England were perennial enemies, that put Scotland in the enviable position of being of great importance to both these countries.

Louis had written that he was sending an embassy to Scotland which would bring certain plans to lay before the King.

James had left the Court to go on a pilgrimage to the shrine of St Ninian; this was becoming a habit and, although it was known that St Ninian was the King's favourite saint, it was also known that he made a habit of combining this practice with a visit to Janet Kennedy.

Margaret was delighted to find that she was pregnant again; at the same time her being in such a state meant that she saw less of the King, which did not please her.

It was while she was with her women, listening to their chatter but picturing all the time what James and Janet Kennedy were doing, that a messenger came to tell her a certain English gentleman, who had come from her father, was below and asking if he might have audience with her.

Margaret, always eager to have news from home, commanded that the man be brought to her without delay.

The Englishman accordingly appeared, and Margaret dismissed her attendants because she felt that what he had to tell her might be of some secrecy.

'I am Dr Nicholas West, Your Grace,' she was told when they were alone. 'I come on instructions from your most noble father.'

'To see me?'

'To see Your Grace and the King. Alas, I have been waiting long at Berwick for a safe conduct, but since this was not granted me I have taken the risk of coming to Edinburgh and presenting myself to you.'

'The King has had much to occupy him,' said Margaret. 'It may be that your plea has not reached him.'

Dr West bowed his head. He did not believe that. He knew that the French were sending an embassy to Scotland and that the King of Scotland was eager to welcome it.

'My master, your most noble father, is not pleased with the way in which matters stand between this country and his.'

'Is that so?' said Margaret, who had never bothered herself with political matters.

'Your Grace will know that His Grace, your royal father, arrested the Earl of Arran and his brother, Sir Patrick Hamilton, when they attempted to pass through England on their way to France without first having obtained a safe conduct.'

'I did not know,' said Margaret.

'This matter has incensed the King of Scotland.'

Margaret thought resentfully: He never tells me anything. Am I not the Queen? He treats me as he does one of his mistresses. He forgets that I am the daughter of the King of England.

'But,' went on Dr West, 'there was naught else to be done. When these gentlemen passed through our country without first having asked for a safe conduct, and we knew they were on their way to France, naturally we arrested them. If I could have an audience with the King and explain this matter to him, I feel sure I could make him see the justice of what we have done.'

'I am sure the King would understand.'

'But, Your Grace, I cannot obtain an audience with the King. I come to ask you to plead my cause – and that of your royal father – for me. Your father has asked me to tell you that he knows you will remember you are his daughter and do all in your power to work for the good of your native land, and seek to dissuade your husband from accepting the friendship of your father's enemies.'

This was a new role for Margaret – political adviser to the King. Why not? She was after all the Queen. She must show James that she was not as one of his light-o'-loves – there to enjoy a night or two of passion. She was the Queen.

She said: 'You may tell my father when you see him that he can trust me to remember that I am an English Princess and the daughter of the King of England.'

Dr West looked about him a little uneasily.

'Speak low,' said Margaret. 'I understand what you have to say is for my ears alone.'

'It is important, Your Grace, that the embassy which the King of France is sending, should not succeed. I come to ask you to use your influence in every way in order to make it fail.'

Margaret nodded slowly.

James came riding back to Edinburgh. Exuberantly he came to his Queen. He had brought velvet and damask for new gowns, and jewels for her to wear with them.

Margaret expressed her delight, while the King gently stroked her swollen body.

'And how is my Queen and her little bairn?'

'Your Queen has been a little sick and very lonely.'

James embraced her, determined to banish self-pity. 'Then

94

she shall be so no longer. I want you to help me plan entertainments such as we have never had before. We have visitors coming to see us and they pride themselves on their skill at the joust. We shall have to show them that in Scotland we are no mean performers.'

'The French?' she asked.

'The French. You will be amused. Such handsome men; and such charming manners!'

'Is it fitting that you should receive the French,' asked Margaret, 'when my father's ambassador has been waiting a long time for an audience with you?'

James raised his brows in a puzzled way. 'Do not tell me that my Queen is turning her attention to politics!'

'Why should she not?'

'For many reasons, one of which is that dancing and music and showing my Court how elegant and beautiful she is, becomes her better.'

'I am no longer a child, James.'

He laughed. 'You grow old. Eighteen, is it?'

She shrugged impatiently. 'You must realise that I am not merely a woman with whom you may amuse yourself, and who has the privilege of giving you *legitimate* children. I am the Queen.'

He rubbed his finger along her cheek. 'A charming queen of whom any king would be proud.'

'Therefore you should talk to me of more serious matters than the plays Cuddy and Dog devise.'

'But are these not serious matters?'

'James, you know they are not. Why cannot you receive my father's ambassador and mend this silly quarrel with England?'

He was at once withdrawn and the obstinacy showed in his

face. He would be gentle and kind, he seemed to imply, but always he would be the ruler. She must understand that.

'My dear Margaret, this pretty head of yours must not be troubled with such tiresome matters. I have no wish to see Dr West.'

'Why?'

'Other matters occupy me.'

'You are ready to dance and joust, to hunt and hawk. Why cannot you meet the ambassador sent by the King of England?'

His eyes narrowed and his lips tightened. 'I do not care that my subjects should be arrested and made prisoner. It is an unfriendly action.'

'Dr West wishes to explain this matter to you.'

'I will tell you this much,' he said. 'Sir Patrick Hamilton has escaped out of England, though his brother Arran remains there. They have not been well treated in your father's domains. That does not please me. And if your Dr West is here to attempt to persuade me not to receive the French embassy, you may tell him he is wasting his time. I understand he has seen you. Now let him return to his master and tell him that in Scotland it is the King who decides what shall be done; and when his subjects have been maltreated he is not to be won over with soft words.'

'You are cruel to me,' cried Margaret. 'And I in my present condition!'

James laughed softly. 'Nay, when was I ever cruel to you? Everything in reason that you ask for is yours. You shall have pleasure, fine clothes, precious jewels. But you must not meddle, my love, in matters which do not concern you.'

He left her then, and when he had gone she stared sullenly before her. Again she had been insulted. In England, they would know that not only was her husband unfaithful to her, but he would not discuss matters of state with her. She was nothing more than a doll to be played with and set aside – she was there merely to become pregnant as soon as possible so that he might dally, in good conscience, with his mistresses.

Some might be content to accept such a position; not so a proud Tudor.

❀ ❀ ❀

James was always remorseful when he disappointed his Queen. She was so much younger than he was that he forgot she had left childhood behind. He always saw her as the girl of thirteen she had been when she first came to him.

He sought therefore to placate her with childish amusements. He spent a great deal of time with her discussing the entertainments, but she was listless because it seemed wrong to her that these pleasures should be planned for the visiting French embassy who were enemies of her father.

To please her, James brought two Moorish girls to her who had come to Scotland from Portugal. They were very beautiful girls and their dark skins and flashing eyes attracted a great deal of attention among the Scots.

'They wish to become Christians,' James told her. 'I am going to give them into your care.'

For a while Margaret was interested in the girls. She took them into her household and they were baptised – one as Margaret and the other as Ellen. Margaret grew fond of them – particularly of Ellen who became generally known as the Queen's Black Ellen. They appeared at the jousts, where they attracted attention, and the Queen took great pleasure in dressing them in gold and scarlet to show off their extraordinary dark beauty. No tournament was complete without the Moorish girls; they would be placed near the Queen, and their desire to serve her was apparent to all.

But Margaret could not be long content with the services of these two lovely girls; she wanted power, the first place in her husband's affections and councils.

James, watching her, began to wonder whether he knew his Margaret after all, and to placate her he did see Dr West, and he allowed the Queen to attend a meeting at which Sir Patrick Hamilton was present and at which he declared on oath that his brother Arran had been ill-treated in England.

After the meeting, James took his Queen by the hand and led her to her apartments; when they reached them he kissed her gently on the brow.

He said little but his meaning was clear. There, he was saying, you see, you should not meddle in politics if you are wise. What can a young girl – albeit she is a queen – know of what is happening at the courts and in the countries of her husband's enemies?

When my child is born, thought Margaret, when I hold my little son in my arms, then everything is going to be different.

The people of Edinburgh had rarely seen such splendour as they did that June when the French embassy was welcomed to Scotland.

The Castle and Holyrood House were the scenes of banquets, masques and plays; in the courtyards of Holyrood House a play, written by English Cuddy, was performed; but what delighted the people more than anything were the brilliant jousts in which Scotsmen tested their skill against the

French. These took place during the warm summer days and they were accompanied by all the pageantry and colour that could be devised.

To the tournament came the Queen's Black Ellen, in a litter carried on the shoulders of fourteen men, from the Castle to the scene of the tournament. The people applauded her and marvelled at her exotic beauty; the strangeness of the French delighted them also and the people declared their loyalty to a king and queen who could give them such pleasure.

Margaret was especially cheered whenever she made her appearance. Her pregnancy was very noticeable now, for her time was near and the people were sure that she carried the heir of Scotland. She had lost her firstborn but that sorrow was forgotten now that she showed signs of giving Scotland the heir.

All through the day it seemed the minstrels played and the trumpets sounded. The French knights acquitted themselves well and it was all the Scotsmen could do to hold their own against them. This was disconcerting because they had been inclined to underestimate the skill of these lithe Frenchmen whose clothes were far more dandified than their own, and whose manners were almost effeminate by Scottish standards.

The Scotsmen would have been defeated but for the sudden appearance of a stranger in their midst. They did not know who he was, but he wore the Scottish emblems and he defeated the first of the French champions with an ease which set the crowd roaring with delight.

He jousted again, and again was the victor.

Soon everyone was talking of the man whom they called the Wild Knight, who appeared every day at the jousts, and one by one challenged the French champions, all of whom went down before him.

The French muttered together that this was no man; it was a god of some kind; it was impossible to beat him at the joust, for he was unconquerable.

At the end of the last day of the jousting, the King announced that there was to be a grand feast which he was calling a Round Table of King Arthur.

This was the climax of the brilliant entertainment. Margaret, seated beside the King, was to give the prizes for those who had won honours in the jousts, and the citizens of Edinburgh crowded into the Palace to watch their King and his guests and to marvel at the splendour they saw.

Margaret was happy, for there was little she enjoyed so much as these displays and there was no question now of her importance. She was the mistress of the revels, the Queen, who would give the prizes and proudly carried the heir to the throne. The heat was overpowering and she could wish that her confinement was behind her and she already the mother of a healthy boy; but she could not complain of the homage all – including the King – bestowed on her. If only he had been a faithful husband! If only he respected her intellect as he did her beauty, how contented she would be! But she must enjoy life while it was good.

The King whispered to her: 'What think you of my Round Table?'

'A fitting end to all the pageantry,' she answered.

'Let us call the child Arthur.'

'Why, yes!' she cried. 'And whenever I look at him I shall remember this day.'

When it was time to present the prizes all declared the first prize should have gone to the stranger, the Wild Knight who was the conqueror of all; and, said the French champions, they felt they should not take their prizes while he, who excelled them all, did not come forward to take his.

There was a hush in the hall, for it seemed that the event for which all were waiting – the prize-giving – would not take place unless the identity of the Wild Knight were revealed.

Then James rose and addressed the assembly.

'My friends,' he said, 'since you insist on my revealing my identity, I will do so. I am the Wild Knight, and I trust our guests will not think hardly of me for the injuries I may have inflicted upon them.'

His words were cut short by a great cheering which shook the hall.

Margaret turned to him, her eyes shining, as the child moved within her.

If he were but my faithful husband, how happy I should be, she told herself.

Margaret was brought to bed in the middle of sultry July. The last weeks had been difficult ones, and she feared that she was a woman who must suffer more than most at the time of childbirth.

Her ladies were about her bed; but the King did not come near her; he could never bear to look on suffering.

'But when my son is born,' murmured Margaret, while her women wiped her brow with a kerchief smelling of sweet unguents, 'it will all be worthwhile.'

At last, after much travail, the child was born.

Margaret heard the whispers in the apartment and her heart sank.

'A maiden bairn.'

'Alas, alas, Her Grace so longed for a son.'

The child lay in her arms and James came to stand by her bedside, to smile at her, to soothe her; and to try to pretend that he was as delighted with the birth of his daughter as he would have been with that of a son.

❀ ❀ ❀

There had been only time to christen the baby before she died. Melancholy brooded over Holyrood House. The lutes and harps were silent; the Queen was desolate and James the King went about with an expression of sorrow on his face.

It was Margaret who tried to comfort him.

'There will be other children, James. We have been unfortunate, but that cannot continue.' Then she burst out passionately: 'I have seen the common people in the streets. Mothers with children at their skirts and at their breasts. Why should this happen to us!'

James buried his face in his hands. 'Sometimes I think I am cursed,' he said. 'Never shall I forget that day at Sauchieburn when I fought on one side and my father on the other. What an unnatural son I was! To go into battle against my own father.'

'James, you were but a boy.'

But he shook his head. 'I was old enough to know what I did. And for this I am cursed . . . cursed with failure to give my country an heir.'

Margaret put her arms about his shoulders; it gave her a certain pleasure to see him thus. At least he laid no blame on her for their ill luck, as many a man would have done. And he was very eager for the comfort she could give.

'Why,' she told him gently, 'we shall get ourselves an heir.'

'But see how these births affect your health. Remember how ill you were last time . . . and this . . .'

'I am young, James, and strong; I shall soon be well.' A cunning look came into her eyes. 'Perhaps it is because you squander your manhood on other women that you cannot give your lawful wife a child who will live.'

'Nay,' was the answer. 'My father loved many women, yet he had sons. It is because of my ill deeds at the time of Sauchieburn. There is a curse on me.'

Margaret put her arms about his neck.

'We will defeat the curse, James. With our love for each other we will defeat it.'

He held her tightly as though he were asking for her protection. Margaret felt strong then, with an infinite faith in the future.

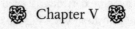

Chapter V

THE WILD KNIGHT

It was April and there was a promise of spring in the air. Margaret sat at a window of her apartments looking out on Arthur's Seat, and she laid her hands on her body and rejoiced because once more she had conceived.

This time all would be well. She was certain it was a boy she carried. She wondered why she had been so unfortunate and why it was that her children did not live. She herself was so strong and healthy – or she had been until she had suffered so from her ordeals. James was strong and lusty. Why could they not get healthy children?

Before the birth of her daughter, who had died so soon, she had spent some months at Lochmaben Castle where Robert the Bruce had been born. James had said: 'Go there, stay there for a while; it would be well if you lived during those waiting months where my noble ancestor drew his first breath.'

She had agreed to go; yet while she was there she had spent as much time wondering with whom James was dallying as she had thinking of the effect the great Bruce might have on her child.

Perhaps last time they had concerned themselves overmuch;

perhaps those women, whom she saw in the streets with their children at their heels, did not fret during their pregnancies. They might even regret them. Could one long for something so fervently that fate perversely denied it?

Thus she was musing when Lady Guildford came to tell her that messengers from England were below and they brought letters from her father's Court.

'Bring them to me without delay,' cried Margaret, and when the letters were brought to her, she read them several times before she could fully grasp their significance.

Her father . . . dead . . . and her brother King!

When she had last seen Henry he had been not much more than ten years old – a swaggering, boastful boy with the words 'When I am King' continually on his lips. Well, now he *was* King. He was also a man. And her father, who for all his coldness had been a good father, was dead.

She put her hand over her eyes. This was real sorrow. She felt apprehensive, a little frightened and alone; and she realised that, all through the years which had been lived in Scotland as James's wife, she had thought of her father on his throne – all-wise, all-powerful, always there in case she should need him.

Now her brother Henry was in his place. She wondered what effect this was going to have on her and James – on England and Scotland.

❀ ❀ ❀

James came to her, for he too was excited by the news.

'What difference will this make, James?' she asked.

'Who knows? Your father was a wise man – not always easy to deal with, but one respected his sound good sense.'

'And my brother?'

'He is as yet untried. You knew him. Do you think he will follow his father's cautious ways?'

Margaret saw him clearly in her mind's eye – rosy-faced, flushed, little mouth prim; the arrogance in his strong young body, the love of flattery and finery.

'I do not think he will be like my father,' she said.

'He writes to me in most friendly fashion.'

'I am glad of that. For I could not be happy if Scotland and England were not good friends.'

'Ah,' said James lightly, 'you should not grieve for such a matter. You are no longer English, remember; you are the Queen of Scots. If there are differences, you should not take them to heart.'

'I trust you will not allow your friendship for the French to stand between you and friendship with England.'

James patted her hand gently and made no answer. Instead he said: 'Your brother is going to marry Katharine of Aragon, so I hear.'

'But she was my brother Arthur's wife!'

'Henry sees no reason why she should not be his also.'

'She is older than he is and I remember she was rarely at Court. She lived aloof from us with her Spaniards. I am surprised.'

'I have heard that your brother's ministers were not eager for the marriage, but he is a young man who will have his own way.'

Margaret smiled. That was true. In the old days people had said they were alike – not only in looks but in temperament. Lucky Henry to be able to say, 'I will have this' and 'I will do that' – and have none who dared gainsay him.

In October of that year Margaret's son was born, to wild rejoicing.

With great pomp he was christened Arthur and declared Prince of Scotland and Lord of the Isles.

Margaret suffered a difficult labour as usual but because the child was alive she came through this in good spirits and quickly regained her health.

She delighted in the child who was named in memory of Arthur of Britain but also of Margaret's favourite brother, who had died so tragically at Ludlow Castle soon after his marriage to that Katharine of Aragon who was now Henry's wife and Queen of England.

This reminded her that Arthur had left her certain jewels in his will, for he had been as fond of her as she of him; but she had never received them. It had been exceedingly difficult to persuade her father to part with anything of value and he had always had some excuse for not sending jewels from England into Scotland; but now he was dead and Margaret did not see why she should not ask Henry to let her have what was hers. She received an affectionate letter from Henry, but he said he could not send her jewels to Scotland. He believed that her husband was very friendly with the French, and the French were no friends of the King of England. If he sent the jewels, how could he be sure that the King of Scotland might not sell them and use the money to make war?

Margaret showed the letter to James whose face darkened with anger.

'It would seem,' he said, 'that we shall not live on such peaceful terms with your brother as we did with your father.'

'But Henry is eager to be friends with you,' Margaret insisted.

'My dear, you do not understand these matters. Your brother is a young king in possession of the great wealth your father amassed over long and careful years. 'Tis my belief that he intends to spend lavishly . . . on pleasure and mayhap war. I hear that he is already planning a campaign against the French. It is easy to see that relations between our two countries will be less cordial than they were during your father's reign.'

'Henry is only a boy,' insisted Margaret. 'He is new to kingship and anxious that everyone shall know how powerful he is.'

'Power is dangerous in the hands of boys,' was James's comment.

❀ ❀ ❀

Margaret ceased to think of politics, for after a few months of life little Arthur followed his brother and sister to the grave.

This was too much to be borne, and the King and Queen were prostrate with sorrow.

James was certain now that he was accursed, and he blamed himself afresh for the part he had played at the time of his father's death.

'Perhaps,' he said, 'I should go on a pilgrimage to the Holy Land. I begin to fear that we shall never have a son who will grow up to be King after me.'

But Margaret refused to despair.

She put her arm about him. 'We have been unfortunate, but has not my brother's wife met with the same misfortune? We will try again, and this time our son will live. I know it.'

'You are right,' James told her. 'It is foolish to fret.'

Hope came to them when, shortly after the death of little Arthur, Margaret was once more pregnant.

'Now,' said James, 'we must take every precaution. I will go at once to St Ninian's shrine and there ask him to take especial care of you.'

'It might be well if you paid no visits on your way back from the shrine,' said Margaret shrewdly. 'Mayhap St Ninian feels it is disrespectful of you to go from him to your mistress.'

James was thoughtful; he decided that he would not visit Janet Kennedy on this occasion.

Now the King and the Queen, together with the whole Court, thought constantly of the importance of the coming birth. Every precaution was taken to placate any supernatural influence which might prove hostile. Relics were brought to the Queen to kiss; some she kept with her at all times. But James and Margaret devoted themselves to prayer and meditation. With only one or two lapses James was the faithful husband. He devoted himself to naval affairs and spent a great deal of time in the company of Sir Andrew Wood watching the building of a new ship which was to be greater in every way than the two – named the *James* and the *Margaret* – which had been recently built. Often he would stay the night on board; and during the first months of her pregnancy, Margaret often joined him there.

If she could only have been sure of producing a healthy child and did not suffer sickness and the disabilities which were always her lot at such times, those would have been the happiest months of Margaret's life. Never since those early days of her marriage had James been so completely hers.

One of the happiest days of all was that in October when the great ship was launched and she stood with James listening to triumphant drums and trumpets as the ship rolled into the harbour of Leith.

It was a day of rejoicing. The Queen pregnant; the greatest ship any of them had ever seen, successfully launched! It must be celebrated with worthy entertainment; and on the arrival of the royal party at Holyrood House a play was performed.

When it was over and the King and Queen had expressed their pleasure, Margaret called the principal actor to her in order to compliment him. This was a young man named David Lindsay who was known as Lindsay of the Mount; he was a poet and had been for some years in the royal household. The King had made him equerry to his first heir, the little Prince James who had died when he was about a year old.

David Lindsay was greatly respected throughout the Court, being a man without any ambition except to live a good life; he was devoted to literature rather than to position and wealth; and both Margaret and James had an affection for him.

'I want to thank you for your performance,' Margaret told him. 'It was a pleasure to watch.'

Delight shone in David's gentle face. ''Twas a good part, Your Grace,' he said.

'And your play coat of blue and yellow taffeties became you well,' Margaret added. 'Pray, tell me the cost, that you do not pay it from your own pocket.'

'It was three pounds, four shillings.'

'A goodly sum, but it was a goodly performance you gave us and well worth the sum.'

James turned to him and added his praise to the Queen's. 'Why, Davie, you are indeed a credit to our Court.'

'You were usher and equerry to my firstborn son who died, alas,' said Margaret. 'I intend to ask the King to make you the same to this child which is soon to be born.'

James cried: ''Tis a good choice. None could make a better.'

'I thank Your Graces,' murmured David. 'I assure you I will never betray the trust you have placed in me.'

'Do this then,' said James. 'Pray for a safe delivery for the Queen and a healthy boy for Scotland.'

'I shall continue to pray thus, Your Grace.'

When he had left them James said to Margaret: 'He is a good man, that Davie, and one whose prayers may well find favour. We cannot have too many prayers.'

❦ ❦ ❦

It was April again and Margaret lay at Linlithgow. Her time had come and in the streets the people stood about and asked themselves what would happen this time. If the Queen failed again, they would say that there was indeed a curse on their royal family.

Some months before, a comet had appeared in the sky – it sent out beams as though it were a sun; and thus it had remained for twenty-one nights.

A warning? A sign of evil? A bad omen?

Now the people remembered it and asked themselves these questions.

There were services in all the churches; there were prayers throughout the country.

A son! A son for Scotland.

Margaret lay groaning on her bed.

'This time a son,' she prayed. 'This time he must live and he shall be called James after his father.'

❦ ❦ ❦

'A boy!'

The triumphant words rang through the Palace, through

the streets of Linlithgow; they were carried to Edinburgh and all over the country the people rejoiced.

The King came to his wife's chamber and demanded to see his son. There he was, lustily crying, a strong little boy with a down of tawny hair on his head and, so said the women of the bedchamber, already a look of his father.

'Let the bells ring out!' cried the King. 'Let Scotsmen rejoice, for this child will live.'

Margaret, exhausted but happy, slept and when she awakened she was refreshed and declared that this was different from her other pregnancies.

As soon as the Queen was able to leave her bed, there must be a feast such as there had never been before. Lindsay of the Mount must come and take charge of the little boy's nursery. The child must be watched over night and day to ensure that he continued in perfect health.

Margaret was now the triumphant mother assuring herself that her little James showed none of the weakness of his brothers and sister. Healthy, lusty, his voice could be heard in his nursery when he crowed and clucked, as though he was determined, as his parents and attendants were, that he should stay alive.

Preparations were made for the feast. Four wild boars were roasted with four oxen; there were ninety-four pigs, thirty-five sheep, thirty-six lambs, seventy-eight kids, seventeen calves and two hundred and thirty-six birds besides pies and cakes of all description.

The wine ran freely and the sounds of rejoicing resounded not only in the Palace, but throughout the country.

James, Prince of Scotland and the Isles, had come to stay.

Little James prospered in his nursery and delighted all who beheld him, though none more than his father and mother; but now that they could believe he was in truth a healthy boy and they need not continually fear he was going to be taken from them, it seemed unnecessary to observe such rigorous piety as they had before his birth.

Margaret no longer prayed for long hours each day; as for James, he had been a faithful husband too long, and abstinence from his favourite game was too much to ask of him.

He was off on his travels once more, and it was whispered that not only did he visit the old mistresses but had added several new ones to those who pleased him.

Anger flared in Margaret's heart. She had been so contented during those weeks of pregnancy when he had been constantly at her side. And now that she had produced a healthy boy, he felt it was enough to visit her occasionally, to share her bed that they might do their best to get more children – one heir not being enough.

She looked about angrily for a diversion.

There was politics. She remembered a conversation which had taken place between herself and her brother Henry before her marriage; then he had deplored the Tudor–Stuart alliance; he did not like what he had heard of her husband. And now that he was King, he seemed to remember that dislike. There was trouble brewing between Henry and James; and it seemed an insult to her that her husband should be more inclined to favour France than the country of his own wife. This is characteristic of the way he has always treated me! she told herself.

It was only reasonable that she should be on the side of her own countrymen and her own brother, and she was going to do everything she could to ruin the chances of the

French and advance those of the English. If she did, Henry might give her the jewels which Arthur had left her. But it was not for that reason that she had decided she would dabble in politics.

She was a woman of spirit, so how could she stand by with indifference while her husband openly visited her rivals.

There was another interest in her life. She was young and beautiful; and now and then she found the eyes of some of her husband's courtiers resting on her, and their looks were meaningful.

She had come to Scotland prepared to love her husband, and she would never have given a thought to any other man had he been faithful to her. But he had wounded her pride – always strong in the Tudors – so, she asked herself, could she be blamed if she, like James, found others interesting?

She had never allowed her fancy to go beyond glances and the imagination. When she bore children she must be sure they were Stuarts of the royal house; but for that, it might have been a different story. She needed restraint in those days – restraint to curb her irritation, her wounded pride and most of all her natural impulses.

James was on a visit to St Ninian's shrine, which meant of course a sojourn with Janet Kennedy; and as Margaret sat at her window in Linlithgow Palace looking out over the loch, she was not admiring the sparkling stretch of water but picturing those two together.

There was a boat on the loch and in it were a young man and woman. Margaret watched him plying the oars while the young woman played the lute. It made a charming picture. She guessed the man to be about her own age, although he might have been a little younger.

I believe childbearing has aged me, thought Margaret ruefully.

She turned her gaze to the men and women who were sauntering at the lochside, but her attention went back to the man in the boat.

She rose and called to her woman. 'I have a fancy,' she said, 'to go on the loch. Go and tell them to prepare my boat for me.'

In a very short time she was lying back in her boat, her lute in her hands, her hair showing golden beneath her headdress; the excitement which had come to her making her look very young indeed.

'Who is that in yonder boat?' she asked Lady Guildford who had accompanied her.

Lady Guildford tried to hide a faint alarm which, knowing her mistress so well, she could not help feeling. So far Margaret had behaved with decorum, although it had to be admitted that she suffered some provocation.

'It's young Archibald Douglas, Your Grace.'

'A Douglas! Old Bell-the-Cat's son?'

'Grandson, Your Grace.'

'Ah, yes, I see he is very young. And who is the lady with him?'

Lady Guildford's mouth was a little prim. 'That, Your Grace, is his young wife.'

'Indeed. And who is she?'

'She is Margaret, daughter of Patrick Hepburn, Earl of Bothwell.'

Margaret began to laugh. 'There seem to be so many Margarets at the Court of Scotland.'

'It is a charming name, Your Grace,' murmured Lady Guildford.

Margaret did not answer, but she continued to watch the young man. She had always had a liking for Old Bell-the-Cat because he had sought to rival James in Janet Kennedy's affection. And this was his grandson. How handsome he was! Gazing at him, she realised that her husband was beginning to look his age. All the Stuart good looks and charm could not give him eternal youth; and what a pleasant thing youth was. He must be near my own age, thought Margaret, possibly younger.

She turned her attention to his wife. Insipid, she decided, and unworthy of him.

Now their boats were close together and the young Douglases were aware of the proximity of the Queen.

'It is pleasant on the loch today,' Margaret called in a friendly fashion.

'It is indeed so, Your Grace.' His voice was melodious, as she had known it would be; and now that she was closer she could see how fresh his skin was, how bright his eyes. She liked the way his hair curled about his neck. By sweet St Ninian, she thought, using her husband's favourite oath, if Old Bell-the-Cat had half the good looks of his grandson, James must have found a formidable rival in him for the wanton Janet.

She played her lute as sweetly as she knew how and the lute in that other boat was silent.

When she had finished there was a round of applause in which he joined most heartily.

She bowed her head in acknowledgement of the applause.

Lady Guildford ventured: 'There is a breeze arising, Your Grace. Should you not consider your health?'

'Row us to the shore,' Margaret commanded; and she turned to smile at the occupants of that other boat.

Trouble had flared up between Scotland and England. James was still smarting under Henry's refusal to let Margaret have the jewels which were rightly hers, when news was brought to him that the English had seized certain Scottish ships and in the fight which preceded the capture an admiral of Scotland, Sir Andrew Barton, had been killed.

Margaret found him pacing up and down his apartment in an anger which was rare for him.

'I'll not endure this,' he cried. 'It is not a matter which can be settled over a council table. This is an act of war.'

Margaret wanted to know of whom he spoke, and when he retorted, 'The English!' her resentment rose afresh. Why would he not take her into his confidence? Surely he realised that she could procure concessions from her own brother which his ministers could not hope to achieve.

'I doubt not,' she said tartly, 'that there were faults on both sides.'

James regarded her thoughtfully.

'This quarrel goes back to the days when my father was on the throne,' he explained.

'Why don't you tell me all about it, James? Don't you see that because I am English I might be able to help?'

'You must admit that your brother is headstrong and hardly likely to listen to advice. But this is what happened. One of our merchants, a certain John Barton, was taken prisoner by the Portuguese and put to death. This happened, as I said, in my father's reign. His family wanted vengeance on his slayers and, since this was denied them, they put to sea in an endeavour to destroy all the Portuguese ships that came their way. This was a dangerous thing to do, for pirates are reckless men and when there were no Portuguese ships available they sought to make prizes of ships of other nations. Some of these happened to be English. That was how the trouble started. The Howards fitted up ships and set out in search of the Bartons. This is the result.'

'It would seem to me that the Bartons deserved their fate, and what has happened is no reason for enmity between you and my brother.'

'The English have no right to destroy Scottish ships.'

'Nor have Scotsmen to act as pirates against English ships.'

'It is certainly a matter which must be brought to a stop. And as a result Lord Dacre and Dr West will be arriving in Edinburgh shortly to discuss some sort of settlement with me.'

'I think you should listen to them in a friendly spirit,' said Margaret.

'Do not forget that your brother holds valuable property of yours which he will not give up.'

'I am sure if I were to plead with him I could make him understand that this strife between our countries is foolish and dangerous.'

'Strife is always dangerous, but I do not trust your brother, Margaret, and I never shall.'

'Yet you are ready enough to trust the French.'

'I have no reason to do otherwise.'

'And with the English . . .'

'Why, you yourself know he will not give up your jewels.'

'James, when Lord Dacre and Dr West come to Edinburgh, will you allow me to see them?'

James hesitated. Then he said, 'Very well, you shall have

your interview with them. Then perhaps you will understand where the fault for this enmity lies.'

Margaret received Dr West and Lord Dacre in her apartments in Stirling Castle. Her son was with her there, for she did not care that he should be far from her and she always found great pleasure in visiting the nursery where David Lindsay was already in charge.

David seemed to be acting as nurse to the boy. He it was who carried him about in his arms, and in spite of young James's age he was already aware of the devotion of this man and apt to be fretful when he was not present. David Lindsay watched over the child with the utmost care and had at last, after several failures, discovered the perfect wet nurse for him in a buxom Irishwoman.

David could scarcely wait for the boy to grow up, so eager was he to introduce him to music and poetry. But he never for one moment forgot how important to the country was this young life; and in those early days he gave his attention to his bodily needs. It was a great pleasure for Margaret to visit his nursery, and hear from David how her son was progressing. He was a beautiful baby, full of good health; and while this was so, other matters seemed of far less importance.

All the same Margaret did want to make peace between her brother and her husband. She had thrown herself into this project with great zest, partly because she was a woman who would always want to rule; partly to take her mind from young Archibald Douglas whom she saw frequently and of whom she was thinking far too much.

When she received the English ambassadors she greeted

them with warmth and asked many questions as to the health of the King and Queen of England. His Grace, her brother, she was told, was in fine good health; the Queen, due to her recent disappointment, a little less so.

'My poor sister!' said Margaret with feeling. 'I beg you, when you return, tell her that I pray for her continually and I hope with all my heart that in due course she will be as happy as I. Now tell me, have you brought me news of my legacy?'

'Yes, Your Grace. The King, your brother, will most willingly send it to you.'

'Ah,' cried Margaret, 'I knew he would. Then when will it arrive?'

'His Grace makes one condition. It is that the King of Scotland makes solemn promise to keep the peace with England and to sign no treaty with France.'

Margaret was startled. She knew that James would not consider such conditions, and she was as far from receiving her jewels as ever; and moreover, relations between her native land and that of her adoption were going to suffer greater strain.

'And if my husband refuses to accept these conditions . . . ?' she began.

Dr West answered: 'Your Grace, it grieves me to say this, but I repeat the words of my master. If the King, your husband, is determined on a state of war between England and Scotland, the King, my master, will not only keep the legacy but take the best towns of Scotland also.'

Margaret was fearful; she could almost hear her brother's blustering boastful voice.

She was seeking for some rejoinder when James entered the room to see how the interview was progressing. She was glad that he had not heard those last ominous words.

It seemed imperative to Margaret that she heal the breach between her brother and husband. This dabbling in politics brought a new excitement to her life at a time when she needed it.

On several occasions in the dance she had found herself partnered by young Archibald Douglas, and she was thinking of him more frequently.

James was inclined to listen to her, but she knew that this was due to his natural courtesy rather than to any desire for her opinions. James was headstrong and believed in making his own decisions; if he would not always take the advice of his ministers it was scarcely likely that he would listen to that of his wife, who must necessarily lack their knowledge and experience.

'Why, James,' said Margaret, 'it is possible that I might persuade Henry to bestow on our little James the title of Duke of York. Poor Katharine of Aragon seems unable to give him male heirs – so why should not our child benefit?'

James was dubious. He had never trusted Henry; he never would. And every day he was receiving the French ambassadors and making excuses to avoid the English.

Margaret was doubly disturbed. News had come to her that her brother Henry had already sailed for France to make war on Louis XII, leaving his wife, Katharine, as Regent during his absence.

How like him to be so impetuous! thought Margaret. He had sought to win from James a promise of peace that he might go to France without thought of an enemy's attacking from the North; but since he could not win this, he had acted without it.

Henry with the flower of his army in France! What would James do now?

She soon discovered. James was longing to make war on his insolent brother-in-law and naturally this was the ideal time to do so.

He was closeted with his ministers who were, Margaret was thankful to realise, not so eager to plunge the country into war as their King was.

James must be persuaded to remain at peace. He must understand that Henry was new to kingship; he had for long been subdued by his father and, now that he was King, was determined to be master. He had always seen himself as a leader of men, so it was natural that now he wanted to see himself as a conqueror. Margaret, who had known the boy Henry so well, believed that the man was not so different. Let him try his wings in France; then he might not be so eager for battle. That was what she wanted to explain to James.

But James's chivalry was touched from an unexpected quarter.

The Queen of France, Anne of Brittany, had written to him to tell him that when her husband's embassy had returned to France they had recounted to her and the king how they had been entertained in Scotland, and how at the jousts there had been one known as the Wild Knight who had beaten all comers. She had often thought of the Wild Knight, a great gentleman; in fact she had thought of him as *her* knight, and she was sending him a token of her regard.

The token was a ring of enormous value. She begged him to wear it for her sake.

She was sorely distressed at this time because the English troops under the brash young English King were on French soil, and she was, in truth, appealing to the chivalry of her Wild Knight. Would he consider helping a lady in distress?

James put the ring on his finger and thought of the French Queen who wrote to him so eloquently. He pictured her at her table writing to him, the tears in her eyes; and his heart was softened. He believed that it was in his power to bring great joy to her, and to himself, by defeating the English.

He answered this appeal immediately by sending his ships – the *James* and the *Margaret* – to the French coast, and he put the Earls of Arran and Huntley in command of them.

Then, because it was against his idea of true chivalry to declare war on a country whose King was absent, he dispatched his Lord Lyon in full herald's dress to Henry's camp at Terouenne to announce that he was declaring war on Henry for the following reasons:

Henry had taken Scotsmen prisoner; he had withheld the legacy of Margaret, Queen of Scotland; he had slaughtered the Scottish Admiral Andrew Barton; and by these deeds he had broken the peace existing between England and Scotland.

Margaret was dismayed. She had so longed to show her brother the influence she held over her husband. And without telling her what was afoot, he had made himself the knight of the Queen of France, giving way to *her*, while his beautiful young Queen was ignored.

Margaret awoke. It was night and, stretching out her hand, gently she touched the sleeping body of her husband. So near, she thought, and yet so far away.

She remembered then riding into Scotland and how she had changed her dress on the roadside because she had wanted to look her best for him; then she had fallen deeply in love with him and for a time had believed herself to be loved.

It seemed now that the whole of her married life had been an affront to her pride.

She began to weep.

'What ails you?' It was James's voice in the darkness.

'Oh, have I awakened you? I crave pardon for that.'

'But tears! Why?'

'It was an evil dream.'

James, who was almost as superstitious as his father had been, was alarmed. He believed fervently in the significance of dreams.

'What was this dream?'

'I dreamed that you were standing at the edge of a precipice and, while I watched you, men came running. They were soldiers and they seized you and threw you down . . . I saw your body mangled and battered, and I could not bear it.'

James put his arms about her. 'You are overwrought,' he soothed.

'Nay, but this dream was vivid. And it did not stop there. I was sitting in my chamber looking at my jewels – my coronet of diamonds and my rings; and as I watched, my diamonds and my rubies all turned to pearls. And pearls are the sign of widowhood and tears.'

Being aware of her desire to turn him from his purpose, James was not as impressed by this dream as she had hoped he would be. 'It is clearly a meaningless nightmare. Go to sleep and forget it.'

Margaret withdrew herself from his arms and sat up in bed.

'What I tell you is of course of no account,' she cried bitterly. 'Now if I were the Queen of France you would listen to me. Alas, I am but the Queen of Scotland . . . your own wife whom you have constantly deceived and ignored.'

James was tired; he disliked such scenes at any time but at night they were doubly distressing. He lay down and began breathing as though he were sleeping.

'Oh, you can pretend to sleep,' stormed Margaret. 'Let us hope you have pleasanter dreams than I. Let us hope that you dream you are reading love letters from the Queen of France . . . fighting her battles for her like her own true knight.'

'Margaret, be silent. You will arouse our attendants.'

'What matters it? They will only hear me say what they know already. Do you deny that you have made yourself the knight of the Queen of France? I wonder you did not go to France instead of Lyon. Then you might have had a chance of sharing her bed.'

James did not answer, but Margaret was not going to be silenced.

'The Queen of France!' she cried scornfully. 'Twice married by means of divorces! A fine lady to arouse the chivalry of her Scottish knight. But she must be served while the mother of your son is cast aside.'

James rose quickly and seizing her pulled her down beside him.

'Be silent!' he commanded, and there was an angry note in his voice.

'I will not! I will not!' she sobbed.

'You are being foolish,' said James gently.

'Why? Because I have loved you too well? Because I have wanted to have a share in your life?'

'Have you not had a share in my life?'

'I have had my moments . . . and then I have been forgotten. I have been here merely to bear your children. Your mistresses have had more of you than I. And now this woman . . . this Queen of France . . . beckons you and against the advice of your ministers you are ready to do her bidding. This old woman – and everyone knows she is in a decline – says, "Be my Knight," and you are ready to serve her.'

'Surely you cannot be jealous of an old woman who is in a decline?'

'I can be jealous of all who take you from me.'

'Oh, Margaret, why cannot you be calm . . . serene . . . ?'

She cried out: 'Like that other Margaret. She was always so calm, was she not? She was so understanding! Well she might be! Grateful for the attentions of a king. But I was the daughter of a king before I was the wife of one . . . and I demand . . . I demand . . .'

She was choking on her sobs again; he stroked her hair and laid his lips on her forehead, and for some minutes they lay silent.

Then at length she said: 'James, you are really going to march across the Border?'

'Yes.'

'My sister-in-law, Katharine of Aragon, will gather together an army to meet you.'

'That is very likely.'

'James, when you go south, let me come with you. Let me meet my sister-in-law. Together we will talk and make peace. There is no need for war.'

James remained silent.

'James,' she went on, 'will you let me come with you? Will you let me talk to Katharine? She will not want war any more than I do.'

'Nay,' agreed James, 'she will not want war. Nor will your brother. They would prefer to wait until he returns from France with the full strength of his army. Then, wife, *they* will not hesitate to march across the Border. By sweet St Ninian, have you forgotten that he has declared he will take the best of our towns for himself if we break not our alliance with France?'

'You should have broken your alliance with France. You should never have sent ships there.'

'I see,' he said ruefully, 'that you are an Englishwoman still, and the English were always enemies of the Scots.'

'Should I be an enemy of my husband . . . of my son?'

'Poor Margaret! It is sad that your brother and your husband should be at war. But for this you must blame your brother.'

She was angry again. 'Nay,' she cried, 'I blame my husband. My husband who, because the French Queen flatters him into becoming her Wild Knight, turns from his true wedded wife to give her pleasure.'

'Nay, Margaret, this is not so. Never should I have taken up arms against your brother if he had treated me as a friend.'

'I could have made friendship between you.'

'Never!'

'You would not let me try.' She sat up in bed and abused him for all that he had made her suffer. She taunted him with his infidelity – the lies and subterfuge during those first months of their married life when he had feigned to be occupied by state affairs and was in truth with his mistresses.

'What sort of marriage is this . . . for the daughter of a king!' demanded Margaret.

She was a little hysterical, because she was afraid. She had related a dream to him which had not occurred that night, but her sleep had been uneasy of late, and although her dreams had taken no definite shape they had been filled with foreboding.

She could not analyse her feelings for this man. There were

times when she hated him, others when she loved him. She loved him for his virile body, for his graceful and expert love-making; but she could never forget that he, who had awakened her to the full sensuality of her own nature, had deceived her, had made her foolish in her own eyes. She had dreamed of an idyll; if he had only seemed a little less perfect during the first days of their marriage it would have been easier to bear. She would have come to a sense of reality before she had built a romantic ideal. She believed that as long as she lived she would feel cheated – and he had done this.

She wanted to tell him so now, because she had a notion that this was the time to tell him. Perhaps she hoped to make him relent towards her, to take her with him into battle. For suddenly she was terrified to let him go.

He had taken her trembling body in his arms and the intensity of her passion communicated itself to him. There could only be one climax for them in such a situation.

When they lay silent and exhausted side by side, Margaret stared into the darkness.

She was certain that that night she had conceived again.

❀ ❀ ❀

The King was preparing for the march south. The Queen was subdued and silent.

She had taken the young prince to Linlithgow and James was with her; but he would not stay long. The country was ready for war.

She did not plead again to be allowed to accompany his army, because she knew it would be fruitless. He was particularly kind and gentle but adamant on that point.

'I feel our son will be safe with you,' he told her. 'I shall make you Regent of my kingdom and guardian of our heir while I am away.'

She nodded sadly and lowered her eyes for fear he should see the resentment which she did not believe she would be able to hide.

He told her that he had called a council to be held in the Palace and that during it he hoped to complete his plans.

'It will not be long before I am back with you,' he said. 'I pray you take counsel with English Cuddy and Scotch Dog. I shall expect good entertainment on my return.'

English Cuddy! Scotch Dog! As though she were a child to be amused with their trifles.

But she did not give up hope of persuading him.

❦ ❦ ❦

Help came from an unexpected quarter, when the Earl of Angus, old Bell-the-Cat, presented himself to her.

Margaret felt stimulated at the sight of the old warrior because she was interested in the Douglas family for two reasons: one that this man was a rival with James for the affections of Janet Kennedy; and the other that he was a grandfather of his namesake, Archibald Douglas, who had so caught her fancy and whom she could not get out of her mind.

'Your Grace,' said Bell-the-Cat, 'I have heard that you sought, most wisely, to turn the King from his intention to attack England, and I have come to ask your permission to work with you in this endeavour.'

Margaret flushed with pleasure. 'You are very welcome, my lord,' she told him. 'I am sure your experience and reputation should be of great help in changing the King's mind.'

'That is what I wish to do, for I am of the opinion that this is not the moment to engage in war.'

'I will ask the King's permission to go with you to him now that you may talk to him.'

The old man bowed his head, and Margaret called to one of her attendants to go to the King and ask if he would receive her and the Earl of Angus who had come on a mission of great importance.

James sent a reply immediately that he would be pleased to receive them in his apartment, and when the Queen presented the Earl, he regarded him with distaste.

He could not help picturing him with Janet, and he knew that Angus felt the same about him. They were rivals – and they always would be, for Janet was a woman whom it was difficult to forget.

Angus too suffered from tormenting jealousy. The Stuart was one of the handsomest fellows in Scotland. Such looks and charm, and a crown to go with them! No wonder Janet had been tempted.

'What is it you wish?' James asked.

'To add my pleas to those of the Queen on this matter of war,' Angus told him.

'My mind is made up,' replied the King coldly.

'Sire, the English have always been a formidable enemy.'

'I am well aware of the strength of my enemy, my lord. But as it happens the flower of the English army is at this moment engaged in attacking my friend and ally, the King of France. And this seems an opportune moment for me to wipe out old scores. As you doubtless know, I have already declared war on the King of England.'

'Sire, will you not call together your old counsellors?'

'Your friends?'

'They will set their reasons before Your Grace, as I will do.'

The King shrugged his shoulders. 'I am in no mood to listen to your advice, Angus. My plan shall go forward.'

'At least,' put in Margaret, 'Your Grace should listen to what these tried and trusty men have to say.'

'Very well,' replied James. 'I will hear you. Let there be a council meeting of those who share your views, and I will attend it; but I warn you, I shall not agree with your arguments and you are but wasting your time and mine.'

'Your Grace is good,' murmured Angus. 'I will bring to the Palace certain members of my family and my friends who share my views, that we may parley with Your Grace.'

'As you will,' said James, but his lips were set in the obstinate lines which Margaret understood; and she knew that he had already made up his mind.

The Douglases came to Linlithgow in their strength. Margaret met the eldest son of Bell-the-Cat, George, Master of Douglas, who was the father of Archibald. She had a glimpse also of the younger Archibald himself, and there was an opportunity of exchanging a word with him.

'I rejoice to see your grandfather at Linlithgow,' she told him when she met him as if by chance on his way to the council meeting.

'I thank Your Grace,' murmured the young man, bowing over her hand.

'I pray that he will persuade the King from this enterprise.'

'I will add my prayers to those of Your Grace.'

'Thank you,' she said, and smiled at him in a manner which embarrassed him slightly because he was not sure of the meaning behind her looks.

It was said in the Palace that the Queen and old Bell-the-Cat were allies, more because of Janet Kennedy than the English.

But there was another thing which was said, and that was that there was a party in the country opposed to war; and this became known as the Queen's and the Douglas faction.

James listened to the objections to war and swept them all aside. He had made up his mind. He was going to march against England.

❦ ❦ ❦

The King had gone to the Abbey Church of St Michael with some of his ministers to pray for a successful enterprise and was attending vespers in St Katharine's Chapel there when an extraordinary incident occurred.

James was kneeling in prayer when, out of the dimness of the chapel, a strange figure appeared. This seemed to be an aged man dressed in a blue gown, with a roll of white linen tied about his waist; his hair hung in yellow locks about his face and fell to his shoulders.

His voice rang through the chapel so that all could hear: 'James, King of Scotland, listen to me and take heed. Sir King, I charge you – do not go where you plan to go. If you ignore this warning, you will not fare well – nor shall any that follow you. Beware. Follow not the counsel of women. Do this, Sir King, and you will be confounded and brought to shame.'

There was a brief silence and before any had time to detain the man he had disappeared.

James rose to his feet. 'Who spoke then?' he cried.

His friends were clustering about him.

'Did you see a figure . . . a strange figure in blue and white?'

'I thought so.'

'Where is he now?'

'He was there one moment . . . and gone the next.'

Frightened glances were exchanged. None was as eager to go to war with England as the King was.

James said: 'Bah! A madman.'

'Perhaps so, Sire, but where did he go?'

'We have other things with which to concern ourselves than the antics of madmen,' said the King.

Margaret awaited the return of her servant.

He was trembling, for he had feared he would not escape. He had planned what he would say if he were caught; he would tell the King that the Queen had commanded him to act as he had; and he knew the King well enough to believe that he would shrug his shoulders and laugh aside the incident.

But he had not been caught. The Queen had planned carefully. It had been possible to emerge from the shadows to say his piece; to step back; to slip behind the curtains and out through the little door at the side of the altar to the privy stairs which led to the Palace.

'Well done,' said Margaret.

She waited now to hear that her husband and his friends had been shaken by what they must have thought was a super-natural vision.

But she was disappointed.

James had gone to Edinburgh, there to supervise his artillery-men who were bringing the military equipment from the Castle where it had been stored. Among this was the great cannon which the King had recently had made and which was known as the Seven Sisters.

It was at this time that the second strange incident took place.

The army was now assembled on the plain of Borough Moor near Edinburgh, ready to march, when at midnight a voice was heard ringing out, it seemed, from the Market Cross.

'These men are summoned to the Bar of Pluto within forty days!' cried the voice. Then there followed a roll call of the names of certain illustrious men who were following the King into battle.

Many of the people of Edinburgh lay cowering in their beds as they listened to the voice; but some ran out into the streets and, although they made their way to the Market Cross, they could not discover whence the voice came.

This was an evil omen, they said. They had heard how a strange figure had appeared when the King was at his devotions. Clearly he was being warned against going to war.

When the King was awakened from his sleep at Borough Moor and told of the voice at Market Cross he merely yawned. 'There are some who are misguided enough to attempt to divert us from our purpose,' he said, and he smiled, somewhat tenderly thinking of one.

Was she responsible for the voice, as he was ready to believe she had been for the mysterious figure in the chapel? He knew of the door beyond the curtain which led to the Palace. His Queen was a woman of imagination and she believed that she could unnerve him through his superstition. But he was only superstitious when he felt he had acted unworthily; and the more he contemplated the war into which he was plunging his country, the more right and logical it seemed to conquer the old enemy at a moment when, by conducting this foolish war on the French, he was at his weakest.

Of course it was a war against his own brother-in-law and Margaret could not bear that her husband and brother should be in conflict. It was a natural feeling. But there was no blood-tie between him and Henry, and if ever Scotland had had an enemy that enemy, he was convinced, was Henry VIII of England.

He would forgive Margaret her little essays into the supernatural. He knew them for what they were, and they were not going to move him one inch from his purpose.

On a hot August day the Scottish army began to move towards the Border. Margaret went with it, riding beside the King at the head of the cavalry. She had accepted the fact at last that it was useless to try to persuade him to give up the campaign. The light of battle was in James's eyes and nothing would deter him now.

With James rode his son by Marian Boyd, Alexander Stuart, a handsome youth in his teens who had already been appointed Archbishop of St Andrews. Glancing at this handsome youth, Margaret was glad that her own small son was safe in the care of David Lindsay at Linlithgow; but Alexander was glowing with health and high spirits, eager to prove himself in battle, and there was no doubt that James was delighted to have his son with him.

They arrived at Dunfermline where they stayed the night. It had been decided that Margaret should go no farther but return to Linlithgow to be with the young Prince.

That was a tender night which Margaret was to remember. James had said to her: 'Margaret, let us forget all rancour. Let it be as it was when you first came into Scotland.'

She had been gentle too; and as they lay clasped in each other's arms James let her know that he bore no grudge against her for the tricks she had played on him; nor had he told anyone of his suspicion that she was involved in them. 'For I know,' he said, 'it was but wifely concern which prompted you to act so. And, if all should not go as I hope, I have left orders that you are to be tutrix to our heir as long as you remain a widow.'

Margaret cried out in horror: 'Do not say such things. It is unlucky.'

'Ah,' he murmured, 'it is you who are the superstitious one now.'

'We are all superstitious where our feelings are concerned,' she told him; and she wept a little, not only because he was going to leave her, but because he had never been all that she had once believed he was.

He comforted her with soft words and told her that he would be back victorious within a few weeks. 'Why, the land will be undefended. A few battles – and England conquered forever, a vassal of Scotland. And then, my love, in years to come it will be said: "That was the work of James the Fourth of Scotland . . . and his Queen, Margaret Tudor, who was a good wife to him."'

'And to whose counsels he paid no heed!'

'When this is over I will pay heed to all you say.'

'Ah,' she murmured, 'when this is over!'

Then they made love, first tenderly, and then with rising passion.

As though, thought Margaret, they who had done these things so often now did them for the last time.

So Margaret returned to Linlithgow and James continued the march south.

It seemed that James had been right. The Border was unprotected. The flower of English chivalry was indeed in France with the King. All along the line the Scots were victorious and all through those preliminary skirmishes James kept Alexander Stuart beside him and rejoiced in his young manhood.

He wished the boy had been his legitimate son. What a king he would have made!

He told Alexander this and was delighted to see the horror dawn in the young face. 'But if I were your legitimate son how could I be King while you lived? And if you are to die, I would as lief die with you, as take your crown.'

Wonderful words from a son to a father. And thus it would have been with my father, thought James, had he treated me as a father should, as I have sworn I will behave to all my children.

Those were glorious days, and James felt young again. Each morning to ride to fresh conquests, teaching his son to make war as a man, with victory crowning all their efforts. Pleasant too to watch old Bell-the-Cat fighting as one would expect such an old warrior to fight, but sour because he had not believed in the war.

He was too old for battle, too old for lovemaking. Perhaps Janet had realised that by now.

And so the war went as Scotsmen could wish. Then they came to the frontier castle of Ford.

The castle stood on the east bank of the Till stream in the north of the county of Northumberland. Alexander, riding beside his father, said: 'It's a grand place, but it'll fall to us as easily as the others.'

James looked towards the two towers at the east and west fronts of the edifice and replied complacently: 'More easily, my son, for the castellan is already our prisoner. He is Sir William Heron who now lies in a dungeon at Fastcastle for his part in the murder of one of our Scottish knights. I do not think this castle will hold out long against us.'

'Then here is yet another conquest!' laughed Alexander.

They were right. There was little resistance at Ford Castle. Into the courtyards rode the Scots, where the defenders of the castle were on their knees begging for mercy.

James, always a generous conqueror, called to them to have no fear, for they would not be harmed unless they acted treacherously towards him and his army. He merely wished to take the castle and rest here for a night before proceeding.

'Take me to him who is in charge,' he cried.

He stepped into the great hall where, her head high, the colour flooding her cheeks, dignified yet unafraid, stood a woman and with her a young girl.

The woman was remarkably beautiful; the girl fresh and charming, scarcely out of her childhood. James's expression softened immediately, and the gallant took the place of the soldier.

'Madam,' he said, 'I could wish we had met in happier circumstances.'

She did not answer but regarded him steadily.

'Have no fear,' James went on gently. 'It is not our custom to harm women and children.'

'We must at least be grateful for that,' she answered.

'My men are hungry and thirsty. Could you give them refreshment?'

'We are at your mercy,' she replied gravely, and, turning, signed to her servants that they must lay the great table and feed the conquerors.

James was at her side: 'While this is being done, may I have a word with you in private?'

She led him into a small parlour, and as he followed her he saw with pleasure that Alexander was seeking to reassure the frightened girl as he, James, intended to reassure her mother.

When they faced each other in the parlour James brought forth all his charm, and he could not hide the speculation in his eyes as, connoisseur that he was, he noted the beauty of her face, her slim waist, her white bosom, her rounded hips. She was a beauty and it was a pleasure to be in her company.

James laid a hand on her arm. 'First,' he said, 'I must teach you not to be afraid of me.'

She lifted her enormous black-fringed eyes to his face and smiled suddenly. 'No,' she said, 'I do not think I shall need to fear you.'

James laughed. 'Now,' he said, 'we are friends?'

'Friends? My husband a prisoner in one of your castles! Our own home besieged and conquered!'

'Look upon this as a friendly call,' James urged.

'Listen to the soldiers in the courtyard. This is war, and however kind the King of Scots may be, nothing can alter that.'

He took her hand and before she could withdraw it – and he was quick to notice, being so practised in these matters, that she had not in truth hurried to do so – he had kissed it.

'There are compensations in all things,' he answered, 'even

in war. Would it be possible for wine to be brought for me here, and would the lady of the house share it with me as though we were friends . . . which I hope we soon shall be?'

'You are in command,' she said.

'But nay!' he answered promptly. 'I would not force my company upon you. I shall wait for you to invite me to share a goblet with you.'

She left him in the parlour, and in a short time returned with a servant who carried wine and two goblets.

'Serve first the King of Scotland,' Lady Heron ordered. 'And then serve me.'

So they sat in the parlour and talked. He spoke of the horrors of war; the need for one country to take up arms against another; and how in the wretched business of wars there were now and then interludes which made of it a glorious adventure.

❁ ❁ ❁

The soldiers lay about the castle grounds glad of a rest; Alexander had found the young girl a pleasant companion, and she was as attracted by him as he was by her.

Meanwhile the King grew more and more enchanted with the company of Lady Heron. She was young, beautiful, and was learning to trust him.

'You without a husband, I without a wife,' sighed James. 'It would seem that we might offer comfort to each other.'

Lady Heron was not coy; she admitted that she found the King of Scotland charming even as he found her, and by nightfall their friendship was progressing so rapidly that it had all the appearance of courtship. The pursuit of a woman had always been a more fascinating project than that of any enemy, and quite irresistible to James.

By sweet St Ninian! he thought. How glad I am that we came to Ford Castle, and what great good luck that Sir William Heron is imprisoned and so not present to spoil the fun.

James had a feeling that he would not sleep alone during his night at Ford Castle.

He gave instructions that the Lady Heron and her family and dependants were to be treated with the utmost courtesy. He and his men were guests in the castle, he would have them know, and any brutality would be severely punished. He asked the Scots to remember their chivalry. Lady Heron was to be free to come and go as she wished in the precincts of the castle; there was to be no suggestion of making any prisoners.

The long day was coming to an end and the friendship between the King and the Lady of the castle now seemed moving towards an inevitable climax. Alexander, who admired his father more than any man on earth, sought to emulate his manners and habits by pursuing the daughter of the house with the same gentle yet persistent charm as his father used in pursuit of her mother.

Old Bell-the-Cat saw what was happening and gnashed his teeth in rage. The King seemed to forget that they were engaged in war. Since he had set eyes on Lady Heron he had behaved as though he were a friendly neighbour paying a visit.

Well, they would leave a few troops in Ford tomorrow and march on. But the amorous nature of his King – reminding him as it did of their rivalry – was galling to the old man, both as a soldier and a lover of Janet Kennedy.

Lady Heron looked out from the window of her apartment over the darkening countryside. She was excited because as a born intriguer and a woman of light morals, she found the position exciting.

She was expecting a message, for she believed this would surely come to her if the King of Scotland arrived at Ford Castle. She was hoping for it; it was going to give her the excuse she needed; but even without it she would not forgo her night's pleasure.

He was certainly attractive and would be an accomplished lover. She would feign reluctance . . . at first. But she would have to act with skill because, for all his outward charm, he was not without shrewdness and insight.

Her maid came to tie her hair and, as she passed the comb through those long curls, she bent close to whisper.

'The messenger is below, my lady. He came with stores for the castle, and he is not to see you for fear of arousing suspicion. He has told me what I must say.'

'Then say it,' said Lady Heron.

'The Earl of Surrey asks your help. He cannot be ready for several days. He wants you to hold the Scotsman here until he sends word that he is ready to meet him. If the Scots march south tomorrow they will find no real resistance, but a few days will alter that. So it is imperative that they are held here.'

Lady Heron nodded slowly. 'You're a good girl,' she said. A lascivious smile played about her lips as she murmured: 'What is asked of a poor woman in the service of her country!'

They were delighted with each other.

'Is there to be just this one night?' asked Lady Heron, her great eyes filled with brooding melancholy.

'I am at war,' laughed James.

'You are conquering all before you . . . the castles of England, the women of England. Must you go so quickly?'

To leave Ford Castle and Lady Heron, now that he had discovered what pleasure she could give him, would indeed be a blow. It had been a night of exciting discovery; yet he felt he had more to learn of the beautiful and willing lady of Ford.

What could one more night matter? He pictured the army camping that night in some cheerless field and he shivered with disgust.

No, as he had told her, it was episodes such as this one which made war a great adventure.

'Perhaps we might tarry one more day and night,' he murmured.

She laughed delightedly. It was so pleasant when one could combine the service of one's country and the satisfaction of one's bodily needs. Surrey would be pleased with her.

❀ ❀ ❀

And if he could dally one night, why not two and three?

So in the castle courtyards the Scots soldiers lay about playing dice, or following the royal example and flirting with the maidservants. They were happy enough in the delay.

Old Bell-the-Cat stormed into that apartment which had been set aside for the use of the King.

'Your Grace,' he cried sternly, 'this is folly. We dally here while the English are mustering their forces to come against us. Already much precious time has been lost.'

'Nonsense!' retorted James. 'The rest and relaxation we enjoy here are preserving our strength so that when the time comes to fight we shall be ready.'

'We are frittering away our strength on senseless pleasures,' retorted Bell-the-Cat, who was too disgusted with his King to mind his words. 'I tell Your Grace, we are giving the English that which they most need: time. Had we gone forward we could have attacked them while their numbers were small.'

'I would be ready to fight the English if they were a hundred thousand more in numbers.'

'Your Grace, you could return to Scotland now. You have shown the English your warlike intentions. You have taken certain of their castles. That will suffice to keep your oath to the Queen of France. I implore you either to go forward now . . . or return. I have reason to know that the Earl of Surrey is gathering more and more men to his banner every day.'

'The Earl of Surrey is a friend of mine. You forget, it was he who escorted the Queen to Scotland.'

'He is now Your Grace's enemy, and he serves his King well.'

'The King of England is fortunate to have such good servants.'

'If Your Grace will either go on to attack or return to Scotland, you will find as good servants as those of the King of England.'

'You forget, Angus, that I am the commander of my own armies.'

'I'll not stand by and see the crown of Scotland placed in jeopardy.'

James's eyes blazed with an anger rare to him. Then he looked at Angus and saw before him an old man. Was he a little jealous of the pleasures shared by the King and the Lady of the castle? Did this remind him of what the King had taken from him when he had taken Janet Kennedy?

James shrugged aside his anger.

'If old Bell-the-Cat is afraid of the English, then let him

return to Scotland. I doubt not that we will win victory without him.'

'Bell-the-Cat was never afraid of the English, but he'll not stand by and let them take the time they need.'

'Then . . . goodbye.'

The old soldier bowed and retired.

Next morning he set out for Scotland; but he left behind his two sons so that, when the King went into battle, there should be Douglases to fight for Scotland.

Surrey's herald had arrived at the castle.

Lady Heron, seeing him come, knew that the brief love affair between her and the King of Scotland was coming to its end. She had done her duty. Surrey had gathered his army and was waiting.

The herald was taken to the King and there gave him greeting from the Earl of Surrey, together with the request that he would name a day for the battle.

This James declared himself delighted to do; and although his generals assured him that it was important they should surprise the English and mow them down with Thraw-mouthed Meg – which was another name they had given to their 'Seven Sisters' cannon – James would have none of this. He was determined to go into battle as he went into the joust. He was the Wild Knight, who must conquer through fair play.

On the morning of the ninth of September the armies prepared to meet at Flodden.

James was exultant. Beside him – on foot as he was – stood his son Alexander. 'Keep close to my side,' he warned. 'And if you are in difficulty remember I am nearby.'

'Yes, Father,' was the answer.

James loved the boy – loved his shining youth, his vitality.

Oh, he thought, if I had but stood beside *my* father as this son of mine now stands beside me, there would have been a different story to tell of Sauchieburn.

He could see the English banner fluttering in the breeze. It would soon be over, this decisive battle which would mean the end of strife between England and Scotland for evermore. Henry would return from France to find his country lost.

He heard the roar of the cannon as the two armies met at the foot of Brankston Hill.

The Scottish army was divided into five divisions with Home and Huntley leading the vanguard; in the rear were Lennox and Argyle; while James, with Alexander, was in the centre; in the rear was the reserve under the command of the Earl of Bothwell.

At four o'clock in the afternoon the battle started and at first it seemed that the English were losing ground, when Sir Edmund Howard, who led the English, lost his banner and his men were quickly in confusion; but Surrey had, on account of the time which had been allowed him, gathered together a strong army, and others were ready to step into the breach and take the place of Howard's men.

James was in direct conflict with Surrey's section where the fighting was at its most fierce. All about them was the noise of battle; the clash of spears, the roar of the cannon and cries of wounded men and horses.

James was conscious of Alexander beside him and for the first time wished that he had commanded him to stay at home, for he had caught a look of startled horror on the face of the boy who had so far experienced nothing but light skirmishes and had dreamed of war which had not been like the reality.

This was no joust. This was war to the death. The enemy was determined to drive the Scots back beyond the Tweed and the Cheviots; and the Scots were determined to go forward.

'Alexander, my son . . .'

James felt a sob in his throat for his beautiful Alexander had fallen and there was blood where there had but a moment before been the freshness of youth.

'Oh, my son . . . my son . . .'

Mercifully there was little time for remorse. He did not see the man who struck him. James was dressed as an ordinary soldier for he had determined to go into battle as one of his men; he had wanted no special treatment. He was a soldier just as they were.

So he fell, as men were falling all about him.

The battle raged; and it was only later when the fighting was done that the terrible truth was known. On that day of glorious victory for the English and bitter defeat for the Scots, ten thousand Scotsmen lay dead or dying on Flodden Field and among them was their King.

🏵 Chapter VI 🏵

THE RECKLESS MARRIAGE

The Queen had shut herself in that turret of Linlithgow Palace which was known as Queen Margaret's Bower. She sat alone on the stone bench which surrounded it and looked out of the window hoping and praying for the coming of the messenger.

When she had heard that James was dallying at Ford Castle with Lady Heron her anger was greater than her fear. Each night she was tormented by vague dreams; each day she came to her bower to watch and wait.

There she relived so much of her life with James. This very bower itself had been created by him for her pleasure. It was reached from his dressing room by means of a staircase, and James had had a stone table erected in the centre. She remembered so well the day he had shown it to her. How charming he was, how tender! And how difficult it was to remind oneself that he had been as charming and tender to other women perhaps the day before he was showing so much solicitude to her.

News was brought to her frequently. She had learned of all the successes, until they had come to Ford Castle. She knew that Old Bell-the-Cat had left the army in disgust; and she trembled. But then she remembered James, the Wild Knight at the joust. He could not fail. Yet his success would mean disaster for her brother, and she had not known until this time how strong were the ties of blood.

What did she want? Peace, she answered. That is what I want. Peace between our two countries, and my husband at my side.

❀ ❀ ❀

She had known before the messenger spoke that he had brought disastrous news; and as she had listened to his words a numbness took possession of her body. Dead! On Flodden Field.

She thought: So I shall never see his handsome face again, never listen to his voice; never again shall I ask myself with what woman he is spending his time now. His beauty has gone; his virile body is but a corpse; and I, his wife, have become his widow.

She went to the nursery, where her little son, who was riding on David Lindsay's shoulders, shouted with joy to see her.

David Lindsay lifted the boy from his shoulders and stood him down; he saw from the Queen's expression that she had had bad news and, because he knew that the messenger had come from Flodden Field, he guessed the nature of that news. He was filled with horror and his first thoughts were of what this would mean to his young charge.

'Davie,' said Margaret, 'this is a woeful day for Scotland.'

'Your Grace . . . Your Grace . . .'

She knelt down and with tears in her eyes embraced her son.

'He is now your King, Davie.'

'This cannot be!'

'Alas, it is so. James the Fourth has died at Flodden and now this little one is King of Scotland and the Isles.'

'So young . . . and tender,' murmured David.

'I trust all will remember it,' Margaret answered bitterly. 'David,' she went on, 'in a few months' time he will have a brother or sister.'

David nodded slowly.

Young James was impatient of this solemnity. He wanted to play.

'Carry me, David,' he cried imperiously.

And solemnly David Lindsay lifted the King of Scotland on to his shoulder.

The whole of Scotland mourned the King. Nor did it mourn him only, for the flower of Scottish manhood had fallen at Flodden and there was scarcely a noble family in the land which was not touched with sorrow. James had won the hearts of his people as few kings had ever done before him. His handsome looks, his great charm, his sympathy with the troubles of all, his chivalry and brilliant performances at the jousts had made of him a public hero. It was forgotten that he was to blame for this terrible defeat against which so many of his advisers had warned him, that it had been unnecessary to fight at all and, having embarked upon the campaign, it had been criminally negligent to jeopardise the lives of so many and the cause of Scotland while he tarried with Lady Heron. They remembered only the hero who had delighted them with the entertainments he had given and in which they had had their share; they remembered only that he whom they had loved was dead.

Old Bell-the-Cat was a broken-hearted man. He had lost two sons at Flodden – his eldest, George, Master of Douglas, and Sir William of Glenbervie; with them had fallen two hundred gentlemen of the name of Douglas. There could rarely have been a disaster to Scotland and the Douglases to compare with that of Flodden. He no longer had the heart to join in public affairs; he was too old, too sad. All his vast possessions would now go to his grandson Archibald, son of George; and Bell-the-Cat retired to his Priory of Whitehorn in Wigtownshire to set his affairs in order, for he did not think he had long to live – nor did he wish it otherwise.

But there was no time to waste. Scotland was defeated; and she had left the flower of her army rotting on Flodden Field. What next? asked those who were left.

The days following the defeat were some of the most anxious the country had ever passed through, until it was realised that Surrey was in no position to march on Scotland; the main army of England was abroad with the King, and the battle of Flodden had been one of defence for England. The Regent, Queen Katharine, was very loath to conduct a war against her husband's sister; all she wished to do was preserve England from invasion during her husband's absence. This had been magnificently done; and Katharine was ready to offer Margaret a truce.

As her numbness left her, Margaret realised that she was now in possession of a certain power – and power was something she had always wished for. James had made her Regent and guardian of their son before he went away, and the nobles of Scotland were anxious to respect his wishes.

First she removed the little King to the strong fortress of Stirling Castle; then she called Parliament, that the will of James IV might be read. There was some murmuring concerning the passing of the Regency into the Queen's hands, for the tradition of Scotland was that this should be a masculine prerogative, yet because the King was so recently dead, none raised a voice against his wishes. A Council was to assist her, and this was made up of old Bell-the-Cat, the Earls of Arran, Huntley, Glencairn, Argyle, Lennox, Eglington, Drummond and Morton; with Beaton, the Archbishop of Glasgow and Elphinstone, Bishop of Aberdeen.

Only twenty days after the death of his father, little James was taken to Scone where, what was called throughout the land, the Mourning Coronation took place. Over the brow of the child was held the crown of Scotland and he was solemnly declared King.

It was the most extraordinary coronation ever witnessed for, as the trumpets sounded, those about the young King burst into loud lamentations; and James was proclaimed King of Scotland and the Isles to the accompaniment of tears and sobbing.

Thus the power for which Margaret had longed was to some extent hers. Jealousy, the most persistent emotion of her life, had been removed. What did all those women who had tempted James from her side matter now? She had heard that Anne of Brittany, who had roused her anger as much as any, had died a few days after the defeat at Flodden. So, thought Margaret, she did not live long to gloat over what she had persuaded him to do.

Margaret herself was now twenty-four years old; she had had many years' experience of Scotland and of the Scottish, and as the weeks following her son's coronation began to pass, her grief passed with them. She forced herself to remember the unhappiness rather than the happiness James had caused her; and once she had given birth to his child she would be free.

She began to think with increasing excitement of freedom.

She was not at this time aware of the feelings of certain members of the Council towards her. They could not forget, first that she was a woman and second that she was English. It was true her nationality meant that the King of England was more likely to show leniency to the Scots while his sister was their Queen; but in spite of the lack of funds in the exchequer and the terrible loss of manpower at Flodden, Scotland was still not eager for friendship with England.

The pro-French party was strong and there was continual and secret correspondence between this party and the French.

There came that day when the Bishop of Aberdeen suggested to the Council that the Queen's task was too much for her strength. It seemed to him that she needed help in her task of Regent; and he proposed that they should invite the Duke of Albany – who, after Margaret's son, was next in the line of succession – to come to Scotland and share the Regency with her.

This was agreed to be an excellent suggestion. Albany, uncle of James IV, should be told of their decision, and they would invite him to tell them what his inclinations were.

Meanwhile the Queen was pregnant and in no fit state to conduct affairs, so first they would approach Albany in secret.

John Stuart, Duke of Albany, was riding round his estates with his friend Anthony d'Arcy de la Bastie when the messenger from Scotland arrived at the château.

John – always known as Jehan – had almost forgotten that he was a Scotsman, although de la Bastie, who had visited Scotland, often talked of his stay there and did his best to arouse Albany's interest in that country. But Albany had been brought up in France by a French mother; French was his native language; he had been in the service of the King of France; and he had married a Frenchwoman. He was now just past thirty and he had been four years old when his father had died, and that had severed, so he thought, all links with Scotland. He was on excellent terms with the French Court; he had been made a knight of St Michael and Admiral of France for services to the King. He was happily married to his cousin, Anne de la Tour, a rich heiress who had brought him these Auvergne estates. He passed the time pleasantly between Court and the country; so he was perfectly content with his life.

It was natural at such a time that they should be talking of Scotland. The news of Flodden was fresh and de la Bastie could not forget what it meant.

He was saying: 'Had you met him you would have felt this as deeply as I. He was so vital; so charming to look at and pleasant to be with. I remember his masquerading as the Wild Knight, and then seeming loath to take the glory he had won. And now . . . he is dead.'

'A fate which must overtake us all,' mused Albany philosophically.

'But not in the prime of our lives, let us hope.'

Albany was silent for a while, then he said: 'They are a wild clan, these Stuarts.'

'All of them?' asked de la Bastie with a smile.

'My Stuart blood has been tempered by that of the French. I boast that I inherited logic and sweet reason from my French mother.'

'And nothing from your father?'

'Heaven help me, not his genius for falling into trouble, I trust.'

'None could say you had inherited that. Here you are, a friend of the King, a brilliant courtier and a happy countryman. What more could you ask?'

'Very little. I was not complaining. I have no wish to live as my father did.' He smiled. 'I don't remember him; but my mother talked of him continually. The last years of his life were almost too fantastically adventurous to bear the stamp of truth.'

'He was indeed a strange man, and an unhappy one – I should think – to quarrel with his brother.'

'Oh, he was ambitious, and when you are ambitious it is not good to be born the second son of a king. It was natural that such a man should long for the crown, and when his brother became James the Third the trouble started. I would rather live in peace than in the centre of revolution. I tell you, I follow my mother rather than my father.'

They had turned their horses towards the château when de la Bastie said: 'Look, there are visitors.'

'You are right.' Albany spurred his horse and the two men broke into a gallop which soon brought them to the gates of the château.

Several of the servants had seen their approach, for they had been watching for it; and grooms ran forward to take their horses and to gabble that foreigners had arrived.

Inside the great hall Albany's wife, who had been the Comtesse de la Tour before she married, was graciously acting as hostess to the foreigners and as Albany went forward, with de la Bastie a few paces behind, he felt a slight apprehension because he saw that the visitors came from Scotland. Moreover they came on an important mission, for the man who faced him was the Lyon King.

He knew, almost before he heard, what the visitor had to say. It was the logical outcome of recent events. An infant king; a woman regent; and he a grandson of King James II.

Never! he thought. Why should I? Here I am at peace. Here I am happy. Why should I leave all this for the strife which would naturally be mine in that strife-ridden country?

But he listened courteously to the Lyon King and gave no hint of his distaste for the mission.

His guests must be royally entertained; Anne would see that they were. She too was looking uneasy. She need not fear. Their life together was not going to be disrupted.

He sat thoughtfully in his private chamber remembering the stories he had heard his mother tell him.

His father had lived a colourful life, but surely happiness, peaceful pleasure, were more to be desired than adventure which had ambition as the spur.

His father, Alexander Stuart, Duke of Albany, had always been in the thick of intrigue, so it was natural that when his elder brother James came to the throne, he, Alexander, and his younger brother, the Earl of Mar, should begin seeking honours and glory. Scotland had been tortured by revolution, due to them; and when Albany and Mar had come into conflict with those Border barons, Home and Hepburn, James III had seized the opportunity to imprison his troublesome brothers. Mar had died mysteriously in prison; some said as the result of an accident when a physician had bled him; others that the King had ordered his veins to be cut that he might bleed to death. In any case that was the end of Mar.

Albany had determined that no such misadventure should befall him, and as he had allies in France, he planned his escape. This took place with a drama that characterised all his adventures. It was arranged that two casks should be sent to him in his prison in Edinburgh Castle; these casks were presumed to contain Malmsey; one did, but the contents of the second were rope, which would make escape possible, and instruction as to where the French ship, which would carry him to France, was moored in the Forth.

Albany made plans with his chamber child, a young attendant who acted as valet during his imprisonment. First he invited the Captain of the Castle to come to his apartment and share the wine which had so generously been sent to him.

The Captain arrived and when he had taken rather more than he was accustomed to, Albany drew his sword and ran it through his body. Then he sent his chamber child to tell one of the guards that the Captain of the Castle was drunk and needed help; and as soon as the guard came into the apartment, Albany killed him. This was repeated twice and in a short time there were four dead men in Albany's apartment.

Albany then commanded the chamber child to descend by the rope, and he himself would follow immediately. The boy was lowered over the walls of the castle, but the rope was too short and he fell, breaking his thigh. Realising what had happened, Albany drew in the rope, lengthened it and himself descended. Although in imminent danger of discovery he picked up the child, carried him to a house nearby, commanded the people there to have his wounds attended to, telling them that if any ill befell the child they would have to answer to Albany, and then made his way to the French ship which was waiting to carry him to France. His treatment of the child aroused the sympathy of the people and he was fast becoming a legend throughout the land. He made his way to the French ship and when he arrived in Paris was treated with respect by the King of France, given estates and a bride – a French heiress, Anne, daughter of the Comte d'Auvergne et de Boulogne.

He had had no wish to settle down in peace, and before long had returned to England where he had entered into an intrigue with Edward IV to oust his brother James III from the throne of Scotland and take the crown himself. The price Edward asked for his help was that Albany should, on gaining the throne, put away his wife and marry Edward's daughter Cecilia. Albany was not one to trouble himself with such details. He had already been married before he left Scotland to his cousin, Catharine Sinclair, by whom he had had three sons and a daughter. He had divorced her on the grounds of propinquity, so legally the present Duke, his son by Anne de la Tour, was his heir.

What strife had been caused in Scotland by Albany's actions! There had been many nobles who were dissatisfied with the King, and they only needed Albany's banner to join in the revolt against James. Bell-the-Cat was at the head of this revolutionary faction and there had been perpetual strife.

Eventually Albany had found it necessary to escape from Scotland and once more sought refuge in France, where his death was as dramatic and unexpected as his life had been. Attending a tournament he was accidentally killed by a splinter from a lance when he was not even engaged in the joust but merely a spectator.

A life of adventure. Had he found it as satisfying as his son found his?

Perhaps it had contented him, for it was the life he had chosen.

'But this,' said his son, 'is the life for me.'

De la Bastie was going to be disappointed in him. He knew what his friend wanted. He would like to accompany the new Regent to Scotland because he had undoubtedly become enamoured of that strange, dour land.

Why not send de la Bastie to act as his proxy? It was a good idea. He would go at once to his friend and lay the proposition before him. It would be better than a blunt refusal. He would say: 'My affairs make it impossible for me to leave France at this time, so I send you my friend who is also a friend of yours, to act for me until such time as I may come to you.'

Until such time as I may come to you?

He was faintly apprehensive and excited.

Was there something of his father in him? Did the thought of ruling a country excite him after all?

He had made up his mind. Not yet . . . but there might come a time when he would wish to go.

How different was that Christmas, spent within the Palace of Holyrood, compared with the last! Margaret had always suffered during her pregnancies, and this one was no exception; and eager as she was to give her little James a brother, she wished that at such a time she could have felt energetic enough to deal with state affairs. She was well aware that there were many noblemen who looked askance at her Regency; she knew that letters had been sent to France and that, since Albany was there, it was logical to suppose certain of her counsellors would wish to see him take over the Regency, or if not completely, to govern with her.

Her fears that this was the case were confirmed by letters from her brother Henry, who had now returned from France.

He was not pleased with the way matters were going in Scotland. There was a truce between the two countries, but he would have her and the Scots know that he agreed to this mainly because he did not wish to make war on a country of which his own sister was Regent. He knew that those about her were putting out feelers to France, and contemplating bringing Albany over. Why, the fellow was a Frenchman at heart and called the King of France his master. Therefore Henry of England would frown on such a man's holding the post of Regent in cooperation with his sister. It must be avoided at all costs. They might seek to marry her to the fellow. It was true he had a wife living, but Henry had heard that she was not strong and might not live long; in any case she was his cousin, so it would not be difficult to dissolve the marriage. He wanted this avoided at all cost.

Margaret sat down and wrote to 'her dearest brother, the King'. She implored him to suppress his hostile feelings towards Scotland and begged him not to harm her little King, his nephew who was very small and tender, being only one year and five months old. She reminded him that she was soon to become the mother of a posthumous child. She could only be happy if she had his goodwill.

Henry replied that if the Scots wanted peace they should have it, and if they wanted war they should have it. As for Margaret's husband, he had fallen by his own indiscretion and rashness and foolish kindness to France. He added that, even so, as a relative, he regretted his death. He went on to say that he liked not to see French influence in Scotland and that if this should be strengthened he would be greatly displeased. He warned his sister of plans to marry her to Albany, repeating that she must avoid this at all costs.

Margaret brooded on this and when she saw young Archibald Douglas among the courtiers at the Palace an idea occurred to her – a wild idea. But was it so wild?

She sent for him and, when he arrived, she told him that she wanted to give him her sympathy, for she had heard that his young wife had recently died in childbed.

He thanked her and said it was a marvellous thing that his Queen, who had suffered so many sorrows, should remember those of her humble subjects.

'Nay,' she answered, 'we have both been bereaved and in a similar manner. It would seem that we should sympathise with each other.'

Archibald bowed his head and she felt a surge of jealousy wondering how deeply he grieved for his young wife.

And when he had passed on, she thought: It might be possible for us to comfort each other.

But I must wait until after my child is born.

There was gloom in the priory of Whitehorn in Wigtownshire where the Douglas clan had assembled at the summons of the head of their house.

Old Bell-the-Cat lay on his deathbed; he had never recovered from the disaster of Flodden Field, that battle which, before it had begun, he had declared was foolish, unnecessary, and doomed to disaster.

He had lost two sons on that field with some of the bravest members of his clan. When it was over he had retired from public life and found that he had no longer any great wish to live. Now he knew that the end was near and he did not shrink from it.

He had summoned to his bedside his two remaining sons, the priest, Gavin Douglas and Sir Archibald Douglas of Kilspindie; there was also his grandson and heir, son of the Master of Douglas who had been killed at Flodden: the Archibald Douglas who had caught the Queen's fancy and who, when the old man died, would be Earl of Angus and head of the House of Douglas.

'Sons, grandson,' muttered the old Earl, 'my time is running out. It is a sad time to go when the affairs of Scotland are in such confusion. There'll be work for you to do and I trust you'll do it in the manner of the Douglases. Grandson, you'll shortly inherit a great title. How old are you now?'

'Nineteen, Grandfather.'

'Alas, 'tis over-young. You will need to heed the counsel of your uncles. My sons, look to your nephew, for very soon he will be the head of your clan. And you, Grandson, are recently widowed. You must marry again and soon. Now it is your duty to get sons for the House of Douglas.'

Young Archibald bent over the old man. 'Be at peace, Grandfather,' he said. 'I am courting a lady whom I hope to marry.'

'Who is this?' asked Bell-the-Cat.

'Lady Jane Stuart, daughter of the Lord of Traquair. She is young, beautiful, and of good birth. I knew I should have your approval of the match.'

'I know her well. A fitting bride, and I rejoice. Marry her soon, Grandson. Life is too short to spend overmuch time in mourning.'

'Give me your blessing, Grandfather.'

The old hand was laid on the young head, and the dying man looked to his sons.

'Let there be no strife in our house. Care for your nephew, as though he were your son.'

'We will, Father,' his sons answered.

'My blessing on you all. Long life and prosperity to the Douglases.'

He lay back on his pillows, exhausted, and the men exchanged glances. It could not be long now.

They were right. In a few days old Bell-the-Cat was dead and young Archibald had become Earl of Angus.

❖ ❖ ❖

The new Earl of Angus lost no time in going to Traquair with the news, where Lady Jane was eagerly awaiting him for she guessed that his grandfather could not live long, and she knew what a change this would make in the fortunes of her lover.

They walked beside the Quair Water together and talked of the future.

'I have his blessing, Jane,' Angus told her. 'He said that it was folly to waste time. We should marry without delay. Are you ready to do so?'

'I am ready,' answered Jane.

'As soon as a few more months have passed then. It would

be a scandal to marry so soon after the death of my poor Margaret and my grandfather. It is useless to expect people to understand how I loved you from the moment I saw you. If we married now they would say we had intrigued during Margaret's lifetime. Who knows what else they might say? They are ready enough to blacken a man's character . . . and a woman's. I'd not care to subject you to that, Jane.'

'We can wait a few more months,' said Jane serenely. 'The time will seem long, but I know that you will long for it to be over, even as I shall.'

'Oh, Jane . . . how long the waiting will be! We'll not make it too long.'

'No,' she answered. 'When you have done mourning for your grandfather . . . when the summer comes perhaps.'

'Oh, how I sigh for the summer!'

❀ ❀ ❀

From Traquair Angus went to Stobhall, as his maternal grandfather, Lord Drummond, had sent for him.

Lord Drummond, who had once hoped to take a large share in the government of Scotland when he had believed his daughter Margaret was going to marry James IV, had been deprived of his dearest ambition. He still mourned the death of his daughter – not so much for the loss of her person, but for the honours she might have brought her family had she become Queen of Scotland.

He had hoped for much from his family. His daughters had been recognised as among the most beautiful women in Scotland. But that fateful breakfast had carried off three of them – Margaret, Eupheme, and Sibylla. Elizabeth, who fortunately had not sat down to that meal with her sisters, had lived to marry the heir of Angus, eldest son of old Bell-the-Cat; she had had numerous children and the eldest was young Archibald, who as Earl of Angus would be a powerful man in Scotland, and because he was so young he would need advice. Who better to give that advice than his grandfather? Now that old Bell-the-Cat was out of the way, that other grandfather, himself, Lord Drummond, should be the one to guide the head of the Douglas clan.

So he sent for the boy in order to impress on him the sudden importance of his rank.

As soon as Angus came into his presence, Drummond was struck by his resemblance to his mother and aunts. His was a family with more than its share of good looks. Angus ought to go far.

'Now, my boy,' said Drummond, 'I trust you are aware of the great importance of your new position.'

'Yes, Grandfather. I have had it impressed upon me, I do assure you.'

'And rightly so. You are now the head of one of the most important clans in Scotland, and it is no good thing that you should have been thrust into such a position so young. Alas for Flodden! Would that your father had lived to pass on the title to you in good time. But what is, must be. While you are here I want to talk to you on Court matters and then I shall wish you to accompany me to Court. There I hope to bring you to the notice of the Queen, and I have little doubt that if you are wise you will do well there. You have good looks and a great name.'

'Thank you, Grandfather. I am ready to go when you wish.'

'That is well.'

'There is one matter of which I would wish to speak to you.

My paternal grandfather advised me that I should marry soon, and that I wish to do.'

'Whom have you in mind?'

'Lady Jane Stuart.'

'Daughter of the Traquair,' mused Drummond. 'Hmm. If you are wise you will shelve that little matter for a while. There are affairs of more pressing urgency afoot, I do assure you.'

Angus felt faintly alarmed. He had a notion that his ambitious grandfather was not quite sure whether Jane was a worthy enough match for the Earl of Angus.

Not that I shall be influenced! Angus told himself. I shall choose my own wife, and that will be Jane.

❀ ❀ ❀

It was April when Margaret's baby was born. She christened him Alexander, and he was given the title of Duke of Ross. He was a beautiful baby, promising to be as healthy as her little James, and she was delighted with him.

Although she felt weak after his birth, this pregnancy had been slightly less arduous than those she had previously suffered; she was glad of this for she was uncomfortably aware of the strife which was going on about her. There were certain members of the nobility who were determined to bring Albany over from France. His deputy, de la Bastie, had already arrived; and her brother Henry was urging that on no account must Albany be brought to Scotland, for he would not tolerate a French influence there. There was another scheme forming in the minds of the pro-French party and that was to marry her to Louis XII of France. Margaret shuddered at the prospect. Aging Louis did not appeal to her as a husband; but there was a grim amusement in thinking of marrying the widower of that Anne of Brittany who had once caused her so much jealousy.

When I marry, thought Margaret, it will be someone young and handsome, someone like young Archibald Douglas. He was the Earl of Angus now – quite a considerable title. Perhaps it would be less incongruous for the Queen to marry the Earl of Angus than young Archibald Douglas.

Lord Drummond, who held the office of Lord-Justiciary of Scotland, had written to her begging leave to present himself. He wished to bring his young grandson to her notice. The boy had recently acquired the title of Earl of Angus; he was still in mourning for his grandfather – and alas, he had been doubly stricken, for he had not long since become a widower – but he was a young man of spirit and yearned to be at Court that he might more assiduously serve his Queen.

Margaret replied graciously. Lord Drummond must come to Court at once. She had heard of the sorrows of the young Earl and the new responsibilities which had been thrust upon him. She wished to give him her personal sympathy.

❦ ❦ ❦

Lord Drummond had not felt so excited since those days when he had believed his daughter Margaret had so enslaved the King of Scotland that he would marry her. He was certain that he had discovered a passion as intense, and for another member of his family.

Why did the Queen keep young Angus at her side? Why did she unsuccessfully endeavour to hide the pleasure his company gave her? Why did her eyes gleam with excitement when he stood beside her? Lord Drummond knew the answers to all these questions.

What a handsome pair they were! Margaret a young and lusty widow. Angus even younger, a widower in need of a new wife. The trouble was that Angus seemed to be wilfully blind to the portents. That was because he was mooning about Traquair's daughter.

By all the saints, Drummond said to himself, what this could mean to our family!

He smiled. Life was ironical. Once it had offered him a similar opportunity. A daughter of his to marry a king. That had failed, through some foul murderer; but now his grandson might be the husband of the Queen.

He considered the matter. Should he talk to Angus? The boy was only nineteen and foolish without doubt, imagining himself in love with Jane Stuart. This had to be handled with the utmost care.

He invited the boy's uncles to call on him, letting them know that he had vital family matters to discuss with them; and when Gavin Douglas, the poet and priest, came to Drummond's apartments accompanied by his brother, Sir Archibald of Kilspindie, Drummond lost no time in telling them what he suspected.

'The Queen is enamoured of young Angus, and this is no surprise to me. I believe him to be the most handsome man at Court.'

'You mean she is his mistress?' asked Sir Archibald.

'Nay, nay. You go too fast. She is deeply conscious of her royalty. The pride of these Tudors is greater than that of the Stuarts, my friends. She is in love with him but I doubt she would be his mistress. Nor do we wish her to. But I see no reason why she should not become his wife.'

The Douglases were too startled to speak.

'Why not? Angus has a great title. Why should not a Douglas share the throne? Have you two so little regard for your family's honour that you would raise objections to this?'

'Why no, indeed,' said Gavin quickly, 'but is it possible?'

'Why not? Providing we act with discretion.'

'How so?' demanded Sir Archibald.

'The Queen is a young woman. She has been without a husband since Flodden. She sees our young Angus and is enflamed with desire for him. Can you wonder? He is a fine figure of a man. I have watched her. I have seen the signs.'

'The Council would never permit a marriage.'

Drummond snapped his fingers. 'Who cares for the Council! If there was a marriage between these two it would have to be made first and the Council told afterwards.'

'It is not a year since the death of the King.'

'We cannot afford to waste time, or they will find a husband for her. They tried to marry her to Louis the Twelfth.'

'They cannot do that now.'

'Assuredly not, since the King of England, determined to have no union between Scotland and France, has married his younger sister Mary to Louis.'

'That we know,' put in Drummond testily, 'but the Council would find what they deem a suitable husband for the Queen . . . and that husband would not be Angus. Imagine Arran, for one, allowing a Douglas to be put above him. Nay, if there is to be a marriage it must be done with all speed, while the Queen's feelings are hot towards our Angus, and before the Council can intervene.'

'Then what do you suggest?'

'That we summon our handsome young man and impress upon him the need to do his duty by his family.'

'I believe the boy to have betrothed himself to Jane Stuart.'

'Then he must un-betroth himself,' cried Drummond. 'Nothing must stand in the way of this match. Have you thought what it would mean to the family? A bishopric at least for you, Gavin Douglas, a fine place at Court for your brother here.'

'And for my Lord Drummond?' inquired Gavin not without sarcasm.

'My dear fellow, all the family could expect to prosper. I want your support when I explain to Angus where his duty lies. He must act with speed and caution. He must let the Queen know that he returns her passion.'

'Which he does not?' questioned Archibald.

'Then he must learn to,' retorted Angus's ambitious grandfather. 'I was once cheated of seeing my daughter share the throne of Scotland; I'll not stand by and see my grandson kept from it.'

'What do you propose to do?' asked Gavin.

'Summon Angus and, with your support, tell him what he must do. Do you stand with me?'

The Douglases eyed each other. They were ambitious men.

'We'd be fools not to,' replied Gavin speaking for them both.

Drummond clapped them both on the back.

'I knew I could rely on you,' he said. 'Now . . . for young Angus.'

Angus was bewildered. He looked in anguish from his uncles to his grandfather.

'You see,' he explained laboriously, 'Jane and I have plighted our troth.'

'Plighted your fiddlesticks!' snapped Drummond. 'I never heard such nonsense. Marry that girl and you are finished at Court, I tell you. Margaret will see that all you hope for is denied you.'

'All I hope for,' replied Angus, 'is to live peacefully with Jane. I don't mind not being at Court. We'll be perfectly happy at Whitehorn or Tantallan.'

'Whitehorn and Tantallan! You forget you are the head of the house of Douglas, my boy, and whether you like it or not your clan looks to you to act accordingly. It is your solemn duty to put honours in the way of your family, and how could you do this better than by becoming the Queen's husband?'

'But she has not said she would marry me.'

'What a young fool you are! It is for you to sigh and simper and show how you would if you dared. She'll be ready and willing enough. If you were half a man you would have read the signs in her eyes.'

'B-but what of Jane?' stammered Angus.

'If she's a sensible girl she'll understand and call you a fool if you missed your opportunity.'

'I have sworn . . .'

'As a Douglas you are pledged to your family, my boy. Now, no more nonsense. How many men do you think there are at Court who wouldn't give ten years of their lives to be in your position? The Queen desiring you! Go to it. You're not a simpering boy now, you know. You're a man.'

'I will not . . .'

'God help us,' murmured Drummond; then his voice rose in a crescendo. 'We are cursed with a Douglas who's naught but a simpering ninny!'

'Grandfather . . .' began Angus helplessly.

Drummond took him by the arm. 'I see,' he said, 'that your uncles and I have to talk to you very seriously.'

Angus believed himself to be the most unhappy man at Court. Why, he kept asking, did his grandfather have to die? Why was he thrust into this position? How much better it would have been to have remained plain Archibald Douglas than become Earl of Angus. Then everyone would have said the match with Jane was a good one. Why had the Queen picked *him* out!

If he went to Jane and married her he would be continually reproached by his family; if he obeyed his family he would be forever reproached by Jane.

All his life he had been brought up to recognise the importance of belonging to a great family. In his family's mansions like Whitehorn and Tantallan there were the Douglas arms and emblems in every room. Old Bell-the-Cat had played a big part in the history of Scotland; as it was deemed fitting that every head of the House of Douglas should do.

What can I do? he asked himself again and again.

He was in private audience with the Queen. His grandfather had arranged it, telling the Queen that his grandson Angus had asked it.

It was untrue; but now that he was alone with her he looked at her with a new interest.

There was no denying that she was beautiful. She looked particularly so today . . . eager and expectant, her eyes brilliant, her long golden hair flowing over her shoulders in a careless fashion that was very becoming. It was so long that she could have sat on it, and he was fascinated by its shining splendour.

She did not seem like a queen; indeed he fancied that she was trying to cast aside her royalty that they might appear as equals.

'My lord,' she said, 'I hear you have something to say to me.'

'Your Grace . . .' he murmured and did not look at her.

She held out her hand, which he took because there was nothing else he could have done; she drew him towards her so that he was standing close to her seductive body; he could see by the rise and fall of her breast that she was a little agitated.

'You are thinking that I am the Queen,' she said. 'Pray, my lord, forget that.'

'It is impossible to forget,' he said quietly.

'Nay. I am a woman and you are a man.' She took his other hand and drew him closer. She lifted her face to his and there was nothing else to do but kiss her. The passion which he met overwhelmed him. She clung to him, her body pressed against his, her kisses fierce, demanding.

She was beautiful; she was desirable, and they were both young; it was not difficult to respond.

At last she withdrew herself, her eyes half closed; she looked as though she were fainting with ecstasy.

'Angus . . .' she murmured. 'My dearest Angus. Nothing shall keep us apart, I swear it.'

'Your Grace . . .'

She held up a hand. 'I have sworn it. I have thought of this matter for a long time. They will attempt to stop us, of course, but we'll not allow it. My dearest love, you must not think of me as your Queen. There shall be no formality between us two. How I long for you! The marriage must take place at once.'

'Your Grace, there is something I must tell you.'

'Not "Your Grace". Say "Margaret". I am Margaret to you now and henceforth. There will be opposition, but I have spoken to Lord Drummond who will arrange this matter for us. He is shrewd and wise. There is going to be no delay. Soon, my love, you and I shall be in each other's arms.' She laughed. 'How you deceived me! There were times when you convinced me that you did not care for me at all. Oh, how wretched you made me! But it is all over now.'

She threw herself into his arms again; the passionate embrace was repeated. And what could Angus do but respond? A man would have to be an eunuch not to, he told himself. She was so beautiful, so eager, and a queen withal! The situation had a piquancy to tempt any man's fidelity.

She would not let him speak; she stopped his lips with her kisses; and who would dare explain his feeling for another woman when the Queen's lips were on his? And afterward he dared not make an attempt. How could he tell her, when she had made such a confession of her own feelings, that he did not share them? How could he so insult a queen?

Margaret was grateful to the grandfather and uncles of her beloved. Lord Drummond had told her that he would arrange for the wedding ceremony to take place, and she could safely leave such matters to him. His nephew, Walter Drummond, was Dean of Dunblane and parson of Kinnoul, so the pair could be married in the utmost secrecy in his church at Kinnoul.

Margaret wanted to show her gratitude to these accommodating gentlemen, and she began by nominating Gavin Douglas as Bishop of Dunkeld. He overwhelmed her with thanks, and she replied that she would never forget his goodness and could wish to have bestowed an even greater reward. She hinted that when it was possible the Primacy of Scotland should be his.

The brothers and Lord Drummond consulted together. Drummond was triumphant. 'You see,' he cried. 'A bishopric already and a promise of the Primacy! I assure you, my friends, that in a short time the Douglases and their connections will be ruling Scotland. It is well that Angus is so young; he will be the more easily guided. But we must get this marriage made before our intentions become known. You are aware, as well as I am, that there are men in Scotland who would rise in civil war to prevent it if they knew what we planned.'

'Then . . .' began Sir Archibald nervously, but Drummond silenced him.

'Nay, Sir Chicken-heart. We play for big stakes. We'll take a risk or two. And if we did not go forward now I doubt not our warm-blooded Queen would do so without our help.'

❦ ❦ ❦

On a warm August day, not twelve months after the battle of Flodden Field, Margaret married the Earl of Angus in Kinnoul Church.

She did not stop to think of the consequences of this marriage. All that mattered was that this handsome boy who had long occupied her thoughts was now her husband.

Her one desire was to abandon herself to the passion which obsessed her.

Later she could consider how she would explain her conduct to her people.

🏵 Chapter VII 🏵

THE DESERTED QUEEN

Margaret was as happy as she had been during the first weeks of her marriage to James. Angus gave no sign that he was not as deeply enamoured of her as she was of him. He was caught up in the wave of her sensuality; she was more experienced than he, having lived for so many years with that expert lover, James IV; there was much she could teach him and he was lusty enough to be a ready pupil. It was too uncomfortable to think about Jane Stuart during those weeks, so he did his best to forget her. He discovered that he was growing up; he was no longer a romantic boy, and he began to realise how wise his grandfather and uncles had been in urging him to this marriage.

Margaret was so deeply in love that she was only happy when she was with him; she promised him all that he could wish. She showered presents on him. 'I want to give you everything you could desire in exchange for all the pleasure you have given me,' she told him.

He replied that the pleasure he had given her could not compare with that which she had given him; and only occasionally did he feel a twinge of conscience on Jane's account.

She would understand, he soothed himself. The Queen had commanded him to be her husband and none could disobey a royal command.

The secrecy which attended their marriage gave it an additional spice. Margaret believed that she had found lasting happiness; but it was foolish to suppose such a secret could be kept for long.

It was in October that the opportunity arose to bestow the Primacy of Scotland on Gavin Douglas, and Margaret carelessly threw the office to the uncle of her beloved husband.

There was an immediate outcry among the nobles. Why should the Queen select this hitherto somewhat insignificant prelate for such a great honour. Only recently she had bestowed on him the Bishopric of Dunkeld. What had he done to deserve it? Old Bell-the-Cat had headed many a revolt in his time. Were they going to stand by and see the Douglas clan leap into power again?

There was clearly some reason why the Douglas clan had come into sudden favour.

It did not take long for the secret to be discovered, and a Council meeting was hastily called. The lords assembled, their feelings outraged by the discovery. It was an insult to them and Scotland that the Queen had married without consulting them; and that she should have married Angus added to the injury. Who did this Tudor woman think she was? they asked themselves. Her only right to the crown was through Scottish James, and before he had been dead a year she had shamelessly remarried.

Lord Home addressed the assembly.

'Hitherto,' he said, 'we have shown our willingness to

honour the Queen, although it is against the custom of our country that women should rule. But because our beloved King and Sovereign, James IV, created her Regent, we have allowed her to remain so. All well and good while she retained her widowhood; but she is no longer a widow. I put forward the motion that we depose the Queen from the Regency, and once more ask the Duke of Albany to come to Scotland to act as Regent; and that we summon the Queen to our presence that we may acquaint her of our displeasure.'

This was agreed, and Sir William Comyn, Lyon King, was sent to deliver the Council's message.

Margaret refused to be shaken out of her idyll. This, she told herself, was what she had longed for in the early days of her marriage to James. It had been denied her, but she did not care now; for now she was happily married; her husband was the most beautiful man in Scotland and she was fast teaching him to be the most erotic. She was completely satisfied with her private life and was prepared to forget, for as long as she would be allowed to do so, that there was another side to a queen's existence.

She was at Stobhall, Lord Drummond's mansion, shut away from the Court, with her husband, feeling young and joyous, trying to make each glorious day and night last for as long as she could.

Lord Drummond looked on well content and made sure that the lovers had every opportunity for solitude. He doubted Margaret had ever before known what it meant to live a private life. Each day she became more and more enamoured of his grandson. They were indeed a handsome couple. Drummond believed that there must by now be a Douglas heir on the way – his great-grandson. This was a time of glory for the Douglases, and for the first time since the tragedy he ceased to mourn the loss of his daughter Margaret.

When rumours came to Stobhall, Drummond did not allow them to disturb the lovers. Of course it was absurd to imagine that the secret could be kept for ever, but let them go on believing themselves safe from controversy.

Then news was brought to him that Lyon King was on his way to Stobhall, and he realised immediately that he could not keep from the young couple the news that their marriage was no longer a secret.

He went to them and told them what was happening.

'Lyon King is on his way to bring a message to Your Grace,' he said. 'He will summon you to appear before the Council.'

'For what purpose?' asked Margaret.

'To discuss Your Grace's marriage.'

'My marriage is my own affair,' retorted Margaret, knowing that it was not.

Angus, who had ceased to be a somewhat timid boy in the last weeks, took her hand and kissed it. 'It is *our* affair,' he said. 'I'll not allow them to insult you.'

She gave him a loving glance and turned to Drummond who added: 'It will be necessary to receive Lyon King when he arrives, and I think we should make of it a ceremonial occasion to remind him that he is in the presence of the Queen of Scotland. Your Grace should wear the crown; and your husband should be beside you. I ask your gracious permission to be present also.'

'My dear Lord Drummond,' said Margaret, 'it shall be as you advise, for I am sure you are right, now as always.'

Thus it was that when Sir William Comyn arrived he found the Queen with Angus and Drummond waiting to receive him.

Comyn came into their presence clad in the insignia of his office, almost as grand a figure as Margaret in her crown and robes of ermine.

His first words were enough to show her and Drummond the intentions of the Council, for instead of addressing her as his sovereign, Comyn began: 'My Lady Queen, the mother of His Grace the King . . .'

Drummond, whose temper, always fiery, was more easily aroused when he knew himself to be in a desperate position, was seized with sudden fury. He had married his grandson to the Queen Regent; how dared Lyon-King-at-Arms address her merely as the mother of the young King!

Impetuously he boxed the ears of Lyon King.

There was absolute silence which lasted for several seconds. Comyn had been solemnly crowned Lyon-King-at-Arms by King James IV and, since he represented the crown and state, his rank was as sacred as that of a royal person. Never in the history of Scotland had Lyon-King-at-Arms been treated, during the course of his duty, with anything but the greatest respect.

Comyn, startled into silence, was in those ominous seconds uncertain how to act. Then bowing to the Queen he turned slowly and walked from the room.

The silence continued. All three knew that this was an insult which would never be forgotten.

This was the signal for revolt, for it was hardly likely that the nobles of Scotland would accept such a state of affairs. The Queen Regent married in secret, to satisfy her lust, before her husband had been dead a year! The hated Douglases, to climb to the highest positions through young Angus! Lyon King himself insulted by the arrogant Drummond!

The first act must be to set before Albany the urgency of his immediate return; and the best person to convey the need for his presence in Scotland was the insulted Lyon King. He should set out for France immediately.

The Lord Chancellor, Beaton, Archbishop of Glasgow, gave expression to his disapproval of the marriage which had taken place when their beloved sovereign was scarcely cold; and Margaret, urged on by Drummond and Angus, decided that she would deprive Beaton of his office immediately. There were Douglases ready to take over all the most important posts in Scotland. So she sent Angus to Perth to arrest Beaton and take the Seal of Office from him.

The warlike lords lost no time in rousing trouble. The Queen's supporters – mostly members of the Douglas clan and their hangers-on – were besieged in their castles by the anti-Queen-and-Douglas party. Gavin Douglas was one of those to suffer, and Drummond was in imminent danger of arrest. The Parliament stood against the Queen and it seemed that there were two rulers in Scotland; the Parliament in Edinburgh, and the Queen in Stirling or Perth.

Margaret was growing shrewd. She had immediately written to her brother Henry, telling him of her marriage to Angus and implying that the reason she had married with such speed was because she believed it was the plan of Parliament to bring Albany over and marry her to him. It was true he had a wife living, but she was not enjoying good health and moreover, as she was his cousin, Margaret believed a divorce was planned. She had realised how much against such an alliance her dear brother would be, for Albany was entirely French in sympathy and if he were ruler of Scotland he would never rest until he had brought war into her brother's kingdom.

The reply from Henry was as Margaret had expected. The last thing he wanted was to see Albany in Scotland, so he gave his approval to the match with Angus and stated that he was happy to accept him as a brother-in-law.

Lyon-King-at-Arms was shipwrecked on his way to France, which caused great hilarity among the Douglases.

'God is clearly of our party!' Margaret said gleefully, and of course the Douglases shared her opinion.

But that did not mean that other messengers were not arriving in France and that Albany was being made aware of his duty to Scotland.

This was the waiting period. The trouble was confined to small skirmishes and had not erupted into civil war. The main reason for this was that Margaret was the sister of Henry VIII who would naturally be watching for any weakness in the Scottish defences.

Scotland was in no state to withstand invasion from England.

❁ ❁ ❁

The Duke of Albany had received a communication that the King would be hunting near his estates and proposed staying a night at his château, which threw his household into a state of tension only produced by a royal visit. François Premier, King of a few months, was a man who had already caught the imagination of his people, even as Henry VIII of England had his. Both these Kings were young, handsome, and lusty; and they had succeeded misers. Everywhere they went their dazzling magnificence delighted their subjects; and their reigns had as yet not been long enough for the people to ask themselves whither such kingly extravagances led.

Albany himself had been a friend of François for many years, all during that time when as Duc d'Angoulême the latter had lived in constant fear that Louis XII would produce a son who would oust him from the succession.

But there had been no son and now François was firmly on the throne; and he was honouring his old friend with a visit, which Albany knew meant that the King was going to give him some command.

Albany was eager to serve François, for the friendship between them was a true one; he enjoyed the witty conversation of the young King – the discussions on art, literature, and architecture, for François, lecherous and a keen sportsman though he was, prided himself first of all on his intellectual leanings.

He arrived at the château and was greeted with respectful affection by his friend. The banquet was almost comparable with those served in Francois's own palaces and châteaux; and it was the next day, when they hunted together, that Albany learned the purpose of the King's visit.

When they were riding side by side, François said: 'My dear friend, I am afraid I am going to ask you to do something for France which may not be to your taste.'

'My liege, whatever was asked of me by François and France would immediately become to my taste.'

'Spoken like a Frenchman,' answered François with a light laugh. 'You are more Frenchman than Scotsman, my dear Jehan. That is why it grieves me to ask this of you.'

'Sire, you are asking me to go to Scotland?'

François nodded mournfully. 'I have received a plea from the Scottish Parliament. Your presence is needed there.'

Albany was silent, looking at the country about him which he loved, thinking of his wife whom he would have to leave behind, for her health was giving cause for great anxiety, and the rigours of the Scottish climate would surely kill her. He thought of the pleasures of his visits to Court which, now that François was on the throne, would be more enchanting than ever.

'My dear fellow,' went on François, 'this is my sorrow as well as yours. I shall miss you. But see what is happening in your barbarous Scotland. The Regent Queen will be her brother's vassal shortly. She has alienated the majority of the noblemen, but they dare not rise against her for fear of that young coxcomb below the Border. He is an irritant, that young cockerel. We can never be sure when he is going to strike, and the last thing we can afford is an harmonious relationship between England and Scotland; so it is necessary that Henry be in perpetual fear of attack from the North. Scotland must therefore be the friend of France and, if you were Regent, my dear friend, I could happily believe that you would never forget that half of you belongs to us. It is for this reason that I ask you to leave at once for Scotland, to take the Regency.'

'Sire, you have spoken. It is enough.'

'Thank you, my friend. I knew I could rely on you. The English Margaret must be stripped of her power, and the best way of doing this is to take the young King out of her charge. Let that be your first duty. Then, when you are the guardian of the little Princes, when you are Regent of Scotland, Henry's sister will be powerless to move against us; and the friendship between France and Scotland will be firm.'

'I shall endeavour to obey my master's wishes.'

'Faith of a gentleman!' cried François. 'This might have been a most happy day but for this sad necessity. Would I could prolong my visit. But I must not delay you. You will have some preparations to make for your journey. This day I shall return to Paris and you will be making your way to Scotland. But we shall meet again . . . erelong.'

So now there would be no avoiding this unpleasant duty. Now he would not be able to send a deputy.

Within three days John Stuart, Duke of Albany, set out for Scotland.

❀ ❀ ❀

It was on 18 May of that year, 1515, when Albany landed at Dumbarton.

Margaret had been forced to agree to his coming because, apart from the Douglases, she had scarcely any supporters in Scotland; and there was one great fear that had come to her, which was that when Albany took over the Regency he would attempt to take her children from her.

Margaret loved her sons devotedly and the thought of losing control of them terrified her. The Parliament had pointed out to her that, although James IV had appointed her Regent and tutrix of James V, he had not known that she would so insult his memory by marrying again before he had been dead a year.

In her anxiety for the future of her children she forgot her desire to cling to power. She was an emotional woman before she was a ruler. Her love for Angus had put her into this difficult position; her love for her children was now making her frantic.

One of her greatest enemies was that Border baron, Lord Home, and when Albany arrived it was Home who set out to welcome him accompanied by ten thousand horsemen of his clan.

Home was magnificently dressed in green velvet, and he believed that by greeting Albany thus immediately as he came ashore, he would find himself highly favoured by the new Regent.

But before the meeting between Albany and Home, the Regent had received his old friend de la Bastie, for he was anxious, before committing himself to any promises or friendships, to hear what his deputy had to report of affairs in Scotland.

De la Bastie told him of the conflict which was raging throughout the land and suggested that he be particularly wary of Lord Home who was now eager to greet him, for like most Border barons he was capable of changing his coat at the first opportunity. It was whispered that Home had not supported the King as he might have done at Flodden; and it was because Margaret had voiced a suspicion of this that he had set himself up as the chief enemy of her and the Douglases. Albany would do well to beware of Home.

Thus, when the two men came face-to-face, Albany did not extend that cordiality which Home was expecting, and as Home rode forward with a smile of welcome, Albany's gaze was cool.

'I'm Lord Home, Your Grace,' explained Home. 'I have most humbly come to place myself and my men at your disposal.'

'Lord Home?' said the Regent. 'I thought one so handsomely attired must be a king. Such a band of followers, such fine raiment, are scarcely suitable for a subject who wishes to display his humble desire to serve.'

With that he turned away, leaving Home discomfited.

Not that Home would accept such an insult. He rode back to his men, savage anger showing on his face.

He had made up his mind. In those few moments he had ceased to be the friend of Albany; and since he was Albany's enemy he must be Margaret's friend.

Margaret, in Edinburgh Castle, knew that she must make a pretence of greeting the Regent. She had agreed that he should come, albeit she had been forced to do so; but she must hide her rancour and pretend to welcome him. She wondered what kind of man he was. He was a Royal Stuart – that much she knew – and they were notorious for their fascination.

She was faintly disappointed, though she would not admit this, in her handsome Angus. While they were enjoying their secret honeymoon he had been all that was wonderful; but now that he saw the strife their marriage had made all about them, he was beginning to be afraid, and instead of the conquering young husband there were times when he betrayed himself as a frightened boy.

He was vain enough and ambitious enough to enjoy being the Queen's husband; but he did not enjoy finding himself at the mercy of powerful enemies such as Arran who quite clearly hated him because of his new position.

But Margaret refused to face this aspect of her husband's character for she was still deeply in love with his handsome body.

At the same time she allowed the women who were doing her hair to chatter about Albany

'They say he is a great hero in France, a friend of the King and noted for his bravery in battle. And there's something else they say. He is furious because of Your Grace's marriage.'

'My marriage is no concern of his,' declared Margaret.

The women laughed. 'Oh, but he has seen Your Grace's picture. And it has been said that he fell in love with it and hoped that there would be a marriage waiting for him in Scotland.'

'What nonsense! He has a wife. I have a husband.'

'But, Your Grace, he did not know of your marriage . . . and they say his wife is ill and cannot live long.'

'Well, even if he had such plans, they must come to naught.'

Margaret smiled at her reflection in the burnished metal of the mirror. She placed her hands on her stomach and revelled in the slight swelling there. His child, she thought, and mine.

She hoped for a boy who would look exactly like her handsome husband, but she could not but be sorry that with all this trouble rising around her she must also suffer the inconvenience of a pregnancy.

It was time for her now to ride out to greet Albany; and she had decided that she would be gracious, for he was her late husband's uncle and a Royal Stuart; but she would be wary, and if he attempted to take her babies from her she would fight with everything she had.

When she saw him she was struck by his handsome looks. There was no doubt of the Stuart blood; that indefinable charm which seemed to be their birthright was there in the broad face with the humorous eyes; his hair and beard were dark, as were his eyes, and his manners were more courteous than those she had come to expect from the Scottish lords. He appeared to be in his mid-thirties, the prime of life, she thought.

'Welcome to Scotland,' she said; and he answered: 'I thank my gracious Queen.'

Then they rode to Holyrood House where the Regent was to have his lodging; and later that day Margaret went back to the Castle.

For all his charm the Regent acted with sternness and speed. His first victim was Lord Drummond who was called before the Council and sentenced to imprisonment in Blackness Castle for his conduct towards Lyon-King-at-Arms. Gavin Douglas was also imprisoned for aspiring to the Primacy; and in fear Margaret awaited the next blow which she was certain would be the removal of her children from her care.

Those Scottish lords who saw the beginning of the downfall of the Douglases, deserted her, and the only supporters she now had were her husband, Angus, and the disgruntled Lord Home who might so easily desert her for the other side if she were to offend him in any way. Still, she must make the best of what she had, and if Home was untrustworthy he was also powerful.

Margaret herself went from the Castle to Holyrood House to plead for the release of Lord Drummond, an old man, she explained, who had acted impulsively when he had struck Lyon King. Albany, eager not to alienate Margaret too strongly, at length agreed to pardon Drummond; this was done, and his estates were restored to him.

But Margaret was growing more and more uneasy because, when his powerful grandfather and uncle had been imprisoned, Angus had become really perturbed. He often thought with remorse of the way in which he had treated Jane

Stuart; and he longed to see her, to explain how he had been carried away by his powerful family and the Queen's insistence. Margaret sensed his lack of ease, and although not aware of his thoughts about Jane, she wondered how strong he would be in a dire emergency. She excused him on account of his youth – the very quality which so appealed to her. She comforted him and told him that all would be well for them if they were loyal to each other.

'As I shall always be to you,' she told him tenderly.

But the Regent and his Council were determined to take her sons from her care, and it was arranged in the Tolbooth that four peers should be chosen to go to the Castle and demand that the children be handed to them.

Margaret's castle spy brought this information to her and, being warned, she was determined not to let the children go without a struggle.

She went to the nursery where young James was being amused by David Lindsay who was singing one of the old Scotch ballads known as 'Ginkerton'. The young Duke of Ross was sleeping in his cot in a nearby room.

'My son,' she cried, 'come here to me.'

'But Davie's singing,' James told her.

'I know, my darling, but we're going to play a game . . . you and I and your little brother. So David shall stop singing now.'

'I like "Ginkerton" best.'

'Your Grace,' began David, who could see that she was in a state of tension, 'is there aught I can do?'

'Yes, David. Go and tell the nurse to bring little Alexander from his cot.'

'It is his hour for sleep.'

'I know. I know. But this is important.' She drew him aside

and whispered: 'Albany is sending certain peers to the Castle for the children.'

David turned pale. 'Your Grace . . .'

'Go and tell the child's nurse to bring him to me. I am going to try to hold them off.'

'Why cannot Davie sing "Ginkerton"?' demanded three-year-old James.

'Because it is not part of this game.'

'I like "Ginkerton" better than this game.'

'Never mind that now, my darling. We are going down to the portcullis. You will see a lot of people. You like seeing the people.'

James nodded and began to hum 'Ginkerton'.

When the nurse had appeared, carrying the little Duke of Ross in her arms, Margaret said: 'Follow me.' And she took James's hand in hers and led the way down to the Castle gates.

She could hear the noises in the streets, for the four peers had set out from the Tolbooth and the townsfolk, guessing what was afoot, had followed them. On the way she was joined by Angus, looking very pale, and some of the ladies and gentlemen of her household. When they reached the portcullis Margaret demanded that it be raised, and when this was done, the four peers and all the people who had followed them saw the Queen holding the little King by the hand. A few paces behind her was the nurse holding the baby, while Angus and the members of her household formed a semicircle about her.

It was a charming and startling picture, and for a few seconds there was a breathless silence before the people of Edinburgh began to cheer wildly.

Margaret, her eyes seeming more brilliant than usual because of her high colour, looked completely regal – but a mother as well; and as such she had on her side every woman in that crowd which had assembled, and almost every man. It was what she had hoped for.

The four peers were approaching, and she called to them to halt.

'I command you to state the cause of your coming before you take one step nearer to your sovereign,' she cried in a loud voice.

'Your Grace,' replied the spokesman of the four, 'we come in the name of the Parliament to receive the King and his infant brother.'

There was absolute silence in the crowd as it watched the conflict of wills, as it speculated as to who would win this first round of a mighty battle – the Queen or the new Regent and his Parliament.

Margaret commanded: 'Drop the portcullis.'

The great iron gate rumbled down between the royal group and the parliamentary representatives.

'The King, my husband, made me governess of this castle,' she cried in a ringing voice, 'and I shall not yield it. But the Parliament of this country I must respect, and I ask that I be given six days in which to consider what they ask of me.'

Then turning, with her train following her, she walked back into the castle.

Angus was alarmed. The scene had been effective in the eyes of the spectators, but he was sure it had been an empty victory. When his grandfather and uncles had persuaded him to marry the Queen he had not visualised such alarming events. He had thought it was going to be all Court pleasures with himself at the Queen's right hand.

He thought of the power which was massed against them, for it seemed to him that the only supporters the Queen had were the Douglases and the unreliable Lord Home. His grandfather seemed broken by what had happened to him, and well he might be, for he had come very near to losing all he possessed.

The thought of losing all *his* possessions alarmed Angus, so on an impulse he wrote to Albany telling him that it had not been his wish to take part in that affecting scene at the portcullis. He had wished to obey the Parliament's mandate, and indeed had advised his wife to do so.

Sweating with fear, he called for a messenger and ordered him to take the letter to the Regent Albany with all speed.

Margaret could not rest. Her thoughts kept going back to an event in her family which suggested a parallel with the position in which she now found herself.

When Edward IV had died his widow, Elizabeth Woodville, had been asked to surrender the young King and his brother. This she had most reluctantly done and they had been lodged in the Tower of London. In that tower of many secrets they had disappeared, and none knew what their fate had been.

How could she give up her little James and Alexander? They were so young and tender. If they died, Albany could claim the throne. She had seen this man; his looks were noble, his manner chivalrous. Yet whom could one trust?

Six days to keep them while she pretended to consider handing them over. During those six days she forgot everything but the desire to keep her children with her.

On the fifth day she wrote to the Parliament telling them that if they would allow her to keep the little King and his brother in her care she would maintain them on her dowry, and that she would allow certain noblemen to share in their guardianship. She guessed of course that the Parliament would not agree to this and, on the fifth day, she told Angus that she dared remain in Edinburgh Castle no longer. 'For they will come and take the children,' she said. 'I know they will not accept my conditions.'

'Then there is only one thing you can do,' Angus insisted. 'Give up the children.'

'Give up the children! I remember what happened in the case of other princes lodged in the Tower of London.'

'I believe Albany to be an honourable man.'

'I trust no man,' retorted Margaret, and she looked at him appealingly as though imploring him to allow her at least to keep her trust in him.

'You daren't go against the wishes of the Parliament.'

'I dare!' said Margaret firmly. 'We are going to leave for Stirling Castle tonight.'

Angus was now really alarmed. 'What good will that do?'

'I do not know, except that I shall have a little respite in which to think. I have told my attendants to make ready. We should leave soon after dusk.'

'W-we . . . ?' stammered Angus. 'I would not come.'

'Would you not?' replied Margaret, her disappointment wounding her so bitterly that it subdued the fire of her anger.

'Nay,' said Angus, ''twill do no good and only anger the Parliament. I shall return to my estates until this trouble has blown over. I'd rather hear the lark sing in the open country than the mouse cheep in prison walls.'

'I see,' said Margaret, 'that I must go without you.'

''Tis better so,' answered Angus with a sigh of relief. 'You have no chance against Albany, mark my words. He has the backing of the Parliament. He'll be less harsh with a woman – being a Frenchman – than he'd be towards me. Do as you wish, but it would not be well if he thought I had any part in this.'

'Then goodbye . . . till we meet again,' replied Margaret.

That evening she and her attendants, with the children, came stealthily out of Edinburgh Castle; and as she rode through the night she was a frightened woman. What will become of my little ones? she asked herself. And she tried to forget that, in this desperate need, the man who should have stood beside her had deserted her lest through remaining with her he might hear the cheep of a mouse within prison walls.

He had been right, of course. What chance had she against a great military leader such as Albany? The flight to Stirling had been the one move left open to a desperate woman, and it could only mean delaying the inevitable climax for a few days – at best a few weeks.

On receiving Angus's communication, Albany had been disgusted.

Poor woman, he thought, and a brave one too. How did she come to choose such a spouse, so childishly young, so ready to desert her side at the first sign of danger?

But for all his sympathy he had his duty to do; while Margaret kept the custody of the King she would be a formidable power; without him hers would be an empty title. Moreover he had to keep his word to the King of France whom he looked upon as his sovereign.

So he prepared to march to Stirling and slyly sent word to Angus that, as he wished to serve the Parliament, he should accompany the army which was about to leave for Stirling, its object being to secure the persons of the young King and his brother.

He felt a little less contemptuous when he received Angus's reply that, although he wished to serve the Parliament, he could not join an army which was marching against his wife.

So Angus stayed on his estates while Albany marched on Stirling.

Margaret, deserted by her husband, knowing that she could not withstand a siege, decided that the only thing she could do was surrender to Albany; and then trust to her wits to bring her children back to her.

Thus, when Albany and his army arrived at the castle, Margaret ordered that the gates be thrown open, and she was revealed standing there with James beside her.

In his little hand he held the big keys of the castle and, walking up to the Regent Albany, as he had been told to do, he solemnly presented them to him.

Margaret's sense of showmanship was superb; and as before the portcullis of Edinburgh Castle, all the spectators were moved to tears at the sight of that small and handsome boy, handing over the keys of the castle.

Albany knelt and took the keys, then he kissed the boy's hand; and as though overcome by emotion he took him into his arms and embraced him while the watchers cheered.

James extricated himself and studied Albany intently. Then he said in his high, piping voice: 'Can you sing "Ginkerton"?'

'I doubt that,' answered Albany with a smile.

'Davie can and so can I,' answered the young James, with

the faintest sign of contempt; but he evidently liked the look of Albany, for he allowed his hand to remain in his as they walked to the Queen, when Albany bowed with all the respect that she could wish for.

Margaret was smiling, but she was thinking: I have surrendered my children. Shall I ever take them away from him?

❀ ❀ ❀

Margaret had handed her children over to Albany in August, and she was expecting Angus's child in October. As always during such times she suffered a great deal, and she was impatient with herself because she felt so weak.

While she planned for the arrival of the new baby she yearned for her sons and at times, frustrated as she was, she cried hysterically for them.

Again and again she recalled the fate of the Princes who had disappeared while in the Tower of London.

'How do I know that a similar fate does not await my own darlings!' she demanded. 'Why has Albany come to Scotland? It is because he wants the throne. He is another Richard the Third. My little ones are in imminent danger.'

Spies flourished in such a situation, and there were many to report her words to Albany.

'She is accusing you of intending to murder the King and his brother,' he was told.

'Nay,' answered Albany, 'do not blame her; she is a woman crying for her children. It grieves me that we must take them from her, but when she married young Angus she brought this on herself. Would that I could do aught to relieve her anxiety, but I cannot.'

In her calmer moments Margaret began to plan; and at last she made up her mind what she would do.

She was going to make a desperate attempt to recover her children and, when she had done so, to take them over the Border into her brother's country where she would ask for refuge.

Angus had proved himself to be overweak; but there was Lord Home whose hatred for Albany was so intense that he was prepared to undertake any action against him. So she sent for Home and laid her plan before him.

'As you know, my lord,' she explained, 'my time is coming near and my pregnancies have always caused me great suffering. I am therefore going into retirement at Linlithgow where I shall observe all the rules laid out by my grandmother, the Countess of Richmond, and thereby hope for an easy labour. At least that is what I wish everyone to believe; and I shall write to my brother telling him, for I know full well all the letters I write to him are seen by my enemies. While I am in Linlithgow I shall arrange for the abduction of my children and our escape across the border, and in this you shall help me.'

This was a project which appealed to Lord Home, for if he could bring about the rescue of the royal children it would be clear to Albany how foolish he had been not to cultivate his friendship.

He therefore threw himself wholeheartedly into the plan, and it was decided that Margaret should escape to Tantallan, the Douglas home near the Border, while Home's Borderers should set fire to a small town near Stirling. Albany would then surely release some of the guards from Stirling Castle, where the royal children were, in order that they might defend the town. Home would then seize the opportunity to kidnap them and carry them to Tantallan where the Queen would be waiting to leave for England.

Now that she had a definite plan, Margaret's spirits rose and she ceased to mourn, because she was certain that in a short time she, with her husband and children and the newborn little one, would be in the protection of her great brother Henry, where none would dare molest them.

She wrote to her brother the letter which she knew would be intercepted and shown to Albany and his ministers.

My dearest brother,

I write to you at this time to tell you that I propose to take to my chamber and lie in at my Palace of Linlithgow within this twelve days, for there are but eight weeks to my time. Matters go well here in Scotland under the new Regent and that is a great comfort to me at this time. I pray Jesus to send me a safe delivery and to have you, my dearest brother, in his good keeping . . .

She was smiling to herself, imagining Albany reading the letter, and his comments as he did so. He would congratulate himself that she had overcome her hysterical desire to keep her children with her; doubtless he would call her a woman of sound good sense.

Good sense indeed! she thought.

She had had the chamber at Linlithgow hung with tapestry and even the windows were covered with it, because her grandmother, the Countess of Richmond, who had had more influence with her son than any other person, had laid down a law as to how royal ladies should be treated in childbed, and one of the first rules was that all light and air should be excluded from the chamber; but the tapestry covering one window, however, might be placed so that it could be easily drawn aside, for in pregnancy women often had strange fancies which it was unwise to deny; and if a fancy for light and air should overtake an expectant mother, unwelcome as it was, she should be humoured. All those who waited on her during her confinement must be women; therefore the tasks of chamberlains, pantlers, ushers, and sewers, which might at other times be allotted to men, must be done by women. Only in the case of dire need must a man be allowed into the chamber.

Such an atmosphere suited Margaret's purpose. In her shrouded chamber in Linlithgow Palace she would work out her plan.

She was ready for the escape, but there was one matter which disturbed her. How could she leave Angus whom she sorely missed? She had already forgiven him his disaffection. He is so young, she told herself. It must have been a great shock to him to see his grandfather imprisoned. I doubt not that he is ashamed of his action by now; and he at least would not march against me.

She longed to see him; but she was supposed to be surrounded only by females, so how could she summon Angus to her? There was one way. If she were very ill and asked to see her husband no one would be very surprised if he came.

Very soon the people of Scotland were talking of the poor

Queen's sickness and the trouble which always attended her pregnancies. Poor lady, they said, she came near to death with the others even when she lived at ease. How will she fare now that she is in such sad state?

And they hourly expected to hear that the Queen was dead.

Angus came riding to Linlithgow in answer to her summons.

She received him in the tapestry-hung lying-in chamber. He was a little shamefaced, but she quickly set him at ease by embracing him, telling him how sadly she had missed him and how happy she was to see his dear face again.

Realising that there were to be no reproaches, Angus's relief was apparent. He returned her embrace and told her that he was happy now they were together again.

'And you will stay with me until our child is born,' she announced.

'Can that be so?' he asked. 'Do you not wish to be surrounded only by women?'

She laughed. 'That was my grandmother's law. I make my own laws. I doubt not that our child will be born in England.

Angus was aghast. 'But how so?'

'Because, my love, tonight we are going to steal out of Linlithgow. We are going to Tantallan and there make our way across the Border.'

'But the Parliament . . .'

'Do you think I care for the Parliament? I am tired of the Parliament. I am the Queen of Scotland, whatever they decree. And I shall have my say.'

Angus was wishing that he had not come to Linlithgow, but now that he was in her presence he felt the force of her character. Her enthusiasms were always so great that he was caught up in them. Thus it had been when she had made him aware of her desire to marry him. He had wanted to refuse then and had been unable to; it was the same now.

She put her arms about his neck and brought her glowing face close to his. 'It will be pleasant to spend a night together at Tantallan. As soon as we have escaped I shall send a message to my brother imploring him for sanctuary. I long to be at the English Court. I have heard it has become truly magnificent since my father's death.'

'You cannot leave your sons in Scotland!'

'Nay, nay. They shall be with us.' She was laughing wildly because she was so happy to see his handsome face again; and she could tell herself that she loved him all the more because of his very bewilderment. She had the same tenderness for him as she had for her little James and Alexander. He was but a boy really. Younger than she was in years . . . and so much younger in experience.

'I will take care of you,' she said. 'I will make you happy.'

'I-I had expected to find you ill,' he stammered.

'It was the only way to get you here without suspicion. I am not ill. The thought of outwitting my enemies makes me feel full of health and vigour. How I should love to see their faces when they discover that we have gone!'

She then told him of Home's plan to make a diversion while he kidnapped the boys.

'This time tomorrow we shall all be at Tantallan,' she told him. 'And then . . . on to the Border.'

'You are in no condition to travel. I cannot allow you . . .'

She patted his cheek. 'My loved one, I shall be well enough for the journey. Our son will be born before we reach London mayhap. But we shall be together . . . my husband and my boys . . . as we were meant to be.'

Angus could see that nothing he could say would dissuade her. He would have to go forward, for there was no way back.

That night, when it was dark, cloaked figures slipped out of Linlithgow Palace to where saddled horses awaited them.

How exhilarating, thought Margaret, to ride through the night, her husband beside her, his child in her womb. And all the time she was thinking of Home in Stirling Castle, snatching up her beloved boys and riding through the night with them, as she rode with Angus.

Then she knew that, much as she longed for power, there was one thing that meant more to her than anything in the world: her own family. That must be so, for her greatest ambition at that moment was to have them all safely under her care even though she never saw Scotland again.

❦ ❦ ❦

Margaret was exhausted when they arrived at Tantallan for the journey had been strenuous on account of her condition, but she did not realise this until they arrived, and she was impatiently awaiting the coming of Lord Home with her children.

When he came she went down to the great hall to meet him and, seeing that the children were not with him, she almost fainted in her dismay.

'My lord,' she cried. 'The King and his brother . . . ?'

'Alas, Your Grace, we were unable to carry out our plan. Albany must have guessed – or mayhap we were betrayed. We fired the town, but never a guard was called off from the castle, and it was impossible to have access to the apartments of the King and his brother.'

Angus put his arm about his wife to steady her. More than ever he wished himself out of this.

Margaret was speechless with misery and, now that her hopes were destroyed, all the discomforts of her condition returned.

Angus, with her women, helped her to her bedchamber where she lay on her bed in melancholy silence; he then dismissed all her attendants and sat by her bed, seeking words which would soothe her.

But she would not be comforted. She murmured: 'My babies . . . my little sons . . . What will become of them?'

'They'll be well enough,' Angus soothed her. 'None will dare harm the King.'

'They dared harm Edward the Fifth when he was held in the Tower with his brother.'

'This is Scotland . . .'

'Ten times more barbarous than England.'

'I am certain the King and his brother will be safe.'

'You but say that to comfort me. There is no comfort for me. How dare they part such babies from their mother. Oh, God, why have you deserted me? Why are they not with me here this night as I had planned?'

'It was a plan doomed to failure,' began Angus.

She raised herself on her elbow and gazed at him dispassionately.

'Yes,' she said, 'you would never have attempted it, would you? You would have preferred to go cap in hand to Albany.'

'The Douglases never go cap in hand,' Angus retorted.

'I rejoice to see some spirit left in you,' she answered. 'But perhaps it is only there when you are facing a helpless woman.'

Angus rose and haughtily left her.

It was the first time she had spoken thus to him, but she did not care.

She wanted only her babies, for she was beginning to fear that she might never see them again.

Silently she wept, and she continued so until exhausted she slept; then her dreams were disturbed by two little boys – not her own two; these were older; and they were not in the apartments of Stirling Castle; they played together within the grey walls of the Tower of London.

There was no time to be lost. Now that it would be known that an unsuccessful attempt had been made to kidnap the King and his brother, and that the Queen was sheltering in Tantallan, an army would be sent to capture her.

She must escape into England; but dared she enter that country without first receiving permission from her brother to do so?

She had written to him of her dire need, but so far had had no reply. But to stay at Tantallan would be folly.

So, early next morning Margaret and her party set out for the Border. Now that she knew her sons would have to be left behind in Scotland all the joy had gone out of the adventure, and everyone exclaimed at the Queen's look of exhaustion.

Angus rode beside her, his handsome face somewhat sullen; and the party's progress was necessarily impeded, for the Queen could not endanger the child she carried by travelling at greater speed.

It soon became clear that they could not go on, and as they were in the neighbourhood of Coldstream Priory they decided they must rest there; and the Lady Prioress, who was related to Margaret's Comptroller of the Household, did all in her power to make the Queen's stay comfortable.

Messages had been sent into England that Henry might be made aware of his sister's predicament and send that much desired invitation to his Court.

It was long in coming and meanwhile Margaret waited at Coldstream Priory.

What anxious days they were which Margaret spent at the Priory! The Lady Prioress made her welcome, but what comfort was there when every moment she must wonder how near her enemies were to the Priory and whether her brother would send that invitation before it was too late.

At last help came from England. Henry had sent a command to Lord Dacre to go to Coldstream and from there to escort his sister to his Castle of Morpeth, where she should remain for her confinement.

When Lord Dacre arrived at the Priory the birth was clearly very near, and it was deliberated which was the more dangerous: to face the strenuous journey in her state, or to remain and risk capture by Albany's forces.

Margaret herself made the decision. 'I would rather put myself at my brother's mercy than that of my enemies in Scotland,' she said.

So the tedious and dangerous journey began.

Lord Dacre, as one of the lords of the North of England who, so far from the Court often made their own laws, was an arrogant man with a profound distrust and hatred of the Scots. He implied that he was ready to serve the Queen because she was an Englishwoman, but he was going to be very wary of her Scottish companions.

He told the Queen that Queen Katharine had sent comforts

for her — clothes and goods which she would need for her confinement — to Morpeth, and these were awaiting her there; there were also letters from her sister-in-law who, having herself suffered the rigours of childbearing, was anxious that Margaret should face the ordeal as comfortably as possible.

So Margaret set out from Coldstream but, before she had gone very far, it became clear that she would not be able to complete the journey to Morpeth.

Dacre made a quick decision. They were not far from the Border fortress of Harbottle, and he decided they must halt there. Harbottle, being one of the English fortresses immediately on the Border, Dacre was determined no Scotsman should enter it. Therefore the Queen must say goodbye to her husband and all her friends who had accompanied her while she stayed in the fortress.

Fainting with exhaustion and already beginning to feel the first pains, Margaret knew that for the sake of the child she must have immediate shelter; so she allowed herself to be taken in, there to be tended by strangers.

She was scarcely aware of this for her agony had begun and, as was usual with her, her labour was long and painful.

Two days later, on 5 October, she gave birth to a daughter whom she decided to call after herself. The Lady Margaret Douglas was a healthy child and, in spite of the trials which had preceded her birth, seemed as if she would survive.

For days Margaret was too ill to understand where she was; and when a gentleman of her brother's bedchamber, Sir Christopher Gargrave, called at the castle with letters from Queen Katharine, Margaret could only hold them in her hands, for she was too ill to read them.

'I could not bring the stuffs Her Grace the Queen sent to

Your Grace,' Sir Christopher told her. 'There are too many robbers in the Border country, and the articles would never have made the journey from Morpeth to Harbottle in safety. But when Your Grace is well enough to leave Harbottle for Morpeth, you will find them waiting for you there.'

Margaret smiled her thanks, but she was too weak to care.

At that time she believed she would never leave Harbottle.

Slowly she began to recover, but then suffered so painfully from sciatica that she was unable to move from her apartment, and it was not until November was nearing its end that she left Harbottle for Morpeth.

❁ ❁ ❁

When she arrived at Morpeth Castle Margaret suffered a relapse. All the excitement and uncertainty which had been hers at this difficult time had been too much for her; not only had she suffered from a difficult confinement but continually she worried as to the fate of her little sons.

She believed that, had they escaped with her, her high spirits would have helped her to regain her health; as it was she was sunk in wretchedness and forebodings of evil.

The ghosts of those other little Princes in such similar circumstances continued to haunt her; and as she lay in her sickbed at Morpeth it seemed to her – and those about her – that she would never leave it.

Angus, with the rest of her friends who had escaped into England with her, was allowed to come to her at Morpeth; and Dacre was inclined to view Angus with tolerance because his master Henry VIII did not disapprove of the young man. Angus, however, was far from happy. Continually he wondered why he had allowed himself to be caught up in such troubles. He believed that Albany would confiscate his estates; and he had no wish to live as an exile in England.

He often thought too of Jane Stuart. His conscience had never really ceased to trouble him about her; and because she was gentle and had loved him so much, he was sure that if he could go to her and explain, she would understand the predicament he was in and how, with the Queen desiring him so ardently, and his family desiring the marriage with equal ardour, he had been in no position to refuse it.

But he had not been happy – apart from those first weeks – though he need not tell Jane about those. Each day when he went to see Margaret she seemed more wan, more exhausted. His little daughter was flourishing so he need not worry about her; she had nurses to look after her now that they were at Morpeth, and all the good things which kind Queen Katharine had sent for her were being used.

There was no need for him to remain at Morpeth. Albany had written to Margaret that if she would return to Scotland she should enjoy all the benefits of her dower lands; and might take part in the guardianship of her children, provided she did not wish to take them from Scotland. Her friends should not suffer for the part they had played in her escapade.

It was that last sentence which appealed to Angus. He wanted to go back to Scotland, to live in peace on his estates, to go to Jane Stuart and explain to her why he had done what he had.

And why should he not return?

Surely if he did he could make matters easier for Margaret.

The idea tormented him so much that he began to make plans.

That was a miserable Christmas for Margaret. Not only was she ill in body and disturbed in mind, and living in Morpeth Castle when she longed to go south to her brother's Court, but terrible news was brought to her.

She was lying in bed, feeling too weak to rise, with her little daughter lying in her cradle beside the bed, sleeping peacefully; wondering why Angus looked withdrawn as though he were occupied with his secret thoughts, why he started to the window every time he heard the sound of horses' hoofs. If he were expecting a message from her brother why did he not say so? She too was constantly expecting such messages.

He was at the window now, staring moodily out, and Margaret called him to her bedside.

She wanted to tell him that they should be happy together. They should remember how they had loved each other in the first weeks of their marriage before their troubles had started. Because the country did not approve of their match, that was no reason why they themselves should not.

Angus had come to stand by her bedside, and she noticed that a fretful look marred his handsome features.

She held out a hand. 'It will soon be Christmas,' she said. 'A happy season.'

'Here in this place! 'Tis like a prison. Can Christmas be celebrated in a prison?'

'It is not a prison,' she replied. 'It is true there are few comforts, but that is because it is really a Border fortress. Dacre is a good host, being commanded to be so by my brother. I doubt not that letters of goodwill, from him and Katharine, will be arriving erelong. Come closer, my dearest.' He sat down and she went on: 'Do you so long to be back in Scotland?'

'I would we had never left it.'

'If we could only have brought my sons with us . . . I would be quite happy.'

He did not answer; and then suddenly was alert. He had heard the sound of horses' hoofs below. Immediately he had risen and gone to the window. When he turned to her she saw the excited look on his face.

'Messengers,' he said. 'I will go and see what news they bring.'

She closed her eyes. Invitations from Henry, she thought. He will be impatient for me to arrive at his Court. He will want to show me how magnificent he has made it.

She smiled, thinking of ten-year-old Henry, and asked herself: Has he changed much?

Then Angus returned with the messenger, and as she looked at the man who had obviously ridden hard – for he was very travel-stained and weary – her heart began to beat faster, for she knew that he brought news which would be unwelcome. Nor did he come from England, but from Scotland.

'You had better tell Her Grace what you have told me,' said Angus.

The man looked appealingly at Angus as though imploring him to help him in his difficult task.

But Angus was silent.

'Tell me quickly,' commanded Margaret. 'You must not keep me in suspense.'

'Your Grace, the little Duke of Ross fell sick of a childish malady. He did not recover from it.'

There was silence in the room.

Margaret lay speechless; all the colour had left her face. It was like waking to find that a hideous nightmare was no dream after all.

What she had feared had come to pass.

❀ ❀ ❀

She was inconsolable. Her women tried to calm her.

'This is so bad for you, Your Grace. Children take these maladies . . . and often they die.'

'Had I brought him with me he would be alive today,' she asserted. 'It is my enemies who have done this. They have murdered him as others murdered my uncles in the Tower. And my little James, what will become of him?'

'Your Grace, you have heard that he continues in fine health.'

'For how long?' she cried bitterly.

There was no consoling her. Her women reminded her of her weakness, but she took no heed of them.

She cried out: 'He has done this, that black-hearted murderer. He has killed my little son. My child . . . dying, and his mother not with him. My little Alexander who was such a bonny child. And what of my James? Oh, this is a bitter day for me. Would I could lay my hands on that murderer. How did he do it? They say my uncles were stifled in their beds. Is that how my little Alex was murdered? You see, do you not, if he murders my little James as he has his brother, then there would be no one to stand between him and the throne.'

They were afraid that in the excess of grief she would do herself some harm, so they sent Angus to comfort her.

He sat by the bed and begged her to stop weeping, for it grieved him to see her thus.

'It is easy for you,' she cried. 'He is not your son.'

'It is not easy for me to look on when you are so sad.'

That softened her. 'Oh, my dearest,' she cried, 'what should

I do without you? But if only our plans had succeeded, if only with this dear daughter of ours I had my sons as well, I would ask nothing more. I swear I would ask nothing more.'

Angus knelt by the bed. 'Return to Scotland,' he said earnestly. 'Make peace with Albany.'

'Make peace with the murderer of my son!'

'You know he is no murderer. What sense does it make . . . murdering young Alexander while James lives? Had he wished to remove all obstacles to the throne he would have killed them both.'

'How do I know what will befall James now that his brother has been removed?'

'You must be reasonable. You are hysterical. Oh, I understand your grief . . . and indeed it is mine, but you know Albany has done no murder. He is not the man to commit murder, and it is my belief that he does not greatly desire the crown of Scotland.'

'It is easy for you. It is not your son who has died. Murderer! Usurper! He is another Richard the Third, I tell you. And my little one is in his hands.'

Angus laid his hand on her brow. He was wondering what she would say if she knew that he had written to Albany asking on what terms he could return, that Albany's reply had been very favourable, and that he had almost made up his mind that he was going to Scotland whether she would come or not.

She was soothed by his touch but she had to give vent to her anger; she had to comfort herself in some way; she could not bear to think that she would never see Alexander again, and she must give way either to sorrow or anger.

But she did not believe in her heart, any more than Angus

did, that Albany had murdered her son. Albany was no murderer of children.

She remembered him when he had taken the keys of the castle from little James – tall, upright, handsome, with a kindly tolerance in his eyes. And how gracious he had been to her – so that he had reminded her of James, her husband; and there were times, although this was another thing she was not yet prepared to admit, when she compared James with Angus and thought: Ah, but he was a king.

And Albany was a king's son; he was a Stuart at that. And in his eyes there lurked that tolerance, that gallantry towards a woman which was almost irresistible.

Angus was convinced that Albany was no murderer, but although she secretly agreed with him, she continued to rail against the man because she was so sick with grief that she must relieve her feelings in some way.

Looking up at Angus, seeing the weak petulance about his handsome mouth, she found herself involuntarily comparing him with Albany and thinking: The Duke is a strong man.

After a few days it became apparent how the shock of this news had affected the Queen's health. She was stricken with a fever and there was scarcely a person in Morpeth Castle who did not believe she was on her deathbed.

Yet even when the fever was at its height and she rambled incoherently, the incessant repetition of her son's name was enough to indicate what was on her mind. She clung to the thought of that small boy as though he were a lifeline; and indeed it seemed as if he were and that Margaret would not leave this life while she believed her son needed her.

Outside the castle the bleak January winds came howling from across the Border; the bitter cold penetrated the castle.

Angus was impatient. His wife was dying, and if he waited for her death, Albany would say he had accepted his terms because there was no other way out for him. He dared not wait. He must show Albany that he deplored the conduct of his wife and that he wished to serve the Regent.

So on that bleak January day, when Margaret's death was hourly expected, Angus with a few of his attendants quietly left Morpeth Castle and were soon galloping over the Border on their way to Edinburgh.

❀ ❀ ❀

'Where is my husband?' asked the Queen. 'Tell him to come to me.'

The woman went away to call him, but she did not return for a long time.

Margaret summoned another woman to her bedside. 'Pray go and find the Earl of Angus and tell him that I wish to see him.'

The woman lowered her eyes and stood silent.

'What has happened?' demanded Margaret. 'Why do you not do as I tell you?'

'Your Grace, the Earl of Angus is not in the castle.'

'Then where is he?'

'He returned to Scotland more than a week ago, when Your Grace lay nigh unto death.'

'Returned to Scotland!' she whispered as though to herself. Then: 'I understand. Pray, leave me.'

She lay still, too numb with sorrow to weep or to rail against him.

She had lain near to death and he had deserted her; and this was the man for whom she had jeopardised the crown of Scotland.

Now she would no longer deceive herself. Her heart should accept him for what her mind had been telling her he was for so long. This is the end, she told herself. I shall never forget what he did to me in Morpeth Castle.

Her attendants were surprised at the calm with which she accepted his desertion. She rose from her bed shortly afterwards and amazingly her health began to improve.

Through February and March letters were exchanged between Morpeth and the English Court; and with them came a warm invitation from Henry for his sister to come to London.

So with the coming of April Margaret began her journey south.

Chapter VIII

DAISY, MARIGOLD, POMEGRANATE
AND ROSE

In spite of desertion by her husband and the loss of her younger son, Margaret felt excited during those April days in Morpeth when she was preparing for her journey south. Henry had written warmly; he was eagerly looking forward to seeing her at his Court, for it was good, he said, that sisters and brothers should meet even though their duties to their kingdoms must necessarily keep them apart for so much of their lives.

His wife, Katharine of Aragon, of whom Margaret had seen little during her childhood, was as eager to welcome her as Henry was. She had heard of Margaret's difficult confinement, a matter regarding which she could offer the utmost sympathy, having suffered so much herself in that respect. The bond of motherhood united them, wrote Katharine, and she longed to see her sister's little daughter, Margaret, who was but a few months older than her own dear Mary who, as Margaret would doubtless have heard, had been born in February.

'And as, my dear sister, you have a long journey to make, I am sending you by my equerry, Sir Thomas Parr, my favourite white palfrey with my own easy pillion which I trust will be of use to you on your way south.'

Margaret had heard that her sister-in-law was a gentle creature, deeply in love with her handsome husband, often sorrowful because as yet she had failed to give him the male heir for which he longed, yet filled with hope because, after several failures, she had produced healthy little Mary.

It would be comforting to talk with her sister-in-law, mused Margaret, for she knew that she was one who would understand full well her grief over the loss of Alexander and her great pride in little James.

She was beginning to believe that she had made a great mistake when she had allowed her infatuation for Angus to overcome her common sense. She had been lonely, she had craved that sexual excitement which had been so necessary to her; and therefore she had been prepared to rush into marriage with a handsome boy.

But experience made one wiser. If she could choose again she would not pick an impetuous boy; she would choose someone mature, a man, not a boy; someone like her first husband; for had he been faithful to her, had he treated her more as an intelligent companion, James would have been the perfect husband. She had not wanted to dominate; only to share.

She had lost James; she had failed to hold her place in Scotland. But it was no use looking back; she must go forward to Henry's Court; she must have conferences with her brother and his ministers; she must, with their help, win back the Regency of Scotland and the right to have the care of the King, her son.

If she had not married Angus, and Albany had not a wife . . . that would have been a different story. She had raged against him, called him murderer; but she thought of him often, and she would have enjoyed more than anything meeting him and abusing him to his face. The thought excited her, but that might be for later.

Now there was nothing to be done but travel south to London.

There was great comfort on Katharine's white palfrey, and Sir Thomas Parr was a pleasant companion, who told her that his mistress had instructed him to take good care of her sister.

Nor was that all; as a mark of *his* esteem, Henry had sent her, by one of his clerks of the spicery, many silver vessels for toilet and table use during the journey.

She was certain therefore of a good welcome, for Henry had also written a letter which accompanied the silverware to the effect that he was planning entertainments for his sister and her spouse when they reached his Court.

The countryside was beautiful in spring; the weather was clement; and Margaret, who was by nature strong, quickly regained her good health and with it her belief that she could win what she wanted.

They had passed through Newcastle and reached Durham, and she was resting in her bed one morning when the door of her apartment was opened and to her surprise Angus walked in.

Taken off her guard she gave a cry of great joy and held out her arms. He embraced her and she clung to him, hugging him in her delight.

Then she withdrew herself to look into his face. She laughed, for he had the look of a shamefaced boy.

'I heard,' he muttered, 'that my absence grieved you.'

'And you came back because you did not wish to make me sad?'

'I never wished to make you sad.'

'Ah, my love,' she said, 'how I have missed you! Do you not want to see your daughter?'

'In good time. First I wish to see my wife.'

She felt young again. It was spring and it was so long since she had seen him. They would make love and talk later, she indicated; and he was willing enough to obey.

The word went through the castle: The Queen is not to be disturbed. Young Angus has returned. They wish to be alone together for a while.

There were long faces among the Englishmen of the party. What did this mean? Was Angus going to try to persuade her to return to Scotland? Such an act would not please their master. They would not want to return to him and tell him what had taken place, for he had a kingly habit of blaming the bearers for the bad news they brought.

Angus was an ally of Albany; and Albany wanted to get the Queen back into Scotland, there to make her subservient to his rule which was, after all, the rule of France, the enemy of England.

They were right in their assumptions. Angus was saying: 'Do you not see the folly of this journey to England? Come back to Scotland with me. Albany is ready to receive you.'

Her eyes flashed in anger. 'Do you think *I* am eager to receive Albany!'

'Oh, come, what good can all this strife between you bring to anyone?'

'I have no wish to go back humbly to the murderer of my son.'

'Your son was not murdered. He died as young children do. It was no fault of Albany.'

'You plead too earnestly for your friend.'

'He will be your friend too.'

'Never. I hate him. But what is that to you? It seems you have his cause at heart rather than your wife's.'

'Margaret, I beseech you . . .'

'Do not be foolish. The only way in which I can hope to regain what I have lost is through my brother's help. Albany is afraid of Henry . . . even as his master, the King of France, is, and with good reason. Stop being so foolish. We are going to England.'

'We?'

'You and I, my dear, for my brother is expecting you.'

Angus turned sullenly away, but Margaret went to him and slipped her arm through his.

'Come, my love, you are going to enjoy the English Court. Our own is a poor place compared with it, I do assure you. My brother loves to masque and dance. He will be fond of you. You will be his friend. He says in all his letters: "Commend me to my brother-in-law, your good husband." And he is eager to meet you.'

Angus did not answer. Go to England? When Albany was prepared to make good terms with him? When Jane had said she understood how he had been forced into marriage with the Queen and that it made no difference to them? Leave Jane . . . now that they had come together again?

But he dared not tell Margaret all this. He stood silent, a little sullen, as though agreeing that she was right.

She gave him a little push. 'Go now. It is time for my women to come and help me dress. I will join you soon; I shall so enjoy your company, my love, on the way to London.'

Angus was afraid. He would have to be very cautious or he would indeed find himself riding south in the Queen's cavalcade, instead of north to Jane Stuart.

He nodded, kissed her and, when she murmured, 'Soon I shall be with you,' he did not deny it.

He went straight from her apartment to the stables where his servants were waiting for him.

He did not speak until he was in the saddle; then he said: 'It was a mistake to come. Now . . . let us ride . . . with all speed to the Border and into Scotland.'

Into Stony Stratford passed the Queen's party, and all through England the people came from their houses to watch the cavalcade. They cheered the Queen of Scots because she was their good King's sister and they knew that it was at his wish that she travelled south.

It was May by the time she reached Enfield, and there she was welcomed to the mansion occupied by Sir William Lovel, who was her brother's Lord Treasurer.

She was now very close to London and she believed that in a short time she would see her brother.

It was a glorious morning when she left Enfield and, as she was coming to Tottenham Cross, she saw in the distance a brilliant cavalcade making its way towards her. Her heart leaped with pleasure for she guessed who this was and, as the party approached hers, she recognised him riding at the head of it. He was a larger, more glorious version of that young boy whom she had known. His doublet was of purple velvet; jewels flashed on his hands and garments, and there were rubies and diamonds in his feathered bonnet. He had grown so much that he appeared to be far taller than any of his companions. On his face was the flush of good health and his blue eyes were as sparkling as water in sunshine and as brilliant as flames.

This was her brother. There was no doubt about that.

And as she recognised him, so did he her, for the resemblance between them had not grown less with maturity.

He rode up to her, smiling.

'My King and dearest brother.'

He sprang graciously from his horse which his groom hastily seized. He came to her and, taking her hand, kissed it.

'This is a great joy,' he told her.

'Henry! How happy I am to be here.'

'We have long looked forward to your coming. But where is my Lord Angus?'

Margaret's expression clouded. 'He returned to Scotland.'

'Returned to Scotland! Why so? Did he not receive my letters of invitation?'

'He thought it wiser to make terms with Albany, I fear.'

The pleasure faded from Henry's plump square face. His eyes narrowed, so that blue chinks shone through the folded flesh. He turned to his sister and gazed at her speculatively, and she knew that he understood full well that Angus had deserted her.

Then he gave a loud laugh. 'Done like a Scot!' he cried. 'He could do without us, eh? Then, sister, I tell you we shall do very happily without him.'

He remounted and brought his horse beside his sister's.

'We will rest awhile at Compton's house on Tottenham Hill,' he said. 'Then we will ride into my capital.'

In the afternoon they started out from Tottenham Hill, Henry on his fine horse with its glittering trappings, a dazzling figure; and beside him Margaret rode pillion with Sir Thomas Parr on Katharine's white palfrey.

The people now crowded the roads. Henry beamed on them, graciously and delightedly acknowledging their cheers.

How he revels in his new state! thought Margaret. He always said that things would be different when he became King, and so they are. And how the people love this merry England he has given them. What a king! How different from our father who was also a good king. And yet it is due to Henry VII that Henry VIII is possessed of the riches which make it possible for him to live in such style.

'To Baynard's Castle,' cried Henry, 'which I have set aside for your private residence, sister. But we shall not stay there. The Queen and our good sister are waiting to see you at Greenwich.'

So the cavalcade paused awhile at Baynard's Castle on the north bank of the Thames below St Paul's; and Margaret, looking at those Norman towers and ramparts, was well pleased with the dwelling Henry had chosen for her.

Here she rested and changed her costume, for Henry had arranged that they should travel the rest of the way to Greenwich by barge.

Margaret looked about her eagerly; now and then her memory stirred. It was so many years since she had passed down this river on the way to Greenwich, and how wonderful it was to see and hear the people on the banks cheering the royal barge, to listen to the sweet music of the minstrels who played as they went along.

Now she saw the Palace with the brick front facing the river;

she saw the tower in the park and the convent which adjoined the Palace.

'We have arranged good sport for you here at Greenwich, sister,' Henry told her gleefully; and she was conscious that all the time he was watching her to see how she marvelled at the splendour of his realm.

They alighted at the stairs, and at the gates of the Palace the Queen was waiting to greet them.

Margaret was warmly embraced by her sister-in-law and the first questions Katharine asked, when she had ascertained that Margaret was well and had suffered no harm from her journey, were concerning the welfare of the little Margaret.

But there was another who came forward to embrace Margaret; this was a dazzling, beautiful young woman who was so like Henry that Margaret knew at once that this was her young sister, Mary, now grown to womanhood.

Margaret kissed her warmly; then drew away from her and looked into that radiant, laughing face.

'Mary! Why, can it be possible?'

'Would you have me remain a baby for ever?' demanded Mary.

'How old were you when I went away? Was it six?'

'Well,' replied Mary, 'you were about thirteen. None of us stand still.'

'And you have had adventures.'

Mary grimaced. 'You too, sister,' she murmured.

Henry was impatient. He liked to see his family in amicable friendship, but he wanted them to remember that, no matter who came, or who met whom after how long an absence, there was one person who must be the centre of every gathering: the dazzling King of England.

❀ ❀ ❀

If she could have had her son James with her, if little Alexander were still alive, if Angus had been the husband she longed for, those would have been happy days for Margaret.

It was wonderful to be with her family again; Henry was eager to impress her with the superiority of the English over the Scottish Court, and one lavish banquet and ball followed another. This was a pleasure, for Margaret too loved gaiety. Katharine, kindly sympathetic, welcomed her as warmly in her way. As for Mary, she was full of high spirits, and delighted to be back in England at the gay and brilliant Court which her brother had made.

Margaret told herself that she needed rest and relaxation before she concerned herself with state matters. In good time she would impress on Henry the need for his help in regaining what was hers by right; but she understood her brother well. At this time he was bent on entertaining her; and had she tried to turn his mind to more serious matters he would have been greatly displeased.

She herself was not averse to a little light-hearted entertainment. Before she reached London she had sent messengers to Scotland to bring her dresses and jewels to her in England, for she would need them if she were to vie with the elegant ladies of Henry's Court.

Albany, evidently eager that she should withdraw her accusations about the death of little Alexander, and perhaps sorry for her, had put no obstacles in the way of her clothes being sent to her; and they arrived in London soon after she had.

Her sister, Mary, was with her on the day her clothes came, and they dismissed their attendants and examined the clothes together.

Mary shrieked with delight as she drew one glittering object after another from the trunk. She pranced round the apartment in a pair of sleeves of cloth of gold lined with crimson velvet; she put a cheveron on her head and turned this way and that to her reflection in the burnished mirror, delighting in the flash of the jewels.

'You were fine enough in Scotland, sister,' she said. 'I had always believed it to be such a gloomy land.'

Margaret sat on her bed, looking at a gold collar decorated with enamelled white roses. She remembered the occasion when James had given it to her.

'My husband was a great king and a fine gentleman.'

'But old,' put in Mary, and her own face darkened. She shivered, and Margaret knew she was thinking of the old King of France to whom she had been married. Poor Mary! At least Margaret had not suffered in that way.

'Not old as Louis was. He was merely older than I . . . and I was very young, so that he was not really very old. He was in his prime. Do you know, Mary, I believe he was the handsomest man I ever saw.'

'Do not let Henry hear you say that,' laughed Mary.

'You are happy now though, Mary?'

Her young sister clasped her hands and lifted her eyes to the ceiling. 'Ecstatically.'

'So it was all worthwhile.'

Mary pouted. 'It need not have happened. What good did the French marriage do for England?'

'It made peace between the two countries, and that is always a good thing.'

'An uneasy peace! And for it I had to endure . . . that.'

'Not for long.'

227

'Oh, no. I could not have borne it. And then he died . . . and Charles came to take me home.'

'And he married you.'

'I insisted, Margaret. I was determined. Henry had promised me that if I married old Louis I should marry my own choice when he died. And Charles was my choice . . . long before I married Louis.'

'So you got your wish.'

'Oh, those were glorious days, Margaret. I'll never forget them. Married to Charles . . . and both wondering what we should be called upon to pay for our boldness . . . and not caring!'

'It was a reckless thing to do. You might have been carrying the heir of France.'

'But I was not. And what fun I had, teasing François and his old mother that I was!'

'It seems to me that you found much to amuse you in this French marriage.'

'But only after my husband was dead, Margaret. What bold and lusty people we are. I wish I could have seen your Angus. He is very handsome?'

Margaret's face hardened. 'Handsome enough.'

'Why did he not come with you?'

'He preferred to stay in Scotland.'

'I know what I should do if I had such a husband.'

'What?'

'Rid myself of him and find another.'

'Easier said than done.'

'What! And you a Tudor. Did you not know that Tudors always find a way? I said I'd marry Charles Brandon – before they sent me off to France – and I have married him. We get what we want . . . if circumstances do sometimes make us wait for it. We're three of a kind, Margaret – you, myself and Henry. Don't you see it?'

'We're strong, we're determined; yes, I see that.'

'Sometimes I am a little sorry for the people who marry us. I was a little sorry for poor Louis. I knew he would not live long. He tried to be young, Margaret. That was a mistake. His pursuit of youth led him to the grave. And now this Angus . . . I am sure you will make him sorry for what he has done to you. And sometimes I look at Henry and Katharine and say: "Poor Katharine."'

'But she is devoted to him.'

'Katharine is such a virtuous woman; she'll always be devoted to him because he is her husband. Her religion tells her she must be. But there is a little friction between them already. He begins to wonder why she cannot give him a son.'

'But she has had several miscarriages, and now she has Mary.'

'Yes, but where are the boys, where are the boys?' Mary took up a silver pomander on a jewelled girdle and set it about her waist. 'Nay,' she said, 'I would not be the wife or husband of a Tudor . . . and displease them. If I were Angus, Katharine, or even Charles, I would be wary.'

Then she began to dance around the room, looking so vital, so lovely, that Margaret could well understand how the King of France in pursuit of youth had been hastened to his tomb by his desire for a Tudor.

There were pleasant hours spent with Katharine, and when they could be alone together they were two mothers fondly discussing their children.

The two little girls were so close in age that when Margaret was at Greenwich they shared a nursery; and it was the joy of the two mothers to visit them and send away their nurses and attendants that they might have the children to themselves.

Margaret, remembering what Mary had said about Henry's growing uneasiness at Katharine's inability to give him a son, felt herself drawn towards her sister-in-law, not only by affection and a common interest, but by pity.

And during those sessions in the nurseries, Katharine confided her great desire to bear a son.

'If I could but give Henry the son he so earnestly needs I should be completely happy,' she told her sister-in-law.

'You will,' Margaret assured her. 'You have had bad luck, as I did in the beginning. There was my little James and my little Arthur, and they both died. Then the present James. Ah, if you could see my James! I never saw such a lovely boy.'

'I would I could see him. What a joy he must be to you.'

'If I could only have him with me.' Margaret was momentarily sad and Katharine was angry with herself for having reminded her sister-in-law that she was parted from her son. But she could not hide the envy in her eyes, and Margaret felt that it was she who should be sorry for Katharine.

'I do believe Mary has grown since we last saw her,' she said. 'And my own Margaret thrives also. Poor child! When I think of her first seeing the light of day in that dreary Harbottle. So different from this little one . . . who was born in royal pomp in this very Palace of Greenwich.'

Katharine could not resist picking her daughter up in her arms. Mary, a solemn baby, regarded her mother serenely.

'I am sure she will be very wise,' said Katharine.

'She certainly has a look of wisdom,' answered Margaret, and she took her own daughter from her cradle; and the two mothers sat in the window seat, each holding her child in her lap.

Margaret asked Katharine to tell her of Mary's baptism; and Katharine was happy, recalling that ceremony. She told how carpets had been spread from the Palace to the font in the Grey Friars' church here at Greenwich; how her godmothers had been the Princess Katharine Plantagenet and the Duchess of Norfolk; how the child had been carried by the Countess of Salisbury with the Dukes of Norfolk and Suffolk walking on either side of her, and Cardinal Wolsey himself had been her godfather.

Margaret listened and cried: 'How different from my little Margaret in Harbottle!'

And as they talked together, Henry came into the nursery, all aglitter in his green velvet spattered with jewels. He greeted them boisterously.

'Ha! The mothers in council, eh! And what bonny children.' He took Mary from her mother and cradled her in his arms, smiling down into those eyes which regarded him as serenely as they had Katharine.

'This is a clever child,' cried Henry. 'She knows her father!'

Katharine smiled tenderly at the two of them.

'You must spare a glance for my little Margaret,' his sister told him.

He came over to her and peered down at the child in her arms.

'A bonny girl,' he said. He put out a finger and touched the little Margaret's cheeks. 'I fancy she knows her uncle,' he said.

Then he walked up and down the apartment, rocking Mary in his arms, now and then chuckling as he looked down at her.

When he had perambulated for a few minutes he came to stand at the window.

''Twas ill luck about your little son, Margaret,' he said.

Margaret's face clouded, and Katharine watched her anxiously. She would have liked to warn Henry not to talk of the matter, had she dared.

Henry's face darkened. ''Twas that scoundrel Albany. By God, it would please me to see him sent back to France.'

'It is what I am hoping will happen,' Margaret replied. 'If I can return, take the Regency and the guardianship of James, I shall forget past troubles and be happy again.'

'You are fortunate, Margaret, to have a son.'

The lower lip jutted out bellicosely, and the face had grown suddenly sullen.

'I am very fortunate in my little James. I would you could see him, Henry. Do you know whom he resembles most closely?'

'Who?' Henry demanded.

'Yourself.'

'Is that so!' The sullenness disappeared and his face was sunny again. 'What colour hair?'

'Tawny. Bright complexion. Eyes blue. Those who have seen you have said "How like his uncle he is!"'

Henry slapped his velvet covered thigh.

'Tell me more of this little fellow. Is he bright? Is he gay?'

'Did I not say he resembles you? It is not only in his looks, I do assure you. I believe he will grow up to be exactly like you.'

'Let us hope that he does,' put in Katharine fondly.

Henry regarded her affectionately, but his moods were always transient. Margaret could see he was thinking: Why do others have sons when they are denied to me?

It was a sunny day and crowds had come to see the tournament at Greenwich.

Margaret sat with her sister and sister-in-law in the balcony which had been set up for them. It was a brilliant scene; the ladies were gaily attired, and Margaret was secretly delighted that she could make as good a show as any of them. Her gown was as gay as Mary's and as fine as Katharine's. The latter of course lacked the love of display which was so conspicuous in Margaret, Mary, and Henry; whenever those three entered an assembly the brilliance of their garments would have betrayed who they were, even if their identities were unknown.

The balcony had been elaborately decorated with their devices. The daisy for Margaret, the marigold for Mary, the pomegranate for Katharine; and dominating them all was the rose of England which was Henry's own emblem.

The shouts of the crowd, the warm sunshine, the brilliance of the knights in armour were exhilarating. It was a glorious occasion and Margaret was flattered that it should be in her honour.

Mary's eyes were fixed on a tall figure among the combatants.

'Suffolk could be the champion of all, if he wished,' she whispered to Margaret.

'And why should he not wish so?' demanded Margaret.

'You have been away for a long time. Naturally he must not shine more brightly than one other. I said to him last night: "As you love me, take care in the jousts." "What," he answered, "do you fear that some agile adversary may slay me?" "Nay," I cried, "but I fear you may outshine the King."'

'So Henry still likes to be the victor, as he ever did.'

Mary laughed loudly. 'It would go ill with any man who

233

proved himself to be a more valiant knight. And we are still being punished for our marriage, you know. We have to pay Henry back for my dowry. We have to walk carefully. You should remember that, Margaret. Whatever you want from Henry, and I assume you want his help to regain your kingdom, you must always remember that, wherever he is, he must be supreme. Impress that on your mind so firmly that you believe it, and Henry will be your friend.'

'How can you speak thus of our brother?'

'Because I am his sister. Because I know him well. I love him, as he loves me; but I know him better than he knows me; indeed I know him better than he knows himself.'

Margaret thoughtfully watched the shining figures riding into the lists. There was truth in what Mary said; and if she were wise she would remember it.

'Who is the bulky knight now riding in?' she asked of Mary.

'Sir William Kingston. None could mistake his size and shape.'

'Well none will unseat *him*, I imagine.'

'It would depend,' replied Mary sagely.

Now the attention of the crowd was focused on two tall knights whose tabards were embroidered with golden honeysuckle, for it seemed that whomsoever these two knights tackled they were the victors.

Margaret noticed that Mary's brilliant eyes never left them, and leaning towards her she heard her whisper: 'Have a care, Charles. Be good . . . so good that all say how good you are . . . and then be just not quite so good.'

Margaret thought: Her stay in France must have changed her; it had made her grow into a cynic. Could that be the influence of young François? Margaret believed that was very likely.

Mary was crying excitedly 'Look, Kingston is in the lists. And the tall knight with him. Kingston is falling . . . horse and all. It is the first time he has been unseated.'

Then she leaned back against the embroidered marigolds on her chair and began to laugh softly.

In the great hall the knights had gathered. Queen Katharine sat on her chair of state with Mary on one side of her, Margaret on the other; and one by one the knights came forward to pay homage to her.

Into the hall came one on whom all eyes were fixed. This was because he was the knight who had overthrown Sir William Kingston; and everyone was discussing that extraordinary feat.

'Now,' said Katharine, 'we will discover the identity of this strange knight, for his helmet must be removed.' She called to him: 'Sir Knight, we would speak with you. We would tell you that we were delighted with your prowess. 'Twas bravely and expertly done, I doubt I have ever seen such skill in the joust.'

Mary said in a voice in which, it seemed to Margaret, the mischief lurked: 'The King will wish to challenge you, I'll swear, Sir Knight. For he is proud of his own daring at the joust.'

The knight came forward, bowing before the Queen, and when his helmet was removed, Henry's flushed and laughing face was exposed.

'So I deceived you, eh. You Kate and you Mary, and you Margaret! Well, you have been away, but Kate and Mary . . . well, methinks they should have known their King.'

Katharine said quickly: 'But now we know the truth, we

235

wonder we did not guess, for never have we seen such skill except that of Your Grace.'

'So you have a fair opinion of my skill, eh?'

'And the greatest pleasure this joust has given me,' went on Katharine, 'is to learn that my King is the champion.'

'Well, well, 'twas done in your honour.'

And so the masquerade was played as it had been many times before and would be again and again.

Henry was in high spirits. At the banquet he drank freely and his voice could be heard above all others. He called for music and played the lute himself; and one of the singers sang a song of his composing.

How he loves his life, thought Margaret. How lucky he is. How different his fate from mine. And yet he lacks that for which he most longs; and although I am parted from him at this time, I still have my little James. And though he be in Stirling and I in Greenwich, he is still my beloved son.

The summer had come and Margaret was anxious, although she could never have enough gaiety, and the entertainment to be enjoyed at her brother's Court delighted her. She missed Angus, and she believed that if he had come to her in England she would have been ready to forgive his desertion; she was longing to see little James; and she reminded herself that her reason for coming to Henry's Court was not to pass the time in pleasure.

Henry, she had discovered, was not eager for friendship with Scotland; he knew full well that while Albany remained Regent, Scotland would be the close ally of France; he hated François as much as ever, being jealous of his successes in war and the reports he heard of his adventures both at home and abroad. His little mouth would grow prim at the mention of the French King's amorous conduct; he often remarked that he did not believe God would long favour such a man. He was now seeking friendship with the Emperor Maximilian, for he believed that if the two of them stood together they could foil Francois's ambitious dream of bringing Europe under his rule.

He was however deeply desirous of removing Albany from the Regency; and he wrote to the Scottish Parliament telling them that he did not care to see his nephew in peril; and that if any harm were to come to the King – as he regretted it had to his little brother – all men would suspect Albany. Therefore it was imperative that Albany should be sent back to France without delay.

The Parliament's reply that the King was well, healthy, and in no danger, and that they had no intention of removing Albany, filled Henry with rage.

But Albany, whose great desire was for peace, wrote to Henry saying he believed that if he came to England he could convince Henry of his honest intentions.

When Henry received this note he came to Margaret's apartments in Greenwich Palace and laid it before her.

'Ha!' he cried. 'Once the fellow comes to England he will be at our mercy. Then I shall insist on his obeying my will.'

'You think the King of France will allow that, Henry?'

'The King of France!' Henry's face grew a shade more scarlet. There was no name in Christendom that angered him more than that one. 'Nay, sister,' he went on, giving her a baleful look which was alarming when she considered how much she hoped for from him, 'I do not consider the wishes of the King of France. I will instruct my Lord Cardinal how he is to treat Master Albany when he sets foot in my realm.'

'You will act with your usual wisdom, Henry,' answered Margaret, 'but I do not think that, when Albany considers this matter, he will come to your Court. He is a shrewd man.'

'I shall couch my invitation in honeyed words,' retorted Henry.

Margaret was right and Albany did not come to England. Instead he sent as his emissary a certain François de la Fayette, who promised that if Margaret would return to Scotland she should have her dowry returned to her, and that her husband, Angus, and his clan should retain their privileges as Scottish subjects – providing they did not revolt against the government.

The terms seemed fair enough, thought Margaret; and as that year passed she began to feel homesick for Scotland. She wanted to see her son; she was anxious to be with Angus again; she was not sure of her feelings for him and although she did not think of him very tenderly, she wanted to be in his company again so that she could analyse her emotions. Moreover, Albany would be there; she told herself that she hated that man, but she thought of him often and had a great desire to come face-to-face with him. Often when his name was mentioned she would abuse him, calling him the murderer of her child; but secretly she did not believe this.

Albany was a Royal Stuart; and ever since she had met her first husband, she had been fascinated by that clan. She wanted to see Albany again, to live close to him; perhaps to discover her true feelings regarding him.

Henry had put at Margaret's service that palace known as Scotland Yard, which was the residential quarters of the Kings of Scotland when visiting London. From the bay windows of the Queen's Treasury she could look out on the river. Not far away was Charing Cross and the Palace of Westminster where the Court was in residence.

Christmas was almost upon her and it was more than a year since she had left Scotland. Young Margaret, now over a year old, was a lively little girl with a personality of her own; it seemed long to be away from home.

Moreover she was in financial distress. She needed money for servants and for gowns since Henry still insisted that the entertainments he gave were in her honour, and she could not attend them wearing garments which had been seen many times before.

She had no recourse but to turn to Cardinal Wolsey and plead for money, which she found very humiliating; but she pointed out that if she could not get it from the Cardinal she must needs approach the King, and that she asked only for loans as, when she regained what was hers, she would pay back all that she had borrowed.

And although she did succeed in getting a portion of the money for which she asked, and that meant that she had more fine gowns which could always put her in good spirits, still she thought with nostalgia of Scotland.

'James will forget his mother,' she told her friends, 'if he does not see her soon. He is over-young for such a long separation.'

She did not mention Angus but she wondered what he was doing during her absence. She did hear that he had entered into an alliance with Albany and was working with him.

There was news too of Albany himself. His wife's health had grown worse since her husband's stay in Scotland and she was said to be dying. Albany, who wanted to be with her, had stood up in the Tolbooth when Parliament was assembled there and explained with anguish his desire to be at the bedside of his wife.

'There is a husband a woman would be glad to have!' sighed Margaret, for how could she help comparing such devotion with the desertion of Angus who had left her when he thought her to be on the point of death?

But the Scots could not let Albany go at this point and, although it was agreed that he should return to France, it was pointed out that he must only go when the affairs of Scotland permitted.

So Albany remained in Scotland and Margaret continued to think yearningly of that land.

Christmas had come and was celebrated at Greenwich.

There must be entertainments in honour of his sister, declared Henry, for it seemed she would not be with them much longer.

So Margaret sat in state with her brother, sister, and sister-in-law while an artificial garden was wheeled into the great hall. It was, Henry whispered to them, keeping his eyes on Margaret all the time to make sure she was suitably impressed 'the Garden of Esperance'.

At each of the four corners of this contraption was a tower, and the banks of the 'garden' were covered with artificial flowers made of coloured silks and brocades and leaves of green satin. In the centre was a pillar set with jewels, and above it was a gilded arch of red and white roses. In the centre of the arch was a huge posy combined of roses, marguerites, marigolds, and pomegranates. And in the garden sat twelve beautifully attired men with twelve women; and when the garden had been wheeled before the dais on which sat the King with his Queen and sisters, the men and women stepped from the garden and danced a ballet.

Margaret clapped her hands with glee and declared that she had never seen anything so exquisite!

'Nor will you in Scotland,' Henry told her with deep satisfaction.

No, she thought, but for all that I would as lief be there. I wonder how James has grown. I wonder what Angus is doing. I wonder if Albany is preparing to depart.

❀ ❀ ❀

The winter had passed in revelries and the spring had now arrived.

Margaret had decided that in clement May she would set out on her journey to Scotland.

'Then,' cried Henry, 'we must have some entertainments as a farewell. I would like them to be elegant and brilliant, so that when you are in Scotland you will remember how we manage such matters here in England.'

'You are very good to me,' Margaret told him.

'Ah, and ready to be more so, my dear sister. When you are back in Scotland you must see that that villain Albany is sent back where he belongs. He's a servant of the French King, and it's a scandal to have him there where you should be.'

Margaret feigned agreement which she did not feel. She was hoping now that when she returned to Scotland she would have an opportunity of speaking with Albany, of trying to make some terms with him.

It was while she was preparing to leave that the riot of the apprentices broke out in London. This was a revolt of

Londoners against the foreign workers in their city; and houses were sacked and burned. The attack was particularly vicious against Spanish merchants living in London; it was said that since there had been a Spanish queen sharing the throne, these people had been particularly favoured, and in such a manner as to jeopardise the livelihood of the English. The foreigners seemed to want to do nothing but work; the English like to work for a while and then enjoy themselves. Thus the foreigners prospered more than the natives, which caused great irritation that came to a head on that day which was afterward known as Evil May Day.

The Duke of Norfolk came to London to quell the revolt. Thomas More, who had been under-sheriff of the city, risked his life to plead with the mob for tolerance towards the foreigners, pointing out that they could only bring trouble on themselves. Henry kept away from London; he hated any show of disapproval among his subjects; and although he was ready to take off the head of any member of his Court who did such a thing, he quailed before the mob. On that sad day 278 youths were taken prisoner, some mere boys of twelve or fourteen, and throughout the city gibbets were erected as a dreadful warning to any other subjects who were considering revolt against the King's peace.

This put an end to the festivities for Margaret's departure; she heartily wished that she had left London before she had had to encounter the sight of those gallows and the wailing women who called in the streets for mercy on their young sons.

She guessed that in his wrath Henry would be terrible; and she was right.

Katharine and Mary came to her apartments, and they could talk of nothing but this melancholy event.

Katharine, the gentler of the two, was very upset. 'Mothers are sending petitions to me imploring me to plead with the King. It saddens me so. But what can I do? Henry will not listen to me.'

Mary shook her head sadly. 'Henry is determined on vengeance. He has said that an example must be made and he is not inclined to show mercy.'

'Is there nothing we can do?' asked Margaret. 'What if we three went together and pleaded for those boys? Henry loves to grant such requests.'

Yes, she thought, it reminds him of his power over us all.

'If it were in public . . .' mused Mary, who understood her brother even better than Margaret. She stood up suddenly and laughed. 'I have a plan. He will come to Westminster Hall to pass judgement; it will be a ceremonious occasion. The Cardinal, the Council, the Mayor and Aldermen will be with him; and so shall we, for you know how he likes to have us with him. Now if, when all are assembled, we take off our headdresses, let our hair fall about our shoulders and throw ourselves on our knees . . . Why, don't you see . . . ?'

'It would be as effective as a masque,' agreed Margaret.

On the high dais in the hall of Westminster sat the King; with him was the great Cardinal Wolsey whose magnificence and pomp rivalled that of Henry; there were the Council, the Mayor, and the Aldermen; and seated with the King and his family – his wife and two sisters.

Then into the hall the prisoners were brought – they were mostly youths, but there were some old men among them and even a few women. They looked wretched, dirty, and hopeless, bound by ropes with halters about their necks. Outside their families clustered, and the sounds of their weeping could be heard within. The ringleaders of the revolt had already been punished and were at this time hanging by their necks from the signposts outside their masters' dwellings; it seemed more than likely that the miserable prisoners would have met the same end before nightfall.

Henry stared angrily at the prisoners, his face scarlet, his frown so deep that his blue eyes were almost lost in the plump flesh about them.

The Cardinal had asked the King to show mercy on these prisoners, the majority of whom were little more than children, but Henry sullenly replied that the peace of his city had been violated and he could not tolerate such conduct; example must be made; he would have the citizens see what happened to those who defied the King's law.

But it was clear to Margaret watching, that Henry was not as angry as he wished it to be believed; he was playing a part now as he loved to do in the masques: the great King, all powerful and terrible . . . yet ready to be moved to mercy.

Mary met her eye. It was the signal. They took off the headdresses which confined their hair, and it fell about their shoulders. The three of them were noted for their beautiful hair.

The King looked startled as they threw themselves at his feet and weeping asked him to show mercy on the prisoners. He stared sternly at those beautiful bowed heads for some seconds before he allowed his face to soften. Then the frown left his face and the little eyes shone bright blue.

'Aye,' he murmured, 'they are indeed young. And how could I refuse to tender mercy when beseeched in such a manner?'

There was a silence in the hall, but it only lasted for a few seconds. Then the prisoners, understanding, took their halters from their necks and tossed them into the air.

The three Queens rose to their feet. Margaret and Mary were smiling at each other; but Katharine was weeping.

It is true, thought Margaret, that it is like a masque!

The farewells had been said and Margaret had started on her journey north. It was pleasant travelling through the green English country in the early summer days, and Margaret would have been in no hurry had she not so longed to see her son. She was excited too at the prospect of reunion with Angus; her feelings had changed towards him; she had often told herself during the last year that had he been with her she might not have passed such carefree days; but all the same she could not suppress her excitement as she came nearer to the Border. She was thinking too of Albany and wondering whether she might not make some terms with him; and contemplating such interviews gave the same lifting of her spirits as she felt at the prospect of meeting her husband again.

When she reached the city of York which greeted her with as much pomp on her return from the English Court as it had when she had passed through on her journey towards it, she found that a servant of Albany's was staying there. This was Gaultier de Malines, and Margaret sent for him and asked him if he had news of his master.

'Yes, Your Grace, my master has departed for France after a long delay. He sailed from Dumbarton on the eighth day of June.'

'And my son the King?'

'He is well and happy, Your Grace; and since it was known that you were returning to Scotland he has been moved from Stirling to Edinburgh where he has his apartments in David Tower.'

'Ah! So he is well and happy. I rejoice. I hope soon to see him.'

It was good news; but she was a little sorry that Albany had returned to France. Not that she would betray this to anyone, for indeed, she only half admitted it to herself.

She learned that, before leaving, Albany had appointed a Regency which consisted of the Archbishops of St Andrews and Glasgow and the Earls of Angus, Arran, Huntley, and Argyle with the Sieur de la Bastie who would of course guard his, Albany's, interests.

Margaret was glad that Angus formed part of that company although it did mean that after her departure to England he had thrown in his lot with Albany. Perhaps it would have been foolish of him to have accompanied her to England; perhaps he was growing up to wisdom. But how much more contented she would have been if he had thrown aside everything to be with her, as she had when she had chosen to marry him.

And when she passed over the Border, there was Angus waiting to greet her – as he had been ordered to do by the Council – and when she saw him she forgot her disappointment. He was as handsome as ever, although he had aged a little. He was no longer a boy, having lost some of his innocent looks, but he was her Angus and still the most handsome man in Scotland.

Impulsive and warmhearted as she was, she thrust aside all rancour. Let them have done with the past. There he was, come to meet her, to welcome her back to Scotland.

He rode away from his men towards her, and she too advanced ahead of her party.

'Margaret—' he began.

But she interrupted: 'Oh, my dearest, how long it has seemed without you!'

The smile that touched his lips was one of relief, but she did not notice this; she only saw that he was smiling at her, that his eyes were warm with admiration, for the year of luxury had restored all her vitality and she was young and beautiful again.

She held out her hand; he took it and his lips were warm against her skin.

'You are pleased to see me?' she asked.

He lifted his eyes to her face and it seemed to her that words were unnecessary.

So together they began the journey to the capital, and in those first days of reunion she did not notice that there was something sheepish in his manner; that often he failed to meet her eye.

She was happy to be back, for soon, she promised herself, she would see her little son. Angus was with her, her dear husband who had made his mistakes and was sorry for them.

Her friends wondered how long it would be before she discovered Angus's secret; and those who loved her, trembled for her, because they knew how great her grief would be.

Chapter IX

THE UNFAITHFUL HUSBAND

It was of paramount importance to Margaret that she should see her son as soon as possible, and she lost no time in making her intentions clear.

This had been expected and the lords of the Council had prepared themselves for it. It had been arranged that young James should be well guarded in Edinburgh Castle and that three Lords – Erskine, Ruthven, and Borthwick – were to take it in turns to live with him there as his guardian, each doing this service for four months of the year. The castellan, Sir Patrick Crichton, ordered twelve guards to watch each night outside the King's bedchamber; and there were guards placed at all salient points, while a master gunner with six cannons was stationed on the walls. The Abbot of Holyrood had his quarters in the outer castle as an added precaution; and before anyone was allowed to enter the King's apartments he or she had first to receive permission from the castellan to do so.

Thus when Margaret arrived at Edinburgh she was at first denied admittance. This infuriated her but, longing as she did to see her son, she restrained her anger and pleaded with his guardians that she was his mother and had been long without a sight of him.

'Take me at once to the castellan,' she pleaded.

She was taken to Sir Patrick Crichton, who was very uneasy.

'Your Grace,' he said, 'I have my orders. I regret that they must be enforced even against you, but I fear I must do my duty.'

'I am the King's mother,' Margaret retorted, 'and I demand to see him.'

'Your Grace, I cannot allow you to enter the castle accompanied by so many attendants. Only twelve may enter and only four of those accompany you to the King's apartments.'

Margaret flushed with anger but, determined to see her son, she again forced herself to control her feelings.

'Very well then,' she said, 'it shall be as you say. Now, I pray you, take me to my son.'

She stood on the threshold of the apartment looking at him. He was sitting with David Lindsay and David was instructing him in playing the lute.

James stared at her for a few moments while David Lindsay rose to his feet.

'Your Grace . . .' he began.

But James had dashed at her. 'Davie,' he cried, 'it is my mother. At last she has come.'

Then he threw himself into her arms.

She embraced him, kissing and holding him as though she would never let him go, while the tears fell from her eyes on to his tawny curls.

She saw David Lindsay wipe a tear from his eye and she smiled up at him.

'Oh, Davie,' she cried, 'it is good to be here.'

Although Margaret was allowed to see her son, she was not permitted to spend a night in the castle. These were uneasy days made pleasant only by the company of her son and little daughter. She was beginning to notice a change in Angus and, guessing that his conscience troubled him for some reason, she believed this to be due to the friendship he had shown to Albany during her absence. Of course that created a rift between them; how could it be otherwise?

But the days spent at the castle brought her great contentment. James was a son of whom any mother would be proud. Every day she saw his father in him. There was intelligence in the blue-grey eyes; his abundant hair with more than a dash of red in it framed a face that was pleasant to look at; his nose would be aquiline when he grew up, Margaret decided, and it seemed likely that he would be another such as his father. She smiled to think of the jealousy his wife would feel; she would sympathise with her when the time came. Who could understand more than one who had suffered it all before? His tutors were delighted with his sharp wits; and besides David Lindsay, Gavin Dunbar, John Bellenden, and James Inglis all supervised his education.

But it was David Lindsay whom the young King loved more than any of his other tutors; this was probably because David was more of a playfellow than a tutor. David made himself the most exciting of companions; and to see them together was to be given the illusion that they were of an age.

David's one idea was to make a man of the King and, even when James had been little more than a baby, he had dressed up as a grisly ghost to teach him never to be afraid, but to investigate any strange phenomenon and so discover the truth beneath it.

David was succeeding admirably.

But although she was allowed to see her son frequently, Margaret greatly desired to take part in his upbringing. David commiserated with her.

'They'll always suspect Your Grace of trying to take him away from Scotland, down to your brother's Court,' he told her. 'You tried once, and they think you'll try again.'

Margaret agreed; and she thought: Aye and I would, given the opportunity.

One day when Margaret arrived at the Castle, she was met at the outer gate by the Abbot of Holyrood.

'Your Grace,' he cried, 'you must not enter the Castle.'

'Why not?' she demanded.

'A child belonging to one of the attendants has the botch.'

'The botch!' Margaret cried in horror, visualising the beautiful skin of her son covered in unsightly boils and swellings. 'Not . . . James?'

'Nay, Your Grace, as soon as it was discovered that there was a case of botch in the Castle he was taken at once to Craigmillar Castle where he is now under the guardianship of Lord Erskine.'

Margaret turned to her companions.

'We are going at once to Craigmillar,' she said.

Lord Erskine made no attempt to prevent the Queen from visiting James at Craigmillar, which was only three miles from Edinburgh. It was strongly fortified but by no means the fortress that the Castle was. As she rode towards it and studied the lofty square keep, Margaret could not help thinking that it would be easier to bring James out of Craigmillar than out of Edinburgh Castle.

James was delighted with the move, as he was growing tired of living so long in David's Tower at the Castle; and Lord Erskine was a lenient guardian.

If only, thought Margaret, Angus were not so strange. If only his aims were the same as mine!

There was no one to whom she could talk of her desires except David Lindsay; and when she hinted to him that she would like to have her son completely in her care, he was horrified at what an attempt to abduct him might mean.

'Your Grace,' he said, 'if you took the child away from his guardians and carried him into England, many a lord would declare the time had come to dethrone James and crown Albany King.'

Margaret pondered this. It might be so. And although she was ready to forgo the right to rule, for the sake of having her family about her, she could not allow James's future to be jeopardised.

She was suspected of plotting to carry him off, and when certain members of the Council heard how frequently she was permitted to enter Craigmillar Castle, they declared it was time James was brought back to Edinburgh.

No sooner was the city pronounced free of the botch than James was hurried back to his old quarters.

This was not the way, reasoned Margaret. While she visited James she would be watched and every movement she made would be suspect. She had once tried to abduct him and carry him to England, and they were expecting her to do the same again.

She decided then to leave Edinburgh and go to her Castle of Newark in Ettrick Forest and there quietly plan her next move.

She believed that, with Angus to help her, she could regain the Regency and the right to be the guardian of her own child.

She wanted to confide in Angus but something in herself prevented her from doing this. Since she had been back in Scotland their life together had been very uneasy. He made excuses to absent himself from her for long periods. He had his estates to look after, he told her; and he was constantly engaged in the work of the Council.

She realised that he had grown up during the year she had been away. He had made a niche for himself in the affairs of Scotland, and was quite clearly recognised to be a figure of importance. Arran's hatred of him was enough to show that, if nothing else.

She must be reasonable. They must work together, for then they would have a good chance of success.

An event occurred which gave her an idea that she might put an important post in the way of Angus. That should please him and show him that he could lose nothing by confiding in and working with his wife.

The post of Warden of the Marches had been bestowed on his good friend the Sieur de la Bastie by Albany before leaving for France; a reward to a friend who had rendered him good service more than once.

Albany – and de la Bastie – could have had little knowledge of the wild Bordermen; otherwise the former might have thought twice before offering such a gift, and the latter before accepting it.

Lord Home and his brother William had mortally offended

Albany and, although he had forgiven them again and again, at length he had decided to do so no more, and had ordered them to be executed. It was thus that the post of Warden of the Marches had fallen vacant.

Home was a turncoat, a wild and arrogant man; but he was a Borderer and, although the Border barons fought each other, they did not care to see one whom they considered a foreigner pass the death sentence on one of their kind. Moreover the Home clan considered it a duty to avenge their leader. Thus when de la Bastie went to the Border to carry out his duties he was set upon and murdered.

This meant that the post of Deputy Governor which had been de la Bastie's was vacant.

Why should not Angus fill it? Margaret asked herself. Then, with Angus as Deputy Governor, it would not be difficult for her to regain her old influence, for her husband would surely support her.

She laid this suggestion before the Parliament.

They would not consider it for a moment.

❀ ❀ ❀

Disconsolate and lonely – Angus was away, engaged on one of his numerous duties – Margaret brooded on the estate to which she was reduced. She was too impulsive where her emotions were involved. She knew this but she could not restrain herself. How could she sit alone at Newark, brooding on the fact that she was not allowed to direct the upbringing of her own son; that when she – the Queen – suggested a post should be bestowed, she was ignored?

As always at such times she found pleasure in making wild plans.

James was the centre of these plans.

He was back in Edinburgh Castle and it was going to be difficult to get him out of that fortress, but she was not one to consider impossible that which was difficult.

Then she remembered that one of her husband's brothers, George Douglas, was the Warden of the Castle.

Now the days had some meaning. George Douglas was eager to serve his Queen and sister-in-law.

He wrote to her. Yes, as Warden he had a certain power within the Castle. He had access of course to David's Tower, and could give her news from time to time of the King. He implied that he knew it was more than news she wanted; and he was ready to help give her that too.

'Dear George Douglas!' she murmured.

She was determined to be careful. She would take no one into her confidence, and was rather glad that Angus was away because it would have been difficult to keep this secret from him.

She might do what she had intended to do before she went into England. That had been a good enough plan. If only Lord Home had been able to divert the attention of the guards he would have rescued the two princes.

Then, she thought angrily, I should have had two sons today, for I am sure my little Alexander would not have died if he had been with his mother.

It was pleasant there at Newark, making plans, waiting for the secret messenger from George Douglas, assuring herself that she could not be unlucky this time.

Perhaps they could substitute another child for James. It would not be discovered until they were away . . . almost at the

Border. Henry would be eager to welcome his dear sister and her little son who was so like himself. Perhaps James would marry the little Princess Mary; then Henry could be relied on to send an army to Scotland, subdue her enemies and place James securely on the throne, there to rule, when he was of an age to do so, with Mary beside him; but in the meantime his mother would be the Regent of Scotland and the guardian of her son.

It was a pleasant dream. To make it come true she would need all the money on which she could lay her hands.

The forest of Ettrick itself yielded four hundred marks a year, which was no mean sum. She wondered how much of it had come in, and sent for her steward.

When the man stood before her and she made known the reason she had sent for him, he seemed surprised.

'Your Grace,' he said, 'the rents have been collected and given to my lord Angus in accordance with his instructions.'

She studied the papers which he had given her, and all the time her anger was rising. How dared Angus appropriate this money! There should have been a goodly sum accumulated by now and she needed it badly.

'I see,' she said; and dismissed her steward.

When she was alone she paced up and down the room. Where was Angus? He must come to her at once. She needed an explanation.

She sent for a man who had been in attendance on her husband.

'Urgent business has arisen,' she told him. 'I need the immediate presence of my lord Angus. Do you know where he is?'

The man hesitated and his furtive looks alarmed Margaret.

'Come,' she said testily, 'where is he?'

'Your Grace . . . I cannot say. I do not know . . .'

She thought: He knows and he is lying.

She wanted to command him to answer, to threaten him with a whipping if he did not speak.

But no, she thought. Let it wait. I will think on this; and I shall discover all in good time.

That very day news was brought to her which made her forget temporarily Angus's perfidy over the rents of Ettrick.

A messenger had arrived from Edinburgh and asked to be taken immediately to the Queen.

He fell at her feet breathless, travel-stained from the journey.

'Your Grace, the Warden of Edinburgh Castle has been arrested and thrown into prison.'

She stood still, her eyes half closed. Another scheme foiled!

She said quietly: 'Why so?'

'Sir Patrick Crichton declared he could not hold himself responsible for the King's safety unless the Warden was removed. He had discovered an intrigue . . .'

She did not need to ask what. She knew.

'So he is no longer at the Castle, Your Grace, and the Earl of Arran has been set up in his place.'

Margaret did not speak. She was thinking: Did ever a woman have such ill luck as I?

Where was Angus? Never with me, she thought, when I need him.

No wonder he seemed guilty. How dared he appropriate the

rents which were hers? Because she had married him, did he think he could rule her . . . the Queen!

She sent for the servant to whom she had spoken before. 'I believe you know the whereabouts of my lord Angus,' she said. 'I command you to tell me what you know.'

'Y-your Grace . . .' stammered the man. 'I know nothing.'

'I will have the truth!'

The man had turned pale but he did not speak.

Wearily she studied him. What was the use of venting her anger on one who was merely trying to be loyal to his master?

She dismissed the man and for some days she was sunk in despair. Her plot with George Douglas was known – to his cost, and to hers most likely. They would watch her more closely than ever. They would probably prevent her from seeing her son.

She felt desperate and alone.

Then Angus returned. As soon as he came into her presence she opened her attack.

'You have been long absent, my lord.'

'I had business to attend to.'

He came to her and placing his hands on her shoulders, drew her towards him, but she withdrew herself impatiently.

'There are certain matters I wish to discuss with you. First . . . the rents of Ettrick.'

A faint colour showed under his skin. 'What of these?'

'I think you are aware of my meaning. I have discovered that these have been passing to you.'

'And why should they not?'

'Because they do not belong to you.'

'You once said that you would give me all I desired.'

She laughed bitterly. 'That was long ago. You once said that you would always be faithful to me.'

Had she not been so angry she would have noticed the apprehension leap into his eyes.

'And,' she went on, 'I shall never forget how you deserted me when you believed me to be dying, how you ran as hard as you could to make sure of a welcome in the opposite camp. And now I discover that during my absence you have appropriated money which belongs to me.'

'I am sure you gave me Ettrick in those early days,' he mumbled.

'I should have remembered,' she said. 'I remember too much of those early days. I know now how ready you are to deceive and desert me, that you give your allegiance to others.'

He misunderstood her, believing her to have discovered more than she had.

He muttered: 'I was betrothed to her before we married.'

'Betrothed,' she murmured.

'I would have married her,' he went on sullenly, 'had I not been forced to marry you.'

She thought she must be dreaming. What was he talking about? Betrothed? Forced to marry?

'So,' she said, 'these absences of yours . . .'

'Of course. What do you expect? You ran away, did you not? What was I supposed to do all that time?'

'Some husbands would have accompanied their wives,' she retorted, but she was not thinking of what she said; she was trying to grasp his meaning.

'Most husbands,' he replied, 'are masters in their own houses.'

'Not all aspire to marriage with a queen,' was her proud answer.

'In which case they may call themselves lucky.'

He was off his guard now. She would get the truth of what lay behind this. 'How long has she been your mistress?' she hazarded.

'Since you went into England.'

'I see,' she said bitterly. 'And I'll dare swear all the Court is aware of this.'

'There are always gossips.'

'And it seems this time there is strong foundation on which to base the gossip.'

'What did you expect?' he cried.

'Fidelity!' she answered. 'Respect. Gratitude for all I have done for your family. Affection for your wife and daughter.'

'I look upon her as a wife, and I have given her daughter my name.'

Margaret could find no words to express her grief and rage. She felt as though she had lived through this scene before. She was back in those early days of her marriage with James when she had discovered that he had illegitimate children. She remembered the pain of discovering that he chose the society of other women in preference to hers.

Why must I suffer this disillusion twice? she asked herself. Why must my second husband treat me as did my first!

She looked at him – the handsome Angus with whom she had planned to live in love all her life. She felt cheated now as she never had when he had deserted her at Morpeth.

She could see it all so clearly; his betrothal to a woman with whom he was in love; the pressure of his family when it was known that the Queen delighted in him; his reluctant agreement to follow the wishes of his family and his Queen.

It was too humiliating to be borne.

'Leave me,' she cried. 'I would be alone.'

❀ ❀ ❀

So now she had the details. He had been betrothed to Lady Jane Stuart, the daughter of the Lord of Traquair; he had deserted her to marry the Queen, but he had never forgotten her, and when his wife left Scotland he made haste to rejoin Lady Jane. He took her away from her family; he insisted that she travel with him wherever he went, as though she were his wife; and her family made no protest. This was not merely Archibald Douglas who had made their daughter Jane his mistress; it was the Earl of Angus, the husband of the Queen.

Jane had borne him a daughter who was known as the Lady Jean Douglas, and it seemed that her mother, and he too, would make this child's position comparable with that of his daughter born in wedlock to the Queen, the Lady Margaret Douglas.

This was not to be tolerated.

Then she made up her mind what she would do.

Angus had been betrothed to Jane Stuart before his marriage to the Queen. Could this be grounds for divorce?

Very soon the news was out, as she intended it should be.

The Queen no longer lives with Angus; she is contemplating divorce.

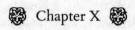

Chapter X

MARGARET AND ALBANY

James Hamilton, Earl of Arran, was on his way to see the Queen. Arran was a proud man; through his mother, Princess Mary, the daughter of James II, he had royal blood in his veins and he never forgot it. It was for this reason that he had been so angered to see the rise of the Douglases through the Queen's marriage with Angus. That he, Arran, who might become a claimant to the throne of Scotland, should have to take second place to that pretty boy was unendurable. There was one person in Scotland whom Arran hated above all others, and that was Angus.

Thus when he heard of the friction between the Queen and her husband he hastened to plead for an interview with Margaret, that he might place himself and his power at her disposal. He was ready to stake his future on this; and he was determined that if she wanted a divorce from Angus she should know that all the influence of the Hamiltons was behind her.

Margaret received the Earl who wasted no time in opening up the subject which was of such importance to them both.

'I come to commiserate with Your Grace,' he told her, 'and to place myself at your service.'

'I thank you, my lord.'

She signed for him to be seated and she marvelled that a man who was an enemy one day seemed to become a friend the next.

'It is a matter for rejoicing among those who are Your Grace's friends that you should have decided to cast off the Douglas. Madam, we have long been aware of his unworthiness.'

'I alas have remained blind too long,' answered Margaret; at which Arran bowed his head in assent.

'But now,' went on Margaret, 'I see him for what he is and, believe me, my lord, I shall not rest until I can no longer call myself his wife.'

'A divorce should be arranged with all speed. The Douglases should be stripped of the power which came to them through this marriage.'

Margaret looked at him and smiled wryly, thinking: That it may be bestowed on the Hamiltons?

Hamiltons, Douglases, Hepburns, Homes – they were all ambitious men, all seeking favours which would strengthen their families and make their clans the strongest in the land. Still, she must try to look to her own advantage as they did to theirs. The Hamiltons were certainly one of the most powerful families in Scotland, and Arran stood at their head. She must use them as they would, if they had the opportunity, use her.

She, who could love fiercely, could hate with the same passion; and now, almost as great as her desire to have the care of her son, was that to rid herself of the husband who had put her in the difficult position she now occupied, and then had rewarded her with his infidelity.

'There is little opposition in the land against the suggested divorce?' she asked.

'There is great rejoicing, Your Grace.'

Yes, she thought, among the Douglases' enemies. She could imagine the consternation the matter would have brought about in her husband's family.

'Why, Your Grace,' went on Arran, 'when you are free of the Douglases, I doubt not that your friends will wish to see you restored to that position which was yours before the unfortunate marriage. I have discussed the matter with the Earl of Lennox who is of my mind; and the Bishops of Galloway and Argyle are as eager to see the bond between you and Angus severed. Your Grace would find yourself supported by many powerful friends.'

'I find that reassuring,' answered Margaret.

'Have no fear, Your Grace. This is the best step you have taken since you entered into that marriage; and in truth I come on behalf of your friends to tell you of the pleasure this has given them.'

They talked awhile of the affairs of Scotland, and Arran asked after the health of the little Lady Margaret Douglas.

Margaret, who could never resist showing her pride in her children, sent for the child that Arran might see for himself what a bonny creature she was.

Arran confessed himself delighted and charmed; and when little Margaret had left them he began to talk of his son with deep affection – and Margaret sensed the implication behind his words. He was telling her that his James, who would one day be Earl of Arran, had the blood of Royal Stuart in his veins; and since one day it would be necessary to find a husband for the Lady Margaret Douglas, the son of Arran should not be considered unworthy.

Margaret allowed him to see that she had grasped his point and was not displeased by it.

When Arran left her Margaret congratulated herself that with the influential lords to back her she stood a very good chance of regaining the Regency, which would mean control of her son; as for Arran, he saw in this the downfall of his enemy Angus.

There were two factions in Scotland now, one under Arran, the other under Angus. The Douglases rallied to the support of the head of their House, and among them were men made influential by the honours Margaret herself had showered on them at the time of her infatuation with her husband.

It was believed by many that the return of Albany was imperative to restore order; and news was carried to him of the trouble between two of the most powerful families in the land and of the Queen's determination to divorce her husband; moreover the suggestion of a betrothal of Margaret's daughter and Arran's son was alarming, for it could unite Douglases and Hamiltons against him.

But the political position had changed, because there was now a rapprochement between France and England. François and Henry had decided to meet and were making preparations for the Field of the Cloth of Gold; and Henry's daughter, the Princess Mary, had been betrothed to the Dauphin. Although François wished Albany to return to Scotland in order to safeguard French interests, he knew that Henry was eager that the Duke should remain in France. It was not the moment to antagonise Henry.

Meanwhile the news of Margaret's intentions to divorce Angus reached the English Court.

Henry grew scarlet when he read his sister's letter.

He could not believe it. He went to his wife's apartment, his eyes ablaze, and signed to her women to depart. Katharine, terrified at his appearance, hurried to him and begged him to tell her what ill news he brought.

'T-that a sister of mine,' he stuttered, 'could so far forget her duty . . . her honour . . . to suggest such an action!'

'Your Grace, Mary . . .'

'Nay, not Mary. Margaret. Listen to this: "I am sore troubled with my lord Angus, since my last coming into Scotland, and every day more and more so. We have not been together these last months . . ."' Henry stopped; it was as though the words choked him.

Katharine said gently: 'Alas, so she is not happy in her marriage. Poor Margaret! I am sorry for her.'

'Whether she be happy or not, it is not for her to talk of . . . divorce!'

'Divorce!' cried Katharine, and she began to tremble with horror.

'I said divorce. Angus does not please her so, look you, she plans to divorce him. She will dishonour her marriage vows. She will disgrace us all. A sister of mine to talk of divorce!'

'Oh, Henry, we must persuade her how wrong this is.'

'Persuade her! I shall forbid her. I shall make her see her duty to her family – if she has so far forgotten her duty to God and the Church. I'll not have divorce in my family, I do assure you. No, Kate, you will sit down and write to her at once. And so shall I. You will tell her how she has wounded you, shocked you beyond belief. While I . . . I will remind her that I am the King of a great country, and not only that, the head of a great House. There shall be no divorce in my family. I'll not stomach the disgrace.'

'Henry, how right you are . . . as always. Divorce! It is too dishonourable to be thought of.'

'Go to, Kate. Write to her, and I will do the same. Then our letters shall be sent by special messenger, that she may profit from them and put an end to this disgraceful plan before it goes too far.'

❀ ❀ ❀

When Margaret read the letters from her brother and sister-in-law she shrugged aside their advice. It was all very well for them to be so self-righteous; they did not know what it meant to be entangled in an undesirable alliance.

She was surprised that she could hate anyone as fiercely as she now hated Angus. There was anger against herself in that hatred. How could she have been so foolish as to lose all sense of proportion merely because of a momentary infatuation for a handsome boy?

How different had been her first marriage. James had at times humiliated her, but in public he had constantly shown her respect. She remembered how he had always uncovered his head in her presence. He only asked that she accept his infidelities which, being the sensual man he was, he could not curb. He would never have deserted her when she was dying. And he had conducted his love affairs with a certain dignity. He had tried to make up for his shortcomings by giving her extra pleasure; Angus had stolen her rents.

She hated Angus and, even if she had to admit that this was largely because he was a living reminder of her own folly and the source of all her troubles, that did not make her hate him less.

There was one who reminded her a little of her first husband; that was Albany. They had some quality, these

Stuarts, which was unique. No, she had never seen others with quite the same charm of manner. James had had it to a large degree; Albany slightly less; but he was certainly a charming, courteous man.

If one were a queen it was necessary to marry wisely. Suppose she and Albany were free to marry – there could not be a wiser match in Scotland, for marriages were often the links which bound countries together, and made friends of enemies. A marriage between herself and Albany – and there would have been no conflict in Scotland; she would never have been cut off from her son; she and Albany would have been joint guardians of the young King. What a happy state of affairs compared with what now confronted her!

And was not too late to put matters right.

She was determined to divorce Angus no matter what difficulties were put in her way; and she was sure there would be difficulties. She could imagine her brother Henry sending off deputations to the Pope, asking him not to grant a divorce to his erring sister, for the sake of the honour of the Tudors. She would have to fight for her divorce; but she would get it in the end. And then if Albany's wife died – for how could she live long; the poor woman had been ailing for some time – he would be free too.

She closed her eyes and pictured him. Black eyes alive with passion. Poor man, married to a woman who for so long had been an invalid.

Arran was persuading her to join with those who were urging Albany to return, because Arran had long decided that when the Duke came to Scotland he would favour the Hamiltons and become the enemy of the Douglases.

She had listened thoughtfully to what Arran had to say;

she had nodded when he enumerated the reasons why the return of Albany would be good for Scotland. And all the time she had been thinking of him — black-eyed, black-bearded, the courteous knight with all the charm of his Stuart ancestors.

She said: 'I will write to Albany and join my pleas to yours. I think that he might be willing to help me in my divorce. He should stand well with Rome, as I believe his master does. Yes, my lord, I am convinced that you are right. Scotland needs Albany at this time.'

She thought: And it may be that Scotland's Queen does too.

It was not easy to obtain a divorce. There were too many people of influence who were against it. Time passed and still Margaret remained unsatisfactorily married to Angus.

Henry and Katharine had crossed the Channel and had had a meeting with the King of France in circumstances of most reckless extravagance, with each King trying to outdazzle the other.

François, mischievous in the extreme, using every means at his disposal to disconcert the King of England, having in his possession at this time the letter which Margaret had written to Albany, thought it would be amusing to show Henry how his sister was working against his wishes and was warmly inviting Albany back to Scotland.

Henry read the letter and quietly handed it back to the King, but when he was alone his choleric anger broke forth.

By God, he thought, this shall be the end of the help she gets from me. What has become of my sister! She shows herself to the world as a wanton. Divorce indeed! She disgraces the name of Tudor and then . . . she deceives her own brother by inviting his enemy to Scotland!

The Scottish matter rankled in his mind during all the balls and banquets, jousts and wrestling matches of that brilliant excursion.

He confided to his wife: 'When we return to England, you shall send a priest to Scotland. Choose him with care for I want him to impress upon my sister that if she persists in attempting to obtain this divorce from her lawful husband, she places her immortal soul in danger.'

Katharine replied that Henry as usual was right. There were few matters which could be so dishonourable, so lamentable as divorce.

❀ ❀ ❀

It was a summer's day when Father Bonaventura arrived in Scotland.

Margaret was then in Perth, and he travelled to her there. He was a gentle priest who had lived away from the world, and Margaret received him kindly when she heard that he had come from her sister-in-law, Queen Katharine.

'It is good of you to have made this long journey,' she told him. And when they were alone together she tried to impress on him that though she appreciated his good services, he was wasting his time if he thought to divert her from her purpose.

'I have come to pray with you,' he told her. 'Your Grace will find the answer to your problem in prayer.'

Margaret, who had never been deeply religious, was a little impatient; but she was courteous to the priest and told him gently that her mind was already made up.

Father Bonaventura tried to reason with her and she

continued to listen patiently, but he realised that he was making no headway and eventually, disappointed and reluctant, he prepared to leave.

Father Bonaventura had no sooner returned to London than Henry decided to send a man of his choosing. No gentle priest this, but a man whose preaching had often set sinners shivering with fear.

Henry Chadworth, Minister General of the Friar's Minor, was summoned to Henry's presence.

'You will go to the Queen of Scotland,' Henry told him, 'and not return until you have wrought in her a change of mind. Tell her that I shall not look on in silence and see a sister of mine lose her immortal soul. Tell her too that I shall hinder her cause in Rome and I shall let all know that those who help the Queen of Scotland to her divorce, help themselves to the enmity of the King of England. Now away with you, and . . . as you value my friendship, let nothing stand between you and your duty.'

Henry Chadworth set out for Scotland, fiery phrases revolving in his mind, determined that he would return in triumph to the English Court. Indeed, how dare he do otherwise?

❀ ❀ ❀

How the man ranted! Yet Margaret dared not further incense her brother by sending him away. There was a certain magnetism about him; perhaps this was because he appeared fervently to believe in the horrors which he said awaited the damned.

He stood before her, his eyes burning with fanaticism. 'Your immortal soul is in peril. Repent before it is too late.

Take this step, and you have bought eternal damnation. It is the Devil himself who is whispering in your ear.'

At first she closed her ears and thought of other things while he ranted on; but his picturesque descriptions of the fires of hell caught her imagination and she found herself involuntarily giving him her attention.

'Life on earth is short,' he thundered. 'It is the trial through which we all must pass to show ourselves worthy of eternal bliss or eternal damnation. Madam, your reputation is in danger; your soul is in danger. Think on these things before you are past redemption.'

She dreamed of the friar; his words haunted her nights. 'I come to warn you,' he had told her. 'For the sake of your comfort in this life and the next, pay heed to my words.'

And she found that she *was* paying heed to his words.

She dreaded his coming and yet found herself looking forward to it. She dreaded hearing his account of the torments which had been devised for the punishment of sinners; and she could not resist listening.

A month passed and still Henry Chadworth visited her each day; indeed his visits grew longer; and she did not seek to curtail them.

Two months after Henry Chadworth had come to Scotland he had achieved his end. Margaret agreed to return to Angus.

The Douglases were triumphant, the Hamiltons furious.

The Bishops of Galloway and Argyle came to Margaret accompanied by the Earls of Arran and Lennox.

'Your Grace cannot mean that you will so demean yourself by returning to Angus,' cried Arran.

'I have been persuaded that it is my duty to return to him,' answered Margaret.

It was difficult for Arran to restrain his wrath.

'Madam, this is the most foolish thing you ever did. Depend upon it, if you return to Angus you will never gain the guardianship of the King.'

'He is my husband,' was Margaret's retort. 'My duty lies with him. I must try to bear my troubles; and I have sent word to him that if he will give up his light behaviour and be a good husband to me, I will return to him.'

She appeared to be as fanatical as her brother's priest, who had already returned in triumph to his master.

Arran and his friends left her presence, cursing the folly of women and the power a priest could have over them. They would wage even fiercer warfare against the Douglases whom, they knew, were now chortling with glee while Angus wrote to his dear brother-in-law thanking him for his timely intervention in his matrimonial affairs.

❦ ❦ ❦

As Margaret was riding towards Edinburgh, which was in the possession of the Douglas faction, the words of Henry Chadworth were still ringing through her mind. She must be reconciled with the man she had married because, whatever he had done, he was still her husband and they were bound together until death parted them. She was apprehensive, wondering how they would greet each other, what their life could be together after all the wrong he had done her, after the abuse she had flung at him.

He met her, riding at the head of four hundred horses, and never had he looked so handsome. He had changed since she had seen him on the loch before Linlithgow Palace and had been struck by his beauty. He had become a man; and he was still the most handsome man in Scotland.

With him rode the Archbishop of St Andrews and the Bishops of Dunkeld, Aberdeen and Murray. The Earls Argyle, Huntley, Ruthven, Morton and Glencairn were also there with Lord Glamis who was Earl Marshal. A distinguished assembly, and she had to admit that none bore himself so well nor looked so fine a man as Angus.

He rode ahead of the party and she did the same. When they met he took her hand and kissed it.

'So, Margaret, we are to have another chance.'

'I have decided that we should make an effort to live happily together, since we are man and wife,' she answered.

'It shall be so,' he replied; and their two parties joined and followed them into the city.

For a week she believed she had recaptured to some extent the ecstasy of the honeymoon which they spent at Stobhall. How wrong she was, how easily deluded! Then she had believed in an ideal; there had been no doubts in her mind. She had believed then that his devotion to her had been as undivided as hers to him. After the first passionate days of reunion she began to picture him, indulging in similar passion with Jane Stuart. When their daughter was with them she pictured him with Jane and her little Jean. No, it was not possible to go back. She quickly began to realise that.

She soon discovered that he did not intend to alter his way of life, and was as devoted to Jane Stuart as he had ever been. He was not going to be denied her company. The inevitable scenes followed.

'I dare swear you have been visiting your mistress,' she taunted him, after one of his absences which hurt her the more because they reminded her of the deficiencies of her first husband.

'And if I have?' He was insolent, believing himself to be in command of her. He knew how the hellfire preacher had played upon her superstitions. She had returned to him because she was afraid of jeopardising her soul if she continued with her plan to divorce him.

'I came back to you on condition that you gave up your light living,' she answered.

He smiled. 'You came back because you feared to put your soul in danger by not doing so.'

'I could change my mind.'

'Your brother would not forgive you if you did.'

'I do not have to obey my brother.'

'You do not have to, but your wisdom tells you that it would be folly not to.'

'So you will not give up this woman?'

'Come, you take these matters too seriously. How many men in Scotland do you think there are who have a mistress or two besides a wife?'

'That may be so, but they are not married to the Queen of Scotland.'

'Should a man be penalised for marrying the Queen of Scotland?'

She saw that he had grown cynical.

She did not answer him, but she thought; I was a fool to take him back, and we cannot go on like this.

There were spies from the Arran faction in the Queen's household who watched how matters went, who listened at keyholes and secreted themselves in the Queen's apartment to discover how the reunion of Margaret and her husband was shaping. They had good news to send to their masters.

Arran laughed to himself. The reconciliation would not last. He knew Margaret well enough to realise that; she had been momentarily alarmed by the prophecies of the preacher, but she had never been superstitious, at heart, and she was tired of Angus.

One of the women said to the Queen when she was helping her dress: 'Your Grace, I heard from my brother who is with my Lord Arran, that his lordship is sorely grieved that he can no longer serve you.'

The woman had spoken so low that no one else in the apartment heard, and Margaret looked at her swiftly. She had not been long in her service and indeed had joined at that time when Margaret had been friendly with the Arran faction. Margaret wondered if this woman was a servant of Arran, as she admitted her brother was.

'He could serve if he wished,' she retorted. 'Alas, I fear he is my enemy.'

'He is ready to be your friend.'

'He has not always been a loyal servant,' Margaret retorted, turning away.

Margaret wondered how many of her servants carried news of her affairs to her enemies, and later that day she sent for the woman and made sure that when she came no one else was in the apartment but the two of them.

'Have you a message for me?' asked Margaret.

The woman looked surprised. 'Your Grace?'

'You spoke of a brother in the service of my Lord Arran.'

The woman flushed and murmured: 'Nay, Your Grace, I have no message.'

'Yet you brought one to me, this day.'

'I, Your Grace?'

'From your brother who is with the Earl of Arran.'

'Oh . . . 'twas naught, Your Grace. It was merely that . . .'

'Pray continue.'

'That I have seen the manner in which Your Grace is treated by my Lord Angus, and methought it was no way in which to treat a queen.'

Margaret's lips tightened a little and her eyes hardened. She was angry, but not with the woman. It was true; she was humiliated again and again. There was not a servant at her Court who did not know of her husband's intrigue with Jane Stuart, of the manner in which he ignored her wish that it should be discontinued.

She said impulsively: 'You have a brother in the service of the Earl of Arran. Doubtless you could pass a message to him which he in his turn could place in the Earl's hands.'

The woman caught her breath. 'I could do that, Your Grace.'

'Very well.' She went to her desk and wrote.

It was suppertime in Edinburgh Castle and Margaret sat with the lords of the Douglas faction while they were served, and the minstrels played softly as they ate.

She was trying to appear serene, but she felt far from that, as she looked about the table at those ambitious men. They were smug because they believed they had triumphed over their enemies, led by the Hamiltons; they were going to have a rude shock before the night was out.

But as yet they must suspect nothing; though it was difficult to act as though she was not all impatience to rise from the table.

There were six people besides herself in the secret . . . three men and three women; all her attendants. They too were alert, waiting for the signal.

Yet she must sit there as she would at any suppertime, listening to the music of the lute and the songs of the favourite singers.

At length she yawned and rose, and when one by one the lords took their leave of her, some of her women accompanied her to her bedchamber.

Seeming sleepy, she bade them good night; but no sooner had the door shut and their footsteps died away than she called to those three of her women – one of them that woman who had a brother in Arran's service – and said: 'Now. The time is come. Bring my riding gown and cloak; and we will escape.'

Her eyes were shining and she looked very young, for a plan such as this could always delight her and give life a new zest.

She had made up her mind that she had been a fool to come back to Angus, to place herself in the position of a deceived wife who must accept the vagaries of a husband. Master Chadworth could go to hell – a place with which he considered himself well acquainted by his accounts of it – for all she cared.

She had changed her mind. She would not stay with Angus; she was going to let the whole world know that she had too much pride to remain with an unfaithful husband who had gained his power through her. She had been forced to endure the unfaithfulness of James IV; but Angus was no Scottish King.

She was in her riding clothes and ready.

'Come,' she whispered. 'By the spiral stairway . . . down to the courtyard.'

One of her women led the way; she followed; the other two came behind.

In the courtyard the three men were waiting.

They led the way cautiously, to where, about a quarter of a mile from the castle, dark shapes were waiting under a clump of trees; Margaret heard the neighing of horses.

Then a voice: 'Your Grace, the Queen?'

'I am here,' she answered.

A man had ridden forward; he was leading a horse.

He dismounted, and taking her hand kissed it.

'James Hamilton,' he said, 'at Your Grace's service . . . now as ever.'

She saw his eyes gleam in the moonlight. He was tall, handsome and so like Arran that she guessed this was the son of the Earl – the natural son of whom she had heard and who was known as the Bastard of Arran.

He helped her mount and then, swinging himself into his saddle, brought his horse beside hers.

'Now,' he cried. 'Away!'

It was a glorious experience to be riding through the night, a handsome man beside her, whose every look and gesture assured her of his respect for the Queen, and his admiration for a beautiful woman.

'My father is waiting for you at Stirling,' he told her. 'I begged for the honour of taking you to him.'

''Twas well planned,' she told him.

'I have thought of nothing else since I knew you would come.'

'Then you are indeed my friend.'

'So much so, Your Grace, that I would willingly do murder for you.'

'Nay, do not talk of murder.'

'Thoughts of murder will enter the mind when rumours of the ill treatment of our Queen disturb it.'

'Ah . . . that is over.'

'Nay, I shall never forgive it, even if Your Grace does.'

She would not discuss her husband, and she was silent. Being quick to sense her mood, he too was silent and there was no sound but the padding of their horses' hoofs as they rode on to Stirling.

Yet memories of that night stayed with her. Arran's bastard during that ride made her feel young again, desirable, so that the wounds which she had suffered from the treatment of Angus – and perhaps that of her first husband – were soothed; and she began to think that perhaps one day she might find someone who would love her as a woman, not as a queen.

That person was not James Hamilton of course; but she would always be grateful to him for reminding her that such a person might exist.

❀ ❀ ❀

With the desertion of Margaret, Angus's position deteriorated, and Arran persuaded the Queen that the way in which she could best obtain her divorce was by joining her pleas to those of the lords who wished Albany to return to Scotland.

Margaret had her own reasons for wishing to see Albany in Scotland and she fell in with Arran's proposal, so that in the letters sent to Albany were some from her, and they were very cordial.

Angus, furious at the manner in which she had left him, and realising that now any number of priests preaching hellfire would not be able to bring her back to him, wrote to Henry, telling him of Margaret's friendship with Albany and that she had again gone so far as to join with those who were urging him to return.

Henry was furious; he was all for disowning a sister who was not only a friend of the French but planning to divorce her husband, but Cardinal Wolsey managed to persuade him to more diplomatic action.

Why not offer to support her with an army so that she might regain the Regency and the care of her son? For that was clearly what she wanted. Offer her this on condition that she returned to Angus and gave up all plans for a divorce.

When Margaret read Wolsey's letter and understood all it contained she shut herself up alone in her apartments and thought about it.

To be the guardian of young James. That was what she deeply desired. To regain the Regency, which would mean that she would be in a position to guide James and teach him to rule wisely. What more could she ask?

But the price was high. Return to Angus! Accept his infidelity! To feel again the desire for him which she had never been able to curb. It was too humiliating. It was asking too much.

But how she longed to have young James living with her!

The offer was tempting; but the price was too humiliating.

'Nay,' she said aloud, 'I shall not demean myself by returning to a husband whom I despise. And I shall go on fighting for my son.'

✿ ✿ ✿

In the château of Auvergne, Albany sat at the bedside of his sick wife. She could not live many more weeks, he told himself, yet he had been saying that for a long time. She had grown frail in her infirmity and it was astonishing that a woman in her condition could go on living.

'Jehan,' she murmured, and stretched out a hand. He took the hand and looked down at it. It was like the hand of a skeleton.

Poor Anne! It was long since she had been a wife to him and on the rare occasions when he had been unfaithful to her it had grieved him. He had had a happy life with her until this sickness had come upon her, this lingering sickness which would not let her live the life of a normal woman, yet would not release her from a life grown irksome.

She was gentle and patient in sickness as she had been in health; and he would sit with her each day and tell her where he had hunted that day and what game he had brought home.

But she knew that he could not stay with her forever. He was a man of action with duties at Court and perhaps far away across the sea.

Scotland! It was never far from her mind, nor from his. They were importuning him now to return, and Margaret the Queen was now adding her pleas to those of the lords who had been his supporters; and that was an astonishing thing, because previously they had been enemies, rivals for the Regency.

He often thought of her – a fine woman, handsome, perhaps overproud, too much like that brother of hers who caused so much trouble in Europe.

He would not tell Anne, but he guessed that erelong a

summons would come from François; then he could delay no longer. There had been a time when François had not wished him to go to Scotland, but that was when he was feigning a certain friendship with England, when the Kings had had that uneasy meeting, which had proved both costly and meaningless to them both, when the Princess Mary was betrothed to the Dauphin. But the political scene had changed. The new Emperor, Charles V, had visited his aunt Katharine in England, and England was inclined to friendship with the Emperor; which must mean that the brief amity Henry had professed with France was at an end. Wolsey was responsible for English foreign policy, and he undoubtedly had his eye on the Papal crown; doubtless he believed that the Emperor would now have more influence in that quarter than François. Thus France would need to court Scotland again.

Anne turned to him and said: 'Jehan, are you thinking of Scotland?'

He nodded. 'Every time I hear the sound of a horse's hoofs in the courtyard I wonder whether it is a summons.'

'And you will go?'

'I fear François will command it.'

She was silent, thinking of herself, a helpless invalid, and of him – tall, strong, vital. We have become an incongruous pair, she thought. He is not a man who should spend his time at a sickbed. Nor would he for long. The messenger would come; she was certain of it.

She was right. Within a week the summons came from the Court of France. Albany's presence was needed in Scotland. He should prepare to leave without delay.

When Albany rode towards Stirling the people had come out of their houses to line the roadside and cheer him. They looked to him to put an end to the petty strife between the Douglas and the Hamilton factions which continually threatened to break into civil war. Only the Douglases and their friends had no welcome to offer. They feared the great soldier and his men, for they knew that not only had he come at Arran's invitation but the Queen's.

Margaret was waiting to greet him at Stirling Castle, dressed in her state robes of purple velvet lined with ermine, and she wore her golden hair loose, because in that way it was most becoming.

Albany bowed over her hand and his eyes told her that she was beautiful.

What a man! she thought. Why was I ever impressed by the looks of Angus? He is like a pretty boy compared with Albany.

This was a man who had been victorious in battle; a strong man, a man who was born to govern. He had the blood of kings in his veins even as she herself had. He was a king in all but name – a fitting mate for a queen.

The banquet she had ordered to be prepared was sumptuous; he sat at her right hand at the table on the dais, with his feet resting on the carpet. She noticed his gracious manners, his courteous smiles, the way in which he took his meat from the carvers, eating with a delicacy never seen in Scotland, so that he spilt no fat on his garments and only his fingers were greasy. These he delicately washed in the bowl halfway through the meal instead of waiting until the end.

French manners! thought Margaret. And I like them well when they are combined with manly strength.

He gave her his full attention; he behaved as though she and only she was of real importance to him. He told her that he had indeed been happy to come to Scotland when he received her letters of invitation.

'My lord,' she answered, 'I see full well that since you are come we shall have peace in the land.'

'My one desire is to keep the King secure and happy.'

'Then we share the same desire.'

Margaret's eyes were shining. He would allow her to be with her son; he would understand how important a mother could be to a growing boy. Oh, how glad she was that he had come! His proximity excited her.

She said in a low voice which was faintly hoarse with emotion: 'I see that there will be friendship between us.'

'It is my earnest hope,' he answered.

The musicians played and they talked of music; they discovered similar tastes. Later he and she led the dancers and, although they talked no more of the purpose of his visit but gave themselves up to the joys of the dance and the masque, she believed that a bond had been established between them.

And when she retired that night she found it difficult to sleep. She was like a young girl who had been to her first ball.

What has happened to me? she asked herself. And she knew that she felt thus because hope had come back into her life.

❀ ❀ ❀

They left Stirling together and set out for Linlithgow. Here Albany was entertained royally; there was more feasting, more dancing, and Margaret was like a young girl in her newly found happiness.

Albany was thinking: Why not? It would be a solution. Yet

he was glad that as yet no decision could be reached. Neither of them was free. He had a wife who was sick and could certainly not live much longer; she had a husband from whom she was trying to obtain a divorce.

She was a beautiful woman; Albany was a lusty man. None would blame him for a little dalliance. He was fond of his wife, but he was far from home and even Anne was realist enough not to expect complete fidelity in the circumstances. All that she would ask was that he should never desert her while she lived; and that he would never do.

So he allowed himself to follow whither Margaret beckoned and if people were watching them and spies were taking an account of their conduct to the English Court, what did that matter? It was his duty to sow discord between the Scottish and English Courts.

As they danced in the hall of Linlithgow Palace he said to her: 'We will go together to visit the King at Edinburgh. If I come with his mother he will know I come as his friend.'

'That will give me great pleasure.'

'Then I shall fulfil two desired objects at the same time . . . See the King and please his mother.'

She lowered her eyes that he might not see the desire for him which she could not hide. It was long since she had been so happy.

The next day they set out for Edinburgh and, as they rode into the city to the cheers of the people, their eyes fixed on the Castle rising ahead of them, Margaret said: 'I wonder if James is at a window watching for us. He will be so excited, but not more so than I.'

'He must be yearning to see his mother.'

'I believe he is, but not more so than she is to see him.'

As they rode up to the Castle gates the Captain of the Castle came out and kneeling presented the keys to Albany.

He took them, and turning to Margaret, gave them to her.

This was a moment of great triumph because it was tantamount to saying: The freedom of the Castle is yours.

She did not know how to thank him; she wanted to tell him what a difference his coming had made to her; so she made the gesture which could imply her full trust in him. She shook her head and answered: 'Nay, it is you who should hold the keys of the Castle.'

He took them and they entered.

Margaret stood by with tears in her eyes while Albany paid homage to her little son. Then she knelt down and embraced James and he put his arms about her hugging her, telling her that he had long waited for her coming.

'This is indeed a happy day,' said Margaret.

They danced late into the night.

Margaret said to him: 'I fear we cause some comment.'

'There will always be comments directed against people who are placed as we are.'

'You understand that I cannot live with Angus.'

'I understand full well.'

'He has not been a good husband to me, and in some ways a traitor to Scotland.'

'We have a way of dealing with traitors. He is already under arrest.'

Margaret caught her breath. For an instant she had a picture of Angus going to his death. She shuddered; she would be haunted for evermore by his beautiful body stark and dead.

There had been times, following Flodden, when she had had bad dreams of James. It was a divorce from Angus she wanted; not his death. She had always hated the thought of death, and she hoped never to have the death of any man or woman on her conscience.

She explained this to Albany who listened thoughtfully.

'I see you have a tender heart,' he said.

'I loved him once,' she answered. 'He is a foolish, reckless boy . . . nothing more. He does not deserve death. I long to be free from him, but I should never rest in peace if I thought I had a hand in causing his death. Help me to divorce him and you will make me a happy woman.'

'Have I made it clear that I would do all in my power to make you a happy woman?'

She lifted her eyes to his. 'I have longed to hear you say that.'

He realised that she was taking his compliments with the utmost seriousness. He shrugged his shoulders. Why not? The wine and the dance had excited him; she was a very beautiful woman, and who could say what the future held for them? When they were free, as he doubted not they must be erelong, a match between them would be a good political move, one which he knew would delight his master, François, and probably put her brother Henry in such a rage as he had rarely known before.

'We will send him to France as an exile,' he said. 'Never fear. I will give orders that he is well treated there, but go he shall.'

'And you will help me in Rome?'

'You may depend upon it; I shall do all in my power to help you in that direction.'

'Oh, how I long to be free of that man!'

'You soon will be. I am sure of this. As for myself . . .'

She moved nearer to him. 'Soon we shall both be free,' she whispered. 'But there is now . . .'

It was an invitation which it would be churlish to refuse.

That night they were lovers.

Those were happy months. There was scandal concerning them, but she did not care. She wrote glowingly to her brother; she wanted to make peace between Henry and Albany, as she had once tried to reconcile the two countries during the lifetime of James.

Henry was furious when he read the letters. He growled that she was shameless and that it mortified him because he had a sister who could so forget all decent behaviour.

He wanted to write to her, ordering her to abandon the Regent and return to Angus. Angus was his protégé and he was ready to make that young man the head of a faction working for England in Scotland. He was even more angry concerning the divorce than he had been when he had first heard of it. He was beginning to believe that he would never get sons from Katharine and that there was a curse on their marriage. As he could not imagine how he could have offended God, he looked for some fault in his Queen and was reminded that she had been his brother's wife before she had been his. His conscience concerning his marriage began to worry him and he too was thinking of divorce.

A pretty state of affairs, he thought, for a brother and a sister to be asking Rome for a divorce at the same time. Therefore Margaret must stop her importuning; she must return to Angus.

That was the very thing Margaret was determined not to do.

Since her friendship with Albany had begun to bloom she was permitted to see a great deal of her son. James was affectionate by nature and fascinated by his lively mother; as she understood that he was as contented with their reunion as she was, her happiness was complete.

So each day she saw James; soon she would be divorced from Angus and she was constantly in Albany's company. When she and Albany were free their union would be legalised to the glory of Scotland and the delight of its Queen.

Angus, having made his promise to leave for exile, was granted freedom to do so; but once free he snapped his fingers at Albany and continued to stay in Edinburgh.

There could be no peace while Angus was in Scotland, and Albany was certainly not the man to see his orders disobeyed.

When he was told that Angus still lingered in Edinburgh he took off his bonnet and threw it into the fire – a habit of his when enraged. No one ever made any attempt to withdraw the bonnet from the fire and Albany would stand glaring at it, watching flames curl about fine velvet. It was thus that he managed to curb his anger against those who offended him; and by the time the bonnet was consumed he was his equable self again. His friends had seen many a good bonnet destroyed in this way.

All the same he had no intention of allowing Angus to flout his authority.

Knowing that Angus frequented a certain wine shop, he sent for the owner of the shop, and said to him: 'My Lord Angus is a patron of your shop, I believe.'

'That is so, my lord. When his lordship is in Edinburgh he

often comes in with a member of his clan. They're fond of the wine, my lord.'

'Hmm,' said Albany. 'Now listen carefully. When next he comes in, I want you to send a message to my guards. Then you are to slip a potion which will be given to you into the wine of my Lord Angus and any companions he may have with him. Is that clear?'

The man said he understood full well and the Regent's orders should be carried out.

❦ ❦ ❦

It was some nights later when Angus entered the wine shop in the company of his brother George, and called imperiously for wine which was immediately brought to him – but not before the potion had been slipped into it and a message sent to the guards.

While Angus and George sat drinking, Angus was boasting that neither his wife nor the Regent would get him to leave Edinburgh. He had as much right in Edinburgh as they had – and more so, for Albany was half French and Margaret was an Englishwoman.

George applauded his brother. George was faithful, although the more sober members of the family had deplored the conduct of the head of their House. Gavin Douglas had called him 'a witless fool, running on his own mischief by the persuasion of wily and subtle men'.

Their uncle, who had died of the plague in London, had been an old man, Angus told George now. Such men were well enough in their day, but times changed and it was young men who knew how best to live in modern times.

George agreed with his brother, as always; and they drank freely of the drugged wine.

'Why, George,' said Angus at length, 'you seem to have grown witless indeed. I declare you have drunk too well.'

George nodded slowly as he slumped forward over the table.

Angus tried to rise, but his legs had become woolly.

'Landlord,' he began, 'this wine of yours is potent stuff . . .' Then he too fell back.

It was time for the guards to enter the wine shop. This they did and, with the ropes which they had brought with them, they bound the Douglases and carried them away.

Outside the shop, horses were waiting and the bodies of the two men were slung across these; the guards mounted and, taking the drugged men with them, they made off with as much speed as possible to Leith.

When Angus and his brother opened their eyes, they were on a boat, bound for France.

❀ ❀ ❀

When he heard how Angus had been banished from Scotland and that his sister continued to live in the utmost amity with Albany, Henry was furious. His own marriage was causing him great concern, and that affair which was becoming known as the King's Secret Matter was already being whispered about, not only in England but abroad.

It seemed to him an act of unfriendliness on Margaret's part to allow Angus to be banished and to continue to sue for a divorce, a relief which he himself now craved.

His fury broke out and without consulting Wolsey he ordered that every Scotsman living in England was to have a white cross marked on his top garment and leave England on foot without delay. The distress this caused was terrible, particularly as the Border barons, who never needed much excuse, immediately engaged in savage warfare against each other.

To Margaret this seemed only a minor irritation. She was now in residence at Stirling Castle, and the young King was with her. She herself supervised his lessons and each day marvelled at his intelligence, declaring again and again that here was his father all over again.

The Regent had matters of state to attend to but they spent much time together and, despite her brother's efforts to prevent the divorce being granted, Margaret had great hopes that she would succeed.

It was pleasant to think that Angus was out of Scotland and that he was not being ill-treated in France. Quite the contrary, Albany assured her, for he had given orders that Angus and his brother were to be given honours in accordance with their rank.

The coming of Albany and the banishment of Angus naturally restored internal peace to Scotland; and this, thought Margaret, is a foretaste of what life here would be like if he and I were married and ruled together until James is of an age to do so.

Then one day as she was passing from her apartments to the great dining hall, and noticing that one of the pages was lying on the stairs in a state of collapse, Margaret went to him and asked what ailed him. The poor boy was too ill to rise and Margaret laid a hand on his hot forehead.

'I will send some of your companions to take you to your apartments,' she told him.

Next day the alarming news was brought to her. There was smallpox in the castle.

Margaret's one thought was for the King.

She was on her way to his apartment when she remembered that she had seen the page on the staircase, that she had touched his brow.

She stood still with horror. It might be so. How could she tell?

She went back to her apartments and summoned one of her women.

She gave orders that the King was to be removed to Dalkeith Palace without delay. She herself intended to follow but not until she knew it was safe to do so.

How glad she was a few days later that she had acted as she did.

The King was safe and well; but Margaret had fallen victim to the dread smallpox.

During the weeks which followed, once more she faced death, and those who cared for her were certain that this time she could not survive.

Margaret, tossing on her bed, often falling into unconsciousness, was not always aware of what was happening about her; when her mind was lucid she asked about her children. Reassuring voices told her that they were well and happy and she had nothing to fear. The King had escaped the smallpox; the Regent sent her friendly messages; and all she must do was concentrate on getting well again.

There were letters from Wolsey written on behalf of Henry, pointing out the desirability of bringing Angus back to Scotland, and there were hints of an almost threatening nature in these letters. Henry wanted her to know that in becoming Albany's friend she had become her brother's enemy.

She did not care. Henry was far away. Let him rule his own country and leave her alone. When she and Albany were married they would live happily together, and because Albany was a wise man, and a strong one, there would be peace in Scotland and the English would be obliged to look to their own affairs on the other side of the Border.

At last, she assured herself, I have come to peace and happiness; and this was the thought which was helping her to live through these terrible weeks. She had the love of her son; she had her dear little daughter; and when she married Albany there would be more children.

She was moving near to that for which she had always longed: the happy family life. The husband on whom she could lavish her passionate devotion; her children whom she could guide, comfort and love.

It has been long in coming, she thought. I had to live through two marriages to reach it. But it is waiting for me now. Albany's life with Anne de la Tour is almost over; he has been devoted to her and would never cause her unhappiness by attempting to divorce her, and I honour him for that. But she cannot live long. As for Angus, the divorce cannot long be withheld and then . . . to contentment.

A letter came from Albany. He must return to France to collect men and ammunition, as Henry was becoming more and more aggressive and the Border warfare was threatening to break out more seriously than hitherto.

He asked for an audience before he left; he wanted to assure her that he would soon return.

She immediately felt better.

'Bring me a mirror,' she cried. 'I must see how I look after this long illness.'

The woman whom she had asked looked at her in dismay; through her illness she had been too sick and feeble to care for her appearance.

'Why do you stand there?' demanded Margaret. 'Did you not hear my command?'

'Yes, Your Grace.'

'Then go and fetch me a mirror.'

The woman stammered: 'Y-your Grace . . . I have received orders . . .'

'What orders? Who gives orders here . . . ?'

'The physicians have said to wait until you were stronger.'

Fear touched Margaret then. She was to wait until she was stronger before she was allowed to look into a mirror. What can this mean? she asked herself. But she could guess.

She must know the truth . . . whatever it was.

'Bring me a mirror,' she again commanded. 'I order you to do so, no matter what the physicians have told you.'

The woman went away and, in a short time, came back holding the mirror, which Margaret snatched from her hand.

'Oh . . . *no*!' The words escaped her as she stared in horror. That was not Margaret Tudor who looked back at her. The lovely skin, pitted, the eyelid drawn down over one eye. 'It cannot be!' she whispered.

But there was no evading the truth. Gone were her glowing good looks. The face which looked back at her seemed hideous and repulsive.

The woman threw herself by the bed, her arms outstretched for the mirror, which Margaret would not relinquish.

'Your Grace, it is early yet. The physicians say you will recover . . .'

Margaret did not answer; she continued to stare at the wreck of her beauty.

'The Queen is too ill to see the Duke of Albany before he leaves.' That was the message she sent to him.

So he sailed away and she was almost glad that he had gone, because she could not have borne that he should see her as she was.

Her physicians assured her that when she recovered her health the effects of the pox would be less disfiguring; her women comforted her that she was growing more like her old self every day.

But in her heart she knew that she would never again be desired for her beauty; and she wondered apprehensively what would happen when Albany returned to Scotland.

🏵 Chapter XI 🏵

THE QUEEN'S LOVER

That dreary winter was over and spring had come. The physicians' comforting assurances had had some small foundation, for as Margaret's health improved so did her appearance to some extent. Gone was the glowing skin which, with her abundant shining hair, had been one of her greatest attractions; the deformation of her eyelid remained although it had ceased to look grotesque. And as the weeks passed she became more reconciled to the lessening of her beauty. She dressed herself even more richly than before; and even when she lay in bed recovering from her illness, she would have her attendants bring out her gowns and hold them up before her. She took great pleasure in them and her jewels; and she persuaded herself that, once she was able to leave her bed, they would do much for her.

Naturally resilient she soon grew to live with her changed appearance, reminding herself that she had a great deal for which to be thankful. Albany would return to Scotland; and although his wife still lived and she herself had not yet obtained her divorce from Angus, soon they must be free. When she was well enough she would be with James again; while she was ill she had received tender messages from him, and there was no doubt that he dearly loved his mother. To be loved by husband and child could compensate for so much, and Margaret began to look forward to the future with hope.

It was inevitable that, among those who surrounded her, were spies put there by those who deplored her friendship with Albany and were in secret working for an English alliance. Angus was no longer in Scotland but the Douglases were a numerous and powerful clan with their tentacles widespread. If Albany's wife died, if Margaret obtained her divorce, the Douglases would indeed be in decline. Therefore every effort would be made by them to turn Margaret from Albany and towards Angus.

A piece of information came to the ears of the Douglas group and they decided that it must be brought to the Queen's notice as quickly as possible. They did not want to mention it themselves, as that would be to earn Margaret's scornful disbelief. But if it were whispered to her as a piece of gossip, she would not rest until she had proved it to be false or true.

Thus it was one of her women who slyly passed on the information to her by introducing the Flemings into the conversation.

'Oh, the Flemings, Your Grace. They always gave themselves airs. Lord Fleming hated his wife, they say, and that was why she died at breakfast with her sisters. And now of course his sister is becoming arrogant.'

'But why so?' asked Margaret idly, thinking of James, never ceasing to mourn Margaret Drummond who had died at that same fatal breakfast with her sister, Lord Fleming's wife.

'On account of my lord Duke, Your Grace.'

'My lord Duke?'

'My lord Duke of Albany, Your Grace.'

Margaret lowered her eyes to hide the fear in them. 'And what of him?'

'Well, Your Grace, 'tis said that he is a man who has been unable to live with his wife, she being an invalid, and that it is natural that he should take a mistress. The Flemings were always a family to look to their advantages, and doubtless they persuaded her to it.'

'To *what*?' demanded Margaret, meaning to whisper yet finding herself breaking into a shout.

'Fleming's sister is the mistress of the Duke of Albany, Your Grace. Well, he is an attractive man and she was nothing loath. As for her family, they could see nothing amiss in being so linked with the Regent.'

'It is idle gossip.'

'Nay, Your Grace, I . . .'

'I tell you it is.'

The woman was silent; but she was satisfied that she had done her duty to the Douglases and the mischief had worked.

Margaret would not rest until she had discovered the truth, and there was no doubt at all that during his last stay in Scotland Lord Fleming's sister had been the mistress of the Duke of Albany.

❀ ❀ ❀

She lay in bed and held the mirror before her face. Her eyes were hard and brilliant; they were burning with the tears which her pride would not let her shed. She was no weak creature to weep and sob because once again she had been cheated.

It was like some cruel pattern. All the men she loved were unfaithful to her. She gave them passionate love; she was ready to give them devotion; but, alas, they turned elsewhere; and always they deceived her. Others knew of their infidelity before she would have deemed such infidelity possible.

It was too much to be borne in silence; and if her love could be passionate so could her hatred.

She hated Albany for so deceiving her. She realised now that she had been the one who had set their love affair in motion; she had invited him and he had courteously accepted her advances, when all the time doubtless he had preferred the embraces of the Fleming woman.

She hated the whole Fleming clan. Nor could she curb that hatred. She began to refer to Lord Fleming as the murderer of his wife and sister-in-law. It was reviving an old slander which had almost been forgotten; but now it was being remembered again, how James IV had desired to marry Margaret Drummond, and she had died after taking breakfast with her two sisters, one of whom was Lord Fleming's wife.

By whose hand did they die?

Could it be true that Lord Fleming, wishing to poison his own wife, had mistakenly poisoned her sisters with her?

To revive that old story was small revenge, Margaret felt, for the wrong which had been done her.

How unhappy she was during those warm summer days.

Never again will I put my trust in men, Margaret told herself.

Now she would devote herself to her son's interests. The boy was in his eleventh year. He was bright, intelligent, and very fond of his mother, who since her friendship with Albany, had been a great deal in his company.

David Lindsay was still his constant companion; the man

would have died for the boy. James knew this and loved him dearly.

David had recently married a young girl named Janet Douglas who was a seamstress of the King's household earning ten pounds a year; but his marriage had made no difference to his duties. James had inherited a love of music from his father and David fostered this, so many long hours were spent in singing and playing the lute and clavichord. David had also taught the boy to love and care for animals and it was their pleasure to play with these in Stirling Park and attempt to teach them tricks; although David would never allow the slightest cruelty, but was very anxious to make the boy understand that, while he took great pleasure in them, he must never forget that it was his duty to care for and protect them.

It was true, Margaret decided, that he was but a boy; but he was also the King, and he was old for his years. Poor child, it seemed that since his father's death he had been in a kind of captivity, never allowed to go where he wished, nor to meet his friends unless he had the permission of others to do so. A pretty state of affairs for a king to find himself involved in!

Why should not the King be released from this semi-confinement? Why should he not be placed at the head of a party – as a nominal head of course – and as he was so ready to trust his mother, why should she not be the real power behind that party?

She would never trust a man again; she had done with men; she was now going to devote herself to politics and restoring herself to the Regency and her son to that life which was due to him as King of Scotland.

She went to Stirling Castle and found James in his apartments with David Lindsay.

When James saw her he greeted her with exclamations of delight.

'It is my mother, Davie,' he cried. 'She will be delighted with our papingo.'

'I am sure she will,' replied David, and Margaret saw that on the boy's wrist, as though it were a falcon, was a brightly plumaged parrot.

'She was sent to me as a gift,' James chattered. 'Is she not beautiful? Have you ever seen such a bird? And Davie says that she may even learn to speak. He is teaching her to whistle.'

'Which she does very well,' added David, as excited as the King.

Margaret's mind was full of her plan, but her interest was caught by the parrot, for she had never seen such a bird before and the idea of its being able to whistle seemed to her fantastic.

When she had marvelled at its oddities and listened to James accompanying David's singing on the lute, she intimated that she would like to be alone with her son, and David retired.

'Why, Jamie,' she said, when they were alone, 'what a strange life it is that you live, and you a king!'

'Strange, Mother?'

'Why, here you are almost a prisoner. Had your father lived, how different it would have been!'

'Then I should not be King.'

'Oh, Jamie, how sad it was that your father should die and you become a prisoner of ambitious men.'

'Yes,' said James slowly, 'I suppose I am a prisoner . . . of a sort.'

'Indeed you are, for if you wished to leave Stirling Castle you would be prevented from doing so. Poor James, you remember little else, so how can you guess what freedom means?' And you a king. There are times when I feel very angry with those who cause you to live as you do. The King should be free and, although you are of no great age, still you are a king.'

James was thoughtful. Then he said: 'Who is it who insists on my being kept a prisoner?'

'The Parliament – and the Parliament is led by the Regent.'

'The Duke of Albany? I liked him well. I thought he was my friend.'

'Your friend?' Margaret laughed. 'He has a charming manner, has he not? Such manners are cultivated by those who plan to deceive us.'

'So he has deceived us?'

Margaret's eyes narrowed, and James stared at her wide-eyed.

'He is the most deceitful man on earth!' she muttered.

'Indeed he must be,' answered James, 'for he had led me to believe he was my friend.'

'It is necessary to be cautious with men such as he is. But, James, I have made up my mind that you shall not be treated in this way much longer. It is my wish that you should leave this prison and take your place in the country of which you are King.'

James's eyes sparkled with excitement. 'How so, Mother?'

'As yet I am unsure. I believe your uncle would help us – now that I have discovered the perfidy of Albany. It might be necessary for us to escape over the Border and throw ourselves on his mercy for a while. Then he would send an army and overthrow the Regent Albany and all he stands for.'

'When, Mother?'

'Oh, there is nothing settled yet, but it is as well to be prepared.'

'Then one day I shall escape. I shall go to my uncle's Court, and then we will gather together an army and I shall be in truth King.'

Margaret looked into his eager young face. 'How I wish you were older,' she sighed. 'But we will be patient. Say nothing to anyone of this – not even David. It is our secret. I want you to remember though that you are the King and that it is not right that you should be treated as you are.'

'I will remember it,' replied the King.

The parrot began to whistle suddenly, and his earnest look left him as he broke into a smile.

'Listen, Mother,' he cried. 'You see how clever she is! Is she not a wonderful papingo?'

He was a child at heart, thought Margaret. But he should not remain so. He was, before all, the King; and she was determined to set him up, that she might the better rid Scotland of one who had poisoned the love she had given him so that it was fast turning to bitter hatred.

The only way in which she could live through those months of bitter disappointment was by making wild plans. She must be in the thick of intrigue to stop herself brooding; so she retired to Perth, where she felt she could act more secretly, and immediately renewed her correspondence with her brother.

In her letters she gave vent to wrath against Albany; she reported his liaison with Fleming's sister and added that she distrusted the Fleming clan, for Lord Fleming himself had murdered his own wife – a mysterious event which had taken place before she, Margaret, came to Scotland – and, with his wife, two of her sisters.

Always ready to listen to attacks on Albany and his French

connections, Henry was interested in his sister's change of front. He implied that if she offered to stop agitating for a divorce and became reconciled to Angus, she would have the wholehearted support of England.

But hating her latest lover as she did, Margaret had no intention of rejoining one who had deceived her even more cruelly. That was one point on which she was adamant. Never would she go back to Angus.

Meanwhile Albany's friends, having an inkling of what was happening, wrote to him and told him that his presence was urgently needed in Scotland and it was unwise for him to delay his return; but Albany, on account of his wife's sickness, was in no hurry to come.

Meanwhile Margaret had succeeded in obtaining terms from the English for a truce between the two countries, and she returned to Edinburgh determined to bring forward young James and allow him to speak for himself in the Tolbooth, demanding, as Scotland's King, the right to go where he would throughout his kingdom.

James, being a fearless boy and well coached by Margaret, entered the Tolbooth that day in a kingly fashion and even the cynical lords were impressed and a little awed. Many of them told themselves that they must have a care how they behaved towards him; he was young yet, but he would one day be King and he looked sharp enough to remember those who offended him.

James spoke in a loud, clear voice. 'I am your King and I will no longer be your prisoner. This realm is of goodly size but it will not contain both me and the Duke of Albany.'

Several of the lords spoke, respectfully explaining to the King that he was accompanied by guards for his own safety.

They had no wish but to serve him, and this they had sworn to do.

James was looking at his mother for his next cue; but at that moment Gaultier de Malines, who had entered the Tolbooth immediately after the King was in his place, came forward to say that he had a message from his master the Duke of Albany and he believed that now was the time to deliver it.

'My master,' he said, 'thanks you for your support of his rule during his absence. He is on his way to you and he has good news for you. Sir Richard de la Pole will shortly be arriving with an army for the invasion of England; and he knows that you will recognise as enemies to Scotland those who have tried to bring about a truce between the two perennial enemies. Let the King remain in Stirling Castle with certain trusted lords as his guardians; but give him license to hunt if he so wishes.'

Margaret, listening and watching the effect of these words on the lords, felt so frustrated that she could scarcely restrain her tears, for anger could make her weep more easily than sorrow. The King had made such a good impression and but for the coming of Gaultier de Malines she would have won James his liberty.

She cried: 'This is no way in which to treat your King. He may be young in years, but see, he is indeed a king.'

But she knew she could not move them with her pleas, so she asked that she might choose the King's guardians and that Lords Borthwick and Erskine might be these, with help from the Abbot of Holyrood and the Bishop of Aberdeen.

The Parliament agreed that Lord Erskine should be the King's guardian but rejected the others.

James, seeing his mother's grief, stamped his foot and cried: 'Do you forget, gentlemen, that I am your King?'

The lords were taken aback. None of them dared meet the King's eye, but they reminded themselves that he was only a child; and they had seen how his mother changed her policy according to her whim. They remembered how she had married Angus scarcely a year after Flodden, and how honours had been heaped on him and his family; now she had nothing but bitter hatred for Angus and his clan. Then she had been friendly with Albany, and now her regard was turned to a venom almost as potent as that which she felt for Angus.

Margaret was governed by her emotions and it was dangerous to follow such a woman.

Still, the boy was the King and he was reminding them of that.

It was proposed then that, if Albany did not return within two weeks, the King's guards should be removed and he be allowed to go wherever he wished; moreover the terms set out by the English for the truce would be again considered.

It was not utter defeat, thought Margaret, as she and the King left the Tolbooth.

Albany had arrived at Dumbarton.

When Margaret received the news she dismissed all her women so that she might be alone to think. She took up her mirror and studied her face. She had grown used to the change now, but it would strike him forcibly. She thought of all the gowns she possessed and which became her most. But since she hated him, why should she care what he thought of her? Yet, she told herself, I must curb my feelings; never must he know how he has wounded me. If I have shown my interest in him, it must be believed that I considered him a worthy match for me – when we both became free – which he would be.

It was important that she should see the King immediately to discuss with him what the return of Albany could mean, to coach him in what he must do and say; and she was thankful that at least her son had such a regard for her that he was ready to obey her in all she asked of him.

She set out for Stirling, and there was warmly welcomed by James. She saw that he had changed; he was no longer malleable; she had made him realise the power which could be his and already he was surrounded by companions who were eager to humour and flatter him. But he was as affectionate towards his mother as ever and she was delighted with him.

David Lindsay however was disturbed and sought to speak to her in private, but she had little time for David Lindsay now; she was grateful to him for his past care of the boy, but he was essentially a companion for a child. James, however, had not changed towards his old friend, although he spent less time with him, there being so many new interests in his life. He liked to hunt with companions a little older than himself, though seeming the same age since he was old for his years.

He had taken the opportunity to hunt every day, and was clearly going to be a great lover of the chase. He had grieved a little because his beloved papingo had escaped into the park where it had been attacked and killed by the wild birds there; but that event had made him throw himself more eagerly into his new pastimes that he might forget his precious bird; and when he was with David he always remembered.

Margaret told him that Albany was in Scotland and they must be wary.

'He will doubtless come to you with soft words, but we must remember he is a very deceitful man.'

James listened carefully, and she rejoiced because his regard for her was so apparent.

He wanted to show her his new household; many of his old servants had been replaced, and when they sat down to a banquet she made the acquaintance of a merry young man, handsome in a brash way, who was the King's Master Carver.

He was very bold, this young man, and he did not seem overawed by the presence of the King or Queen. In his livery of silk, his doublet of crimson satin and his red hose which were furred with black budge he was quite a dazzling figure.

He carved for the King and the Queen on that occasion, and kept them amused by his merry wit.

'Tell me,' said Margaret to her son, 'who is this young man who seems so pleased with himself and life?'

'I will get him to speak to you himself,' answered James, and beckoning the young man, added, 'Her Grace the Queen would speak with you.'

The young man bowed low and opened his eyes wide with pleasure. He murmured: 'The Queen wishes to speak with *me*! This is the happiest day of my life.'

'Tell me your name,' said Margaret.

'It is Henry Stuart, Your Grace.'

Margaret smiled. 'A goodly name and one which is not unfamiliar to me. Tell me to which branch of the family you belong.'

'My father is Lord Avondale, Your Grace, and I am his second son. My brother James is in the service of the King with me. We count ourselves fortunate to be in such good service.'

'And it would seem to me that you perform your duties in a commendable manner.'

He raised his eyes to the ceiling and murmured: 'Your

Grace, who could fail to . . . when serving the King? And now to enjoy the additional pleasure of serving the Queen . . . !'

There was something in the boldness of his looks which she found amusing. She signed for him to carve for her, which he did with alacrity and, when he held the meat for her to take, his eyes were on her in a manner which, though bold, she did not find offensive. He was young and he had made her feel young.

When she retired that night she felt more light-hearted than she had for a long time.

Albany was on his way to see her and she could not restrain her excitement. The fact that she knew he had had a mistress while he was making love to her could only grieve her, she supposed; it could not make her hate him. She had chosen her gown with the utmost care; her hair at least had lost none of its beauty, it was carefully dressed and she was adorned with jewels. But she could not completely hide the ravages of the smallpox, and he would notice how changed she was. Yet when she was at the height of her beauty he could not be faithful; neither could James, her first husband, nor Angus her second.

She had left the King at Stirling and returned to her lodgings in Edinburgh, for she knew that Albany was on his way to the King and she thought it fitting that she should not greet him in James's presence. Her friends had told her how Albany had knelt before young James and sworn that he had returned to Scotland to lay down his life, if need be, for his sake.

And now he was on his way to Edinburgh and Holyrood Palace which he would make his headquarters.

She could hear the sounds of acclamation in the streets; he was immediately popular even though he did seem like a foreigner to the citizens of Edinburgh. It was the Stuart charm which was so irresistible and seemed to be possessed by everyone who bore the name. That young Master Carver of James's had it. He was a bold fellow and perhaps she had encouraged him overmuch; but he had so pleased her; he had made her feel that she was young again and that her women were right when they assured her that the pox had made little difference to her looks.

Albany paused on his way to Holyrood to call on the Queen. She waited, her head held high, until he came and stood before her. He bowed and, when his eyes met hers, there was no sign that he noticed any difference in her appearance.

'So you have come back to Scotland!' she said.

'I should never have left, had it not been necessary.'

She wished that her heart would not beat so wildly, that she did not feel so absurdly glad that he had come. Yet mingling with her pleasure was a fierce anger against him. She wanted to say: And when do you propose to visit your paramour, the Fleming woman?

But their conversation was cool, as was becoming in the presence of others.

'How long will you remain in Edinburgh?' she asked him.

'For but a short while, I fear. I have matters to attend to.'

'On the Border?' she suggested, but he only smiled.

'Yet,' he went on, 'I hear that my friends have prepared some entertainment for me at Holyrood. I could not enjoy it if the Queen were not present to make my joy in this return complete.'

She smiled. The desire to dance with him in the state apartments of Holyrood Palace was too great to be denied.

They led the dance as they had on previous occasions.

'It has seemed long,' he said.

'Doubtless you had much to occupy you in France.'

'So much – and yet it seemed long.'

'I was very sick when you left.'

'I did not know how sick, or I should never have been able to leave Scotland.'

'Nay,' she retorted, 'one mistress sick, what matters it? There was another to amuse your leisure hours.'

He was silent; then he gave her a remorseful look. 'Alas,' was all he said, smiling wryly as he did so.

'My enemies told me,' she continued. 'I would rather have heard it from you.'

'One's flesh is weak,' he admitted.

'It seems a very hard task for a man to be faithful to one woman. I begin to believe it is an almost impossible one to fulfil.'

'That,' he said with a snap of his fingers, 'is of no great moment. It is the affections, the tenderness, which are important.'

'I agree. To love would mean never to hurt the loved one by deed or word.'

'I beg you to understand that what happened in a moment of weakness need have no lasting effect on the relationship between us two.'

'Perhaps you are of a lighter mind than I, my lord. You may understand your feelings; you cannot understand mine. You gave no sign of your horror when you saw what illness had done to me . . . just as you gave no sign that you had another mistress. I congratulate you on your superb control. I should have liked you better had you displayed more human feelings.'

She could feel the anger rising now. She wanted to shout at

him, to wound him as he had wounded her. She wanted to scream: Why do I have to love these faithless men? Why cannot I escape from my emotions as easily as they can from theirs?

He was watching her, and she wondered whether he knew how near she was coming to an hysterical outburst. He would know a great deal about a woman's feelings, she was sure. He, with his devotion to a sick wife! Devotion indeed! No doubt he sat at her bedside and soothed her . . . when he was not visiting some new mistress. She believed she had the measure of him. He was a man who wanted peace; but he wanted to satisfy his lusts also. He did so in secret, keeping this from his sick wife, playing the faithful husband, as he played the passionate lover to each of his mistresses in turn.

She was praying now for calm and for courage. She must not obey the demands of her senses; she must cling to her pride; she must let Albany know that he could not treat the Queen of Scotland as one of his lights-o'-love and expect her to be willing and eager the moment he beckoned.

'I will make you understand . . . when we are alone,' he murmured.

She was fighting his allure with all her strength, and against her will she forced herself to say: 'I do not know when that will be, my lord, for I have no wish to be alone with you.'

He looked regretful, but calm as ever. Why should he care that she would no longer have him in her bed? He would doubtless quickly seek solace with the Fleming woman.

Albany was only faintly disturbed by the Queen's discovery of his infidelity. He believed that, if Anne should die and Margaret obtain her divorce, a marriage between them would be considered so desirable that she would succumb and marry him. Moreover he knew that she had been very loath to deny him her bed. He had read the anger in her eyes; he knew she was a passionate woman; that was jealousy he had seen tonight, and if she had not cared deeply for him she would not feel the fierce anger which she obviously did.

If it were necessary he would have no difficulty in regaining her affection.

But at the moment he had other matters which demanded his attention. He had men and arms at his disposal and he was going to wage war on the enemy of Scotland and his master, the King of France.

He spoke to the Parliament in the Tolbooth and he was very eloquent.

'Have you forgotten,' he demanded, 'how your King and your fathers were slain on Flodden Field? How many Scottish towns have been destroyed; how many Scottish churches desecrated? How many Scottish homes, perilously near the Border, have been sacked? The time has come to defeat these enemies once and for all. We have the arms. What are we waiting for?'

The Parliament listened. It was true that they hated the English, and now Albany was back in Scotland with news that Sir Richard de la Pole, who called himself the Duke of Suffolk, was preparing an army which would invade England. The cockerel Tudor would be driven from his throne; there would be peace for evermore between the two kingdoms. No more fighting on the Border, no more fear throughout the land that the English were preparing to invade.

Very soon after his arrival in Scotland Albany was on the march, and when he reached the Border he sent a challenge to the Earl of Surrey to come on and fight.

Surrey however declined the invitation. He was ready to fight, he said, but he would do so on English soil. Let the Scots come to him.

But the weather had changed and the Scots were fearful of entering England. They murmured together, asking themselves why they should be living uncomfortably thus in camp when they might be at their own firesides. Albany declared his devotion to Scotland, but wasn't he really fighting for France, and shouldn't the French fight their own battles?

Albany was filled with rage against these Scotsmen, particularly as he had reason to know that the English were in no state to withstand an attack. They could have settled the old score; they could have healed the wounds they had suffered at Flodden.

But no, said the Scots. They were not crossing into England.

Well might he snatch off his bonnet and throw it into the campfire.

Watching the flames curl about the velvet he felt, as ever, his anger burning out.

He was wearying of Scotland; he wanted to be at home in France. Anne needed him. He was tired of the virago Margaret, the cloying Fleming woman. What did they mean to him? Nothing compared with Anne.

He wanted to go back to her bedside, to sit with her, for he knew that the pain was less acute when he was there. He wanted to take her hands – those thin, transparent hands – and say to her: 'Anne, they are nothing, those women . . . they satisfy the desire of an hour . . . and then there is the remorse. But you would understand. You know . . . and you have never reproached me.'

Holy Mother of God, how tired I am of this bleak land. How I long for Auvergne and the sickroom of my beloved one.

❀ ❀ ❀

As soon as Albany had left for the Border, Margaret went to Stirling. She had made up her mind that she would not be separated from her son, and if any tried to do so they would have to use force.

Her indignation against Albany was growing. What had he cared because she had refused his advances? Any woman would serve his purpose, she told herself. And I, the Queen, demeaned myself by showing him how much he meant to me.

The only manner in which she could fight this ache in her body was to abuse him, to tell herself that she would not relent if he came begging on his knees.

'I hate him!' she told herself. 'Let him go to his Fleming. What do I care?'

It was ridiculous, and if she had not been so sorry for herself she could have laughed at her foolish deception. Why could she not keep the men she desired, faithful to her? Were there no faithful men in the world? Was it because the men she chose were desirable to so many women? James, Angus, Albany! She admitted that they must be three of the most attractive men in Scotland.

What balm to be with young James who was so eager to see her. At least, she told herself, I have an affectionate son. It was the same with her daughter, Margaret. Her children returned her love, and in that she was fortunate.

Whenever she was with James she thought of her brother Henry who was growing more and more apprehensive every day because he had no son – except one bastard. Poor Henry! It was pleasant to be able to pity him when she considered her wrongs.

She talked to James again and again of her distrust of Albany.

'Why, my son,' she said, 'it is a disgraceful state of affairs when you, the King of this realm, must wait upon the pleasure of your subjects!'

James listened eagerly; he was weary of restraint; he had begun to realise that as King he should not have to give way to the will of others. He longed to take what he considered to be his. This was no life for a king, and his mother assured him of this.

'Depend upon it,' she said, 'we shall not long endure it.'

She was very conscious of the King's Master Carver, and she was inclined to think that Harry Stuart was very conscious of her. Often she would look up to see his eyes fixed upon her, and there was a mixture of boldness and reverence in the glance.

She began to look for him as he did for her, and she would find her heartbeats quickening whenever he was near her. Sometimes at a meal their hands would touch and she was certain that the contact affected him as deeply as it did herself.

One day when she sat with the King, and Harry Stuart was among his attendants, she found him close to her and she bade him sit beside her.

This he did with alacrity and rather closer than he should. But she had always been attracted by his boldness.

He whispered: 'Your Grace, I know your anxiety on behalf of the King's Grace and the manner in which he is kept a prisoner. I wish to say that if there is aught I could do in the service of the King . . . in the service of Your Grace . . . willingly would I give my life.'

'Thank you,' she answered quietly.

'Your Grace, there are matters with which I would wish to acquaint you, but here . . .'

'You wish to see me privately?'

'If Your Grace would grant me such an honour . . .'

'Come to my apartments when I leave the King. I will arrange for you to see me alone.'

She could not entirely interpret his reception of such a favour. He looked like a young man in a dream – fearful yet ecstatic.

She caught his excitement and could scarcely wait for the moment when they should be alone. A notion had occurred to her that he was in love with her; she would have to deal with him very gently. All the same she was looking forward to listening to what he had to say.

❀ ❀ ❀

He stood before her; then he knelt and taking both her hands kissed them.

'Well,' she asked, 'what is this great secret you have to impart?'

He rose without her permission and, still keeping her hands imprisoned in his, he stood very close to her. She could see the long, dark eyelashes that set off his brilliant eyes; she saw the warm colour in his cheeks. He was extremely handsome; so young and ardent.

'I dare not say it, now that I am in the presence of Your Grace, though I have rehearsed it a hundred times.'

'You had better speak,' she answered. 'It would not please me to have granted this interview for no purpose.'

'Your Grace, I fear you may consider me overbold, but since you came to Stirling to be with the King I can neither eat nor sleep for thinking of you.'

'You are very young . . .' she began.

'Your Grace is young also. And if you were in truth old it would make no difference to my feeling. To me you seem without age . . . You are a Queen and I but the second son of a lord who is not of the first rank. But I am a man for all that, and Your Grace, you are a woman and it is not as Queen and subject that we can speak together this night.'

His emotions seemed to overcome him; he put his hand across his eyes and turned away; she thought he was about to stumble from the room, so she put out a hand to detain him.

Immediately as she touched him he swung round; he lifted her in his arms, for he was strong; she was conscious of his virility and her senses demanded that she meet his passion with her own.

With his arms about her, his lips on her throat, she could not uphold her pretence of reluctance because he could read the signs of passion as easily as she could.

'This is . . . f-folly,' she stammered.

'What glorious folly,' he cried. 'I would willingly die on the morrow following a night of such folly.'

She was trying to remember that she was the Queen; that she was being driven by her emotions once more; but she could remember nothing but her body's urgent need.

'Where could we be alone?' he whispered.

'Here,' she answered. 'I have given orders that I am not to be disturbed.'

'Your Grace . . . my love . . .'

'Oh, but you are a charming boy.'

'Not such a boy, as you shall discover,' he answered boastfully; and she was acquiescent to his demands, for they were her own.

And as they lay together she thought: Why not? There are some faithful men in the world. Why not this charming boy who is socially so far beneath me that he must always be grateful? He had been as passionate as any of her lovers; but a deal more reverent. He reminded her of Angus in the days at Stobhall – those days which she was longing to relive with a partner who would give love for love, fidelity for fidelity.

He said: 'When can we be together again?'

'I do not know. We must be careful.'

'I feel reckless. I will take any chance rather than miss one minute of your company.'

'You are a foolish boy,' she told him fondly.

'Is it foolish then to love like this?'

'It would be if we were discovered.'

'Do you think I care what could be done to me? I would count death poor payment for the joy that has been mine.'

Such charming words from such charming lips! There should be many such meetings, she promised herself. The wounds inflicted by Albany were healing.

What did she care for Albany? Let him spend every night with the Fleming woman. She had a new lover; he was young, he was passionate, and he adored her. He betrayed it in every word and gesture.

Unsuitable? So far below her in rank? Young? Younger than she was?

What did she care?

The Queen was in love.

Albany had returned to Edinburgh and he had discovered that Margaret had become his enemy, that she was now seeking reconciliation with her brother and plotting for his, Albany's, destruction.

He had made an enemy where he had had a friend, which was unfortunate. He longed to return home. The news of Anne was bad; he was furious with the Scots for refusing to carry war into England, and he was wasting his time here.

It was alarming that the Queen should be so often in the company of the King. He could see great danger there, for reports were constantly being brought to him that Margaret was inciting James to rebel against the restraint which was put on him.

He stood up in the Tolbooth and requested leave to go back to France where his wife was dangerously ill. This was denied him; he was told that his presence was needed in Scotland, and there lay his duty.

'Then,' he replied, 'the King must be taken from the care of the Queen, for I see great trouble ahead of us if she is allowed to imbue him with ideas of rebellion against the restraint which we have been obliged to impose upon him.'

The lords of the Council agreed with this and it was arranged that Margaret should be separated from James, and his personal attendants replaced by others.

When the news was brought to Margaret, she was alarmed, and she did what was fast becoming a habit with her – she talked over her troubles with Harry.

Harry was proving himself to be more than a passionate lover; he clearly enjoyed giving her his advice and, as she wanted to please him as much as she possibly could, she always asked for it.

'What can we do?' she said. 'Our enemies are so strong. I will not be parted from my son.'

'The King himself is reluctant to be parted from Your Grace; which is easily understood. We must be strong but wily. We must think about this very carefully and not act rashly.'

She smiled at him. 'Oh, Harry, how good you are for me. You know that I can be a little rash at times. Yes, let us ponder this and decide together how best we can outwit that man.'

'It is said,' Harry went on, 'that he intends to make Lord Fleming one of the King's guardians.' He looked at her covertly, for he knew that not very long ago there had been scandal touching her and the Regent. 'And Lord Fleming's sister is Albany's mistress. That seems to me a dangerous situation.'

'Why so?'

'Because Fleming has a bad reputation. It is said that he murdered his own wife and her sisters with her. He would like the Regent to be King, which he might well be if the King were dead.'

'Do not speak of such a thing!' cried Margaret in horror.

'My love, such a possibility fills me with horror as it does you, but we must not ignore such possibilities. Fleming would prefer to see his sister the mistress of a king than of a regent.'

'Oh, the vile creatures!' murmured Margaret.

'It may well be,' went on Harry, 'that Albany has chosen Fleming for this reason: he wishes someone to do this evil deed for him, and Fleming could be the man.'

Margaret sat listening with narrowed eyes. She knew that to be false. She knew he would never connive at murder and that he had some affection for James; that he was not a man so ambitious that he would wish to see his young kinsman murdered for the sake of a crown.

But it was pleasant to revile him with Harry, knowing herself beyond need of him, knowing that she had a young and handsome lover who adored her.

The winds of December were battering the walls of Stirling Castle when Albany arrived there.

Margaret, with James, was waiting for him. As he entered she noticed how drawn he looked. He is getting old, she thought; and she rejoiced in her Harry who had helped her to recover from that bitter love affair.

James, primed by her and always ready to do her bidding, received Albany coolly. Albany on the other hand treated the boy with the utmost reverence.

Margaret stood watching, delighted that she could do so without emotion; and when Albany came to her and bowed, she acknowledged his greeting without warmth.

'I greatly regret,' he said, 'that I have displeased you.'

'You have none but yourself to blame for that regret,' she retorted.

'Cannot we come to some amicable agreement?'

'It seems unlikely,' she retorted. 'The King is in no mood to brook further restrictions. He feels them to be impertinent and an insult to his crown. In this he has the support of his mother.'

'I regret that His Grace should harbour such opinions.'

'Indeed my Lord, you seem to feel nothing but regrets.'

She smiled maliciously and she thought: Oh, Harry, my beloved boy, how happy you have made me! Let Albany do his worst. Let him go to France or the Fleming . . . what do I care, now that I have you!

'I hoped that I could turn you once more to friendship,' murmured Albany.

She shrugged her shoulders. She felt gloriously free. He no longer had the slightest power to move her. She had finished with him as she had with Angus; and when hatred turned to indifference, then could a woman call herself no longer the prisoner of her emotions.

❀ ❀ ❀

Albany fretted as the weeks slipped by. He had come to no decision. The King was still with his mother in Stirling; he himself had made repeated requests to leave Scotland, and each time they had been refused.

He sat in his apartment looking out over the snowy landscape, thinking of that sickroom in the château. He had written to Anne promising that he would be at her bedside as soon as he could bring some order into the troublesome affairs of this country.

He knew that she would be thinking of him as he was thinking of her, and he longed to assure her once more of his devotion.

It was while he sat thus that messengers arrived from France with the sad news that Anne had died; she had blessed him before she did so and had wished to thank him for the happy life he had given her.

Albany covered his face with his hands when he heard the news.

I failed her, he thought; even at the end I was not at her side to bid her farewell.

❀ ❀ ❀

There was whispering throughout the Court. The Regent was a widower; it only remained now for the Queen to obtain her divorce and they would be free to marry.

It was a situation to give rise to speculation.

Margaret heard it and smiled. Harry was quite obviously

alarmed. She laughed at him when they were alone. 'Nay, my love, do you think I'd take Albany now!'

'It might be considered a desirable match by the Council.'

'Do you think I will allow them to make a match which would be quite distasteful to me?'

'I greatly fear they will try to persuade you.'

'Then you are a foolish boy.'

'I live in terror.'

'My poor sweet Harry!'

She was delighted with him and so touched, yet sad because she was unable to give him all she longed to.

'I have not obtained my divorce from Angus yet, you know,' she said to comfort him.

'I rejoice in that, for at least you cannot marry Albany yet.'

'I never shall, I tell you. Though when I get my divorce I may marry again.'

'Your Grace . . . my dearest . . . but whom would you marry?'

'A certain young man.'

She was reckless, but it was delightful to watch his face. She loved him too much to tease him for long. She went on: 'His name is Harry Stuart.'

She watched the wonder dawn slowly in his eyes.

🦁 🦁 🦁

It had been necessary for Margaret to leave her son in Stirling Castle while she came to Edinburgh. She was restless and unhappy because this meant that not only did she have to say a temporary farewell to James, but to Harry also.

She was determined that it was a state of affairs which she would not endure and, when Albany invited her to meet him at the Gatehouse of Holyrood Palace, she went there eager to hear what he had to say to her.

Theirs was a private meeting which she found to her satisfaction, but when she heard the news he had to tell her, she was alarmed.

'I am afraid,' he warned her, 'this will prove a shock to Your Grace. Angus has escaped from France and is on his way to England to seek refuge in your brother's Court.'

Margaret was horrified. Since she had fallen in love with Harry she had been agitating more determinedly than ever for her divorce. She knew how delighted Harry would be, as she would, if she could openly claim him as her husband. She hated the present separation and all the subterfuge which, even when they were under the same roof, had to be put in motion before they could spend a night together. She, as much as he, longed to regularise their union. There would be great opposition to their marriage, she knew; but they would face that afterwards. She had acted before on impulse and taken the consequences. If Angus had proved to be the husband she knew her dear Harry would be, she would have had no regrets. It was Angus's perfidy which had caused her such sorrow, not her own impulsive action.

It had been pleasant to believe Angus to be well out of the way, and the thought of his return and all the trouble it could mean was alarming.

Albany watched her closely. 'And your brother will offer him sanctuary and help.'

'I fear so,' she answered.

'Margaret, your brother is no friend to you.'

'I shall agree with you if he is ready to make Angus his friend.'

'That he is eager to do. Moreover, he would give Angus the help he needs to come back to Scotland and form a party to work for English interests and plot the downfall of the King. So you see, he is working against you.'

She was silent. There was so much truth in what he was saying.

'France would be a better friend to you,' went on Albany. 'The King of France would grant you a pension; and if at any time Angus returned, and he made life difficult for you in Scotland, honours would be waiting for you in France.'

'Could I be sure of this?'

'I promise you it would be so, upon mine honour.'

'Your honour, my lord?'

'Come, I do not break my word. When did I ever swear to you that I had loved no other woman?'

''Tis true enough,' she answered.

'We must be reasonable, Margaret. A marriage between us would doubtless do much to bring peace into Scotland. I am now a widower, and if you obtained your divorce you would be free.'

She did not speak; she was thinking how much she would have given such a short time ago to hear him say those words. Now she could listen to them calmly; and she was thinking: Never would I marry you. I have no wish to marry you. You are ageing and jaded, and my Harry is so young and tender. He thinks it the most wonderful thing in his life that a queen should love him. When I am free, it is Harry who shall be my husband.

She pretended however to be persuaded. She would let him think that she would marry him; then she would show him how much he meant to her, in the same way as he had shown her.

Revenge was still sweet, so perhaps even now, with Harry's

caresses fresh in her memory, she still had some feeling towards this man.

She would go along with him, hide her true feelings; for if her brother was going to be the friend of Angus so that he regained his power in Scotland, her divorce might be delayed still further, and it would be well to see what France had to offer her.

'There shall be a bond between us,' said Albany. 'I will have it drawn up and you will see what advantages will come to you through friendship with France.'

'Yes,' she answered, 'let there be such a bond for me to see.'

Now that she was on friendly terms with the Regent, Margaret returned to Stirling to her son and lover. Albany had impressed upon her the need to obey the Council's injunctions, which were that the King should be kept under restraint for his own safety. She listened quietly and had appeared to acquiesce, but she and Harry together discussed their plans, which were that as soon as the opportunity offered itself the King should be nominal head of the party which they themselves would lead.

That was an uneasy winter.

A quarrel flared up between Margaret and her brother, for her enemies arranged that a copy of the bond to which she had agreed with Albany should be sent among her papers to England.

Henry was furious. Whom could he trust, he stormed, if not his own sister? To think that she was considering making terms with France after all he had done for her.

Margaret shrewdly replied that she herself had had the bond sent to Henry in order that he might understand Albany's intentions; but Henry was not mollified, because he did not believe her. He guessed that she had heard of his invitation to Angus and because of this was seeking friendship with France. It was a sorry state of affairs when brother and sister must quarrel, grumbled Henry, but he had done all he could to keep his sister from losing her kingdom and her soul; he saw that he might be forced to abandon her if she did not mend her ways.

All this seemed unimportant to Margaret, because of her love for Harry Stuart.

Meanwhile Albany was getting desperate because he was not allowed to return to France. He had written to his friends there, assuring them that it was impossible to persuade the Scots to fight against England. He could no longer serve France, and he begged permission to return.

At last he was allowed by France and Scotland to do so and, before departing for Dumbarton where his ship was waiting for him, he went to Stirling Castle for a last interview with Margaret and her son.

He asked to be alone with Margaret for a few moments so that he could say goodbye to her. She granted this request, exultantly recalling the last time he had left and the sorrow she had felt then.

'This is not goodbye,' he said to her, and he held out his hands.

Margaret pretended not to notice the gesture, and walking to the window, looked out.

'We are sorry to see you go, my lord,' she answered.

'I hope that soon you will be free,' he went on.

'I too hope, as I have for so long.'

'And then,' he added, coming to her and standing close, 'we shall be able to make our plans.'

She inclined her head. Her plans were already made, but she was not going to tell him what they were. It would give her some pleasure to refuse his offer of marriage when it came, because, she realised now, she would never really feel indifferent to him.

'Margaret, my dear . . .'

She turned and smiled at him vaguely. 'I must wait until I am free before I can make my plans,' she replied, and moved away from him.

'How you have changed towards me,' he said sadly.

'Time never stands still for any of us, my lord.'

He sighed and, realising that it was no use talking to her as a lover, said: 'Margaret, the state of a country is always uneasy when the King is not of an age to govern. There are too many ambitious men waiting to seize power. I pray you have a care.'

'The care of my son has always been my first and most important task.'

'That I know well, but it is necessary to act with the greatest caution. I beg of you, do not attempt to bring him out of his boyhood too soon.'

'You must trust me to study his welfare in every way.'

'Margaret.' He put his hands on her shoulders and turned her to face him. It was the gesture of a lover towards his mistress. 'Let us part as friends.'

She smiled and, gently disengaging herself, offered him her hands.

'Farewell, my friend,' was all she said.

He drew her to him and kissed her with passion. He still had a slight power to move her. But she was thinking of Harry and their plan to make the young King head of a party which they would lead. All this would be possible, once the Regent had left for France.

Let him think that the kiss she gave him was the kiss of a friend. She could feel little rancour towards him now. Let him go. What did it matter? She was happy with her Harry; and thus she intended to remain for the rest of her life.

Now that Albany had left Scotland, the time had come to carry out that plan which Margaret had cherished for so long.

Closeted with her son and Harry Stuart she told them what they must do. 'The King is coming into his own,' she declared. 'I, no less than he, am weary of this delay. We must seize our opportunity, and as we have many friends it will soon come.'

Young James and Harry were enthusiastic, and their eyes shone with anticipation, because both saw through this a change in their present situation. James had his eyes on a future when he should be King in more than name. Harry was dreaming of the day when Margaret would keep her promise to make him Treasurer of Scotland, and give the Great Seal into his charge. Nor would that be all; as husband of the Queen great titles as well as honours would be his.

'When?' cried young James.

'As soon as I am sure that we can act with safety,' was the answer. 'Now I propose to go on a pilgrimage to the shrine of St Ninian when in truth I shall be mustering the lords of Galloway whom I have reason to think will be faithful to our cause.'

'And soon,' cried James, 'I shall leave this prison. Soon I shall show my subjects that I am in truth the King.'

There was a wildness in the tawny eyes that might have alarmed Margaret if she had not been so elated. She looked from her beloved son to her lover and put an arm about each of them.

'We are together in this,' she murmured, 'and we cannot fail.'

There were many to rally to the Queen's cause. Albany was gone and loyalty to him was waning as it always did when he was no longer in Scotland.

Moreover it was obvious that James would be a King who, in maturity, would make up his own mind and would not thank those who stood against him now. There was the future to think of. James was determined on freedom and would remember those who helped him to it. So there was very little opposition when the King decided to break through his guard at Stirling Castle. When he rode in triumph to Edinburgh his people came running from their houses as he entered the capital city.

'Long live the King!' they shouted. 'We have a king to rule us once more.'

And indeed James had the look of a king. What did it matter that he was so young? Youth passed all too quickly. The boy would soon be a man. Another such, they said, as his father. And they remembered the bonny man; remembered how his eyes would gladden at the sight of fair maidens, and his handsome looks and the show he gave them at the jousts when he was always champion. They forgot that he had led their men into unnecessary battle; they forgot that he had died before his time on Flodden Field.

They only remembered his charm and beauty and they said: 'James the Fifth is another such as James the Fourth. Long live the Stuart. Long live the King!'

So James with his mother rode through his capital and came to the Palace of Holyrood; here they stayed because they had decided to use it as their residence while they remained in the city.

Harry Stuart swaggered about Edinburgh. Rarely had a young man risen so rapidly to power, and many were asking why.

What had this Harry Stuart to bring him such posts as Treasurer and Lord Chancellor? What of those able lords whose experience and rank entitled them to these honours? Why should these be given to a younger son of an obscure nobleman, who had only just begun to be noticed about the Court?

Of course he was handsome; he gave himself airs; he had a knowing look.

They remembered the rise of Angus, and asked themselves if this was an old story repeating itself.

So just as Margaret was beginning to win the respect of the lords she was doomed to lose it. Scotland was prepared to accept the boy King as their ruler; and since he was devoted to his mother and desired her to act as Regent, they were ready to acquiesce. But to set up this nobody – simply because he had a handsome face and a bragging manner – was unendurable.

There was not a lord at Court who was ready to knuckle under to the Queen's paramour. They complained together of the Queen's loose living and told themselves that they had not supported her that she might rule Scotland with the help of Harry Stuart.

Margaret was unaware of the grumblings. She was so happy to have her son and lover contented. They were three happy conspirators – all certain of success.

She wrote to Henry in England telling him that she had successfully flouted the restrictions placed on James by Albany, and that the boy was now in Edinburgh recognised as King. She thought that James should be turning his thoughts to marriage, for although he was as yet young, his betrothal was of great importance to him and to Scotland. Nothing would delight Margaret more than to accept her dear niece, the Princess Mary, as her daughter; and knowing her dearest brother's affection for his nephew (who bore such a striking resemblance to himself) she felt that he would not be averse to accepting him as his son.

Thomas Magnus, Henry's ambassador, arrived in Scotland with Henry's reply to this proposal, and when Margaret heard that he was in Edinburgh she was eager to see him without delay.

James and Harry were with her when she received Magnus, who told her that his master was pleased to hear that James had freed himself from the restraint put on him by Albany and that he hoped that now there would be an end to the strife between their two countries.

'My brother must be assured that this will come to pass,' Margaret replied. 'Pray tell me what was his comment on my proposal concerning the Princess Mary.'

Magnus glanced at Harry, but Margaret waved an imperious hand. 'All that you have to say may be said before the Lord Chancellor.'

Magnus was clearly surprised that such a young man should hold the office, but he said: 'My master, the King of England, declares himself to be overjoyed at the prospect, of the match you propose. At this time a marriage alliance exists between the Princess Mary and the Emperor Charles; but this is a match which my master would be happy to see abandoned for the sake of one with Scotland.'

'This is news I have longed to hear!' Margaret told him.

'But,' interjected Magnus, 'it would be necessary to keep the proposed alliance between Scotland and England a secret until that between England and the Emperor has been officially abandoned.'

Margaret nodded; she turned to James and Harry.

'I am so happy,' she said. 'I have always longed for this. My son the true King of Scotland, and friendship between my native land and that of my adoption.' The glance she gave Harry was warm and secret. She wanted to say: And I love and am loved.

But of course he understood.

'I know,' she went on, 'that my brother has my welfare at heart. He has not understood my desire for a divorce and has opposed me in this matter, but I feel sure, now that there is this understanding between us, he will no longer put obstacles in my way. I do not forget how he keeps the troublesome Angus in England, knowing how it would embarrass me if he returned to Scotland.'

And then, my love, her loving glances told Harry, there will be an end to this secrecy. I shall let the whole world know how matters stand between us two.

Magnus took out the letters and gave them to her.

She sat at the table with James on one side of her, Harry on the other; and while they were thus engaged there was a knock on the door.

Margaret looked up startled; she had given orders that she was not to be disturbed except in an emergency. She could not believe that she had been disobeyed.

'You may enter,' she called.

One of her pages opened the door, and a man with the stains of travel on his clothes stood there.

'You have news?' asked Margaret, rising.

'Yes, Your Grace, and I thought it should be brought to you without delay. The Earl of Angus crossed the Border this day and is now in Scotland.'

Chapter XII

THE QUEEN'S THIRD MARRIAGE

In the dark of night a band of horsemen was making its way towards Edinburgh. At its head rode Angus, his face grim with purpose. Beside him rode Lennox and Buccleugh; they had joined him because they were not prepared to take second place to Harry Stuart.

What a foolish woman she is! thought Angus. Again and again she throws away that which she values. First with me; now with this Stuart fellow. Thank God for a fool!

'We're within a mile of the city,' he murmured to Lennox. 'Who'll go ahead and scale the walls and unlock the gates to let us in?'

'There'll be plenty of volunteers for that duty,' answered Lennox.

Angus nodded. Circumstances had changed him from the young boy with whom the Queen had fallen in love. He was an ambitious man now, yearning to rule Scotland. And as the Queen's husband – he was determined to hold out against the divorce – it was his place to control the Queen's son.

He was determined to get James into his possession; then he could demand what terms he liked to make with Margaret.

He had heard that she constantly referred to him now as my lord Anguish. Let her. She would see that he could cause her anguish enough. He had Henry of England behind him; he had made sure while he was at the Court of England that Henry had understood his sister's leanings towards France through Albany. Henry disapproved of Margaret's obtaining a divorce; he had accepted Angus as his brother-in-law from the first, and continued to do so.

The walls of the city loomed ahead in the darkness and Angus called a halt.

Lennox gave a sign and several men dismounted and crept toward the walls. There was silence among those who waited which seemed to go on for a long time; then the gates of the city were thrown open. Dawn was beginning to show in the sky when Angus and his men marched into Edinburgh through the High Street to St Giles's Church.

❀ ❀ ❀

There was an atmosphere of expectancy in Holyrood that night.

Margaret was conscious of it. It was due to the fact that Angus was in Scotland, and she could not feel safe while he was there.

Harry Stuart was in her bedchamber; it had become common knowledge that he was her lover, and Margaret's passion was too ardent for her to submit to subterfuge. Her love for this young man was apparent in every look she gave him, and she knew it was no use attempting to hide it. Better to show it in – as some called it – a brazen manner. She was not ashamed of her love, nor was he.

'Harry,' she said, 'I have not felt at ease since I knew Anguish had crossed the Border.'

'We'll be a match for Anguish when the time comes,' Harry assured her.

She took his hand and kissed it. 'My blessing,' she murmured. 'What comfort you give me!'

'That is my great desire and always will be,' Harry told her.

He was very pleased with life which offered him so much honour and so much devotion from the Queen.

'It seems oppressive,' Margaret said, 'in spite of the November cold.'

'Let us to bed,' replied Harry. 'I promise to drive off the oppressive atmosphere and the November cold.'

She laughed and kissed him.

'Harry,' she said, as they lay in each other's arms, 'I fancy you have been quiet of late. Is there something on your mind?'

'It is not easy to keep troubles from you. Your eyes are so sharp.'

'Then something is worrying you.'

'I'm afraid, my love.'

'Afraid! *You*, Harry? I do not believe it.'

'Afraid of offending you. If I did, I think I should walk out of this apartment and leap down from the topmost point of the Palace.'

'Don't say such things! I can't bear it. Tell me, what has made you feel thus?'

'Something which happened long ago and of which I have not told you.'

'Someone you loved?'

'Or thought I loved,' he said. 'I did not know love until I knew my Queen.'

'And this . . . someone you thought you loved?'

'I married her.'

'I see. So she is your wife. And you visit her?'

'Not since we told each other of our love. In truth she is no longer my wife. I have divorced her. It was easy enough.'

Margaret was silent for a few seconds, then she said: 'Tell me her name.'

'You would not know her. She is Lady Leslie. My love, my Queen, you are angry with me for keeping this secret?'

'Oh, no, Harry, my darling. I could never be angry with you. And why should I be now? You married her before we met. You kept her existence a secret from me, fearing to hurt me; and you tell me now because she is no longer your wife.'

'Oh, Margaret . . . if you were the humblest maiden within these city walls, I would love you and count it an honour to be your husband.'

She lay against him. 'Thank you for telling me, Harry. It is always so much better to be told than to discover. I have been hurt by the men whom I have loved. Let us swear now that we will never keep secrets from each other. If our love fails we will tell. If we are unfaithful we will tell. Do you promise?'

'There will never be occasion to tell.'

'I know, my love, but let us swear all the same.'

So in the quiet of that night they swore; they made love; and they slept. But not for long.

Margaret released herself from her lover's arms as the disturbance outside her door roused her from her sleep. There was a faint dawn light in the room and she could hear the sound of shouting in the streets.

Hurrying into the antechamber, she called to her women who helped her to dress, their teeth chattering, their fingers fumbling as they did so.

Now there was a hammering on the door.

'Who is there?' called Margaret.

It was one of the guards. 'Your Grace,' he cried, 'my lord Angus is in Edinburgh. His men have scaled the walls and let the invaders in. They are already in the streets on the way to the Castle.'

Margaret understood. They would take the Castle. They would take James from her.

She ran from her apartment, calling the guards as she did so.

'The invaders must not enter the Castle. Send a message at once to the guards that the cannon are to be fired on them as they advance.'

The quiet early morning was broken by the roar of the cannon.

Margaret stood tense, waiting. And after a while news was brought to her that the invaders were retreating from the castle precincts.

❦ ❦ ❦

Angus and his friends, alarmed when the Queen had ordered the cannon to be fired on them, left Edinburgh and took temporary refuge at Dalkeith and then retreated still further to Tantallan.

As soon as the city was free of them Margaret made plans to leave Holyrood, and that night, with her son, led a procession by torchlight to the Castle. There, in that strong fortress, she felt safe, but only temporarily.

She knew that the Douglas faction was too powerful to be easily vanquished, and what she dreaded more than anything was that Angus should force her to return to him.

It was ironical to contemplate that the return of Angus had been made possible by her own brother; Margaret was very uneasy regarding the relationship between herself and Henry, and she decided that her first move must be to alienate Henry from Angus.

The situation was filled with dangers. Scotland was teetering on the edge of civil war. The Douglases were growing bolder than ever now that Angus was back and it was believed that he had the support of the King of England. They had already shown their intentions by murdering Lord Fleming on the very threshold of St Giles's, solely because Fleming was a friend of Albany's and his sister the Regent's mistress; the Douglas faction had determined to thwart the French, and for this reason alone would have had the support of the English.

Never had it seemed more true that a friend one day might be an enemy the next. Margaret, who had previously longed for peace between England and Scotland, was now wondering whether France would not be the more substantial ally.

It was all very well for Henry to offer the Princess Mary to James; but Margaret believed that Henry was contemplating divorcing Mary's mother, Katharine of Aragon, because, as she had been the wife of his brother Arthur, her marriage with himself was invalid. Then would Henry offer a bastard princess to the King of Scotland!

Letters from France reached her. Albany had a suggestion. His wife's niece, the daughter of the Duke of Urbino and Marie of Boulogne, was one of the wealthiest heiresses in Europe. It was true that Catherine de Medici was not royal, but Albany believed she would be a very good match for the King of Scotland.

Margaret feigned to consider this but James's marriage could wait.

In the meantime there remained the menace of the

Douglases; and it seemed to her that the most urgent matter of all was the need to obtain her divorce from Angus.

In exchange for a divorce she offered him a portion of her dowerlands which would bring him in a good income. He refused the offer and his refusal was ominous. The more so because the Parliament, realising the power of the Douglas faction, had decided that he should be included in those selected to take over the guardianship of the King. It had been arranged that Angus and the Archbishop of Glasgow should have the guardianship of James for three months; Arran and the Bishop of Aberdeen for the next three; Argyle and Chancellor Beaton next, to be followed by Lennox and the Bishop of Dunblane. Thus it seemed that none of these ambitious and able nobles should have the King for too long a period in his care.

❀ ❀ ❀

On a bleak February day the King was escorted to the Tolbooth in the state procession. With him rode his mother; and before them Angus solemnly walked, carrying the crown, while Arran held the sceptre and Argyle the sword.

It was the first time in years that Margaret had seen her husband, and she found it difficult to look at him without emotion.

He had not lost his handsome looks for, although the freshness of youth was no longer his, he would always be extremely distinguished in appearance.

If he had been a faithful husband, she told herself, we could have found great happiness together.

She was aware of Harry among those riding with her. Poor boy! He looked apprehensive, fearing, she knew, that she might return to Angus. She wanted to comfort him. Never would she forgive Angus for the unhappiness he had caused her. No! She had given her love to Harry Stuart now, and as soon as she could she would marry him. He was to be her last love.

In the Tolbooth, when the ceremony of opening Parliament was completed, Margaret rose to tell the assembled lords that her greatest desire was for peace throughout the realm.

It was arranged then that a Regency should be formed, with the Queen as the principal member, which should be made up of lords temporal and spiritual. The latter consisted of St Andrews, Glasgow, Aberdeen and Dunblane; and the former were headed by Angus, Arran, Argyle and Lennox.

On the surface it was a peaceful meeting, but there were many hard looks directed towards Harry Stuart; and several of the lords whispered together that although they accepted the Queen as a member of the Regency they would not accept her paramour.

The meeting over, the King made his way back to Holyrood with the Queen. Not far from Margaret rode Harry Stuart, very pleased with himself, and not in the least disconcerted by the curious and hostile glances cast in his direction.

Young James was uneasy, knowing that he was to be passed to the custody of Angus for the next three months, and because he adored his mother and knew how she hated her husband he was displeased. He would have preferred to be in the care of Lennox whom he liked best of all of those selected to guard him.

Margaret sought to comfort him.

'Never fear,' she said, 'we will find some means of rescuing you. But I doubt not that he'll be a lenient guardian. He'll not dare be otherwise. You are the King and even though as yet you are a boy who must obey these men, it will not always be so and they'll remember that. And while you are with him you can do your best to persuade him to the divorce.'

James said he would do his best; and while they were together Harry joined them.

'You are looking disturbed,' said the Queen tenderly.

'I have just been warned,' he replied, 'that the Douglases have sworn to murder me and my brother James this night – if we remain in Holyrood.'

'Harry!' cried Margaret, and she began to tremble. 'But,' she went on quickly, 'they must not find you in Holyrood. You must leave at once.'

'Leave you and the King!'

'I know you would stay to defend us, but these Douglases are a ruthless clan. Harry, you must leave at once. Take your brother with you. I shall not know a moment's peace while you are here.'

'But to leave you . . .'

'It is a command,' said Margaret firmly.

Harry looked from her to the King, who said: 'Yes, Harry, you must go. My mother and I would be deeply grieved if harm should befall you.'

Harry bowed and retired, but Margaret followed him to his apartment and they remained some seconds in a close embrace.

'My love, how can I go?' demanded Harry.

'How can you stay when it might mean your death?'

'I would not care . . .'

'But I would. Nay, Harry, this is farewell but not for long. Go to Stirling and remain there. I shall be with you erelong, for I cannot bear to live apart from you.'

There was another passionate embrace which was interrupted by the arrival of Harry's young brother James.

Margaret regarded him sadly — such a handsome boy! — then she kissed him on the brow.

'Take care of each other,' she cautioned. 'And now . . . go quickly.'

They both kissed her hands and, when they were gone, Margaret was for a time cast down.

Her lover gone to Stirling; her son in the care of Angus. This was a day of mourning; but it was not her way to accept defeat.

She was certain that soon she would be divorced from Angus and married to Harry; soon the power of the Douglases would be overcome; soon her son would rule in truth with herself and Harry in the background to guide him.

❦ ❦ ❦

The rule of the Douglases had begun.

When the period of Angus's guardianship had elapsed, he simply refused to give up the King. He had by this time set the members of his clan in the highest posts and as Douglases from all over Scotland rallied to his banner his followers grew in number. Any ambitious man who hoped for honours placed himself in the service of the Douglas; Angus had the King, and although it was said that James V ruled Scotland now, the real ruler was Angus.

Margaret, angry and alarmed at her husband's growing power, watched events from the shelter of Stirling where she had joined Harry and his brother. The subject which dominated her mind was the divorce. She longed for it passionately and she was desperately afraid that the growing power of Angus would enable him to prevent her obtaining it.

James himself was fast growing away from boyhood. He

was going to be as handsome as his father; he was strong-willed; very skilled in the joust and the hunt, he surpassed his companions in these fields. In order that he should not allow himself to become a mere tool of ambitious men, Margaret had impressed on him his need to assert himself, and James had learned that lesson thoroughly.

He had learned also to hate Angus, and the arrogance of his stepfather did nothing to endear him to the young boy. Deeply he resented firstly being made Angus's prisoner, for that was how he regarded himself, and secondly being obliged to give his assent to matters with which they scarcely bothered to acquaint him.

While he was under the care of Angus he was continually plotting as to how he could escape. He believed that, once he could rid himself of Angus's rule and escape to his mother, he would rally the loyal lords against the Douglases who must be hated because they were feared so much.

When an opportunity came to speak to Lennox of his feelings he did so; and although Lennox was cautious there was a tacit agreement between them that when the time was ripe the King should escape from Angus's care.

Angus made a habit of taking the King about the country with him; and on one occasion when they had travelled to the Border in order to suppress the robbers there, they were intercepted by two thousand men who, under a certain Scott of Branxton, made an attempt to kidnap the King and free him from Angus. This attempt was defeated.

Lennox was present when it took place, but he made no effort to ward off the kidnappers; and it was not due to him that they were repulsed.

Shortly afterward Lennox joined the Queen, who was

always ready with plans for escape. They decided that next time an attempt to free the King should not fail, and they began to plan.

It was agreed that Lennox should ride to Borough Moor near Edinburgh with only a few horsemen, and take with him eight spare horses which would be for the King and seven of his trusty servants who would escape with him. It should not be difficult for a message to be conveyed to the King at Holyrood, and with the help of certain members of his suite, who were in league with Lennox, for James to make his way out of the Palace.

Margaret, with Harry, waited impatiently at Stirling to receive James.

'And once he is with us and we have raised the lords against Angus, the power of the Douglases will be no more,' she announced confidently.

❀ ❀ ❀

James was at the window ruefully looking out at Arthur's Seat. Each day he grew more restive. He often told his attendants that he would like to have Angus hanged on the nearest tree. How much longer was the Douglas going to be allowed to rule Scotland? Was there no one in the land who had enough love of his King to set him free?

He knew some who loved him enough to attempt it. There was his mother for one. There was Lennox for another. He knew now that Lennox was his friend. He could not long remain a prisoner. Then let Angus beware. He would hound him from Scotland. For, he thought, there will not be room in this country for Scotland's King and the Earl of Angus.

One of his pages was plucking at his sleeve.

'Your Grace, there is someone at the door.'

James started up and said: 'Who?'

But before the page could answer, the door was opened and a man burst unceremoniously into the room. His eyes were wild and, seeing the King, he came straight to him.

'Your Grace,' he said, 'forgive this intrusion. I am the Master of Kilmorris and I come from my lord Lennox.'

'Speak on,' said James eagerly.

'My lord Lennox is at Borough Moor; he has horses waiting. If, under cover of darkness, you can leave the Palace and find your way to him, he will conduct you to safety and the Queen.'

'This is good news,' cried James. 'Kilmorris, my friend, I shall remember this when I am free of Angus.'

'Your Grace, I serve you with my life.'

'I thank you. Now tell me of the whereabouts of Lennox, and I will summon those whom I can trust to help me.'

There was a commotion at the door and another of the King's pages ran into the apartment.

'Your Grace,' he cried, 'it is known that a stranger has entered the Palace. The guards are being called out. They are coming now.'

Kilmorris turned pale, guessing what his fate would be if he were discovered. James looked at him with horror, for he also knew. It was clear to them both that there could be little chance of escape now, but James was not going to allow the faithful Kilmorris to be taken if he could help it.

He looked about him eagerly and said: 'Quick! Follow me.'

He ran from the apartment with Kilmorris at his heels; he slipped through a door and they ran down a spiral staircase. They were both breathless when they came to a door which the King pushed open. 'This is the coining house,' said James.

'You can get away through here. They will not think you could go this way. Go at once and I will return to my apartment.'

Kilmorris thanked his King and James hurried back to his apartment to find that Angus had already arrived with some of the guards. When the Earl saw the King he gave a shout of relief.

'Your Grace,' he cried, 'thank God you are safe. I heard that our enemies had invaded the Palace.'

'Is that so?' answered James coolly.

'It was doubtless a false alarm. So eager are my men to preserve Your Grace's safety that they are sometimes overzealous.'

James inclined his head and walked somewhat haughtily to the window.

He stood there looking out, glad that Angus could not hear how loudly his heart was beating.

He will have left the Palace by now, James was thinking. Now he will be safe.

But although Kilmorris escaped, Angus did not believe that it had been a false alarm. He doubled the guards about the King, and the result of that little escapade was that James was more of a prisoner than ever.

But James was not going to endure such conditions. Hearing that his mother had come to Linlithgow, he sent for Angus and told him that it was long since he had seen the Queen and he wished to do so.

Angus, realising that his enemies were gathering against him and that Arran was only with him because he was the enemy of Lennox, decided that the King must be humoured;

and he gathered together a small army to accompany the King to Linlithgow.

On the road between Edinburgh and Linlithgow Angus's army met Lennox and his, and a skirmish ensued. Lennox and his men were determined to take possession of the King; Angus and his were equally determined not to let James go.

'Keep the King in the rear,' Angus ordered, and the bridle of James's horse was taken by George Douglas, whom Angus could trust as he could few others.

James, watching the battle, was looking for the opportunity to slip out of George Douglas's grasp and make his way to the other side, when George, realising this, laughed grimly.

'You should bide where you are, sir,' he warned. 'For if they get a hold of you, be it by one of your arms, we will seize you by the leg; and we'll pull you into two pieces rather than part with you.'

'I'll not forget that, George Douglas,' said James.

''Twill be well if you'll remember it, sir,' was the answer.

Rarely had the young King known such fury as that which now gripped him. He, the King, to be so treated, to be told they would rather see him dead than in the possession of their enemy. Indeed he would remember this. As long as he lived there would be no place in his kingdom for a Douglas.

But when he heard that Lennox had fallen, his anger changed to sorrow. Lennox, the guardian he had loved, the man whom he had believed would rescue him from the hated Douglases.

Angus, triumphant with victory, was riding towards him. The battle was over, and James was a prisoner still.

Margaret was in despair. The power of the Douglases was as great as ever, James remained in the custody of his stepfather, and the Douglases were in all the important posts of Scotland.

She hated the cold of December in Stirling Castle, and she was beginning to despair of ever attaining her freedom, proclaiming Harry as her husband and enjoying the company of her son.

Then the miracle happened, when dispatches from Rome arrived for the Queen.

From Rome!

Margaret cried out that the messengers should be brought to her without a moment's delay.

She read the documents and felt the hysterical laughter rising within her.

It had happened at last. The Cardinal of Ancona, whom Clement VII had appointed to judge her case, had given judgement in her favour.

She had her divorce.

She was no longer married to Angus.

❀ ❀ ❀

Those were wonderful weeks which followed. Harry was constantly in her company; they planned their future and her first act was to redeem her promise.

She and Harry were married.

But, she reminded him, there would be opposition to the marriage, for there was bound to be jealousy among the lords, and they must act cautiously. She remembered how disastrous life had become when she had secretly married Angus, and they agreed that they must be more cautious this time.

Her divorce was being discussed above and below the

Border. Her brother Henry wrote of how the news had shocked him. He wanted her to remember that the divine ordinance of inseparable matrimony was first instituted in Paradise, and he could only protest against this shameful verdict which had been sent from Rome.

Margaret laughed hilariously.

'Do you know, Harry,' she said, 'my brother Henry is the biggest hypocrite living. He is seriously thinking of ridding himself of poor Katharine. Of course he is going to say that he was never truly married to Katharine. Well, nor was I to Angus. He was betrothed previously to that woman of his. Henry should remember that.'

But she and Harry were too happy to care. The glorious thing had happened. She was free and she had married the man she would love as long as she lived.

Of course they could not keep the marriage a secret for ever.

The news that her divorce had been granted reached her in December. In March she made a declaration to the country: 'Now that I am free I have married again; and my husband is Henry Stuart.'

❀ ❀ ❀

Angus was furious when he heard that Margaret had been granted the divorce, but when he learned of her marriage to Henry Stuart he could not control his rage.

'How dare she so demean herself!' he shouted. 'She shall be sorry for this. It is an insult to me and to Scotland.'

He went to the King and asked him what he thought of his mother's action.

'I do not presume to judge the Queen,' answered James coldly.

'Your Grace, she has lost all hope of keeping her place in the Regency.'

'Has it occurred to you that soon there will be no need of a Regency?'

'Indeed that is so, but just now there *is* need for a Regency, and we are going to Stirling to see that this upstart, Henry Stuart, receives his just deserts.'

'And what are those?'

'Your Grace jokes. He shall be thrown into prison. He has no right to marry the Queen.'

'But she gave him that right which was hers to give.'

'Your Grace is too young to understand the implications of this.'

'Ah,' retorted James. 'It is the old story. I am always too young.'

Angus was so disturbed that he did not notice the King's coolness. They must set out at once for Stirling, he said, and the King must accompany the party which should go, because it was in his name that Harry Stuart should be arrested.

How angry was young James as he rode towards Stirling. He thought of Lennox, dying from wounds inflicted by the hated Douglases. He thought of his beloved mother and his friend Harry Stuart. They loved and married; and because the Douglas had not wished them to do so they were to be parted.

If he were but King in truth!

He thought of all the things he would do. He would embrace his mother first, then Harry, and tell them he hoped for their happiness. And then he would cry: Throw that man in prison. And he would laugh aloud to see the astonishment on the face of Angus.

'I hate the Douglases,' he muttered as he rode along.

But power was still in the hands of the Douglases.

Angus strode into Stirling Castle and demanded to see the Queen.

She faced him defiantly, but when she heard his demand that Harry be brought forth, and when she saw his guards lay their hands on her husband, she was alarmed.

She cried out: 'James, you are the King . . .'

James wanted to intervene but he knew it was useless; there was nothing he could do, and he could only stand by, black hatred of the Douglases in his heart.

So they took Harry Stuart and threw him into a dungeon.

And they left Margaret weeping for her newly married husband.

❀ ❀ ❀

It seemed now that the country was completely in the control of Angus. He was the uncrowned King. The Queen, who had retreated to Edinburgh, was forced by him to give up the Castle. She so feared for her life that she hid herself on the moors and lived the life of a shepherdess, surrounded by a few faithful friends who adopted the same disguise.

Harry escaped from his dungeon and, when she received a communication from him, she joined him at Stirling and they made the Castle their refuge.

James was scarcely a boy now, for he would soon be seventeen. Time enough, he believed, for him to throw off the yoke.

The lords surrounding him watched his hatred of Angus growing and, ever ready to change sides, they believed that it would be wise to do so now.

Margaret with Harry and his brother James made a new plot, and messages were smuggled in to the King. Margaret let him know that she was taking the precaution of fortifying Stirling Castle so that very shortly it would be completely garrisoned; a good place for the King to come to and make a stand against his enemies.

She wanted him to know that there was none who worked more zealously for him than his mother and his stepfather, Harry Stuart; she hoped that when it was in his power to do so he would remember all Harry had done, and reward him. The Lordship of Methven, she suggested, would be a suitable honour. James should think of it.

James did think of it. He would be very ready to reward Harry, or anyone who could help him escape from his hated position.

Angus had moved him to Falkland Palace, and one by one James was winning over the servants to his side. He knew whom he could trust, and it would be a simple matter to slip out with the help of guards who had ceased to be the servants of Angus and wished to serve their King. Horses would be waiting for him; then away to Stirling.

It proved to be as simple as he had thought it would because he had been right when he had believed that there were few now who wanted to disobey the King.

So one night James walked out of Falkland, mounted the waiting horse and rode full speed to Stirling, where he was received with great rejoicing by his mother and her husband.

Next day the royal standard flew high over Stirling Castle. The King was a boy no longer; he had come into his own. He was ready now to rule Scotland. He was going to reward his friends – and woe betide his enemies!

How happy Margaret was now.

James, her son, was King in truth, and there would be no more separations; Harry had been rewarded and was now Lord Methven and Master of the Royal Ordnance; men were deserting the Douglases and rallying to the King; there was nothing to do but rejoice.

James, who would never forgive Angus for the years he had spent as his captive, declared his intention of throwing him into prison. But Angus was not easily captured, though he was put to the horn and declared a traitor in every town in Scotland and a prize of a hundred marks was offered to any who could bring him, dead or alive, to the King. His estates were seized and divided among the loyal nobles who were only too eager to receive them.

Yet none caught Angus, and news eventually came to Margaret that he had escaped into England. This was good news, except for one thing. He had taken their daughter, the Lady Margaret Douglas, with him, and Margaret's hopes of regaining the guardianship of the girl were frustrated.

She was very anxious about her daughter until she heard that the Princess Mary had taken her into her household. Then she consoled herself that, as cousin to the Princess, she would be well treated. As for Angus he would be received well at Henry's Court for Henry had always been his friend.

Well, she had lost her daughter, but she had her son, who showed in a hundred ways his regard for her; she had Lord Methven, her dear Harry; and there was no longer the need to plan James's rescue because James was free and in his rightful place.

She had enjoyed intrigue, but she was growing too old for it. Perhaps now she would settle down happily to the life of wife and mother, for she was young enough to bear children. She would retire from the glare of public life and be content to shelter in the brilliance of her son.

She was no longer Margaret the Queen, fighting to retain an untenable position; she was Harry's wife, contented and at peace.

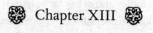

Chapter XIII

THE LAST DAYS

The years of retirement passed in happiness as Margaret had known they would. She bore Harry a son and a daughter; and her only sadness was that her daughter Margaret was far away and becoming more and more a stranger to her mother as the years passed.

Yet young Margaret was well cared for, the friend of Princess Mary, and a favourite, it was said, of her uncle. She was by all accounts a rare beauty, and Margaret would have given a great deal to see her again.

But it was not possible to have all one wished in life and she must learn to be content with what was hers.

Harry was a devoted husband; she was very fond of his brother James who was so like him in every way. The King was an affectionate son; he was loving by nature as many young women had discovered. Ah well, thought Margaret, it was hardly to be expected that a son of James IV and herself would be otherwise.

There were few shadows in life up to that time when news came to Scotland that the King of England had married again and was asking acknowledgement of Queen Anne Boleyn.

James came to see Margaret to discuss the matter with her.

As usual when she saw him after a brief absence she was filled with pride as he entered her room at Methven Castle. He was startlingly like his father and every bit as handsome. His hair had never lost the reddish tinge; his eyes were bluish grey, long and alert; his aquiline nose gave dignity and manliness to a face which otherwise would have been almost feminine in its beauty. He was of medium height, slender and well-shaped – a son to be proud of.

He kissed her hand – so gracious and courtly – another reminder of his father.

'So my brother has at last freed himself of poor Katharine and married the Boleyn woman,' she said.

James laughed. 'Well, you must admit he has been patient.'

'Patient! 'Tis something Henry could never be. He must have suffered torment. I pity those about him.'

James nodded. 'He wishes us to acknowledge her as Queen of England.'

Margaret spread her hands. 'Henry has made her his Queen. That is an end to the matter. But I know how he always loved approval. He could never be happy without it.'

'The clergy are displeased,' James told her. 'They sent a friar to preach before me and, although he did not mention names, he made it very clear that what has taken place in England has deeply shocked him and his brethren.'

Margaret made an impatient gesture. 'I am sorry for Katharine, but I always knew she was too meek. And she was very condemnatory of my divorce. It is all such nonsense. When a marriage is finished, it is finished and that should be an end to it.'

'As you proved with Angus. Mother, I am in agreement with you. I shall write to congratulate Henry on his marriage and to wish him and his Queen a fruitful union.'

'Do so, my son, but with discretion. There are too many people in Scotland who imagine divorce to be a major sin, and it is better not to offend them.'

'They will have to change their minds.' He hesitated for a few seconds then hurried on: 'Mother, I have made up my mind to marry.'

'It is time, my son. Do you plan to visit France yourself to claim your bride?'

'No, I do not intend to go to France because I have no intention of marrying into France. I have chosen my wife and she is Scottish.'

Margaret stared at him in astonishment. 'But you have been promised to the daughter of the Duke of Vendôme. What are you saying, James?'

'That I have decided to marry where I please, and I have chosen my own bride.'

'James! This cannot be so. Whom have you chosen?'

'Margaret Erskine. She has already borne me a son and I would make him legitimate if that were possible. He is a fine healthy boy and I love his mother as I could love no other.'

'But is she not married to Douglas of Lochleven?'

'We have just agreed that when a marriage is irksome it should be dissolved, have we not?'

'James, this is madness!'

'Was it madness when you divorced Angus?'

'I was only the mother of the King. You are the King.'

'Nevertheless I am determined to marry whom I will.'

'So it is for this reason that you congratulate my brother and his new Queen.'

James was silent, and Margaret felt peace slipping away from her. She tried to look dispassionately at that handsome face which was almost womanish. The aquiline nose could not altogether disguise the weakness of the chin. James *was* weak where women were concerned, as his father had been.

He must not make the mistakes that she had made. Looking back she saw that hasty marriage with Angus as the beginning of all her troubles.

In that moment she wanted to help James achieve his desire, but she believed that by arranging a divorce for his mistress, marrying her himself and by attempting to legitimise his bastard, he was, at the beginning of his reign, making trouble for himself. What of the French? How would he placate them for the insult done to them?

No, she must make a firm stand.

'It is impossible,' she said.

His brow had darkened, his lips tightened. He turned on her in a rage.

'It was well enough when you wished for divorce. So there is one law for you and another for me?'

'James . . . you are the King.'

'And you were the Queen. What did you care? So you will stand against me now. I had not believed it of you.'

She tried to explain but his impetuous nature was in revolt. All those who would not help him in this matter were his enemies.

It was the first quarrel they had had; and it was a bitter one.

Margaret was filled with grief; and that was the end of the peaceful years.

James did not marry his mistress. 'When the Parliament stood firmly against him he was wise enough to realise that he could only court disaster by doing so.

So he gave way and went to France, in the role of romantic lover, to court the lady who had been chosen for him. He was received with warmth in the Duke's household, but he did not fall deeply in love with Mademoiselle de Vendôme. His thoughts were still with the mother of his son James on whom he doted although he had put aside his desire to marry her, for the sake of duty. It was not surprising therefore that he lacked enthusiasm for this woman who had been chosen to be his bride.

Travelling through France he was entertained at the Court of François, and there he met the young Princess Magdalene who had at one time been suggested as a bride for him. She was a delicate child who, no sooner had she set eyes on him, adored him.

As for James, all his chivalry was aroused by her fragility and her admiration of himself; and he confessed to her father that she was the lady whom it would delight him to marry.

The King of Scotland was a worthy *parti*. So the proposed marriage with Vendôme was put aside for the more desirable one with the daughter of the King of France.

James was delighted. Only this fragile child could compensate him for his inability to marry his dear Margaret and legitimise his bonny James. The Parliament of Scotland had no objections. A French marriage was what it desired, and a daughter of the King of France was more suitable than one of the Duke of Vendôme.

❦ ❦ ❦

Margaret sighed with relief. Once James was safely married, all would be peaceful again.

News came from England that Henry, tiring of his second wife, had accused her of adultery and she had lost her head on Tower Green. He was now married to Lady Jane Seymour.

'He cannot blame me for having had three husbands,' commented Margaret, 'now that he has had three wives.'

She was a little anxious about her daughter Margaret who by this time had become a prominent member of the English Court. In those days of intrigue one could never be sure who was going to arouse the King's anger next. Henry VIII was a fickle man; his anger was terrible, and he had supreme power with which to make it felt. Who would have believed that the vital and dazzling Anne, for whom he had fought desperately over so many years, could in three short ones have passed from glory to dishonour and death? It was ironical that glory, honour, disaster and death had been dealt by the same hand.

And there, in the centre of intrigue, was young Margaret. Her mother's anxiety had increased because the girl had been favoured by Anne Boleyn, which doubtless meant she had lost favour with her original benefactress, the Princess Mary. It must be impossible to live at the English Court and not take sides.

It seemed that no sooner was the anxiety concerning one child lessened than that concerning another must distress her.

She often lay awake at night, thinking of the dangers which could beset her daughter at the Court of her terrible brother. It was true that Angus, as a pensioner of Henry, was at that Court and, whatever else he was, he was fond of his daughter and would do his best to protect her.

Without doubt the peaceful era had come to an end.

But she was not prepared for the greatest blow of all.

During one of the rare journeys she made, she visited the home of the Earl of Atholl. A splendid banquet was prepared for her and she took great pleasure in wearing her most dazzling gown; her person sparkled with jewels as she sat at the table which was laden with beef, mutton, venison, goose, capon, swan, partridge, plover, moorfowls and every kind of food that could be thought of; with Malmsey and muscatel, white and red wine, beer and aqua vitae with which to wash it down. It was rarely, said Atholl, that he had the honour of entertaining the Queen.

Harry had been with her as usual and, as they sat together at the places of honour, a woman caught her eye. This was Janet, widow of the Master of Sutherland, and eldest daughter of the Earl of Atholl; in that moment it was as though some extra sense warned her to take especial note of Janet; and when she met Janet's young son, a most engaging boy, she kept him at her side. There was something in the lad which appealed to her strongly.

'What is your name?' she asked him.

'It is Henry, Your Grace,' he told her.

She smiled at Harry. 'A goodly name,' she commented, 'and one which I like well.'

Harry laid his hand on the boy's shoulder and it was almost as though a secret message passed between them.

Margaret turned her eyes to the Mistress of Sutherland who was watching them, and she noticed that the woman's hands were slightly trembling.

She remembered then that she had heard of the death of the Master of Sutherland some years before. Could he have had a son of Henry's age?

She mentioned the matter to her women when they were undressing her that night, but strangely they seemed reluctant to speak of the matter.

Then it was almost as though she had gone back in years and was reliving certain episodes, as though her life was a vast tapestry, the essential point of which was that the pattern should be repeated again and again. A stupid fancy, she told herself; and tried to dismiss the matter from her mind.

But the evil suspicions persisted, and she found herself watching Harry as she never had before. Emotions which she had long forgotten seemed to be stirring within her.

One evening when they were alone together in her apartments at Methven Castle she burst out: 'What is the Mistress of Sutherland to you, Harry?'

As she watched the blood drain from his face, she knew. Had she not lived it all before?

❀ ❀ ❀

So her life was shattered. She was no longer young, being nearly fifty. The pain was as great as it had been when she had discovered the infidelity of James and of Angus. Why, she demanded, was she called upon to bear this yet again? Why was it that her marriages always ended in this way?

Ended?

Yes, this was going to be the end of her third marriage. She was not going to be deceived and deluded again. She supposed that all the Court knew of her husband's treachery as they had known of that of Angus and James before she did. Then she had given way to passionate weeping. But she was older now; her emotions were no longer so easily stirred.

Harry should be made to suffer though. All his honours should be stripped from him.

'You will be sorry for this, my Lord Muffin,' she said, using the contemptuous term which her brother Henry had bestowed on her third husband when he had first heard of the marriage, and had indeed persisted in calling him ever since.

There was one word which kept hammering in her brain: divorce.

Was there no end to trouble? News came from England that her daughter, the Lady Margaret Douglas, had incurred the King's displeasure by betrothing herself, without his consent, to Lord Thomas Howard, the uncle of Anne Boleyn.

Young Margaret's position had changed when the King had declared his marriage to Katharine of Aragon invalid. It had altered once more now that Anne Boleyn was disgraced. Since both the Princesses Mary and Elizabeth were declared illegitimate, Margaret Douglas was heir to the throne if Henry did not beget legitimate children. It was true that King James of Scotland came before her; but Margaret had been brought up at the Court of England and had until now enjoyed the favour of her uncle.

Therefore to betroth herself to Lord Thomas Howard without the consent of Henry would be to bring his wrath down upon her.

Her mother's fears were not without foundation.

Deeply wounded from the knowledge of Harry's treachery, Margaret was distracted when the news came from England that her daughter and the girl's lover were in the Tower of London, the King's prisoners.

A little while ago she would have gone to Harry for solace. Now there was no one to whom she could turn. James had lost some of his affection for her when she had not helped him to win a divorce for Margaret Erskine that he might marry the woman he loved; moreover James was in France.

She paced up and down her apartment. She longed to have

her daughter with her. She wept, remembering the girl's birth in Harbottle Castle, which now seemed so many weary years away.

She stopped by her writing table and, taking up her pen, wrote to her brother imploring him not to be harsh with her daughter. 'If you will send her to me in Scotland,' she wrote, 'I will answer to you that my child shall never trouble my brother more.'

She did not seal the letter when it was written; she sat with her head in her hands, while a feeling of utter desolation swept over her.

Harry, whom she had loved and trusted, had betrayed her as the others had. And now she was no longer young and beautiful. Still, she was vigorous; she was a queen.

She began to think of young James Stuart who was so like his brother Harry and, she told herself now, of a less sly countenance. No, she could not marry her husband's brother. She thought of Angus, whom when she had last seen him had changed from the callow boy she had married. Angus had been most reluctant to be divorced.

Suppose she went to England. Suppose she married Angus there and brought him back to Scotland. Then my Lord Muffin would so tremble in his shoes that his Mistress of Sutherland would be hard put to it to comfort him.

She picked up her pen and wrote once more:

'Dearest brother, I suffer much misery at this time. I have been very evilly used by Lord Methven and I am seeking now to put an end to my marriage . . .'

She put down her pen and found that she was weeping, for suddenly, sitting there, the full force of her desolation swept over her, because she realised that the peace and happiness had never truly existed outside her imagination. The complacent years were revealed to her for what they were.

No happy married life; all lies; all deceit.

Why has Fate set me this tragic pattern? she asked herself. Is there a reason?

❦ ❦ ❦

James brought home his little Magdalene – a dainty creature, looking too fragile to be real. He adored her, which was comforting. Poor James, he needed to be happy for he had been denied the bride he had wished for and he constantly grieved because his bonny James must remain a bastard.

But he was happy for a while with the delicate child. How pretty she was in her closely fitting gown of white damask embroidered with gold, and the small round cap made of pearls and jewels set on her light brown curls. A fairy child, too delicate for the winds of Scotland.

She coughed and after coughing there was blood on her kerchief which she tried to conceal, and did for a while. It was soon discovered that Holyrood was too damp and low-lying for her comfort; she coughed a great deal there. But the Castle was too bleak and she coughed there for that reason.

Will this delicate creature bear Scotland heirs? asked the brawny Highlanders. Magdalene of France was the daughter of a great king, but would she give James of Scotland a son to compare with Margaret Erskine's bastard?

James worried about the health of his bride, and was irritable when his mother told him that she intended to divorce his stepfather.

'A divorce at your time of life!' he cried. 'Why, you would be a laughing stock.'

'You would take your revenge because I could not help you obtain a divorce for Margaret Erskine?'

What a tragedy that she and James were no longer the friends they once had been.

Magdalene had landed in Scotland in May; by July she was dead. Had she lived a few more days she would have reached her seventeenth birthday.

Scotland mourned her; but none more deeply than her young husband.

❋ ❋ ❋

The Queen's depression lifted a little when she heard that her daughter Margaret had been moved from the Tower to Sion Abbey. She had caught a fever while in prison and evidently the King did not wish her to die since he had agreed to her removal to a more comfortable place of confinement.

Margaret had written again to her brother imploring him to allow her daughter to return to her. If she came back to me, she told herself, I should have her future to plan. I would live again through her.

Occasionally she thought of Harry's brother James. Dared she risk a fourth marriage? Sometimes she said no; at others she asked herself, Why not? The old pattern could not go on repeating itself. There must be a man somewhere who would be her faithful husband. James was handsome, but so young. And there would be an outcry if she married her husband's brother.

Angus?

She thought often of Angus as he had been in the days of his youth. Scenes from the honeymoon at Stobhall often came back to her mind and made her feel young again.

But James continued to ridicule the idea of another divorce, and she could not marry again without one.

Take a lover? She craved for a happy and legitimate union. She was so lonely nowadays; and she found that she could not feel as angry with Harry as she had with Angus. Her pride had been wounded more than her emotions. Was this a sign that she was growing old?

Life went on about her. Her brother wrote jubilantly that he now had a son: Prince Edward. True, the child had cost his mother, Jane Seymour, her life; but he found it more difficult to get sons than wives.

Young Margaret's lover had died in the Tower and she was freed because, with the birth of a prince, she was no longer of the same importance. In fact, Henry VIII did not care to have about him young people who might be said to have a claim to his throne, so he declared her illegitimate, adding that the marriage between her mother and Angus had been no lawful one.

Margaret's rage was great when she heard this, and once more she planned a remarriage with Angus that they might fight together for her daughter's legitimacy and for her place in the succession to the throne of England.

Yet nothing came of these plans. She no longer found intense excitement in plotting as she once had; and, looking into her mirror, she told herself that she was growing old.

'I am growing old,' she said one day.

She sat at her table, her pen in her hand, writing letters, a habit of hers.

She was very tired and felt vaguely unwell. Words would not come easily to her mind as they used to, so she laid down her pen and thought; and as usual at such times her mind went back to the past.

Her daughter Margaret was happy in England, she supposed, now that Henry had given her a place in the household of Anne of Cleves. James had married a French widow, Mary of Lorraine, and although the two children whom they had had, both died, they would have others.

Poor James! How hard it was for royal people to beget healthy legitimate children. His illegitimate ones were bonny creatures, in particular that young James whom he loved so dearly. What a pity that the boy had Margaret Erskine for a mother instead of a Queen of Scotland!

Her own children by Harry were not strong and their health gave her cause for concern, but there were so many anxieties, and she felt too tired to think of them any more.

Instead she thought of her youth, of coming into Scotland and riding on the palfrey James had sent. She could see him now, so handsome, so beloved by his people, riding into his capital with his bride on the pillion behind him.

Her hands had begun to shake and she could not stop them. She stared at them in dismay and called for her attendants, but when they came running to her side, she could not see them clearly.

'Help me to my bed,' she said. 'I feel ill.'

As they undressed her the palsy intensified; and when she lay on her bed she said: 'I have never felt so ill before. Send to Falkland Palace for the King. Tell him of my state and that I should like to see him.'

Her orders were obeyed and she lay on her bed, waiting.

Soon he would come – her beautiful son whom she had loved so dearly. She would see him come striding into her chamber. But when she thought of him it was that other James she saw – the laughing, handsome husband with whom on her first coming to Scotland she had fallen violently in love.

She had forgotten that she was in Methven Castle, imagining herself to be in Holyrood with James standing before her while she accused him of deserting her for his mistresses. Then it was Angus who stood there . . . or was it Albany . . . or Harry? She was not sure. They were as one now. The men whom she had loved; the men who had deceived her.

She murmured so quietly that none heard: 'If I had not been the daughter of a King should I have been loved for myself?'

She tried to rouse herself because there was so much she had to say.

'My daughter . . . the Lady Margaret Douglas . . . James must be good to her. Angus . . . Let James forgive Angus . . . Let him remember that he had suffered much . . . Peace . . . I want peace among them. Peace.'

Those about her bed exchanged glances. She had been well a short while ago. Could one be struck so suddenly?

It seemed so, for it was deemed advisable that the last rites should be administered. This was done, and when James arrived – although he had come to her bedside with the utmost haste – he was too late. Margaret, the Queen, was dead.

🏵 Bibliography 🏵

Brown, P. Hume, *A Short History of Scotland* (New Edition by Henry W. Meikle)

Everett Green, Mary Anne, *Letters of Royal and Illustrious Ladies of Great Britain* and *Lives of the Princesses of England*

Fisher, H. A. L., *The Political History of England (1485–1587)*

Froude, James Anthony, *History of England: Henry VIII*

Gairdner, James (ed.), *Memorials of Henry VII (The Chronicles and Memorials of Great Britain and Ireland during the Middle Ages)*

Hickman Smith Aubrey, William, *The National and Domestic History of England*

Lindsay, Robert, *The Chronicles of Scotland*

Mackie, R. L., *King James IV of Scotland*

Pollard, A. F., *Henry VIII*

Stephen, Sir Leslie and Lee, Sir Sidney (eds.), *The Dictionary of National Biography*

Strickland, Agnes, *Lives of the Queens of England* and *Lives of the Queens of Scotland and English Princesses*

Wade, John, *British History*

Madame Serpent

Broken-hearted, Catherine de' Medici arrives in Marseilles to marry Henry of Orléans, son of the King of France. But amid the glittering banquets of the most immoral court in sixteenth-century Europe, the reluctant bride changes into a passionate but unwanted wife who becomes dangerously occupied by a ruthless ambition destined to make her the most despised woman in France.

The Italian Woman

Jeanne of Navarre once dreamed of marrying Henry of Orléans, but years later she is instead still married to the dashing but politically inept Antoine de Bourbon, whilst the widowed Catherine has become the powerful mother of kings, who will do anything to see her beloved second son, Henry, rule France.

Queen Jezebel

The ageing Catherine de' Medici has arranged the marriage of her beautiful Catholic daughter Margot to the uncouth Huguenot King Henry of Navarre. But even Catherine is unable to anticipate the carnage that this unholy union is to bring about . . .

arrow books